D1473005

HOMEFRONT

Also by Scott James Magner

Seasons of Truth (Book One of the Hunters Chronicle)
Blood & Ashes (a Foreworld SideQuest)
Hearts of Iron (a Foreworld SideQuest)

HOMEFRONT

A NOVEL OF THE TRANSGENIC WARS

SCOTT JAMES MAGNER

Arche Press

Homefront is a work of fiction. Names, characters, places, and incidents are the products of the author's imagination or are used in an absolutely fictitious manner. Any resemblance to actual events, locales, or persons—living or dead—is entirely coincidental.

Copyright © 2014 by Scott James Magner

All rights reserved, which means that no portion of this publication may be reproduced or transmitted, in any form or by any means, without the express written permission of the publisher.

This is A001, and it has an ISBN of 978-1-63023-003-6.

This book was printed in the United States of America, and it is published by Arche Press, an imprint of Resurrection House (Puyallup, WA).

Send our children to the stars.

Edited by Fleetwood Robbins
Cover Art by Jennifer Tough
Cover Design by Darin Bradley
Book Design by Aaron Leis
Copy Edit by Darin Bradley

First hardback Arche Press edition: November 2014.

www.resurrectionhouse.com

HOMEFRONT

For the dreamers of dreams. The future is there for us all, if we choose to meet it with eyes open and heads held high.

And for Jay Lake, who never stopped believing in it.

(Partial Transcript)

CHAIRMAN DAVIS:

So I guess we're just looking for a little clarity here, Dr. Harrison. You said in your report that the Transgenic virus was a part of the natural course of human evolution, but in your testimony today you are indicating otherwise. Were you lying then, or are you lying now?

(silence of approximately 12 seconds)

Nothing to say, Doctor?

(further silence of 10 seconds)

DR. MICAH HARRISON:

I have a great deal to say, Senator, but I'm trying to figure out exactly which parts of my study your aides decided to misinterpret. If they had read the entire report, they might have gleaned the relevant words, rather than just the ones you wanted to hear.

DAVIS:

Please, enlighten us. And don't be afraid of the big words. We're all intelligent people here.

HARRISON:

With respect, sir, there are no words big enough for what's been done to us.

DAVIS:

To us, Doctor?

HARRISON:

If you, or your lackeys, had actually read the report, instead of the summaries meant for exobiology students, you'd already understand my position. But for the record, and to dispel the confusion you yourself have now injected into the issue, I will state definitively that the human race has not evolved as a result of contact with the virus.

DAVIS:

So you are reversing yourself then!

HARRISON:

Hardly, sir. Evolution is a long, chaotic process of genetic mutation in living creatures. Over time, favorable mutations are more likely to survive and reproduce. What's happened, what's happening, to the human race is not evolution. It is a biological attack by an unknown factor.

(silence of approximately 20 seconds)

SENATOR CLARK:

Doctor, are you suggesting . . .

DAVIS:

Preposterous! In over two hundred years of space exploration there has never been any conclusive proof of . . .

(general shouting, gavel pounding)

Order, order! Doctor Harrison, please explain yourself!

HARRISON:

Again, I refer the committee to my study. Evolutionary mutations are a response to environmental factors or species imperatives. They do not occur in adult organisms, nor could random chance produce mutations like functional body parts. Additional arms and legs, third or fourth eyes that can read radio waves, that sort of thing. And evolution certainly does not produce these results essentially overnight in widely separated populations and genetically diverse individuals.

The Transgenic virus, as you name it, affects— is affecting—specific portions of the human genome. In fact, it might be more accurate to say that it targets them. It transforms a normal human being into a fully functional member of another species.

No technology we possess does this. No process we have can stop or reverse these mutations, nor can we explain why some people are affected and others are not. Moreover, we—

(gavel pounding)

DAVIS:

Doctor Harrison! This is a serious inquiry, not a . . . a . . .

HARRISON:

What it is, sir, is the end of the human race. Ladies and gentleman of the committee, I cannot stress this point enough. The virus is real, and did not originate on this world. The more planets we explore, the more likely it is that we will find other organisms like this one, which will have similar interactions with our biology.

No sir, the virus is not evolution, but it's foolish in the extreme to assume the evolution of our species has ended. It will happen, must happen because of the virus. It's inevitable.

Superior forms of life now inhabit this planet with us, and there's a clear pattern for what happens next. Like our own species displaced those that came before us, we will eventually give way to these new forms of human.

DAVIS:

Unless we take steps to stop it. Quarantine the infected, limit new exposures . . .

HARRISON:

Steps? Steps? Mr. Chairman, every man, woman and child on this planet is infected. For now, most of us have not expressed any effects. But our children, and our children's children, will quite literally see things we cannot imagine.

You can attempt containment, but you will fail. You can hound and harry and treat your children like animals, but in the end you will only destroy yourselves.

CLARK:

Doctor, for the benefit of those who have not read your study and are watching these proceedings, how would you recommend we proceed?

HARRISON:

With patience, Senator. This is all so new, and there's so much we do not understand. In time, we'll learn to manage the effects, perhaps even guide them. But the one thing we must not, cannot do is act out of fear.

DAVIS:

And why is that, Dr. Harrison?

HARRISON:

Because for now, they still remember being human. And there's one thing that children, animals, and all living things have in common.

When threatened, our transformed descendants will defend themselves . . .

BOOK ONE

BOOK ONE

JANTINE

AS SUICIDE MISSIONS GO, THOUGHT JANTINE, *THIS ONE could do with a bit more excitement.*

Maybe it was the lack of activity, or that she and her team had no way to alter their course through hyperspace. Maybe it was that she really didn't understand their mission, or that despite their training her team seemed ill-suited for it.

Maybe if they'd given us a proper spaceship, instead of stuffing a bunch of mods barely old enough to leave the crèche into a cargo container and firing us into another dimension. But three weeks of travel for what might only be seconds of activity makes even the best of us a bit restless.

"Malik, time to insertion?"

Her second-in-command's face glowed in the light of his computer screen. She and Malik were alone, but he made a point of looking around before answering.

"Fifteen minutes less than when you last asked. Three hours, twenty-five minutes, and odd seconds remaining. You should make the call."

Malik was right, of course. The others needed to prepare as best they could. But delaying the call meant she could push back the reality of their mission a short while longer, and savor what little life she had left.

Jantine got up from her chair and stretched, careful not to extend her arms all the way and touch the fabric of the temporary shelter that served as their command center. She'd made that mistake on their first day out, and Malik had barely made it outside with the portable terminal before the tent collapsed around her. Everything about this mission was temporary, including its personnel. But Jantine couldn't fault the Alphas for their accommodations. After all, why spend money on equipment you'd never need again?

"I need to take a walk. Give a shout if something happens."

"Will do, boss."

Jantine shut down her own computer. It was a near duplicate of Malik's, built into a carrying case of ballistic plating and powerful enough to run an entire city if necessary. But instead of scanning the not-landscape of hyperspace for threats as her second-in-command did, her daily routine consisted of comparing crew readiness reports and preparing training schedules.

My first command, and it's like I never left the training center. Reports for everything, including how many reports there are.

Closing her eyes and twisting so as to not touch the sides of the opening, she eased herself out of the tent. It was one of many tiny exercises she'd assigned herself every day to keep sharp, and her engineered body was as responsive as ever.

As Betas, Jantine and Malik were the finest soldiers the Colonies could produce. Her specialty was operational command, and he was designed for tactics and interpersonal relations. Physically, their strength and speed were nearly matched, but despite a higher combat aptitude she'd never been able to best him while sparring. Malik always found a way to win, no matter how hopeless the situation was.

Eyes still shut, she let the red glow on the other side of her lids move her dark-adjusted eyes back to normal. When she opened them, the simulated light of the cargo container came at her from every direction, banishing shadows and approximating the ground-level light of their destination. If the surface currently serving as a floor weren't darker in color than the walls around them, the appearance of their camp would be even more surreal.

At present, her command consisted of a handful of tents and a few dozen crates of equipment neatly arranged on the deck plating—everything they'd need if the mission lasted longer than a few seconds after landing. Only her command team and the support crew were awake during this phase, and a group of them were far enough away at the other end of the container that the gently arcing floor put them above her.

The remainder of her people were in cryosleep in a second container, waiting for Jantine to make the most important decision of her young life. Of everyone's lives, really, but the responsibility was hers. She'd been training for this moment almost since she took her first steps, and it still didn't seem right to her.

A dozen mods, with the weight of the worlds on our shoulders. And only half of us have military training. Me and Malik, Katra, Jarl, and the Deltas. What were the Alphas thinking?

About half the support team civvies were watching Crassus and Artemus walk through their paces under Katra's watchful eye. Unlike the Gamma's subtle genetic advantages, there was no mistaking the Deltas for baseline humans. Almost four meters tall, their extra arms and hardened gray skin were easy indicators of their primary function as combat infantry.

Both mods were carrying an unpowered squad weapon in the upper set of arms, and deflection panels in the lower. By the looks of it, Katra had them executing a defensive sim, projecting holographic opponents directly into their eyes. The Gamma's fair hair was a shade lighter than Jantine's, but she had a similar lanky build.

The speed at which the Deltas moved was impressive, and the civvies watching them seemed a bit confused as to what they were actually doing. To Jantine's trained eye, the Deltas were adjusting to incoming fire from imaginary combatants, moving the barriers in front of simulated beams and bullets that would otherwise make sticky paste of the unprotected scientists and technicians sitting behind them. The audience was an unknowing part of the training exercise, and in the long run, the most important part of their mission.

Assuming, of course, that we survive the landing. And then make it out into the open. And then find a place to defend. And then . . .

Three hours, twenty-some minutes. She needed to make the call.

Jantine thought about keying into Katra's sim, and giving the Deltas some real opposition. Not physically—either one could rip her apart if she let them get close enough—but strategically. Katra's sims were straight out of the training manuals. Although the Gamma was a talented instructor, she didn't have the right mindset for improvising a chaotic battle—Katra and Jarl were combat infiltrators, not commanders.

Speaking of whom . . .

The hairs on the back of Jantine's neck stood up, and her senses went into overdrive. She bent her right knee and kicked out with her left leg, while at the same time tasting the air around her for some hint as to Jarl's direction of attack. She smelled nothing but the sterile blandness of recycled air and the slightly greasy feel of tent material.

Jantine rolled forward when she hit the ground, adjusting for the curving surface of the container. But her maneuver came to an abrupt halt when her back slammed into something that shouldn't be there, and she knew she'd guessed wrong as to Jarl's location.

Again.

Before she could twist away, strong hands pulled her arms behind her back and the full weight of her opponent pressed her into the floor. She scissored her legs in an attempt to get free, but Jarl was a heartbeat faster, and locked one of her thighs behind one of his knees.

"Stabby Stabby. Dead."

Jarl's throaty whisper was close enough to her ear that she could feel his breath moving across her skin, and still she couldn't smell him. He held her down long enough for her hypothetically slit throat to bleed out, and then pulled her to her feet.

When she looked at him, the dark outfit Jarl was wearing told her how he'd done it. Instead of the non-descript brown coveralls the rest of the team was wearing, he'd somehow fashioned a spare shelter into a flowing garment that not only broke up the lines of his body, but allowed him a full range of movement. She'd smelled a tent because she was attacked by one, and the knowledge made her smile at her earlier thoughts regarding Gammas not being able to improvise.

"How long?"

"Two hours. Malik spotted me when I came inside, and scored a kill. So I waited for you to come out instead."

Damn. Should have thought of that. Make the score Jantine 0, Malik more than 0, and Jarl 37.

Jantine gave Jarl a small bow and ducked back into the tent. He'd heard Malik's timetable announcements and knew as well as she did where the mission stood. It was time to make the call, and prepare for the rest of her life.

She didn't bother sneaking up on Malik—his senses were better than hers, and he'd likely heard everything that transpired outside. Malik's intense focus on the screen in front of him didn't blunt his perceptions of the world around him, and this heightened awareness was one of the many reasons she liked working with him.

Settling back into her chair, she spent some time looking at Malik's face in the dim light of his screen. It was similar to her own, but with enough differences to mark him as belonging to another crèche.

Betas were bred to serve, be it as officers, underlings, ambassadors, or teachers. Gammas like Jarl and Katra were carefully designed tools meant for a specific task, but Betas were the ones qualified to use them. Most of the command team outside were Betas, as were about ten percent of the sleepers in the second container. But before partnering up with Malik, she'd never really considered what it meant to just like somebody for who they were.

And she did like him. His casual efficiency at everyday tasks, the way he kept her on track, and the occasional smile that escaped his inbred professionalism. If she didn't know better,

Malik could almost pass for an Alpha, but they were far too valuable to send on a mission like this.

Jantine saw a slight movement of Malik's left eye before he spoke, the only acknowledgement he ever gave that he noticed her scrutiny.

"Are you ready?"

The implications of those three words were almost too much for Jantine to handle. Malik knew the most likely outcome of their mission, and the prospect of permanent exile on a hostile planet should they survive it didn't seem to bother him. He only wanted to know that she was prepared to command him to his death when necessary, and was more than capable of activating the container's destruct sequence if she was not.

Because a Beta who would not do her duty was as big a threat to the Colonies as the enemy, and Malik would certainly do his. The rest of the team would never know it had happened, and their mission would disappear from the universe as if it had never launched in the first place.

"Yes. Open a channel for me."

Malik nodded, and mumbled a command phrase that both disarmed the destruct system ready to burn them to ashes and activated the communications array. As a result of her choice, life in the containers would become interesting over the next few hours.

The next words Jantine spoke to her team would pale in comparison to the message she was about to send, possibly the most important words ever spoken aloud since humans first went out into space. She knew the message so well she could recite it in her sleep, and she would deliver the words of the Alphas to the universe without a single change.

"It's ready, Jantine."

Jantine was still watching Malik for some sign that he returned her almost-affection, and was surprised when he turned his head to look her in the eyes. It had been eighteen days, seventeen hours and thirty-seven minutes since they'd been sealed into the container and fired into hyperspace, and in all that time Malik had displayed nothing but perfect Beta obedience and efficiency. But as the last day of their lives slowly counted down, she saw in his eyes how much he'd wanted to not activate the destruct sequence, and in his smile how happy he was to be alive for just a little bit longer.

Malik gave her a nod, then rose and left the tent. Jantine pulled his portable unit over to her, placing her palm on the scanner and verifying her willingness to die for the Colonies.

"This is JTN-B34256-O. Streamship 7 is a go. Time to insertion is three hours, ten minutes, twenty-six seconds. Message begins.

"This is JTN-B34256-O. In accordance with Interstellar Compact and the Magellan Accords, I state now for the record that my actions are mine and mine alone. I hereby declare myself free of the tyranny of the Outer Colonies, and ask that my actions be viewed in the context of the greater good.

"On March 17, 2640 OER, I commandeered the freighter Argo and killed its crew, appropriating its cargo of workers and colonists for my own use and freeing them from lives of genetic servitude.

"Do not attempt to find us. Do not attempt to reclaim us. We are armed, we are free, and will defend ourselves to the utmost of our abilities.

"You have been warned . . ."

MALIK

Malik stepped out of the tent, wary of another encounter with Jarl. The Gamma rarely tried an ambush twice in the same cycle, but Katra once told him that in training, Jarl was known to attempt touches at any time.

It's a good command. A bit small, but with a bit of luck we'll have everything we need for success down on the surface.

Malik did a quick scan of the immediate area, then moved himself into the open. The scattered tents of their encampment cast no shadows to speak of, and if Jarl was lying in wait he'd shed his tent camouflage in favor of something even more inventive.

He'll probably try for someone inside a tent next. It's no use stalking Katra, she's far too good at this, and he knows not to bother her while she's running sims.

And the Deltas don't care in any event.

At the other end of the container, Katra and the Deltas were performing for a nearly full audience. Only the Omegas were missing, but their translator Doria was front and center with a huge smile on her face as always. The other civvies were watching with a mixture of concern and confusion on their faces, but Doria was just relaxing and enjoying the show.

Perhaps it was her empathic abilities that made the difference. Malik wasn't exactly sure how it worked, but she seemed to get more enjoyment out of life than anyone he'd ever met.

Malik started walking toward the group, looking around for the Omegas. The shape and size of the container were such that to really conceal oneself took a great deal of skill and ingenuity, so the two hulking mods must be engaged in some private project inside their shelter tent.

The Transgenic virus hadn't done humanity any favors overall, but compared to the base stock the Omegas' appearance was truly alien. For reasons lost to time, the hulking pair looked even more extreme than did the Deltas. Instead of gray skin and extra arms, their skin was a vivid orange, and they were almost half a meter taller. Their broad faces had extra pairs of eyes, and a double set of ears on each side of their heads.

In contrast, their mouths were comically small. Again for unknown reasons, the Omegas had very different respiratory systems than other mods, one that allowed them to work in a variety of hazardous conditions, including the vacuum of space. As a result, though they understood language well enough, their mouths and throats couldn't form responses in normal frequencies. Rather than use translation devices, they preferred to communicate with empathic facilitators like Doria.

Responding to his thoughts, Doria turned and looked at him. Her knowing smile hinted at a lifetime of other people's secrets, including his own.

Without saying a word, Doria patted the space beside her and then turned back to watch the Deltas. Malik walked up and took the place she'd indicated, interested in what she might have to say.

"They're designing." Doria's whisper was unprompted, but Malik knew her well enough to know she was answering the questions most people asked her when she was sitting alone: "Where are the Omegas?" and "Is everything okay?"

While Malik wasn't particularly worried about the Omegas, he always felt a bit frustrated that the other mods defined Doria by her association with the Omegas instead of engaging her on her own merits. She was funny, intelligent, and insightful—all traits a trained medical specialist needed. But despite her easy-going nature, since she was "the voice," she tended to give status updates instead of greetings.

Just like the rest of us. Until long after landing, anyway. There won't be much time for casual interactions until we're fully established and out of danger.

"Anything in particular?" As he spoke, Malik kept his eyes focused on Katra rather than the Deltas. She had a look of intense concentration he rarely saw in a Gamma, and he wondered if something had gone wrong with the training simulation. But Doria's next words made him forget all about that.

"They won't tell me. They usually don't if the project is going to take a while. They don't want to burden us with disappointments."

Malik now gave his full attention to Doria. Rather than sputter out the words of his many questions all at once, he waited for the Gamma to continue. She'd turned to face him, and the warmth of her smile was all the communication she deemed necessary. When she didn't speak, Malik was ashamed that right now he was treating her just like the rest of the mods did.

Doria's hand came up and caressed the side of his face. The gesture was so unexpected that the only thing Malik could do was cover it with one of his own, and continue looking into her eyes.

"Thank you. For acknowledging it—most people don't bother. It's all right not to know how to react around an empath. It's also okay to ask questions if you have them, I don't mind. The Omegas don't think on the same timescales as we do, or about the same sorts of things."

Malik reluctantly pulled her hand away from his face, but didn't want to let go of it. Somewhat surprised by his reaction, he kept holding her hand while considering his next action, and decided a full conversation on this topic was probably a good idea.

Malik rose to his feet, and Doria came up with him without any urging. She cocked her head toward the tents, then slipped her hand from his.

In another community, the pair's departure might have been met with raised eyebrows and hushed whispers. Both Malik and Doria were healthy and mature, and given the probable outcome of the next few hours no one would fault them for seeking some comfort in sexual activity. But the very nature of this mission required the team's members remain professional at all times, and Doria's role as a counselor put her off-limits in any event.

Besides, she's not the one for me . . .

Malik followed Doria to her shelter tent. Ducking his head to step inside, he saw the same basic camp furniture he had in his own tent, although Doria had arranged it into a much more comfortable space. Where Malik, Jantine, and the other combat mods had set up their quarters in nearly identical fashion based on years of training and discipline, Doria's personal space was an organic extension of herself.

Unlike the command tent, Doria had opened up all the ventilation flaps to let in air and light. Her gear wasn't set up based on how fast she could exit the tent in an emergency, or with an eye to where her weapons were stored. Instead, Doria's layout invited him to sit down and relax for as long as he wanted to visit.

"I don't usually see people here like this, but you and Jantine are always welcome." Doria waved him to one of the chairs and sat down facing him half a meter away in the other. Malik noticed that she'd chosen the one that kept her face fully visible in the tent's half-light, while he was more in shadow.

How does she do that? Always coming up with the right thing to do or say?

"I can't read minds, not exactly. Empathic communication is more about predicting behavior than telepathy, but you're very easy for me to read. You and Jantine are so used to command that people do what you want them to as a matter of course; it's almost like working with Them."

When Doria said the word like that, Malik knew she meant the Omegas. They had designations like every other mod, but since there was so little cosmetic variation among them they decided to embrace their similarities and rejected individuality altogether along with their names. Over time, a skilled observer could tell them apart, but even through intermediaries like Doria, few mods tried to engage them in conversation.

"Um, thank you. But . . . you do communicate directly with the Omegas, right?"

"Of course. I was bred for it. They have wonderful minds, and their desires are very easy to sort out. I use words and terms I'm familiar with, and they guide me to the right meanings. It's functionally the same thing."

Malik tried to keep the confusion off his face, then remembered that with Doria it didn't matter. If she really could interpret his emotions, she'd know better than he what he wanted to say.

Doria smiled, and leaned forward to rest one of her hands on his knee. She gave it a gentle squeeze, then sat back in her chair. The slight disturbance in the air as she did so carried a scent to him from deeper in her tent, something spicy and soft and full of mystery. He was just about to comment on it when she continued.

"There aren't a lot of us in the Colonies. Part of it is that the Omegas live very long lives, and prefer not to deal with our chaotic personalities. One, maybe two Gammas like me can support an entire community. For the most part they do their own thing, and they don't need facilitators to communicate with one another. And like you, people generally understand what they want on the little stuff."

"Why don't they cover this during education?" Malik was genuinely curious now, and leaned forward slightly to hear Doria's response.

"They do for some. But I don't know how to use the gun your hand just went to, or how Jarl got so close to you before you realized he was there." Doria's smile didn't falter, but her gaze shifted to a point just over Malik's shoulder. "Oh, sorry, you hadn't figured it out yet. Not consciously anyway."

Malik's eyes widened as a strong hand squeezed his shoulder. He didn't turn his head, but instead looked down at his right hand, which was indeed curled around the handle of his sidearm.

I wonder which of us he came for?

"Jarl, if you'd like to join us I can sit on the cot." Doria gestured to the side, and cocked her head slightly before continuing. "We're talking about the Omegas, who are impressed at how quietly you moved around in their shelter. They want me to let you know that watching you has helped them with their design problem for the Colony's outer defenses, and that you're welcome to try and kill them again any time."

Malik felt the hand leave, and this time did turn to look. Jarl was back in his normal coveralls but had dusted his skin with some kind of dull powder. Given the visual range of the Omegas, it was likely something meant to change his skin temperature.

"No, I'm good. Malik, Boss says to call a meeting."

Jarl was speaking to Malik, but the Gamma's eyes never left Doria. Malik wasn't sure if his expression was one of disappointment or admiration, or some mixture of both.

Doria would know, of course, and Malik decided that was what was bothering Jarl. Empathics made an infiltrator's job a lot harder, but at the same time they gave him a reason to do it.

"Thanks, Jarl." Malik saw that the infiltrator was waiting for further orders, and continued. "Get cleaned up, and meet us in the group tent in . . . let's say twenty minutes."

That should be more than enough time for you to prepare your next "surprise."

Jarl nodded, and left without saying another word. On the way out he didn't bother with stealth, and his shoulder somehow brushed the tent's entrance flap. It cut off some of the outside light as it fell into place, and Malik turned his attention back to the ever-smiling Doria.

"That was well done, Malik. Whether you realize it or not, you can read people too. I think it's a part of your training as much as your mods."

Doria's face softened after she spoke, and Malik tried to imagine what it would feel like to do what she did. Jarl and Katra were easy enough to understand, and Jantine . . . Jantine was different in her own way. She wanted some kind of reaction from him whenever they spoke, and half the fun of his day was finding ways to almost give one. But the civvies didn't have a lot in common with the combat mods, and he didn't expect that to change after landing. JonB was an excellent example of how the two groups were just . . . different.

But then there's Doria . . .

Malik decided to switch topics. He'd come here to learn more about Doria, but they'd spent most of the time talking about the Omegas or himself.

"Why did you do that? Ask Jarl to join us?"

"Because he wanted to. He wants to understand you, much like you're here trying to understand me. You see him as more than a killer, and he's not used to that in a commander."

Malik sat back in his chair, trying to process what Doria was saying to him. He hadn't thought about it in exactly those terms before, but it seemed that Doria knew his mind better than he did.

"Are we all that obvious?"

Doria paused before answering. When she did, her voice was a bit softer than before, almost childlike.

"No. Like I said before, I can't read minds. Not exactly. But you and Jantine see us—Gammas, I mean—not just as tools for a specific job like other Betas do. We notice. And you in particular are . . . special. I sometimes can read a bit more from you than the others."

Now Malik was truly at a loss for what to say. After almost three weeks of close contact with them, in the last few minutes he learned more of what it meant to be a Gamma than he'd thought possible. He didn't feel special—he wasn't sure exactly what he was feeling.

Is there a word for this? Maybe it's what Jarl was feeling. Something between disappointment and anger. Not toward myself, or the Gammas. But towards our society as a whole maybe? I don't know, and that's . . .

He hadn't seen Doria move, but suddenly she was next to his chair and that same spicy-sweet smell came with her. He found himself on his feet, and as soon as he was standing Doria was crushing herself to him in a fierce hug. Her left cheek was pressed against his right, and the warmth of it was as unexpected as the words she was whispering in his ear.

"Don't think like that. Never like that. It's all right, you've done nothing wrong. It's all right, it's all right. . ."

The words trailed off in his ear, but Malik felt Doria was still speaking to him somehow. He could feel her jaw moving against his own, and small puffs of air were tickling his skin.

Unsure of what to do, Malik put his arms around Doria and just held her. He tried not to think about the mission, or his orders, or anything at all but her in his arms. In that shared moment he was as much a part of her world any of the objects around them, but it couldn't last. He knew what was expected of him outside the walls of the tent, and though his body was certainly interested, he couldn't help being who he was.

I'm a Beta. And Doria is not the one for me.

They stood there in silence for several minutes, until Doria relaxed her arms around him. He let his hands fall away from her back, and before she pulled away she surprised him one last time by turning her head and kissing his cheek. It lasted only for a moment, but in that time Malik's universe contracted to the few square centimeters of his body still in contact with her warmth.

Doria moved a short distance away, and took a moment to compose herself with her head turned to the side. When their eyes met again her smile was back in place. Malik didn't know what to say, but he was sure she understood. He watched her eyes in the shadows for a few long seconds, and then said the only thing he could.

"I should go tell Carlton and Harren to prepare a meal. I . . . I'd like to talk to you again sometime, but I don't think we'll have a chance before landing. Would that . . . would that be all right with you?"

Malik was almost disappointed at the speed, and professionalism, of her response.

"Yes, of course. I'll see you at the meeting, Commander."

Malik nodded, and turned to leave. Out of respect he waited until he was outside to smooth his coveralls, biting down hard on his emotions as he realized that no one would be looking at the entrance to Doria's tent.

It may be all right, but after we land things are going to be different for you, Doria. I can promise you that for sure.

Malik pulled out his handheld and keyed in a general meeting call. He had fifteen minutes now to prepare for the next phase of the mission, and the rest of his life would just have to wait.

JANTINE

"... AND THAT'S WHERE WE STAND. I KNOW IT'S NOT a surprise to any of you that we'd be considered rogue agents, but I felt you should know that we are now officially at war with the human race."

Jantine scanned the faces of her team, looking for any signs of dissent brought on by her revelation. She expected none—even the civvies had volunteered for the mission—but other than Malik and Jarl none of them had known about the destruct sequence before just now.

The crew—if they could be called that—of Streamship 7 was gathered in the large tent they used for communal meals. One last round of tasteless nutrient wafers and a speech before dying was all she had to offer her people, and now she'd given them both.

Sitting on chairs, crates, and deck plating, both the combat and support teams were silent. Everyone but Malik seemed to be waiting for more information, though no one wanted to be the first to ask. Even the Deltas and Omegas squatting in the back seemed ready to say something, though it was hard to tell with the Omegas.

Doria looked enough like Katra that they could be crèche-sisters, at least while seated. But the contemplative Doria rarely spoke out in a group meeting. And when she did, it was to relay any concerns the Omegas might have. Jantine could see her throat pulsing as she subvocalized her thoughts, but whatever communication she was having with them wasn't meant for the entire team.

The message she'd sent was pure diplomatic fiction, but it was a carefully scripted and executed one. The Alphas needed to disavow their actions, and Jantine and her team, along with the three hundred sleepers in the other container, were a small price to pay to give plausible deniability to the other Streamships.

The real ships. The ones that might actually survive their missions.

Surprisingly, the first person to speak was Katra. She wasn't the most intelligent Gamma Jantine had ever worked with, but Katra was definitely one of the more perceptive.

"Did the words mean anything, other than as a cover story? Are we actually free?"

Interesting. Wasn't expecting that at all.

Jantine looked at the other mod's face, searching for her real questions. The answer to both her spoken ones was no, but at the same time a solid case could be made for yes. They really were disavowed, and since the penalty for going rogue was death, being condemned as rebels wouldn't mean all that much in the end.

After a few seconds, Jantine decided Katra was more afraid of not having a command structure than anything else. It was unlikely she had any truly treasonous thoughts, and could be counted on to do her duty.

"It means we have a mission to carry out, and a license to do so as we see fit. We know the target planet has Colonial sympathizers, and whether or not we get down safely my broadcast will tell them that at least we tried. But our priority is still to establish a secure base, and cycle the sleepers as fast as possible. We'll deal with any political ramifications once we complete that objective."

Katra nodded, and Jantine was about to dismiss the team when JonB spoke up.

"When you say, get down safely, does that mean you don't expect us to?"

JonB hadn't made any friends since coming aboard, even among the other civvies. His pessimism always seemed out of place in a scientist, and Jantine hoped that if—when—they landed, one of the sleeper Betas would be a better fit to act as her chief science advisor. It's not that she disliked the dark-haired mod, but she'd rather deal with someone she felt a real connection to as her civilian liaison, instead of someone assigned to her by the Alphas because he did well on tests.

"It means that right now, I'm in command of twelve mods and not a lot else. We've got exactly two buttons left to push that can control our destiny, and a whole bunch of hopefully empty space between us and our objective. Once we jettison the hyperdrive module and re-enter normal space, best case scenario has us a few hundred million kilometers from the planet, and on target. If all goes well, Malik will orient us as soon as we're in normal space and start our burn accordingly."

Jantine tried not to think about how insane it was to be traveling through space—hyper- or otherwise—without any way to change their destination. The cargo slug the containers were attached to had no maneuvering thrusters, no navigation sensors, and worst of all, no weapons.

Not that any were necessary. The slug itself was a weapon, a mass of rock and iron moving at relativistic speeds. Aimed directly at a planet, it was so potentially destructive that until now the human race had avoided using anything like it in five centuries of space travel.

Jantine's team was another kind of weapon, one meant to be fired and discarded after use. According to the Alphas' plan, her crew container and its twin containing the sleepers would detach from the slug as they approached the target planet. Their projected insertion point was far above the plane of the ecliptic, so slug itself would go on traveling into interstellar space once the containers were away. If the plan worked, they'd come down intact on gravity buffers, blast their way out into sunshine and clean air and start killing anything that moved while the civvies and Omegas started building them a stronghold.

If. Lots of ifs. But the Alphas had big brains, and they said it would work. So Jantine believed it would too.

Mostly.

"Carlton, Harren, are you ready?"

The civvie Betas actually were crèche-sibs, and responsible for reviving the sleepers as soon as it was determined safe to do so. Unlike JonB, they were open and jovial, and tended to finish one another's sentences.

"You bet, Boss. Find us a spot to work in, and we'll get the job done."

Harren nodded at Carlton's words, and she knew they'd get it done. All of them would, even JonB.

We have to be more than our numbers. At least for a little while.

"Then that's all for now. We've got a little more than two hours until the transition. I want our camp broken down and final readiness reports in one hour."

And with that, the meeting was over. Jantine stood as the crew filed out, running a hand over her jumpsuit in search of crumbs. There were none, but generations of Betas before her had done the same thing after a meal, whether or not they were in the field. It was the little things that got you killed. Even though they would likely be dead soon anyway, there was no reason to abandon discipline.

Carlton and Harren were hanging back from the others, and it took her a moment to process that they were waiting for her to exit the tent. This space needed to be collapsed as well, and since the team had already eaten there was no need to leave it standing.

Jantine picked up several crates to carry outside. Everybody helped on this team—there were no ranks or egos to interfere. Jantine was in command, Malik backed her up, and everybody else did their jobs. Jarl would likely assume command if both of them were incapacitated, but given how few combat operatives they had it wouldn't be for very long.

Out in the too-white light of the cargo unit, Jantine watched the camp collapse around her. As each gray-green shelter came down, the mission got more real. They were going to invade an inhabited world, establish both an initial base and a hidden colony, and then defend them to the death with only the barest hope of support from the local population.

No problem. Yet.

Jantine had dealt with her own gear right after she'd made the call, so she had time now to circulate and talk to her people one-on-one. For her first conversation, she selected Doria and the Omegas.

The trio was securing the other team members' crates as they were assembled, in preparation for a hard landing. There was no guarantee Malik could get them down in the same relative orientation they had now, and to power the external buffers he'd need to kill the internal gravity.

Watching the Omegas work filled Jantine with something akin to the wonder the civvies felt when Crassus and Artemus ran sims. There was no wasted movement in their activity— just a quiet grace she wished she could emulate.

Jantine was a hair slower than most other Betas, a bit more awkward and unsure of her body. But her mind worked much faster than she could explain to the others. She could see each Omega's actions for the poetry it was, knew exactly how much force they were using, and how much they were holding back.

Doria knew. Doria knew everything, though she rarely let on. Her empathic mods let her speak for the Omegas, but they also gave her unparalleled insight into the mental health of all the team members.

Doria didn't look up from her handheld when she spoke, continuing to catalog the mission's supplies. The Omegas had seen Jantine approach, and likely had relayed that information to the Gamma through their link.

"They really like you. They want me to make sure you understand that. They're sorry you're so sad."

Sad? I'm not . . .

"You're not like the other Betas, and they know it. You're special, but alone."

Jantine stood silent, unsure of exactly how, or to whom, she should reply. Doria tapped out something on the handheld and then turned to look at Jantine. As if sensing the nature of her conversation, the Omegas turned away to wait for the next crate. Jantine knew they could hear every sound in the container if they wished, but also that they understood the other mods needed privacy now and then.

"It's okay, the damper is running. We're as alone as you need us to be."

Doria waved a hand toward a pair of chairs that had yet to be stowed, and smiled. Jantine returned the expression, and took one of the offered seats.

"Is this an official session, then?"

"If you'd like. The chairs are here for everyone, and I expect you won't be the last visitor we have over the next hour. What we're doing isn't . . . small."

Jantine nodded, as much at Doria's phrasing as the words themselves.

"No—no, it's not. You were communicating with the Omegas during the meeting. Is there something they want?"

"Katra asked more or less the same question they had, and you answered it well enough. They wanted to be sure the team understood the full meaning of the message. But they were more concerned about you than anything else. Like they said, you seemed sad."

There's that word again.

"I'm fine, really. This *is* a big thing. An impossible thing, really. Everything has to go exactly right for this to end well, and so little of it is in our control."

"And the Omegas know that. We all do, even JonB. But we volunteered for a one-way trip knowing we might not even make it that far. The Alphas could have picked anyone for command. They chose you, and that's enough for us."

Jantine exhaled, pushing herself back a bit into the chair and wishing it were a warm pile of blankets she could hide in until the mission was over. It wasn't sadness the Omegas felt in her, but doubt. She could admit to herself, if not to Doria, how overmatched she felt for what was to come. Why she'd delayed making the call for so long, when she knew she had to do it from the moment the cargo slug launched.

The Omegas are perceptive, and they talk to Doria. But can the others figure it out?

Jantine was older than Doria by a couple of years, but she'd spent those years absorbing tactics and history, while Doria had spent almost all of her time since leaving the crèche listening to people's problems. It made the Gamma seem so much older and competent by comparison, even though Doria was among the physically weakest mods on the team.

"Thanks. And let them know I appreciate their concern, will you? I know that I wasn't all that approachable in the command tent."

"I will." Doria smiled and gestured toward the Omegas. "And don't worry about the Builders. They're the most well-adjusted among us. They don't worry about the same things the rest of us do in the Colonies. To hear them tell it, they've been preparing for a mission like this for a very long time, almost since the exile."

Jantine took pause at this, trying to remember exactly when the Omega line stabilized. It was one of the last mods to really distinguish itself from the baseline, the first expressions arriving a good fifty years after the Gammas bred true. The Omega community adapted well to life in the Colonies, and were full partners in the Accords. Jantine couldn't imagine a society without Omega architects and builders, where artists made music and drew pictures with senses designed for one planet only.

If any of us could plan on that scale, it would be the Alphas. But the Omegas might be capable of it as well. They build great things. Would a shaping a society be any different than planning a city? If only we—I—knew them better.

Jantine started to stand, but Doria's hand came over to rest on hers, and despite the seeming kindness of the gesture Jantine tensed up.

"It's important to them that you understand. It's all right if things go wrong. They are here to help you, and are ready to do whatever you need them to do. All you have to do is ask."

Something in Doria's eyes made Jantine wish for the blankets again, along with a big bowl of something warm that didn't come out of a tube. There was a meaning in the words that was pure Omega, layered and nuanced and beyond the understanding of most mods. Doria herself might not really understand the message she was delivering, but Jantine suspected she did, and that the Gamma was frightened by it.

The peaceful, gentle Omegas were ready to fight and die at her command.

Doria's hand withdrew, and Jantine watched the other mod's smile settle back in place.

"I understand." Jantine wanted to say more, but those two words were all that seemed appropriate. She'd answered their question, now she had to make sure the Omegas never needed to fulfill that promise of sacrifice. Instead she nodded to Doria, and walked away from the staging area.

She didn't need to check her handheld to know how much time there was to insertion, but she'd need to talk to every member of the team like this before Malik pushed the button.

And if everyone uses their time to tell me how much faith they have in me, I sure hope we live long enough for me to thank them properly down on the surface.

JANTINE

"ALL DONE WITH YOUR PEP-TALKS, BOSS?" MALIK'S whisper was barely in the audible range, but Jantine could hear the smile he normally kept hidden. He was busy strapping himself in to the cargo harness, eyes never straying from his computer. The rest of the team was making the same preparation for insertion, aligning themselves along the outer edge of the "raft" of crates the Omegas had assembled. Assuming Malik could get them to the surface intact, the harnesses should keep everyone secure as they descended.

"Why? Feeling the need to unburden yourself?"

The "pep-talks" had taken most of the two hours she'd allocated, the bulk of which was confirming all post-landing activities with JonB. Jantine could see him now in animated conversation with Doria, and by extension the Omegas, on the same topic.

Wearing encounter suits with the faceplates open, the pair of civvies almost looked like combat mods. But there was something in their eyes, a softness that betrayed their genetic programming.

They're not ready to kill. Not as long as we're here to do it for them.

"I'm good, Boss. Ten minutes, give or take. The readings are a bit different now, but I don't know if that's the end of the hyperspace corridor or something else. If we ever make a return trip, I'll let you know."

"I'll keep that in mind. How long until you kill the lights?"

Malik's response was slow in coming, a personality trait to which she'd never quite grown accustomed. He wasn't a slow thinker, he just liked to be thorough. And he had a habit of translating his very accurate responses back into plain speech to put people at ease. Jantine had no real preference, but understood that others did.

"I can probably manage the power load fine with them on. It's the grav that uses most of the reserves. And we won't start tapping those until we jettison the hyperdrive module."

Jantine considered several scenarios before speaking again. If it truly didn't matter, the civvies would probably appreciate not being in the dark. They'd made the adjustment to living in constant illumination well enough, and it was their idea to stop using the simulated sky projections. Jantine definitely approved of that change—no matter what the weather was supposed to be like at their destination, seeing clouds move with no accompanying breeze just seemed wrong.

"And the other environmental systems?"

"Same general idea. We shouldn't have to use them long enough to make a difference. We'll either be able to land or not."

Something was bothering Jantine about insertion, more so than her earlier doubts. She felt she should be doing something right now, even something small, to increase their chances of survival. In the end it all depended on Malik's ability to land a falling building using nothing but readouts and fast reflexes, but Jantine was responsible for keeping everyone alive, and the team had made sure she knew they had complete faith in her ability to do so.

"Kill them in five, and the other systems too. Save every erg you can. Patch me into the handhelds."

Jantine surprised herself with her confidence, but only a little. This is what she was bred for, and after so long with nothing to do she was now in her element.

Her handheld beeped twice, and checking it she saw eight ready icons waiting for her words. While the Omegas could read just fine, they preferred to communicate through Doria rather than transcriptions.

Okay, here we go.

"In five minutes, we're going to shut down all environmental systems in preparation for insertion. Get your helmets on and breathers calibrated, and then power down all nonessential equipment. I want no stray signals. We will be weapons-hot in five minutes starting . . . now."

Jantine nodded approval at the countdown that appeared on her handheld, but then frowned at the comm request from JonB. Surrendering to the inevitable, she keyed in a privacy code and answered it. She barely had time to register his face on the screen before he started speaking.

"Is this really necessary, JTN-B34256-O? I'm reading full capacity on all power reserves, and we're well within safety margins."

"It's 'Jantine,' JonB. Or 'Commander' if you must, but yes, these are my orders. This is still a combat mission, and I don't think I have to remind you of the stakes here."

Jantine could almost see JonB's brain working inside his head. After her almost-rebuke, his lips were pressed tightly together and his eyes had narrowed. He was running options in his head, trying to figure out why she would want the extra power.

There was a very thin line between advice and insubordination, and JonB had higher intelligence scores than she did, if less practical experience. Everything he'd said so far was correct, and she was impressed that he'd been monitoring the situation so closely. But the decision was hers to make, and he had to accept that.

I'm really hoping one of the sleepers can replace him.

"I understand . . . Jantine. I'll message you once I confirm everyone's breathers and suits are properly calibrated."

The connection terminated abruptly, and Jantine felt her own lips pressing together. The next few minutes were crucial to the survival of the Colonies, and if it came down to it, she had to make their sacrifice matter. One by one her team signaled their readiness, well within the deadline she'd set. Doria sent a text-only message along with her confirmation, and reading it sent another chill down Jantine's spine.

They understand, and are ready.

How much, or how little, the Omegas really grasped about what was happening was something only Doria could tell her. But Jantine suspected it was the former, and it probably wouldn't take much longer for the rest of the mods to come to the same conclusion they had.

All, or nothing.

"Boss?"

"Do it. Scenario Five Alpha is a go."

"Acknowledged."

On schedule, Malik disabled the environmental systems. Her encounter suit responded instantly, adding a small puff of air in her helmet every time her chest moved and keeping it the same temperature as her skin.

Jantine didn't think she'd miss the subsonic hum of the container's air exchangers, but without it she felt a little bit naked. With her faceplate sealed, she could only hear the sounds of her own body, and it was a bit unnerving. Nothing would change in the module for a few hours; there was plenty of shielding, and it was a completely enclosed system. But without that constant vibration stimulating the edges of her perception, the mission was now more real than ever, and she tried not to think about the fifty thousand or so things that could go wrong in the next few minutes.

She especially avoided thinking about the destruct charges Malik had just re-enabled.

From her position, Jantine had a clear view of Malik's screen, and the sight of his faceplate illuminated by its glow was a comfort. Just before insertion, he closed his eyes, counting down the seconds until the sequence he'd programmed jettisoned the hyperdrive module and brought them hurtling back into normal space.

Five . . . four . . . three . . . two . . .

MALIK

MALIK SLAMMED INTO HIS RESTRAINTS AS HIS SCREEN went wild. He had no more than a second to decide whether his rifle or the computer was more important to hold on to, and given the team's location it wasn't a hard choice at all. His right hand shot out and barely reached the case's handle before it went spinning away. Pulling it closer, he kept his eyes on the readouts as the container tumbled.

The sudden return of gravity to his world was a completely unexpected development, and until he could confirm what had gone wrong with the insertion, his priorities were still to get a lock on the planet and get the containers free of the cargo slug.

Their exit from hyperspace should have been no more dramatic than a few new data points appearing on his screen. But now they were spinning wildly through space, and the mass readings indicated that fragments of whatever they'd impacted were tumbling along with them.

And also that they were definitely not alone in this supposedly empty area of space.

"Boss . . . not . . . done . . . with . . . bad . . . news."

"What . . . happened?"

Jantine's words were as strained as his own, and at least one other member of the team was screaming. Through the chaos, he thought it might be one of the sibs, but there was no telling which one.

"Hit . . . something. Above . . . ecliptic . . . not . . . natural. Have to . . . retask . . . scans."

"Do you . . . have . . . planet?"

Malik got his other hand to one of his restraints and released it, dragging the strap across the case to provide a bit more stability. Up and down were still relative and uncertain terms, but at least now the screen was level with his eyes, and he could enter some commands. A few seconds of hurried tapping gave him answers, but not the ones Jantine wanted.

"No. Ships. Lots. Big . . . ones."

Half a dozen, in fact. But he couldn't spare the syllables to explain fully.

"Want . . . grav?"

Whatever Jantine was going to say was lost when another impact shook the container. In addition to an expanded debris field from the ship they'd hit, a handful of new contacts appeared on his screen, and none of them the planet he was looking for. But these new arrivals were moving in familiar ways, enough so that he didn't need to wait for the computer to tell him what they were.

"Missiles!"

On the screen, the missiles were converging on a single point, thankfully one on the other side of the cargo slug. So far, the enemy was treating their improvised spacecraft as nothing but an unexplained rock in space, and the targeting made sense. They were trying to break it up before it could do any more damage to their fleet, but Malik could see that their plan wouldn't work.

On target, but definitely too late to do them any good. We're not finished hitting spaceships yet . . .

Malik stabbed a finger at the broadcast key on his handheld, and was rewarded with a humming inside his faceplate as the suit comms went live.

"Brace . . . yourselves!"

He could see Jantine from his position atop the crates, and knew generally where the rest of the mods were fastened.

When the missiles hit, the subroutine he was running on their suit telemetries gave him a much clearer picture of the team's status. And an unfortunately smaller head count.

Harren and Doria are flatlining . . .

Malik's grunt of recognition was all he allowed himself to voice before bending his head and starting a new set of burn calculations. There were bigger things to worry about right now. If the civvies were dead, so be it. Unless he could stabilize their flight, they'd have plenty of company soon enough.

Doria, I . . .

The missiles' impact didn't do much more than blast off a few hundred tons of rock, but as an unexpected benefit the explosions killed most of the slug's angular momentum. Jantine must have realized this as well, and was already unfastening her harness.

"Grav! And find me that planet."

Malik programmed one-quarter gravity, but didn't activate any other environmental systems. All he really needed to do was establish a separate frame of reference for the container and buy them a little more time. Once it came online, he felt a great weight lift from his shoulders, but didn't raise his head from the screen.

Jantine would see to the others—that's what she was here for. Now that he could use both hands Malik began searching for any trajectory that didn't include a very large spaceship directly in their path.

And when he found one—as with the missiles—it was too late to matter. Using as calm a voice as he could muster, Malik addressed the rest of the team over the open channel.

"Anyone who's not still harnessed should find something to hold onto. We're about to make contact with the enemy."

There wasn't much point in telling Jantine they were about to collide with a Redstone class dreadnaught, or that they'd already plowed through three of its tenders. All any of them could do now was hold on and hope for a quick death.

As he watched the range to target decrease, his thoughts weren't of the mission, or Doria, or even the people aboard the enemy ship that would die along with him. Instead, he imagined the surface of the planet he'd finally located, and how nice it might have been to stand on it.

Despite the artificial gravity field, Malik was thrown hard against the restraints by the impact, and this time they were insufficient to the task. He rocketed off the raft of crates toward one of the unseen walls of the cargo container. As he flew through the thinning air, he tightened his grip on the portable unit and drew it close to his chest. If he couldn't save his own life, at least he could protect the only chance the rest of the team had for survival.

All right, JonB. Let's see how smart you really are. Maybe you can figure out why an attack fleet is trying to stay hidden this close to—

ALOYSIUS

"DAMMIT, WHERE'S THAT EMERGENCY POWER?"

Captain Aloysius Martin, commander of the System Defense Force dreadnaught *Valiant* was not happy. First a giant rock came out of nowhere and smashed through his battle group. Then he'd lost his grip on the railing. And then just when he'd oriented himself for a secured position along a bulkhead, one of the wetnose middies panicked and bounced him back out into open air.

If I find out which one it was, I'm going to enjoy showing the kid just how much dirt can hide on a deck, even when you're inches away with a tiny wire brush.

Floating blind through his command center, there was nothing he could do until one of the dozen or so screaming people in the same situation either guided him to a wall or followed his damned orders.

And I'm getting a little tired of waiting for answers.

"Sir, I don't know . . ."

"Captain, I can't . . ."

"I'm not sure, but . . ."

Martin felt something solid against his back and used the hand he'd kept on his belt controls since he started tumbling to activate his boot magnets. The solid SSSSHUNK as they made a connection with whatever surface he'd found was the best

43

thing he'd heard in the last five minutes, and it finally gave him something to work with.

Taking a deep breath, he puckered his lips and gave a shrill whistle. The earsplitting noise had the desired effect, and he let the silence linger for a moment before speaking.

"Listen up! The next person who tells me what they don't know or can't do had better not let me recognize their voice. We have a problem. I want solutions, not excuses. So who's willing to start?"

There was a long moment of silence as his subordinates pondered the rest of their careers. Martin was about to speak again when he heard four knocks against some surface across the room. Three seconds later, they repeated, standard damage control procedure aboard starships.

There's someone out there!

Martin was about to order a response when someone in the same area found enough leverage to give an answering three knocks.

Alive. Pressurized. Ready. Looks like one of you new recruits was paying attention in class after all.

Martin closed his eyes and waited for the command center's access door to cycle. Whoever was out there likely had a portable power unit and came up here to get some idea of what happened. He'd have the answers he needed soon enough.

Martin heard the door squeal in protest as his rescuers cranked the manual release. There was a soft sound of escaping air, and through his lids he registered a soft glow.

Opening his eyes onto the green light of a chemical hand lamp, he smiled at the realization that he'd come to rest inverted from ship normal. The hatch was cranked halfway, just enough for a half dozen crew in hardsuits to come in, but not so far that it couldn't be closed in a hurry if necessary.

The team leader's suit had what Martin thought was a red blaze across the shoulders, but in the chem light it could easily enough have been blue. What mattered most there the two circles on either side of their collar, and the professional way the officer was taking stock of the ruined command center.

And very close after it on the list has to be the induction pistol fixed to that chestplate. Whoever you are, you're not taking any chances, are you?

After slapping a tether box to the bulkhead, the lieutenant stepped aside and let the rest of the team go to work. A clear contralto came from the suit's external speaker, and Martin smiled when he recognized who'd come to find him.

"Who's in command?"

"I am, Lieutenant Harlan. What can you tell me?"

Mira Harlan had been with Martin for almost five years, and was a strong candidate for the captains list the next time there was an opening. Her normal duty on the *Valiant* was supervising the fire control center, and her team efficiency ratings were the highest aboard the ship. If anyone could shed light on their current situation, it was she.

But she's not one of us. Not yet, anyway. There's still a lot that she doesn't know. And there's too much at stake to throw it all away on someone we haven't fully vetted.

The damage team spread out from the tether box, grabbing and stabilizing crewmembers as they went. One floated up to the center's nominal ceiling and anchored themself much as Martin had. Whoever it was planted an emergency lamp, and seconds later the compartment was full of light.

"Sir, at 1245 ship time, an unidentified object approximately 250 meters in length and massing almost 100 kilotons made a hyperspace transition at close range with the *Harrow* and proceeded to destroy not only that vessel but the tenders *Cessnock* and *Gadwell*. I pumped six Geysers with full warheads into the bogey and didn't even slow it down."

"Are you sure about that, Harlan?"

"Yes, sir. At first we thought it was a rogue comet, but the composition was all wrong, and then the hyper emergence was confirmed. The object collided with us forty seconds later, and then we lost comms and external sensors."

Martin took in this information while he looked around the command center. Charred panels warred with floating clouds of blood for his attention. His ship was dead, and several of his officers along with it. Commander Williams he knew about:

Martin was standing next to him when his panel exploded. But the additional losses of Lieutenants Mackie and Charles effectively gutted his senior staff.

Martin waved Harlan over to him, then walked himself down the wall. It felt like running through ankle-deep mud, but at least he wasn't floating wild anymore. Harlan crossed the room by launching herself at the ceiling, then caroming down in a perfect shot to a space next to him. Her boots attached to the decking right about the same time Martin was upright relative to everyone else, and he had to admire her skill.

Showing off for the boss, Harlan? Or are you like me, and just don't like wasting time?

Martin motioned to Harlan's helmet, and the blank glass faceplate nodded. She raised gauntleted hands to her neck and released the helmet's seals, allowing him to see inside and have a more private conversation. The face inside was a match to her voice: sharp and uncompromising. Martin held her gaze for a few seconds while he deliberated. Finding something in her eyes he liked, he made his decision.

"Okay, Harlan, you've got my full attention right now. What was it?"

Harlan nodded, then lowered her voice so that it wouldn't carry. Her damage control team was herding the injured out, but Martin didn't want the speculation to get too out of hand. The fact that they were still alive meant something, and he needed level heads around him to figure out what it was.

"Sir, it was moving too fast for a positive ID, but I can definitely tell you it wasn't a ship. No power signature, no outgassing after the Geysers hit. A salvo like that would have cracked a courier vessel wide open, and a hostile would have fired back instead of ramming us. My gut tells me it's a mined-out planetoid, but the mass is all wrong."

"Explain." Martin could hear Harlan's damage control team as they worked to restore order, but they kept clear of the two officers while they spoke.

"There are rocks that size all around the system, but for the most part they're in stable orbits and fitted with claim transponders. We cleaned the roamers up a few centuries ago, and the rest belong to the mining companies. If something like that was flying around loose, we'd know about it long before it hit one of our ships, and it definitely wouldn't be this far above the ecliptic.

"So we're back to my gut. I think it was a mass weapon, but I'm still clueless as to where it could have come from, or who would have fired it."

Martin was about to offer his own theory when a vac-suited crewman with an open helmet slammed into the half-open access door from the corridor, checking himself before he came tumbling into the command center. Both the captain and Lieutenant Harlan swiveled their heads to see what was going on, and Martin recognized the man as a junior engineer on Master Chief Henderson's watch. The name escaped him, but there were over two hundred people on the *Valiant*, and most of them were new.

Were being the word of the day. As far as I know, I've got a little over a dozen people still alive on this ship, and all of them are in this room.

"Sir . . . Ma'am, we got hit! There's something stuck in us, and it's cutting off power through the ship. We can't . . . well, I don't know if . . ."

Martin tried not to roll his eyes, focusing instead on the first part of the breathless crewman's report. At his side, he saw Harlan also keenly intent on what the man was saying. Martin was a heartbeat faster with his question though, and Harlan wisely waited her turn.

She's got definite promise.

"Stuck? Tell me what you saw, son. That's all I can ask."

Martin signaled the man to float over, for much the same reason he'd summoned Harlan to his side. There was no need to shout across the compartment if they didn't have to, and he had a feeling that whatever the crewman had to say, he wasn't going to like it very much.

In his haste, the crewman almost knocked Harlan loose from her perch, but she was ready for him and applied enough force to cancel his inertia and leave him floating next to a support railing. He nodded his thanks, snapped a tether from his work harness to the rail, then launched into his report.

"Sir, ma'am, the chief told me to get up here right away, said you'd definitely want to know about it. It's a ship, sir. They must have rammed us, but we've got no way of knowing who or how big."

This time, Harlan jumped right in.

"How do you know it's a ship, Mr. Carson? And where exactly did you come from?"

The engineer was able to handle the captain's scrutiny for the most part, but the ice in Harlan's voice left him momentarily speechless. To her credit, she didn't immediately dismiss the man's report as not fitting her facts, but like any trained tactical officer she wanted specifics, and not everyone thought in those terms during a crisis.

Plus, she knew his name. Carson swallowed nervously, and his mouth worked a couple times before more words came out.

"Ma'am, we were rotating tertiary power modules on the maneuvering jets up in the hullspace when all hell broke loose. We couldn't hear anything, of course, but we sure as hell felt it. Since we were already into the lines, we ran a trace back until we found the breach.

"There was too much damage to see exactly what it was, and in that compartment we could only see a cross section of it. But it was definitely metal. And curved. It's a hull of some kind, or I'll eat my stripes. The breaching systems sealed up around it good and tight, but once we got back inside we found more of it on other decks. I can't tell you much more, other than it's not radioactive, and it's not one of ours."

Harlan's face twisted in a scowl, but Martin didn't think she was upset about her theory being proved wrong. He suspected she was working up a new explanation, and just couldn't get all the facts to line up.

"Harlan?"

The lieutenant cocked her head slightly, flicking her eyes to the captain before squaring her expression and turning her full attention on the engineer.

"Sir, I'm . . . Carson, how many decks did you check out before Chief Henderson sent you up here?"

"Three, ma'am. We found some other debris as well, some space rock and such, but it was the same kind of metal. Definitely a ship of some kind."

When the engineer finished speaking, Harlan stared past him at the destroyed command center. The silence went on a bit long for his liking, so Martin prompted her with a question.

"What are you thinking, Lieutenant?

Harlan blinked twice and turned her head to look at the captain.

"Sir, I'm thinking that I very much want to know more about this supposed hull."

Martin nodded, and was about to send her to find out when Carson interrupted him.

"But ma'am, it's . . ."

Harlan cut him off with an upraised gauntlet and fixed him with a withering gaze.

"Carson, I'm sure the chief needs you right now more than we do up here. Tell him I want emergency power for this deck on standby, and to back away from whatever it is you found for now."

The engineer swallowed, then nodded.

"Yes, ma'am."

Carson looked at the two officers as if expecting some further commands but, after a few long seconds, realized that neither Harlan nor the captain were going to talk with him around. With more skill than he'd shown on arrival, he maneuvered himself so he was facing the out hatch, unhooked, and launched himself back into the ship.

Martin took a step forward and grabbed the rail, almost chuckling to himself at how close it had been while he was floating in the dark. The feel of it in his hands was reassuring, and helped to quell the roiling sensation in his gut. His eyes scanned the ruined command center

What happened to my ship? And why now, when I'm so close to . . .

"Sir, I want to scramble as many security teams as we can to midships. We have to assume a hostile incursion at this point, and I want to . . ."

Martin held up a hand to cut off Harlan's statement, and then moved it down to his belt controls and released his boots. He then motioned for the lieutenant to follow him as he shoved himself down the rail.

A few quick pushes, then a hard grab brought him to his destination. Several members of Harlan's team were working to free a body from under a mass of wrecked equipment, but Martin waved them away. Activating his boots again, he knelt and searched at Bill Williams's neck for something. He heard Harlan touch down behind him, then her involuntary gasp as he pulled back his hand with a bloody circuit key in his fingers.

"Lieutenant, I need for you to designate one of these crewmen as your replacement. As of . . ." Martin tried to establish a timeline in his head based on what Harlan had said, but one of the men nearby realized what he was doing and supplied him with an answer.

"1806, sir."

"1806 ship time, you are now the *Valiant*'s executive officer, with the acting rank of Lieutenant Commander. Do you acknowledge this order?"

"Sir, yes sir. Ramirez, the squad is yours. Get me comms and power, then a shipwide status report."

"Aye aye, ma'am."

"Get to it, Alonso. We're dead and blind right now, and I'd like to fix both ASAP."

Martin made as good an attempt as he could at cleaning the blood from the command key before handing it to Harlan. She was a good officer, just not part of his inner circle. He already knew she could handle herself in a crisis, but nothing about her politics.

Well, only one way to find out.

"Harlan, you're right. We need a lot more intel before our next move, but there are a couple other things to do first. Get teams down there like you said, and have one meet us at my quarters. I want to get into my hardsuit as soon as possible, and we can talk on the way."

Harlan looked the captain in the eye for a few seconds, then nodded. She put the key into one of the small pouches and pockets affixed up and down her left arm, then resealed her helmet. Her hardsuit's speakers squawked back to life, and everyone in the command center stopped to listen.

"All right, people, you heard the old man. Ramirez is in charge up here until we get back. Find me every trooper still mobile and scramble the best of the best to the captain's quarters. Get everyone else amidships weapons hot, and I want to hear someone's voice on channel three whispering in my ear before too much longer. Let's do it!"

As the repair crews acknowledged her orders, Martin oriented himself on the out hatch. But before he could float over to it, a squad of security troopers appeared just on the other side in with full defense gear, including laser cutters. He turned to Harlan, who shrugged.

"Well, that's one less thing to worry about. You men are with me and Commander Harlan now. Let's go."

A chorus of 'sir' came back at him, and Martin moved past the troopers into the corridor. Once out, he saw that someone— most likely Harlan's people—had slapped emergency beacons all the way down the corridor on their way up.

Martin started for his quarters with a practiced leap, sailing down the corridor ahead of the security escort with Harlan just a few meters behind. At the first junction, he held his release just long enough for her to draw a little closer, and once they were floating free again he spoke in a voice he was sure her suit mics could pick up.

"I don't have time to properly read you in on what you have to know, so for now just smile and keep following my orders."

Without hesitation, Harlan popped her faceplate again and answered in the same tones.

"Sir, I'm with you. We all are."

Martin smiled, but did not look back at her.

Of course you are, Harlan. That's what we told you to say back in training. It's certainly what they told me, and look how well that's turned out for us.

"Good, I appreciate it. Believe it or not, we have something more important to do right now than process damage reports, or even investigating whatever it was that hit us. There's a prisoner aboard who is vital to our survival. We are going to collect that prisoner now, and then move her to a secured shuttle."

Harlan slapped her chest to activate the suit's emergency lighting as they approached the end of the corridor. They were moving into areas she and her people hadn't secured yet, and Martin wondered to himself why he hadn't brought her into the fold before now.

Harlan did something with her left hand, and her boot jets flipped her heels-over-head. She landed on the bulkhead with her boots already magnetized near the emergency release and started working the hatch open. Martin stopped himself by grabbing a transit ring while several troopers performed maneuvers similar to Harlan's. Once the hatch was open enough to get gauntleted fingers into the gap, they added their suit-assisted strength to her purely mechanical efforts.

Once the hatch was open, she swung herself inside, brandishing a weapon he hadn't seen her draw. Once Martin was through himself, he activated his own boots and attached them to the wall on the other side. He studied the faces of the men and women filing through the hatch, meeting the gaze of a sergeant who stopped on the other side of the hatch next to him.

"Dog it, and seal it tight. We're not coming back this way."

"Yes, sir." The trooper waited until Martin was through, then got to work. As Martin launched himself down the passageway he heard the sounds of an emergency hand welder in action.

Good man. No questions.

Martin waited until he came up beside Harlan before continuing his explanation. "In case you were wondering why we we're out here in the middle of nowhere in the first place, it's because no sane person is supposed to be looking in this direction. It's cost us twice as much fuel as it should have and most of my political capital to get us within striking distance of the planet below, and it's just our bad luck that someone else seems to have had the same idea."

"Sir?" He didn't have to see her face to know what expression she was wearing. It wasn't fear, it was the hard stare of an officer committed to a course of action she didn't fully understand

"We're at war, Commander, whether the people down there know it or not. And I've gone too far down this road to let a broken ship and some lunatic firing mass drivers defeat me. We're going to secure our prisoner and regroup while I figure out how much firepower we've got left."

"Yes, sir. I was going to ask if there's anything I should know about the prisoner."

As Martin sailed through the still air of his dying ship with an armed force at his back, he felt almost as young as the officer he'd just recruited into his shadowy, interplanetary rebellion. She was asking the right questions, and that said a lot about who she really was. But as he'd said, the road to here was neither short nor straight, and there was no going back now.

"How much do you know about the Transgenic virus, Harlan? Because whatever you were told in school, I'm pretty sure we've found a cure."

MALIK

SOMETHING'S WRONG. I CAN'T MOVE MY . . .

Knives of pain stabbed through Malik's chest, and he decided to stop trying to speak. His eyes refused to focus, and he couldn't quite make out the voices speaking nearby. But they were somewhat familiar, so it stood to reason that at least two other members of the team survived the impact.

Broken arm, broken ribs. Cranial damage, possible infarction. Vision seems to be getting better, I can see some . . .

". . . pupillary response. He's definitely trying to communicate, but there's no telling how much damage there really is. I'd need to unpack some of the . . ."

". . . of the . . . tion. There's no telling how long we've got until we . . . pany."

Doria? Jantine? I think I hurt myself. You have to . . .

"I said, can he be moved? We can't stay here."

Jantine's voice was getting stronger, but Malik still couldn't see her face, or much of anything else. All he could really make out was a blue-white flashing from somewhere off to his left, but he didn't want to risk more pain by turning to see what it was.

"No. Neither of us are in any shape to go anywhere. But I think I can reach him, with just a little more time. Malik, can you hear me?"

"Na. Na!" Malik's tongue wouldn't move he way he wanted, but from what he could tell Doria understood him. Then JonB's voice came from Malik's left, complaining as usual.

"What do you mean, you think you can reach him? Commander—Jantine, we need to start the descent process. He's got most of it programmed in, but I need your disarm codes. They're almost through, but I can do this!"

JonB, no. We're done. You have to, you have to . . .

Malik tried to move his arm again but couldn't. When Doria spoke again, her words seemed to strip away some of his pain.

"Relax, Malik. I'm here with you. Just picture in your mind what you want me to tell them, and I'll do the rest."

Picturing his computer closing on JonB's hands, Malik tried to focus on what she was telling him. Doria said she couldn't read minds earlier, but he could hear her voice a lot clearer than he could Jantine's or JonB's—almost as if it was coming from inside his own head. He felt her hand on his cheek, and more of his pain slipped away.

"NnnnNuooo."

"That was a no," said Doria, "in case you hadn't figured it out, JonB. He says not to proceed with his calculations."

"But it's plain as day! It's all right here."

"He says it won't work."

I do? Yes, no. No! That trajectory isn't for us. Tell Jantine to find another way down. Tell her, Redstone dreadnaught. Tell her . . .

Malik felt a pinching pain in his right shoulder, then a spreading warmth. Doria's hand moved from his cheek to the back of his neck, and something like feathers was moving around inside his skull. He had the impression of something else, something very sad nearby. Two somethings in fact, but Malik filed them away as problems to deal with later.

Redstone. Tell her!

Before Doria could relay his message, Jantine spoke.

"JonB, can you tell me anything about where we are? What's around us?"

"There's a big planet down there that we can get to, that's all I need to know. Mass readings match what we have on file for . . ."

Malik felt something slide into place in his mind, and he heard Doria's voice stronger than ever.

"I'm not exactly sure what it's called, but Malik wants you to know that we hit a ship. And that we need to find another way down to the planet."

"That's ridiculous! How are we supposed to complete the mission if we don't—"

"JonB," Jantine interrupted, "tell me right now if you think you can use those equations to pilot both containers. And remember that Doria's not the only one around here who's good at figuring things out."

Malik felt something new, a vibration of some kind coming from behind him. His back was against a hard surface, and since Doria was unwilling to move him it was likely one of the container's walls. What had JonB said?

"They're almost through . . ."

JonB wasn't saying anything now, and Malik tried to smile. He'd done it; he'd saved the sleepers. Jantine would take care of the rest—that's what she was here for.

There wasn't any more pain, but Malik still couldn't make his mouth move properly. Then the hand on his neck shifted, and he felt something brush against his right ear.

Doria's voice was soft, warm, and this time on the outside of his head.

"We don't have a lot of time, Malik. Is there anything else you want her to know? I'll be here to help you. Just tell me what to do."

Doria, I . . .

"It's okay. Jantine and JonB know how badly I'm hurt, but the others don't. The stims are handling most of the pain, and I can stay with you until it's done. Tell me what she needs to know. Just stay focused, and I'll be your voice for now."

Malik felt the paired sadness move inside him, and the strength of it was nearly overwhelming. But at the same time, it gave him some comfort, and the longer he was in contact with it, the less it hurt. Although he couldn't say how, he recognized the presence of the Omegas in his mind alongside whatever it was Doria was doing to him. He pictured their faces as best he could, and when he asked his question, he was sure they heard it as well

I never knew. Is it . . . are they like this all the time?

It felt to Malik as if the words were plucked out of his mind as soon as he thought them. When Doria's whispered response came a few seconds later, he had the distinct impression that she was smiling.

"All the time," she said. "Don't be sad. And that goes for the two of you as well. This is a natural part of life. This would have happened eventually in any event; you two will live longer than any of us."

Malik tried to find words of his own to share with the Omegas, but as soon as he decided on the right ones, he felt them flow away and knew the mods understood.

Okay, here's what we have to do.

DORIA

DORIA FELT HER BROKEN RIBS GRINDING INSIDE HER chest. The pressure bandage Harren applied before the second impact was likely doing more harm than good, but at least he'd dealt with the bones that had pierced the skin and slowed her bleeding down.

For now. There was no way to confirm the diagnosis without alarming the rest of the mods, but she could feel the cuts inside her body. Every movement let a little more blood flow, and there was nothing she could do to stop it.

Though she was still crouched over Malik, she could feel waves of anticipation pouring off Jantine and JonB standing behind her. Fighting to keep her voice calm, she relayed what Malik had seen on his screen in the seconds before the impact.

"It's hard to be sure, but he thinks there's probably just a few tender ships left out there. The slug was on a trajectory to hit the larger vessel. He keeps showing me something, a small rock of some kind. It's a . . . oh, I understand now. A red stone. Does that mean anything to you, Commander?"

Jantine gave an uncharacteristic gasp.

"A Redstone dreadnaught. Intelligence says the enemy has about a dozen of them, and they never travel alone."

Malik's thoughts signaled agreement, then he summoned up a series of images that took Doria a few seconds to process.

"If I understand him correctly, he says if you move fast, you may be able to commandeer a scout ship, possibly a shuttle. But you have to leave us here. It's . . . it's the only way."

Doria lowered herself to the deck and turned to put her back against the wall next to Malik. In the flickering light of the computer screen, JonB's face matched his emotions, concerned, impatient, and more than a little frightened. But even though Jantine wasn't handling the situation well herself, she was in command, and needed the others to know it.

Like Malik said, it's what she's here to do.

"Can you handle this, Doria? Or should JonB stay with you?" Jantine said she was back in control, even though Doria could sense doubt creeping in around the edges.

JonB's confusion deepened, then his expression hardened as he realized what was about to happen. Doria felt a touch of regret that he'd never truly opened up to her, but given who he was and why he was on the mission, there really wasn't a lot she could do for him until the colony was established.

And now . . .

"I can . . . *we* can do it. Malik's got an excellent visual memory, and my hands are still functional. It's not the kind of detail work I'm used to, but I'll adapt. And if you'll bring the computer a little closer, I should be able to make things a little easier for you in the short term."

Doria gestured to the computer, and JonB slid it closer to her hands. The screen was cracked, but still functional, and by guiding Malik's memories she brought the lights up enough for the mods to see each other clearly, instead of by dim emergency beacons.

It seemed like a lot longer than thirty minutes since she'd seen Jantine's face, but it seemed different now. It wasn't just the low light, her demeanor had definitely changed. It wasn't the uniform either; even with the faceplates open, the encounter suits gave everybody a little more confidence. This was something different, more fundamental. Reaching out to her mind, Doria felt none of the uncertainty Jantine had struggled with just a few hours before. She was every bit the commander now, and Doria tried to share some of it with Malik.

She'll be okay. They all will.

Jantine leaned closer. Her eyes conveyed her concern for Malik and Doria, but more for her second-in-command than for the Gamma. Doria shared as much of it as she could with Malik. His response was both immediate, and heartbreaking.

"It's okay, Jantine. He wants you to. Has for some time."

Jantine closed her eyes, and bent down to press her lips to his mouth. Malik couldn't move in response, but he didn't have to. This was about feelings, and feelings were what Doria did best.

The Omegas were already moving along the wall, orienting themselves by the heat generated by what must be cutting torches on the other side. They weren't big on goodbyes, another thing she liked about working with them.

The rest of the team was lined up behind the Deltas, waiting for the attack to begin. Katra wasn't in very good shape either, but the Omegas were helping her place the breaching charges, and Doria knew they'd be fine too. It wasn't going to be an easy adjustment, but they'd been at this a while.

Besides, Jarl wouldn't let anything happen to Katra. Not while he was alive.

When Jantine finished, she moved over to Doria's side and handed her several grenades from a pouch on her harness. Even though it hurt, Doria pushed them away, and smiled. She answered for both herself and Malik.

"We're covered. And something tells me that you're going to need those a lot more than I will."

Jantine smiled, and stood up. Without another word, she walked over to the rest of the team and crouched into a firing position. She snapped her helmet's faceplate closed, and the rest of the team did the same.

Doria leaned a little closer to Malik and whispered to him.

"Malik, Do you want me to watch her for you?"

Malik surprised her with an image of a handheld, with text scrolling across the screen. It took her a second to figure out what he was trying to do, but when she did she gave his hand a small squeeze and read his message.

No, it's all right. We have to finish the launch sequence. She'll buy us enough time to get the sleepers down safely, and once I confirm the team's launch, we can let go.

"Malik, I . . ."

What was it you said? It's going to be all right. We can do this.

"No. That's not it."

Before she could tell him, the breaching charges went off. Jantine and the Deltas sent a three-second burst of hell through the resulting hole, then stopped firing long enough for Jarl and Katra to go to work.

Doria couldn't hear any screaming from the other side of the wall, but the Omegas could see just fine. Through their eyes she watched the thermal blurs of her fellow Gammas tear through the much cooler forms of the enemy. The hallway was clear five seconds later.

The Omegas waited until Carlton and JonB were through, and then paused to look back at her and Malik. Then she felt them enter her mind, sharing their lives with her and showing Doria her part in them.

Doria had spent her life interpreting the emotions of others. The joy she felt when communicating like this was almost as good as the drugs Carlton had given her, but this time the Omegas weren't holding back. Doria finally experienced the full impact of feelings that they always held back from other mods. Doria let it fill up the corners of her mind, taking away her pain and giving her a few more minutes of clarity to work with.

She didn't bother to send her thanks through the link—none were necessary. She'd already said her goodbyes, and they were carrying away a part of her with them to share with their next Gamma.

Instead, Doria turned her thoughts back to Malik, and the job they still had to complete.

"Malik, I think you should show me how to set a timer on the destruct charges. I don't think I've got that much time left . . ."

ALOYSIUS

"WHAT EXACTLY AM I LOOKING AT HERE, SIR?"

Harlan's confusion was understandable. Martin had his own doubts about the sleeper tank installed in the Environmental Systems bay, but as the person who'd put it there and arranged for an independent power supply and round-the-clock guards, he had at least some of the answers she was looking for.

Harlan was using a private suit channel for the question, so he responded in kind. So far, neither had received any signals from the main comms, but Harlan's damage control teams were the best in the fleet and it was only a matter of time before they'd need to have their stories straight.

"That, Commander, is humanity's future. It's what the gennies call an Alpha, one of their leaders."

Martin didn't offer more information, letting Harlan draw her own conclusions as to why it was aboard the *Valiant*.

The techs were fitting the bulky unit with a grav harness, but Martin's eyes went as always to the doll-like face of the being in deepsleep inside. Whatever dreams he and his co-conspirators had of taking back their destiny rested inside that perfect head, and had done so for longer than he'd been alive.

"It's one of the first ones, actually. We found it in a crashed gennie transport on a frozen planet I'm not cleared to tell you about. But it had been there for some time, so long in fact that the Alphas in the Colonies now are much, much different biologically."

This time he'd aroused her curiosity, and Harlan turned her suited head to look at him directly. Martin saw the reflection of his own helmet in her visor, and found the metaphor apt.

Go ahead then, ask it. It's what I'd do in your position.

"With respect, sir, how is this thing supposed to help us?"

Martin jetted forward, motioning for Harlan to follow. His hardsuit was the same model as hers, minus all the pouches and extra weapons. And although the extra time he spent reclaiming it and a few personal effects from his quarters might still bite him in the ass, it was worth it to be fully mobile again. He used a gauntlet jet to stop himself, then placed the same hand on the sleeper unit.

"The gennie bloodlines, or mods, as they call themselves, stabilized about two centuries ago. Every one of them comes out of the womb perfectly designed for their role in Colonial society, and then they spend a dozen or so years in a crèche downloading all the education they need to fulfill it.

"This one though . . ." Martin's voice trailed off as he thought about the magnitude of what he was saying, "this one isn't done yet. Its genes are still in flux, being acted on by a version of the Transgenic virus we haven't seen in centuries. When we found it, well, it changed everything."

Harlan's shoulders shifted slightly, and Martin wished he could see her face.

Do I really have to right to involve her in this? So far she's just following my orders, but soon there'll be a line she can't uncross.

Martin nodded to a vac-suited tech, who released the clamps securing the sleeper unit to the *Valiant*'s environmental systems and power grid. The damage to his ship hadn't propagated this far, and the unit's independent power supply was still operational. Watching the techs work, Martin was glad Harlan had come looking for him first—he doubted the guards he'd posted would have deterred her for very long if she'd chosen to restore the ship's air and heat instead.

Martin switched over to an area broadcast and spoke to the crew. His real crew, the ones he'd selected for loyalty over the past few months. That group also now included Harlan and part of the security team that followed them from the command center.

One other benefit of stopping off at his quarters was a quick consultation of their personnel files—all but three of them were on Bill William's expanded list. He'd had Harlan send those he wasn't sure about to the squads forming up around the intruder object, one to each deck, to deliver his orders.

Stand fast. Observe.

"All right people, let's move out. We're making for transfer bay six, the captain's shuttle. No delays, we'll apologize for any bruised shins or feelings later."

Martin watched the security team move into place both ahead and behind the now-mobile piece of history, as well as taking up positions behind himself and Harlan. Like Harlan, they had a lot of gear affixed to their hardsuits, and Martin was sure it was all meant for causing damage. Harlan's kit was a combination of extra ammunition and a variety of tools the captain didn't recognize, but he was sure she had quite a few nasty surprises hidden away as well.

Ammunition. Should have brought some more of my own, but I'm hoping it won't come to that. If I can't get the job done with only one pistol . . .

As soon as it was clear of the bay doors, he nodded to Harlan, who jetted up to kill the portable lighting unit. She detached one of the boxlike compartments on her back and stowed the light away, returning everything to its proper place in a fluid movement.

Harlan twisted through the air as she came back down to land beside him, and the two officers started floating after the rest of the team. Several troopers were waiting on the other side of the hatch; after they dogged it behind them, it would be as if they were never there.

"Still with me, Mira? This can't be an easy thing to learn about, especially today."

Harlan floated silently alongside him for a few meters before speaking.

"Yes, sir. No problems here. I'm assuming you'll give me the full story on who 'we' are before I get shot for treason, but I'm with you."

"I appreciate that, Harlan. More than you know. And it's not treason we're facing, but extinction. We have been, ever since the first gennie mutants expressed. But that one"—Martin waved ahead—"it's still cooking. Still mostly human, and with the technology we have now we can properly analyze the changes it's going though and reverse the process."

"Reverse, sir? Are you suggesting we . . . this . . ."

Martin had a very real sense that Harlan was about to dig in her metaphorical heels, and spun himself to face her directly.

"No, Lord no. You have to believe me, Harlan, we're not talking about vivisection, or weaponization. We, our people, are looking for a vaccine at best. I don't want to eliminate the gennies, I just want to save the human race! Those of us who are still human, still able to call ourselves that."

This time Harlan did stop, jetting to a halt. Martin did the same, bringing up his internal visor lights and making his face-plate clear so she could see his face. Almost instantly, Harlan did the same, and for the first time since she'd joined him in the command center he could see real doubt in her eyes. She reached out and grabbed his shoulder, locking herself into the same plane of reference. Though they were drifting slightly, they were doing it together, and he thought that was just fine.

Here it is, Aloysius. Decision time. She's already made up her mind, but she needs to hear the words.

"You said we were at war, sir. I need to know right now with whom, and for how long."

Martin leaned forward to touch his helmet to Harlan's. Once he was sure she he had her complete attention, he made a show of moving his eyes down to the left. Martin narrowed his focus on the holographic icon that turned off the private channel they'd been using, and waited.

Harlan's eyes tightened, searching his face for some clue as to his intentions. Through their joined faceplates he could hear her breathing, then heard it stop as she made the same mental connection. Without turning her head, she scanned the edge of her peripheral vision for the security troopers that were still behind them in the passageway. When they made no overtly hostile move, she dropped her focus to the lower left of her own display, and killed her comms.

"Go." Her voice was muffled after passing through two face-plates, but its tone was colder than interstellar space.

"Harlan, the reason we're out here, out of contact with the rest of the fleet and far enough above the ecliptic that no one will even think to look for us is because there are people who want to do the exact same thing you were just about to accuse me of. There is a faction in the fleet that's not content with keeping the most important human being in the universe on ice, and from this moment on you have to assume that anyone you know could be the enemy."

Martin watched the realization set in, how carefully her eyes stayed fixed on his, how fast the breaths started coming when she finally remembered to breathe. He remembered the cold line of sweat at the back of his neck when Admiral Worthy pulled him aside during a hyperspace hull survey just after he'd been given command of the *Valiant*, when he realized the man he'd idolized for half his life was prepared to shove him off into interdimensional space if he gave the wrong answer.

The same moment he realized that that man was contemplating genocide, and that Martin would do anything in his power to stop him.

"I didn't find the Alpha, Harlan. I stole it. Then I stole this whole battle group, and parked it out here until I could be sure of who I could trust. You can hate me for what I'm planning, you can hate my methods, but you have to believe me when I say that I'm one of the good guys here."

"How?"

Martin was taken aback by the simple question. There were so many things she could have asked, so many different ways he could have answered why. But Harlan didn't want justification. She didn't want an explanation. She wanted a reason to trust him, and to believe.

He had an answer. Of course he had an answer. But it pained him to even think about it, and explaining it was even worse.

"Because gennies always travel in pairs, and the fleet has already tried to kill one of them. Tried, and succeeded. If we can't protect that little gennie girl in there, I think they're going to use the virus to kill us all . . ."

JANTINE

JANTINE FELT THE LAUNCH VIBRATIONS SHAKE THE corridor, but didn't have time to reflect on what it meant for her and her team. Her attention was wholly focused down the sights of her pulse rifle at the enemy.

That's it, just a little closer . . .

She could make out eight figures limned in soft green light. They were floating in a staggered formation, almost exactly in the center of the corridor. They were each carrying some kind of bulky rifle, easily twice the size of the weapon in her hands.

She fired a shot high over their heads, almost pitying them for their lack of mobility. The hardsuited opponents drew up fast with hasty course corrections, but ended up floating slowly down the corridor instead of moving into secure firing positions. They were essentially helpless in the seconds before they could redirect themselves with boot or hand jets. Just like the first group, they were no more threatening than target drones.

Jarl and Katra waited until the last enemy was past them to disengage their active camouflage, then they opened fire with hand pulsers. In less than three seconds they'd neutralized all eight enemies, and Katra was bounding down the corridor back the way they came.

You people have to have grav generators, otherwise this area of your ship wouldn't have a "floor." Why do you keep wasting your tactical advantages by coming in weightless?

Malik would have an answer, he always did. Jantine tried to bury her sadness, but his loss was too raw to process right now.

How am I going to do this without you?

Jantine took a moment to steady her breathing then opened her faceplate. The cold air of the corridor was like a slap in the face, and an urgent reminder that they needed to get off this ship as soon as possible.

"Wrap it up, JonB. It's time to go."

Jantine's whisper was barely audible, especially compared to the sounds of combat that filled the corridor just moments ago. JonB shot her a worried look then turned his attention back to the pile of technology laid out in front of him.

JonB started tapping on his handheld, while at the same time intently studying Jantine's portable terminal. He'd had to power both down while the mods set the ambush and now was catching up on what was happening outside the ship.

When he didn't acknowledge her order, she waved Artemus ahead and then chanced a look at the rest of her team. Even in the soft light of the terminal, she could see that Carlton was in bad shape. One of the Omegas had a hand on his shaking shoulder in a gesture strongly reminiscent of Doria. Jantine understood—she wasn't doing much better, but wishing wouldn't bring her friends back.

JonB was another matter. He seemed more annoyed than upset that three members of the team were either dead or permanently incapacitated. The scientist wasn't on the mission to make friends, none of them were. But he hadn't gone out of his way to do so either, even with her. If anything, he'd kept the other mods at a distance intentionally, as if predicting this exact situation.

"JonB. We need to move."

"Another minute, Commander. Please. I need to confirm the container's course. The debris field out there is huge, and any number of things can go wrong."

Jantine understood what JonB was saying, but she didn't have to like it. Malik was good at what he did, and even using Doria's hands she trusted him to get the sleepers out of danger. But no one could have predicted the presence of enemy spacecraft at their insertion point, and there could be even more surprises coming their way.

"Take two, and then we're leaving even if Crassus has to carry you."

JonB returned to his energetic tapping. Jantine couldn't pretend to understand the calculations necessary to track the container—she wasn't born that way. Her responsibility now was to get the team down to the planet and recover the sleepers. She needed the scientist, now more than ever. But she also needed to know her orders would be carried out.

Malik is—was—so much better at this.

The thought spawned a fresh wave of grief and self-doubt in Jantine. She needed to start thinking of Malik in the past tense, and let go of the memory of her second-in-command propped up against the wall with a massive head wound. The knowledge that Doria was dying alongside him didn't make it any better.

I need to be doing something. Moving, killing enemies, anything. Waiting around here is just making this worse.

Harren's death was unfortunate, but what bothered Jantine was that her reaction to it was so clinical. Carlton was barely upright after the loss of his sib, and she'd simply written Harren off when she saw the body. It was more that their specialties weren't immediately useful to her, so Jantine regarded the support Betas differently than she did JonB.

If they ever did get down to the planet, Carlton would be far more valuable than just another pair of arms. Jantine's job right now was to make sure that happened. And to do it, the team had to get moving.

Crassus waved a free arm to catch her attention. The Delta was a bit cramped in the corridor, but at least he and Artemus could still stand upright. The Omegas had it much worse, almost doubled over when not moving. The enemy ship seemed to be designed for a fairly narrow range of human being, and no one they'd seen so far was out of the ordinary.

Jantine gave Crassus her full attention.

"Commander Jantine. Scout Katra reports the corridor is clear for two hundred meters then opens into an intersection. Scout Jarl has secured a cache of enemy equipment and awaits further orders. He believes we can use scattercomms undetected but worries about the atmospheric integrity in the rest of this vessel."

Jantine nodded. The thought had crossed her mind as well. The air here was too cold for comfortable living, though she'd encountered worse during training. Even the most undisciplined commander made environmental systems a priority in an emergency.

"Thank you, Crassus. Is there anything else?"

Jantine had worked with Deltas before and knew they tended to prioritize information. She couldn't think of anything else Artemus might have relayed from further down the corridor, but she wanted to make sure.

"No, Commander Jantine. Do you require me to discipline Scientist JonB?"

JonB blanched at this but did not say anything in response. Jantine didn't hide her smile.

"That will not be necessary, Crassus. Everyone here knows what we have to do."

"Yes, Commander Jantine. I have taken personal responsibility for Support Technician Carlton and the Builders. No harm will come to them while I live."

The Builders. Such an elegant name for the Omegas, even when spoken so formally. Crassus, you are a poet at heart.

If JonB was bothered by his omission from the Delta's vow of protection, he didn't show it. It was simple mathematics— the Deltas had divided responsibility for the civvies, and he wasn't on Crassus's list. Artemus would have him covered, even from his position up the corridor next to Jarl.

Jantine looked over her command and judged it ready for travel. Katra and Jarl would find them a path; Artemus and Crassus would make sure they got there. Her job was to give the orders, especially the unpleasant ones. So far her choices had gotten three of her people killed, but the rest still needed her.

"Time's up. Let's go."

JonB closed the computer's case and handed it off to Carlton. The civvie Beta stood and tapped out something on his hand-held then held it up to the Omegas. One of them looked at it, and then picked up several of the bulky packs the first wave of enemies had been carrying.

When Jantine gave him a questioning look, JonB sidled over and tipped his head toward her.

"The laser cutters may be useful. Just about everything else they've got is garbage, but they burned almost all the way through the container's hull in a lot less time than it would have taken us."

Jantine thought about the other tactical advantages the mods had over the enemy. The team's grav generators were the biggest ones, and the suit technology they'd seen so far was laughable. The enemy's vac-suits were twice the thickness of even a civvie encounter suit, and offered much less protection. The armored suits were a little better, but even more bulky. And unlike the recoilless pulsers the combat mods used, the enemy's induction slug throwers seemed ill-suited to fighting in a weightless environment.

It's a wonder you people ever made it out into space. You're like children playing with knives.

Now that she had time to think about it, Jantine's curiosity was aroused. It also helped that for once, JonB actually seemed to be helping her, rather than complaining.

"What else can you tell me about them? While we hop."

JonB fell in beside her as she started moving. Crassus dropped back to shield his charges, and Jantine knew he'd make sure they kept up.

Jantine pushed off, keeping her strides small so as to not overrun Jarl and Artemus. At the preferred quarter-grav the team was using, she could easily cover a dozen meters with each jump. Katra's report said there was an intersection ahead. The Gammas would have to scout both directions before they could move on, so there was no need to hurry.

"I think Jarl's right about the scattercomms. The first group wasn't carrying any personal transmitters, but in the damage control packs they had a relay unit of some kind that I think keys into the power system. The cargo slug's impact must have taken out their primary infrastructure. Essentially, everyone we encounter will be operating independently, and I don't believe they've got a lot of surprises for us."

Jantine had only glanced at the packs in question, but what JonB was saying made sense. The first group had been carrying far more gear than was necessary to breach their container. They must have been a repair crew, and she felt a momentary twinge of guilt at killing noncombatants. But from what she knew about the Redstone class dreadnaughts, there should be a lot more and a lot better resistance arrayed against them.

It's as if someone decided to crew a ship with untrained recruits, rather than combat veterans. The techs certainly knew what they were doing, but that patrol was a joke.

Jantine saw Jarl and Artemus shoulder several of the downed enemy troopers and carry them forward. It was a reasonable precaution, and she wagered that JonB was as interested as she was in examining their gear.

By the time the two Betas reached the intersection, Katra and Jarl were already gone. Artemus was standing guard over the enemy corpses, bodies Jarl had selected based on the amount of damage they'd suffered.

The first corpse was nearly intact save for the shattered faceplate. A pair of pulser shots had destroyed the second's chest, most likely killing it instantly. Or, more accurately, her. JonB wasted no time in wrestling off the helmet of the dead woman's hardsuit.

The woman's features were fascinating. She might have been in her late teens, with an unlined face and hair that ended neatly at the base of her neck. Jantine studied the contours of the dead woman's face, searching for something, anything relatable to her own life. In the green glow, it was surprisingly asymmetric, instead of the designed and proportioned faces she was used to.

Jantine resisted the urge to raise a hand to her own face and feel her cheekbones and orbital ridges; her mental picture was as accurate as any mirror could be. Instead, she knelt and moved the woman's head further into the light.

The appearance of the dead trooper was unnerving, a fact that bothered Jantine in and of itself. Not three meters behind her were mods whose faces were much more removed from the human baseline. But this woman was . . . almost familiar. There was no one thing wrong with her features; it was just that none of them were "right."

Jantine let the body fall, and she scanned both sides of the passageway for some sign of the Gammas. When none came, she closed her eyes and listened instead. She could hear JonB tinkering with the helmet, and filed the sound away in order to narrow her focus.

In similar fashion, she catalogued the sounds of the bundles the Omegas carried moving against one another, Crassus's careful footsteps, and even Carlton's compulsive fidgeting. Finally, she focused on the sound of her own heart beating, letting it drop below her normal resting rate of forty beats per minute until she could feel it pulsing throughout her entire body. With each heartbeat, she considered another of the facts before her.

We have met no solid resistance.

Our opponents are inexperienced.

This ship is either dead or dying.

This area of space should be empty.

Malik said ships, plural.

Our opponents are inexperienced.

We are not alone.

"JonB. I need blood samples from both these bodies. Artemus, Crassus, get the Gammas back, at least to comm range. Carlton, I want a full, functioning suit of this armor and some of their weapons for analysis. I don't care how many pieces either is in, just as long as they work."

Jantine was about to include instructions for the Omegas, but she had a sense they were already busy with something. Turning around, she saw they were moving their heads back and forth, as if trying to zero in on something with their exceptional auditory range.

Jantine watched the pair of mods for another few seconds. It didn't seem right to stare at them, but Doria's smiling face wasn't there as a buffer anymore. The Omegas didn't seem concerned by the noises JonB and Carlton were making while they dealt with the bodies, or by the sound of the Deltas' feet skipping down the corridor. It was if the thing they were searching for was just beyond their ability to sense, and that thought was a sobering one.

Whatever it is, they'll let me know about it when it's relevant. Until then, I've got a job to do.

Undisguised footsteps from both sides brought her back into focus. Katra and Artemus were together, but the Katra's eyes and shaking head were just as effective a report as any words would be.

From the other direction, Crassus came back alone, with something small and dark held in a lower hand. He raised it to his head once he was sure she could see him, then extended a long forefinger and trailed it along his jaw.

Scattercomms were standard issue for combat ops. The organic circuitry was easily applied along the underside of the jaw, with one end resting just under the chin and the other tucked in behind the left ear.

Though the devices were powered by piezoelectric charges from the skin of the wearer and nearly undetectable while active, it was impossible to have a truly secure conversation while using them. The main advantage of scattercomms were instant group conversations over a medium distance, when a helmet channel or handheld wasn't practical.

Jantine ran a finger down her jaw to activate her unit, then pumped her mouth twice without speaking to open a channel. She heard three clicks in her left ear, one for herself and each mod already in the loop. Crassus set whatever he was carrying on the decking, and then moved back down the corridor to act as a relay. When he was almost at the edge of her visual range, she heard four clicks. She swallowed, and began talking from the back of her throat in a whisper that barely escaped her lips.

"Jarl. Go."

"Encountered another repair group, boss. No weapons or cutters, but this one had emergency lights, a power relay, some handheld comms, and a map."

Jantine felt her heartbeat speed up at the news, but she kept her voice calm.

"Is that what Crassus brought back?" She nudged JonB with her foot, making the comm motion with her left hand and gestured at the object with her pulse rifle in her right. He signaled understanding and moved forward to collect it. Five clicks sounded in her ear, and Jarl spoke again.

"No. Comm unit. It's unlocked, but don't . . ."

A high-pitched squeal rang out from the black object in JonB's hand, and Jantine dropped into a firing crouch. Over her sights she watched the civvie fumble with the device for several seconds until he managed to reverse whatever he'd done to make it react like that.

". . . turn it on while using active scatter. There's a feedback loop."

Jantine frowned slightly, marking up yet another reason not to use the supposedly untraceable comms.

"Were you detected?" She heard four clicks, and saw JonB hunch his shoulders somewhat. His lopsided smile was all the apology she needed, and as she and the other combat mods lowered their weapons, he relaxed his posture and went to work on the captured device.

"No. They had no time to send a signal. Map shows a maintenance entrance ten meters from here, but I have no visual confirmation. Found what looks like a transit bay, but it's the long way around and one level up."

Jarl didn't waste any breath on the fate of the repair team, and Jantine didn't bother to ask. If he was being observed, Jarl was too good to risk comm chatter, especially after discovering the feedback loop.

"Hold position. We're coming to you. Next comm in sixty seconds."

Jantine used her left hand to swipe her jawline, killing the connection. As she stood up, she held the same hand out to Carlton and the Omegas, then gestured down the passageway in Jarl's general direction. JonB started back to the group as Carlton finished packing away the hardsuit's components.

Out of her armor, the dead woman looked even younger than she had from the neck up. She had well-muscled arms, but she still had a softness that indicated she'd only been engaging in intensive exercise for a short time. She lacked the definition of Jantine and the Gammas, but most humans did.

This last thought cemented what Jantine found so troubling about the bodies, and made JonB's blood samples mostly irrelevant.

It's as if she's virus-free. But that's not supposed to be possible . . .

JonB reached her just as Carlton finished, and he packed up his gear in seconds, leaving the portable enemy comm out on the deck. Jantine looked at it, weighing whether or not destroying it was the right call.

"Can you make that thing work?"

"Yes. It has an internal power cell, but the default setting is to function on broadcast power. It's just bad luck that it thinks the scattercomms are part of that system. As long as I can bypass the protocol, it should be fine. And I found a volume control; we should be able to listen in at a rational level."

"All right. Don't experiment without telling me first. I don't want any more surprises."

"Of course, Commander. But . . ." JonB looked nervously at the other mods while he shouldered his pack.

"JonB, you and I have to trust each other for this to work. If there's a concern, it comes straight to me now. And if I'm not around, to Jarl. Understand?"

Jantine watched the Omegas and Carlton move ahead to join Crassus, while Artemus took a position that allowed the Delta to still see JonB. Katra was guarding their rear, and if she took any offense at Jantine's statement, she gave no sign. Technically Jarl was next in command, even though Katra was older and more experienced. But the same lack of imagination that made her sims predictable also kept Katra out of the command structure. She was a creature of instinct, not intuition.

A distinction probably lost on JonB. But this mission doesn't require that we all like each other.

"Yes, Commander. I was wondering why you wanted the blood samples? You already know the answer . . ."

Jantine held up her hand to stop him then gestured down the corridor. JonB was a bit slow in following her meaning, and instead of repeating the gesture, she grabbed his shoulder and gently shoved him after the rest of the team. The scientist stumbled briefly, but he still had a Beta's grace and was able to keep up with her long strides as she started skipping down the corridor.

Jantine didn't bother looking at him when she spoke. There'd be time enough to whip him into shape once they got through the current crisis and onto the next one.

"Look around us, JonB. These people, this ship. They're not advancing, not as fast as they should be. If this is the best they have to offer, our mission is pointless."

Before he could answer, Jantine activated her scattercomm, trusting that JonB had disabled the enemy device as he'd said. She received five clicks in response.

"All clear."

"No change, boss." Jarl's whisper was controlled, and Jantine imagined he was under active camouflage again.

"Rear secure." Katra's check in was expected, and Jantine knew the other listeners were the Deltas, spaced out to function as signal relays. Part of her had hoped that JonB would follow protocols for once and join in, but the Beta was silent at her side.

"Out."

Jantine shut down the comm, and she thought a bit more on what she was going to do with JonB. Her original plan to replace him once the sleepers were activated seemed somewhat petty now that they'd taken casualties. He might ask too many questions, but that was his job. An analyst had to have as much information as possible, otherwise he couldn't formulate effective plans.

In many ways, he was the polar opposite of Katra, and that comparison as much as anything else told Jantine what she had to do. It was incumbent on her to get better at answering JonB's questions, not the other way around. The Alphas' plan included them working together for a long time, and he hadn't been selected at random. Further, if she felt Katra's planning skills were deficient, it was Jantine's duty as her commander to improve them.

The corridor ahead grew lighter, and as she felt the ship's gravity field take hold, Jantine slowed her steps and powered down her personal generator. Both JonB and Katra were long-term projects; getting her team off this vessel intact was a more immediate one.

The scene she came upon was textbook perfect. Jarl had taken out a team of six techs and then arranged the bodies among the bulky repair gear so cleverly that a casual observer would think the area abandoned. There was no sign of the Gamma himself, but Jantine knew he was there all the same.

Carlton moved up to the assembled gear, examining each pack briefly for useful items under Crassus's watchful eyes. The Delta stood over him with pulsers in all of his hands, covering the corridor in front of them. Artemus took up a similar stance facing the other direction, while Katra skipped past everyone to scout further ahead.

The Omegas were swiveling their heads around again, and Jantine was starting to worry. Something was bothering them. Doria had said they would get by fine without her, but Jantine suspected her absence was affecting them a lot more than they let on.

"Show me the map."

To his credit, JonB did not scream when Jarl appeared seemingly out of nowhere between them. But he was visibly shaken, and Jantine lost a battle with her smile.

Jarl held up a thin sheet of flimsy, translucent material in both hands. With a small flourish, he unfolded it along an invisible seam, and a holographic representation of a Redstone dreadnaught appeared in the air above it. JonB's eyes widened, and Jantine had to admit she was impressed as well.

Finally, some sign of advanced technology. But why are the techs so well equipped, while the combat operatives are so inexperienced? Who are these people?

Jarl clearly had been experimenting with the map, because he moved to the side of the corridor and placed the clear sheet against a bulkhead at chest height. It stayed in place, allowing Jarl to place his hands into the image then spread his arms. The holographic ship expanded, and both JonB and Jantine leaned into examine the details. The civvie was first to speak, but since he and Jantine had the same question it didn't really matter.

"So where are we now?"

Jarl's fingers were spread wide. He twisted his wrists, and the ship rotated. They could see a line of green dots making its way through the ship.

"They've restored power along this route. I can't simulate the cargo slug, but we're logically closer to the hull than the center of the vessel. So, this end must be us."

JonB caught Jarl's eye, and raised his own hands to manipulate the image. The Gamma stepped back to stand at Jantine's side. JonB was focusing on the edges of the image rather than the details of the ship, poking at some unfamiliar icons with an intent expression.

Jarl kept his eyes moving, taking in not only what the scientist was doing but also the actions of the rest of the team.

"Commander. These people. I . . ." Jarl's voice was unsteady for the first time in Jantine's memory.

"I know, Jarl. Something about this ship is very wrong, and we need to leave it as soon as possible. Once we're away, we can take time to worry about who and what we had to kill. You said there was a maintenance access hatch?"

"There is, but I don't think it's an option for us. They're not going to . . ."

Jantine turned to look at him; he was wearing an uncharacteristic expression of surprise. It took her a moment to understand what had affected him so, and she realized that the rest of the team had gone silent as well.

Most of them, anyway. The Omegas had stopped their slow head motions and were moving toward JonB and the holographic projection. One of them placed a broad hand on his shoulder, gently pushing him aside

What are they doing? This isn't like them at all.

The Omegas took up seated positions on either side of the projection and expanded it even further. Unlike the rest of the mods, they still wore their jumpsuits, and the orange skin of their arms and faces was exposed. Jantine, JonB and Jarl moved into the center of the assembled repair gear, marveling at the speed and grace of the Omega's hands.

Fingers that could crush rock danced through the holographic ship, spinning it almost too quickly to see. Jantine recognized some of the icons JonB was studying only seconds before as they enlarged and contracted, seemingly at random. The ship was taking on more definition, additional lines of light forming as they worked.

More green paths spread through the ship, and a large solid section of red appeared. Jantine felt a wave of deep sadness wash over her as a blue dot appeared inside the red and then expanded into a solid line. She watched the team's path move down several corridors to their present position, and then resolve into nine softly pulsing glows.

It took Jantine a moment to realize they'd stopped working, and that the image also showed two glowing dots back at their starting point, and one in approximately the area Jarl had identified as a landing bay.

Then she noticed that both Omegas were staring at something. Or rather, someone. Following their eyes, she saw Carlton standing alone, with his handheld in one hand and the oversized pack he was using to carry captured enemy gear in the other.

"What? What is it? What do you want?"

Carlton's voice was trembling, and Jantine could hear the pain of their collective losses fully expressed in it. He was on the edge of losing control, and she had no idea how to help him.

She looked back to the Omegas, searching their orange faces for some clue of what to do next. The nearer one stretched out a hand to Carlton, and pointed.

"I don't understand! I'm not a Gamma. I can't . . . I can't help you!"

Carlton walked forward, but the expression on his face indicated he really didn't want to. Every step he took was punctuated with another denial, and by the time he reached the Omegas he was nearly in tears.

The analytical part of Jantine's mind noted that he left the oversized pack behind but was still wearing his own and carrying his handheld. The Omega reached out to Carlton and gently relieved him of both, placing them on the deck. The Omega then placed his hands on Carlton's shoulders, using four eyes to stare into the Beta's two. Carlton started shaking, and the Omega leaned forward until his broad forehead touched the top of Carlton's helmet. The support tech was sobbing openly now, and he collapsed into the Omega's arms.

"Thank you. Thank you. Thank you."

Hearing the raw emotion Carlton had been holding in since his sib's death made Jantine want to cry herself. Not knowing what else to do, Jantine looked at JonB. The scientist's face was streaked with tears, and he made no move to wipe them away.

Carlton disengaged himself from the Omega and walked back to join the rest of the mods. Jantine kept watching the Omegas, but pulled him back a step to make sure he was okay.

"Carlton, what just happened?"

The one who hadn't comforted Carlton reached for the handheld and began tapping in commands. The other one opened the pack and withdrew the case containing Jantine's portable computer terminal.

"He helped me, I think. Since Harren died, I've been . . . I was . . . lost, I guess. He took some of that pain away."

Jantine wasn't entirely satisfied with this explanation, but what the Omegas were doing now needed all of her attention. From Jantine's vantage point, she could just make out the terminal's screen, and saw it was still running JonB's course tracking program. JonB must have seen the same thing, because he powered up his own handheld and gasped.

"They can't—they shouldn't be able to do that!"

Jantine watched the projection as small red objects began appearing around the ship. The image contracted, and then a new green line stretched out from the cargo slug and to the edges of the projection. It contracted again, adding more red objects until they nearly filled the corridor.

Nearly. There were green objects making their way through the debris field as well, and their inexorable progress sent a shiver down her spine.

JonB's next words echoed Jantine's thoughts completely.

"We have to get off this ship!"

Jantine turned and addressed the team. "Pack it up, everyone. We're leaving. I want—"

The Omega's hand on her shoulder was an unexpected interruption. She raised her eyes to the other mod's, preparing herself in case the Omega was going to do to her whatever they'd done to Carlton. Instead, it pointed to the projection. The other Omega spread its hands wide, zooming in on the wounded ship represented at its center. Jantine started a mental clock on how soon the closest of the green icons she'd seen would reach the ship, uncomfortable with both the size of the image and the time she had left.

The dreadnaught's familiar wireframe was back, but the Omega wasn't done yet. The projection focused on the transit bay, then the Omega brought its hands close together. The projection collapsed into a cloud of colored lights then resolved into a video image.

Jantine saw a column of armored figures walking down a wide passageway, escorting some piece of bulky equipment into a large room. The Omega squeezed her shoulder for emphasis while pointing with its other hand at the image. Jantine tried not to think about how much pressure the Omega could exert on her if it wanted to, focusing instead on the intense feeling of need that pulsed through as the long finger indicated the equipment.

"I think I understand," Jantine said, "but our priority has to be getting off this ship. If we can secure whatever that is, we will, but . . ."

The sound of the other Omega's hands slamming together at full speed was like a small explosion, and it nearly stopped Jantine's heart. The projected image disappeared, and the feeling of need changed to a sense of dread.

Jantine desperately wanted to escape, but the Omega's hand on her shoulder held her fast. She was keenly aware that the rest of the mods in the corridor were staring at her, but like them she had no idea how to deal with an angry Omega. The very concept was inconceivable, but there was no mistaking the expressions on their faces.

The Omegas were giving the orders now, and they weren't taking no for an answer.

Doria had told Jantine they didn't think about the same things other mods did, but it was apparent now that they were more than capable of doing so. She'd also told Jantine they had faith in her leadership, and would do whatever she asked of them. But nothing Doria said could have prepared her for this.

Squaring her courage as much as she could, Jantine put her hand on the Omega's wrist and pushed. The hand came off her shoulder, and she backed up a step so she could look at both Omegas at the same time.

"Fine. But you have to tell me why. If we don't get off this ship, all of us are going to die. You understand that, don't you? You have to."

Both Omegas raised their left hands to their jaws, trailing a finger down the line of their broad faces in a gesture that did nothing to soften the hard expressions they wore. Jantine was about to repeat her question when Crassus's low rumble came from the other end of their makeshift encampment.

"Commander Jantine. Scout Katra on the scattercomm. Says it's urgent."

The Omegas made the gesture again, and Jantine realized they were trying to answer her question. She mirrored their action and heard seven clicks in her ear.

I guess I can't blame any of you. I'd want to hear this too.

"Go."

"Boss, I've acquired another enemy comm. You need to turn yours on. Now."

Jantine's eyes darted to JonB, who moved forward holding the small, black box. He pointed to a switch on the face of the comm and gave her a weak smile that did little to mask his fear.

"Should be fine. We're back on their power grid, no feedback."

Jantine nodded, and pressed the switch. An unfamiliar voice sounded from the comm, but the tone of the speaker was one she recognized instantly.

This man is in charge, and is not happy.

". . . eat. This is Captain Horace Kołodziejski, of the System Defense Force. I hereby assume command of your battle group and order Captain Aloysius Martin be placed under arrest as a traitor. Power down all weapons systems, and prepare to be boarded. Any person or persons attempting to assist Captain Martin will be considered enemy combatants and subject to the Interstellar Compact's rules of war. This is your final warning."

Jantine turned off the device and looked at the Omegas. The one on the left picked up Carlton's handheld and tapped a command. The holographic image sprang into life again, and this time she could see what looked like the nosecone of a shuttle, and the edge of an open cargo ramp.

But more importantly, she saw a large number of weapons in people's hands, half of which were pointed at a tall figure in a hardsuit whose own hands were empty and raised in the air. At its side was a slightly shorter individual holding two hand weapons, constantly shifting targets in what looked to Jantine like a defensive pattern.

Drawing on her memory of the ship's schematic, Jantine made her decision.

"Katra. Look around your present position for a maintenance access panel. There's a flight deck one level up and two hundred meters from my current position with multiple hostiles. Get there and secure the situation."

"Yes, boss."

Six clicks sounded in her ear as Katra deactivated her comm. Jantine turned to Jarl, who was starting to fidget.

"Go. We'll catch up."

Jarl sealed his faceplate and started running. He stopped briefly to rip a panel off the wall, then disappeared inside the revealed maintenance shaft before it hit the deck.

The hole was too small for either Crassus or Artemus to follow him, which was probably why Jarl had dismissed the shaft as a viable path. The Omegas certainly wouldn't fit through the opening, so the rest of the team would have to go the long way around to the flight deck.

It's time.

"The rest of you, get ready for a fight. Make sure you've got your handhelds and packs, but leave any captured gear you're not sure of behind. Crassus, on point. Move out."

The Delta started running down the hall at an impressive pace, weapons ready. JonB stepped forward to retrieve the map panel, and the Omegas watched him with burning eyes. Whatever was going on inside their heads, they were still clearly intent on the projected image, and when it powered off they turned their attention to Jantine.

Jantine matched their glares as best she could, but she didn't have any time to waste on power games. Breaking eye contact, she tightened her grip on the pulse rifle and started running after Crassus. She trusted Artemus and JonB to get the rest of the mods organized—Katra and Jarl needed her more than they did right now, and she wasn't going to lose anyone else today if she could help it.

If the Omegas were no longer under her complete command, she'd deal with it when the time came. She had to trust that whatever agenda they were following now was in her best interests, and those of the Colonies.

Because if they're not on our side anymore, I have no idea of how to stop them . . .

ALOYSIUS

"ALL RIGHT, EVERYONE. LET'S NOT DO ANYTHING WE'RE going to regret later."

Martin tried for his most amiable smile, turning his head from side to side in an attempt to win over any of the security troopers on the flight deck who were wavering. It was hard to look like a trusted commander with your hands in the air, but he'd been a line officer for a lot of years and knew that just about anything was possible if you refused to give up.

Kołodziejski's broadcast couldn't have come at a worse time. Another few minutes, and he and Harlan would have been off the ship and commandeering one of the remaining tenders. They would have been able to disappear into interplanetary space, and the Alpha would have been safe.

Well, as much as it could be, under the circumstances.

The way Harlan kept shifting her targets certainly wasn't helping matters, and Martin was of two minds about his next step. He was still processing Horace's words when she snatched his gun off his waist, and her aggressive posture was making his negotiating position very difficult.

He could surrender, and hope to negotiate some sort of mutually beneficial deal, or he could try and charm his way out of immediate danger and proceed with the original plan. But as long as everyone was pointing guns at one another, it was only a matter of time until something happened he couldn't talk his way out of.

From the looks of things, about half the troopers on the flight deck and all of the techs were on his side. They'd already stowed the gennie on the shuttle—if he could just get himself and Harlan aboard with a minimum of casualties he might still be able to salvage the situation.

"There's a completely rational explanation for all this. What you just heard is only half the story, and I'd like to think that I've earned enough respect to tell you the rest. Can we just take a few minutes and talk?"

It was hard to get a read on people with blanked faceplates and wearing hardsuits, but Martin saw some of the troopers aiming at him shift their feet a little.

It was the newer, younger members of his crew that he needed to win back—men and women who hadn't lived enough to understand how many shades of gray there were in the universe. He'd made a point of sending the more reactionary troopers elsewhere; if he could appeal to just one of them, the rest would follow.

"Sir, ma'am, lower your weapons, get down on the deck, and remove your helmets. Captain Kołodziejski's orders are valid, and I am required to enforce them."

The trooper's voice was somewhere between cold confidence and abject terror, and if the rest of the people currently pointing weapons at him felt the same way, Martin had more to work with than he'd originally thought.

Smile still in place, Martin turned to face the speaker. He was one of three troopers with their slugthrowers raised, and they didn't seem at all fazed by either Harlan's steady aim or the pair of their comrades aiming at the back of their heads.

I'd be proud of you all, if I wasn't so damn scared this will end in a bloodbath.

Martin kept his eyes fixed on the troopers. It was easier to be brave when no one could see the fear in your eyes, and that fear had to have these troopers asking some hard questions right now.

Okay, time to roll the dice.

"Son, everyone, I'm going to remove my helmet now, all right. No tricks, I just want to talk this thing through."

"Sir."

Harlan's one-word statement was a question, caution, and declaration of support. So far she hadn't technically aided and abetted him, but as soon as the shooting started there would be no going back for her. If this plan had any chance of succeeding he needed at least one other senior officer free to act.

"It's all right, Commander Harlan. I don't have anything to fear from these people. They're following orders, just like I am. We all want the same thing here, to understand what's going on. Here I go, I'm taking my helmet off, nice and easy."

Without the suit mics relaying his voice over both the comms and external speakers, he'd have to pick his words very carefully over the next few minutes. Every second Martin wasn't winning back his people, Horace Kołodziejski got that much closer to coming aboard and taking physical control of the *Valiant*.

The seals at his neck released, and Martin lifted the helmet up and over his head. He hadn't been wearing the suit all that long, but he was shocked by how cold the air in the launch bay felt. The flight deck had its own power and gravity generators, but the air temperature was regulated by the same systems that maintained the rest of the ship.

If Harlan's people haven't got them online by now, they're probably too far gone to salvage. In that case, it won't matter how much power they can reroute—the Valiant *is dead and so is its crew. We're too far away from any friendly faces out here for hope of rescue.*

Martin felt a momentary twinge of guilt—after all, it had been his orders that put the *Valiant* and her support ships in this region of space in the first place. He'd picked this position specifically because nothing was supposed to be out here, and no one could have predicted the random appearance of a rock or ship or whatever it was, or that it would cause so much damage to so many systems at once.

"What's your name, son?"

"Maranov, sir. Please, don't move."

Martin had been about to step forward, in an attempt to block the man's view of Harlan aiming for the middle of his faceplate.

"It's okay, Maranov. No one wants this to get ugly. I'm putting my helmet down, but I want you to promise me something, all right?"

Come on, son. Think this through.

"I can't do that, sir. Please get on the ground. Ma'am, lower your weapons. Captain Kołodziejski's orders—"

Martin turned to look at Harlan, still holding his helmet in his hands. He knew that if he couldn't get the situation under control, and fast, there was no way out for anyone.

The boy's right about one thing. People have got to stop pointing guns at one another.

In a move that must have appeared far braver than he felt, Martin turned his back on Maranov and his two flankers. He held the helmet out to Harlan, fixing her with a knowing stare. The woman's dedication to his safety was admirable, but he wondered how much of it was loyalty and how much pure adrenalin.

Stick with me, Mira. We'll live through this if we can just stay calm a little longer.

Harlan made a face like she'd swallowed something vile, but seemed to understand his intent. She slowly placed the gun in her right hand into a holder on her chest plate, then took the empty helmet from her captain. She didn't let go of the other pistol, but at least she wasn't pointing it at anyone.

All right, that's one . . .

Martin made a slow turn, noting the positions of everyone on the flight deck. There were twenty people besides himself and Harlan, most of whom were pointing at least one weapon at someone else. As he turned, Martin kept his hands at shoulder height, palms down and making gentle patting motions.

Apart from his personal shuttle, this deck held a few smaller vessels under repair, along with the machinery and supplies necessary to work on them. But Martin and Commander Williams had seen to it that no crews ever got assigned to those ships, and it was about as private a place as one could find inside the hull.

Good. The last thing I need right now is someone I'm not sure of charging in here and shooting people.

"Everyone, please, do what the man said and lower your weapons. No one needs to die here; I just want to talk. Maranov, is it? Any relation to Commodore Maranova? She's good people, and I'd like to think she would want you to listen to what I have to say."

Maranov was silent for a few seconds, and then he lowered his rifle halfway. The gesture caught his comrades by surprise, one of whom spoke up.

"Ivan, what are you doing? We have our orders."

Martin recognized the trooper as Randall Jensen, another name on Bill Williams's list of potential recruits.

"He's thinking, Jensen. Like all of you should be doing right now. I'm no traitor, and neither will you be if you lower your weapons. Horace Kołodziejski is mistaken, and I want to hear what he has to say as much as the rest of you. But I can't do that with a gun in my face."

From Jensen's aggressive tone, Martin didn't think he'd stand down without a lot more convincing. But Maranov wanted to talk, and since at the moment the others were taking their cues from him, Martin wanted to hear him out.

Stepping in front of Harlan for a second time drew a muttered curse from her, but the longer Martin could keep the troopers talking, the better it was for everyone.

"Sir, my great aunt, sir. She's spoken fondly of you in the past. She was very proud when I was assigned to the *Valiant* after graduation."

Martin was glad he'd guessed right. Ykaterina was more than good people—she was on the right side of all this.

"As am I, son. As am I. Now, if you can just convince Jensen there and your other friends that the guns aren't helping, I can try and explain what's going on. You all know I've taken great pains to secure that sleeper unit aboard my shuttle, and the rest of the information you need to see is aboard as well. If we can just go inside and talk . . ."

"Not gonna happen, sir." Jensen took a firmer grip on his weapon, the exact opposite of what Martin wanted. "Now get on the ground, hands on your head. Do it!"

Worse, it was exactly what Harlan was afraid of, and she'd apparently had enough of waiting. Martin heard his helmet hit the deck, and he could only assume she'd filled that hand with a gun immediately.

"Mac, Callen. On me!" Harlan's order blasted out at full volume, and Martin flinched away from the sound. He spun to face her directly, but before he could countermand her, the sight of several techs sneaking up behind a security trooper changed everything.

"No, you fools. Don't—"

Martin's warning was too late for the unarmed techs. The first stumbled as he ran forward to make a tackle, and the trooper nearest to him whirled and fired his weapon. The tech went down in a heap, and Martin knew from the angle of his head he wasn't going to get back up again.

Oh shit.

Something hit Martin in the chest, and for a moment he thought he'd been shot as well. But the pressure continued all the way to the deck, and the sight of Harlan kneeling on his chest while firing both her weapons was truly impressive. He marveled at her cool competence, right up to the point where he followed her line of fire and saw Maranov's chest plate disintegrate as grav-accelerated micro-slugs punched through it.

Shock didn't do justice to the captain's state of mind. He'd almost done it, almost talked everybody back from the edge. Now he was trapped in a worst-case scenario, and his newest recruit was the one doing the most damage.

The deep-throated growl of Harlan's guns was nearly deafening, and the accompanying electric tang of ionized air stung his nose. It wasn't until she stopped to insert new ammunition canisters that he could make out her shouted commands.

"...'ve got to fall back! Everyone, get to the shuttle!"

Before Martin could stop her, Harlan sent another short volley at Jensen, who ducked behind a maintenance frame just in time for one of Martin's faceless allies to come up behind him and put a dozen micro-slugs into his back. The trooper had no time to celebrate, though, as someone else walked a deadly line of fire up her body from waist to armpit. The last few micro-slugs shattered the hardsuit's faceplate, and the look of complete surprise on the young woman's face tore at Martin's soul.

What have I done?

The noise over his head dropped in intensity, and Martin turned his attention back to Harlan. Her faceplate was blanked, and the mirrored finish made her seem inhuman. He thought he heard something like a grunt come through her external speakers, but he had no idea what the sound meant.

Before he could speculate, Harlan slapped one of her guns back into its holster and used the now-free hand to grab Martin's collar and drag him towards their escape craft.

It took several meters for Martin to process that the muzzle of the gun on her chest was glowing cherry red. When the one in her left hand stopped firing as well, she dropped it and started running, with Martin bouncing heavily behind her as she made a dash for cover.

Somebody watching the lanky fire control officer dragging her middle-aged captain along the deck in the middle of a fire-fight might have found the sight amusing, but as the drag-ee Martin was glad when she let go of his collar and he rolled to a stop behind a workbench. He couldn't make out the rest of the flight deck from where he was, but from the sound of things it was still going at full tilt.

I have to stop this. If they'll only just listen!

Martin got to his knees, but he couldn't see over their impro-vised cover. From the sounds of the rounds slamming into the other side, she'd picked right. But Harlan wasn't firing back at the moment; she was busy repairing her remaining weapon.

First, Harlan ejected the fused barrel of her induction pistol and replaced it with a spare drawn from one of the many hard pouches on the front of her suit. She then snapped a new ammunition canister into place, held the weapon at arm's length, then triggered the acceleration module. He heard the miniature gravity generator whine to life, and the amber light on the side of the pistol switched over to green.

Martin played back the frenzied activity of the last two minutes, and realized why she had to fix the gun in the first place.

One, two, three . . . was that really her fifth reload?

Quickly doing the math, Martin realized that Harlan had just fired at least two thousand micro-slugs at members of her own crew in an attempt to save his miserable hide, and the thought that she was prepared to do so again moved him to action.

"Harlan, Stop. Everybody, stop! You don't understand what's at stayiaaaaagh!"

Hot metal rained down on Martin as a section of the bulkhead above them shattered. He couldn't see Harlan's expression behind the mirrored faceplate, but he was pretty sure what it would look like if he did. He was making it increasingly harder for her to save his life, and there was only so long they could hold this position. But the lives of every man and woman in human-controlled space depended on the outcome of this encounter, and despite his desire to stop the killing Harlan might have the right idea after all . . .

Harlan fired her remaining weapon dry over the maintenance bench, then slapped in yet another canister and continued shooting. From his position on the floor he could see a distorted version of the flight deck reflected in her faceplate, and the people fighting across it.

Harlan shifted her aim, and the gun growled as one of the hardsuited figures running across the floor dropped. She moved again, and a trooper positioned at the base of the cargo ramp doubled over.

A fresh round of impacts slammed into the workbench as she ducked back down to reload, and Martin wondered how Harlan could tell friend from foe in all this chaos. She wasn't hesitating in her target selection, but neither was she firing indiscriminately. That discretion was somewhat encouraging, and Martin decided to take another approach.

"Harlan, that sleeping Alpha is the only priority here! You have to survive and get it to a safe harbor. So forget about us. Leave me here to deal with this, and I promise you'll get away clean."

Harlan wasn't paying attention to him, or if she was, she didn't turn her head in his direction. Her faceplate was angled out over the top of the bench, as if she was looking at something in the firefight. Martin chanced a peek of his own around the side of the workbench to try and figure out what it was.

About six meters away lay a fallen trooper. At first he thought Harlan might be eyeing the weapon lying next to the body, until Martin saw a second suited figure moving towards it. Then the trooper's head just disappeared. The body slumped forward, and when it hit the deck a crimson fountain erupted from its neck.

Martin stared at the corpse, noticing that the sounds of combat had diminished. He dove back behind cover and turned to look at Harlan. Her faceplate was tracking slowly to their left now, while her hands were busy reloading her pistol underneath the bench.

Harlan hadn't said a word since they'd taken cover. He chanced a whisper in her direction, although it was more for his own sanity than concealment. Anyone with eyes and ears knew where they were, yet no one was coming for them.

"What is it?"

Harlan stopped moving her head, apparently looking at something in the direction of the shuttle. Then she was back under the bench almost too fast to see, and another section of the bulkhead exploded with a small shower of sparks. Martin looked up at the two shining craters in the supposedly indestructible surface, and shuddered.

"There's someone out there shooting at both sides. And one of these," she said, hefting her induction pistol, "can't do that." Harlan gestured at the gouged out sections of bulkhead, and the captain nodded his understanding.

It's too late, they're already here. And they don't care about taking me prisoner anymore.

"Whoever it is, they're herding us. I count five groups out there, and all of us are afraid to stick our heads out. We have to get aboard the shuttle as soon as possible, but it's too far. If we go out without cover, I don't think both of us will make it."

Martin tried to think of some way to distract the sniper so that Harlan could take him or her out. Other than just stepping out into the open, none came immediately to mind.

"Harlan, how many of our people are still up?"

"I clocked Sergeants Callahan and Sykes holed up against the far wall. I'm really not sure who the ones without heads are at this point, but there are at least six hostiles active, three of whom are more or less dug in at the ramp."

Damn. I guess it's not a hard decision after all.

"Okay, I'll make a dash back the way we came and try to get a weapon off somebody. You get to that shuttle, and get the Alpha away from here. Once you're free, contact—"

"No."

"What?" Harlan's refusal caught him completely by surprise.

"No, sir. Even if I do get off this ship with the Alpha, I haven't got a clue what to do with it. And as we've seen over the last few minutes, I have no idea who I can trust, or even who's in on your little secret."

"On the ship, Harlan. It's all there. Your command key will—"

"Negative, sir. We go together, or we blow the damn thing up. But I'm not leaving you behind in either event. You have to make those casualties out there right, and whether I like it or not I'm in this now up to my neck. So it's both of us, or not at all."

A flurry of gunfire brought their attention back to the flight deck. Two hardsuited figures were running broken lines toward their position. Martin was alarmed, but they weren't firing as they ran, and Harlan wasn't aiming at them.

Must be Callahan and Sykes. They've probably come to the same realization Harlan has.

A third trooper popped up from behind a partially disassembled thruster and sent a line of micro-slugs after the sergeants before his chest exploded.

Martin ducked back behind the workbench as micro-slugs started bouncing around, but two very different facts made him feel even worse about his situation than he had before.

First, one of the sergeants was down, though Harlan's cover fire let the other roll behind the workbench to join them.

But the second thing he'd just learned was more important than congratulating the scrappy sergeant.

I didn't hear a shot when the trooper's chest exploded. What kind of a weapon has that much power, and makes no sound?

Harlan reloaded quickly, and raised her head for another look at the flight deck. If she was struggling with the same question, she gave no sign of it in her voice.

"Callahan. Report."

"There's motion in the corridors, ma'am. If we're going to do something, it needs to be soon."

Callahan ejected his rifle's grav accelerator and replaced it with a spare drawn from a pouch on his abdomen. Once it was in place, he repeated the same aiming and activation ritual Harlan had used with her pistol.

When he was satisfied with his weapon, Callahan clenched a fist and let it fall, and Martin saw Harlan nod in response. Callahan's faceplate went clear, and Martin saw earnest blue eyes crinkle in a smile as the sergeant addressed him.

"Sir, stay behind me. I'll get you aboard in one piece."

Before Martin could answer the trooper, the flight deck's speakers sputtered to life again, and his heart sank. Given how quickly his plans had deteriorated after the last shipwide announcement, he was sure time that this one would only add more fuel to the fire.

"This is Lieutenant Ramirez in the command center. Captain Kołodziejski and his men have come aboard through the port cargo bay. I repeat, Captain Kołodziejski's men have breached the port cargo bay. Sir, if you can hear me, we're all with you. Crew of the *Valiant*, resist these invaders to the best of your ability! Don't let them—"

The sharp report of an induction pistol cut off Harlan's former second, and the sounds of a scuffle closed out the transmission. Martin closed his eyes, wishing he'd seen Alonso's face at least once before he and Harlan left the command center in his charge.

"Harlan, I—"

Harlan vaulted the workbench with an easy grace and was running at full speed toward the shuttle before Martin had a chance to continue his apology. Callahan was right behind her, and Martin stumbled to his feet after them, keenly aware that he had neither a helmet nor a weapon.

Callahan's weapon was braced at his shoulder as they moved. The sergeant was sending streams of micro-slugs not at the troopers at the ramp, but seemingly at random angles as he advanced. Martin did his best to stay behind him, but as the trio grew closer to the shuttle, he noticed return fire coming from several directions.

"Down, sir." Callahan stopped suddenly, and Martin dove for cover. The captain heard the pinging of slugs all around him as Callahan fell to his knees. A second burst spun him around so he was face up, and Martin watched the light leave the sergeant's eyes.

Harlan's gun went dry, and this time instead of reloading she threw it ahead of her as she ran. Martin scooped up Callahan's rifle and aimed over her head, hoping to add some kind of distraction to her insane charge. But when one of the two troopers left on the ramp was suddenly missing a head, he decided that his poor marksmanship would only complicate matters.

Not knowing what else to do, Martin sprinted after her, firing the rifle blindly off to his right. Harlan launched herself at the remaining guard, who was staring at the downed and headless corpse of his partner when her outstretched arm took him in the neck. Both of them slammed into the cargo ramp, but Martin saw Harlan's arm raise and start slamming a gauntleted fist into the other trooper's faceplate.

Martin was almost to the ramp when his weapon ran dry, and he was so focused on Harlan's struggle that he didn't see the figure hurtling from his left side until it was too late. The new opponent's tackle was hard and fast, and Martin's head bounced against the edge of the ramp hard enough for him to see stars.

He felt, rather than saw, additional figures piling on top of him. Everything was spinning, and the sounds of fighting slowed until they were a distorted growl. A mirrored faceplate was shouting something at him, but Martin couldn't make his mouth work anymore. He was cold, and tired, and his suit weighed a ton.

The faceplate bobbed again, and something grabbed at his suit collar. Martin felt himself being dragged up the ramp, accompanied by a hideous slow-motion screeching sound. The faceplate disappeared, and Martin felt something hot and wet on his face as everything went red, then black.

As the *Valiant* slipped away into darkness, one last thought went through his mind.

That could have gone better.

JARL

JARL HEARD GUNFIRE ECHOING DOWN THE MAINTENANCE shaft, and slowed his advance. He didn't believe anyone was looking for him, but his active camouflage would do nothing to muffle the sounds of his footsteps if an enemy happened to be standing near his exit point.

The sounds of combat were coming from the other side of a ventilation unit, and as he approached, Jarl saw that Katra had fused a two-meter fan in place with a low-powered pulser blast, and then scored a centimeter-long arrow pointing down into the metal.

Jarl listened at the panel. The sounds of the unseen combat were mainly confused shouts and the growls of the slugth-rowers he'd seen earlier. The whine of Katra's pulse rifle was an indicator of her status, and he allowed himself a smile.

Picking her shots. Not under any particular stress. Good.

Jarl applied pressure to the base of the panel. From this angle he could see a free space directly under the vent, about a three-meter drop from the maintenance shaft. Wishing he could see more of the immediate area, he dropped through feet first.

As he hit the floor, there was a flurry of gunfire. Something hit the wall behind him—a lot of somethings. Jarl let his legs go limp and continued his fall until he was lying flat on the decking with his rifle out in front of him. A volley of tiny projectiles ricocheted through the space he'd just vacated and tore through the surrounding crates and equipment.

When he wasn't killed by a follow-up volley, he rolled until his back was against something solid and aimed at a gap between crates about two meters from where he'd landed. Jarl counted out ten seconds, then eased himself to his feet. He was careful to keep himself completely covered by the surrounding crates as he took a few soft steps forward. The helmet's pickups registered another shot from Katra's pulse rifle, but there were no more slug throwers firing in his immediate vicinity.

Jarl readied his fingers on the firing studs and spun around the corner. Instead of a crouching enemy waiting to kill him, he saw two downed combatants, one missing part of its torso and the other apparently dead from several hundred small punctures. The rifle in the first body's hands had a red-hot barrel, from which rose small tendrils of smoke.

Interesting.

Jarl was concerned with the blood covering all the nearby surfaces and its likely effect on his camouflage. Judging passage through the narrow space to be too risky, he looked up at the wall of crates enclosing the free space under the vent. It looked sturdy enough to support his weight, so Jarl slung his rifle across his back, aligning it with his spine and triggering the static charge that stiffened the weapon's strap and fixed it in place.

He pulled his hand weapon from its chest sheath and then leapt for the top of the nearest stack, using his free hand to steady himself once he landed.

Jarl blinked twice as he scanned the room, giving his brain two quick images to analyze for immediate dangers. With his faceplate closed, he couldn't use his own senses to their fullest potential, so he set his subconscious mind to the task instead.

Jarl didn't *feel* threatened, so he took two long strides across the piled supplies and swung down to the deck on what looked like maintenance scaffolding. Mindful of the rifle on his back, he didn't roll forward when he landed, but to the side to take cover under a landing strut. Keeping his hand weapon out in front of him, he listened for the whine of Katra's pulser to orient himself. The rapid-fire growls of multiple types of slugthrowers told him the approximate locations of the enemies he couldn't see.

The center of activity seemed to be a shuttle located directly opposite his position—apparently the only intact craft in the bay. A large group of suited figures were wrestling on a ramp that angled back into the vessel.

Lining up a shot, he announced his location to Katra with a pulser shot into an exposed enemy back, and ducked behind the landing strut in anticipation of return fire.

Katra's answering shot killed a second enemy, and some of the remaining figures scrambled up the ramp dragging several others.

Two factions. What have we stepped into?

Jarl worked his way under the small vessel's hull to Katra. Her fire was coming from inside a partially disassembled machine on the other side, the function of which was a mystery to Jarl. It looked too large to be a component of the ship above her, and though something about its construction seemed familiar the pile of parts nearby seemed to be of different manufacture altogether.

Jarl pulled a gravity grenade from his harness and thumbed it active. The fist-sized cylinder was a stripped-down version of the personal generator built into his encounter suit, designed to create distractions rather than casualties. They were dangerous to use aboard spaceships, but Jarl wasn't particularly concerned about the enemy's safety. If a few of them got crushed by their own gear as two grav fields worked out their differences, so be it.

Jarl moved to the front of the small craft, listening for hostile activity. Picking a spot near where he'd last heard a slugthrower, Jarl threw the grenade and sprinted back along the hull. As he moved, he replaced the hand weapon in its sheath and released his rifle.

Jarl spun to face the rest of the bay before sitting down, and ducked behind a workbench, and a second later Katra settled into place beside him.

The reunited Gammas deactivated their camouflage and came together in an interlocking, seated embrace. Both kept their weapons at the ready, aligning themselves so that they could see all of the immediate area.

Their faceplates touched, and Jarl noticed Katra's face was slick with sweat. Her pupils were also larger than they should have been given the light level in the bay. It wasn't enough to interfere with her aim, and her arms seemed strong around him. But unless something had happened he didn't know about, the signs of stress were troubling. Before he could say anything, she gave him a tactical overview.

"Eight left, two factions. More coming. Hear the announcement?"

"No."

They were speaking barely above a whisper, trusting their helmets to insulate the sound of their voices. Jarl had seen three actives heading up the ramp with two prisoners; he stopped looking at Katra's face and scanned for one of the others. He hadn't heard any firing since the grenade went off, but that didn't mean they were out of danger.

"*SDF Valiant*. Coup in progress. Boss?"

Jarl processed Katra's summary quickly, knowing she preferred action to planning. His response was equally brief.

"Inbound. Three minutes, no trouble."

Jarl's estimate was based on the route the Omegas outlined before he left the main group, and his belief that Jantine and the Deltas could handle any force outfitted like the enemies they'd encountered so far. But a second, possibly third hostile force aboard the ship complicated matters.

Katra shifted, and Jarl was surprised when some of her weight fell onto him. She didn't change the angle of her arms or lower her weapon, but the sounds of her breathing were . . . odd.

I don't like this. Something is wrong.

Jarl's mind raced through new tactical situations, working out fire plans requiring only one active. But the longer he dwelled on the subject, the more he had to know what had happened to Katra.

"Status?"

Jarl decided the risk of attack from his left side was negligible and turned to read Katra's expression. Her eyes were still wide, and he wished he could see enough of her neck to time her pulse.

"Three hits, micro-slug ricochets. Collapsed lung, impact fractures in left arm. Suit sealed up, stims. Operational."

Jarl understood her firing solutions better now. Firing prone, all of the rifle's action was channeled into her right side. She was still more than a match for these opponents, but she'd need to get out of her encounter suit sooner rather than later for treatment.

Jarl considered what to say next, counting down the seconds until Jantine, and now more importantly, Crassus and Artemus, would arrive. He could capture the shuttle on his own, but he'd rather have a Delta with him to be sure. And no matter what, they needed more intel on the situation aboard the *Valiant*. If there was a third force of actives heading their way, it was even more imperative that Katra receive proper treatment.

In the end, he decided to take her at her word. She'd never lied to him before, and with the stakes so high, wasn't likely to start now.

"Noted. Flush?"

"Negative. High ground."

Jarl nodded, then leaned back, twisting to the side as he broke their embrace so that both Gammas could disengage without spoiling their aim. Katra sat up straighter, and now that he knew what to look for, he saw that her movements were a little stiffer than normal. If things got worse before the rest of the mods arrived, he trusted her to let him know.

Jarl scanned the area for new firing positions. Whoever had organized the repairs on the *Valiant*'s small vessels had done a good job of leaving the center free of obstructions, but their discipline wasn't absolute. For some reason, the area felt more abandoned than active, and scaffoldings like the ones surrounding the crafts being repaired were everywhere.

Jarl aimed his rifle at several positions that would offer him good sightlines of both the intact shuttle and the bay's main entrance. Katra indicated a third inside one of the partially disassembled vessels, which Jarl realized would also let her cover parts of the corridor outside.

He pumped his clenched fist once, and the Gammas split off. As he ran, Jarl saw a hardsuit moving closer to the shuttle's still-open ramp, and he snapped off a shot in its direction. Katra must have seen the motion as well, because her shot changed the body's direction as it fell.

The enemy must have been about to fire when it died, because its rifle discharged when it hit the deck and sent a stream of micro-slugs toward the shuttle. Jarl couldn't tell if the vessel was damaged as a result, but one of the bodies still lying on the ramp was hit a few times, and the results were impressive. Portions of the hardsuit simply disintegrated, severing one of the legs and sending painted shrapnel bouncing around the immediate area.

Jarl reached the scaffolding he'd selected and swung himself upwards with his left hand. If Katra's count was correct, there was still one hostile at large, and he needed to locate it as soon as possible. Settling into his perch, he realized he could see through the forward window of the shuttle.

Three armed and suited individuals had their backs to him. On any other mission, Jarl would send a volley of pulser fire through the window and be done with it. But they needed the shuttle to complete their mission, and it would probably be hard to fly even without unnecessary damage.

Malik would know what to do. He was our tactician. I'm just a gun with legs.

But that's not how Malik had treated him or the other Gammas. Malik's attitude was far above that of a typical Beta, more tolerant than even Jantine. Jarl and Katra were the only ones left now, and it still felt odd to be outnumbered by Betas in such a small group.

The whine of a pulser brought him back to the present. Jarl shifted as subtly as he could to see what Katra was shooting at, and the sight of two dozen fresh opponents both excited and troubled him. They were clustered at the entrance to the bay, and Jantine was due within seconds.

Katra had waited until the newcomers were all the way inside before firing, and it looked to Jarl like the bodies on the floor had been moving to meet them. Jarl took aim at a face-plate, steadied his hands, and fired.

The shot took one of the enemies high in the throat. While not as spectacular as Katra's precise shooting, it had the same general effect and dropped the enemy instantly. He sighted on his next target, tracking it as the enemies split into several groups and sought cover.

Katra's next shot was as accurate as ever, and Jarl noticed she'd waited ten seconds after his shot before firing. Counting down that same period, Jarl cleared his mind of distractions and surrendered to the moment. His heartbeat slowed down, and when the time came he stopped his breath and made his body perfectly rigid.

Seventy meters away, a helmet exploded in a shower of bloody white fragments. The enemies around it went into a panic, splitting their forces once again. There were now three distinct target groups—four, counting those inside the shuttle. A corner of Jarl's mind registered that only one suited figure was standing in the shuttle's window now, positioned sideways in an attempt to see the deck outside and also keep a weapon trained on two other figures inside.

Prisoners. Nice of the enemy to police themselves.

Jarl shifted his aim to the base of the ramp, counting down the seconds until another head presented itself. As if responding to his needs, two enemies came down the ramp. Jarl waited for a clear shot, then sent a pair of pulser blasts at them.

The first hit one of the suited figures in the shoulder, spin-ning it to the right. The second destroyed its target's left arm before carving a hole in its chest.

Not a warrior's death. But it serves.

Jarl switched his focus to the entrance, marking the posi-tions and numbers of the two enemy groupings. He selected a target for his next shot, confident he'd guessed Katra's choice as well. He shifted his aim towards the front of the launch bay for a follow up shot, but Katra's target dove aside right before she fired, revealing Jantine and Artemus charging down the corridor.

Katra realized she was firing into her own people just in time, but too late to stop the pulser shot. She did manage to pull it off to the right, causing a shining crater to appear about three meters off the ground. Unfortunately, walls made more sound when struck by a phased plasma pulse than people did, and both enemy groups turned to see what had happened.

Jantine hit the deck instantly, firing her rifle as she dropped. One of the Deltas ran across the opening to draw fire while the other opened up with a weapon in each of it upper hands.

Jarl heard another weapon fire, this time from the base of the shuttle's ramp. He thought it a pointless gesture at first, given the observed range of the enemy's weapons. But then he realized there was another possible target, and saw Katra's uncamouflaged body fall out of her perch.

Jarl was moving almost before he'd fully registered what had happened, pulser on rapid fire and aimed at the base of the ramp as he dropped from the scaffolding. He lost line of sight when he reached the deck, but he was satisfied the shooter was dead.

Another volley of combined pulser and slugthrower fire sounded in the still air, and then he heard nothing else. He reached Katra just in time to see several punctures in the encounter suit sealing over on her upper back.

Jarl put down his rifle and cradled Katra in his arms. She wasn't moving, and when he turned her over he saw her faceplate was broken in several places. Fearing the worst, he popped the seals at her neck and removed her helmet entirely. It came away trailing a line of blood, and Jarl sat back heavily on his legs. He removed his own helmet and watched her bloody face in stunned silence for several seconds, and it was only when he saw her eyelids flutter that he remembered to breathe.

"Pulled . . . shot. Jantine . . . okay?"

Jarl's instinct was to brush away the clear fragments of faceplate embedded in her right temple, but he couldn't bring himself to touch her.

Not her. Not now.

Looking at the blood flowing freely down her face reminded him for some reason of what else was touching her skin, and his. He swiped a finger down his jawline, then Katra's, and heard five clicks in his ear just ahead of Jantine's voice.

"Report."

"At least one hostile inside shuttle. One group of reinforcements already arrived. Katra injured, multiple suit punctures."

Jarl heard Katra's voice both from in front of him and in his ear as she gave her own status report.

"Op . . . Operational."

Jarl helped her to a sitting position, keeping an eye out for more hostiles. She had a pained expression and raised a hand to feel around the area where the faceplate fragments had cut her face. He offered a helping hand, but she waved it away and continued speaking.

"I can . . . Good to fight, boss."

"If you're sure, it's good enough for me. We should take the . . . what are you do—"

Four clicks sounded, then three, then two as Jantine's voice cut off mid-sentence. Jarl grabbed for his pulser and vaulted over Katra, rolling into a combat crouch as soon as he could see the bay doors.

"Jarl. Jarl, what's happening?"

At the bay entrance, Crassus was standing in front of Jantine and holding all four arms wide in an attempt to stop the Omegas from entering the bay. Artemus was pulling at one of them, but the Omega shrugged him off with a casual motion that belied the force necessary to send the Delta staggering across the corridor.

"Jarl, report!"

Before he could respond, a volley of slugs hit the scaffolding behind them and filled the air with deadly ricochets. He felt hits in his side and leg, and fire spread inside his chest. He fell to his knees, left hand clutched to his abdomen. The gauntlet came away bloody, revealing three ragged tears in his encounter suit. He watched the smart fabric seal around them, and then a flush of endorphins widened his eyes as the auto-doc's stims kicked in.

So that's what it feels like . . .

He felt a hand on his shoulder and turned his head to see Katra's face hovering centimeters from his own.

"Jarl, what are our orders?"

Jarl looked into Katra's widened eyes, and he wondered just how much time the two of them had left. The stims were only partially dulling his pain, and he felt something grinding inside his left knee as she helped him into a crouching position.

Neither of them could see Jantine from where they were, but the renewed sounds of pulser fire gave them a fairly accurate idea of her position. Jarl knew more than that, though. He knew the Omegas had been acting erratically since they'd abandoned Doria and were very insistent on getting to this part of the ship.

And since there was only one thing worth having in the compartment, Jarl also knew what Jantine wanted the Gammas to do.

"We take the shuttle."

DORIA

DORIA SAT IN THE DARKNESS, WATCHING HER LIFE counting down on the handheld. The numbers were comforting, and promised an end to her pain.

Not long now.

Malik was resting comfortably with her right arm curled around him. She felt a tinge of regret that he wouldn't be with her when the time came, but in the end his pain was too great, and she'd had to massage his mind into unconsciousness. Even while asleep, she could still feel his strength, and that's all that mattered

The handheld was the only light in the compartment that had been their home for the last few weeks. Malik had helped her configure a switch for the destruct charges before succumbing to his injuries, and as long as she kept her left thumb on the activation panel, they stayed alive.

Doria smiled, amused by how fiercely she clung to each one of the 59 seconds of life she had left. Then a cough shook her, bringing up blood to fill her mouth and nose.

55 . . . 54 . . . 53 . . .

Wait. What was that?

At the edge of her vision, the faint green glow she'd grown used to was getting both brighter and whiter. Sharp lines now outlined the hole through which the others had left, and as it grew in intensity Doria could hear voices.

"What the hell happened here? It's like they were torn apart."

"I don't know, but Captain Kołodziejski wants visual confirmation of all *Valiant* personnel. Get their helmets off, and scan the faces. Martinez, you're with me."

Two spots of light bobbed through the hole, and Doria saw answering spots form on the raft of crates in the center of the container. A human form started in and then fell to the deck with a small cry

"What the—Lieutenant, there's grav in here! And the floor's different."

Oops. But to be fair, we weren't expecting visitors, were we Malik?

A second form came through, a bit more cautiously than the man picking himself up off the deck. Doria saw the light it was holding swing around the room. She tried to focus on their faces, but after so long in the dark even their small lights were blinding.

When one of the lights swung over her and Malik, her right hand came up reflexively to shield her eyes. Malik groaned softly as he slid down into her lap, and the combined movements started her coughing again, this time much louder and wetter.

"I've got survivors over here! Anderson, get in here with the scanner, and mind the first step. The floor and grav field in here are both angled away from the *Valiant*."

The speaker moved forward, followed by his two companions. Doria tried to reach out to their minds, but her own pain was almost overwhelming. It was all she could do to keep sitting up straight and maintain her grip on the handheld.

She tried to speak but couldn't manage more than a pained wheeze. When the man holding the lamp kneeled in front of her, she flashed him a bloody smile.

"I don't believe it. Guys, they're just a couple of—"

Doria's smile widened as she lifted her thumb. The countdown stopped at 15 seconds, but she didn't mind.

It's going to be all right, Malik. It's over n—

JANTINE

JANTINE SENT ANOTHER BURST OF PULSER FIRE TOWARD the enemies surging through the bay doors, wondering just how many more she'd need to kill before the day was over. She saw Crassus drop behind a scaffold to slot energizers into his rifles, just as Artemus intensified his fire from the other side of the room. The Delta had claimed several enemy rifles from the fallen, and the noise as he emptied them into the oncoming foes was incredible. Jantine also noticed dark blood falling from Artemus's shoulders, fat droplets shaking loose with the recoil of the captured weapons.

How long will it be before we're reduced to throwing rocks? They just keep coming . . .

If not for the Omegas' bizarre actions they might be aboard the shuttle by now. She had no idea if the Gammas were successful in eliminating any resistance inside the small vessel, only that her force was pinned down and separated.

The warning beep from her own rifle's energizer sounded, and she dropped behind the stacked crates she was using as cover. Whether the containers would offer her any protection at all from the enemy's ridiculously overpowered slugthrowers was somewhat in question, but the skill level of their opponents was finally matching up to her expectations.

With the sounds of battle raging around her, Jantine ejected the spent module. Slotting in a fresh energizer took only a few seconds, but waiting for it to generate a charge took a bit longer. She used the time to do a sight check on her people. JonB was crouched beside her with his eyes closed, mouthing some silent mantra she couldn't make out. Carlton was across the bay next to Crassus, and the Omegas . . .

The deck pitched wildly to the side, and the crates toppled onto her. The unexpected impact forced the air from her lungs, and all she could do for several seconds was stare at her rifle on the deck, half a meter from her outstretched hand.

"Jantine. Jantine!"

JonB's voice seemed far away. Darkness was closing around her as she fought for air, and she felt rumbling of some kind through the deck. The rumbling became a pounding, and then the weight on her back was gone.

A pair of tree trunk legs was standing in front of her, and Jantine rolled over to take in a painful, gasping breath. One of the Omegas was holding the crate high over her head, then spun around rapidly before releasing it. It sailed away like a rocket, and she felt rather than heard its impact. She raised her head, and saw a jumble of arms and legs struggling feebly beneath the crate as it came to rest in the corridor outside.

Dazed, she couldn't make out what JonB was saying. Something about charges and detonations, but all she really wanted to know was where her weapon was, and how many of the enemy were left.

Another crate went flying, then another. Jantine couldn't help but stare at the casual way the Omegas were thinning the enemy ranks.

Even now, they're beautiful. All that strength finally unleashed, and it's still just the smallest part of themselves.

The Omegas were moving now, and with each step they took they transformed from peaceful architects into orange-skinned engines of death. Powerful arms were swinging, swatting enemies aside like flies. One trooper had enough time and presence of mind to fire a weapon, and Jantine's amazement grew as the slugs bounced harmlessly off an Omega's chest.

JonB was shouting now and trying to pull her up from the floor. Artemus shouldered him aside, using one lower hand to yank her to her feet, and placing her weapon in her hands with the other.

Jantine accepted it mechanically, unable to tear her eyes from the sight of the angry Omegas. Meter-and-a-half arms came together with a trooper in the middle, and she heard the hardsuit cracking from across the bay. The Omega spun again, now using the dead trooper as a club to batter the remaining enemies to the floor.

The fight was over, but the deck shook as both of the Omegas ran toward the shuttle. But for the blood streaking their coveralls, they might be children chasing a ball. She felt JonB shaking her shoulders, and finally heard what he was saying.

"Commander, we have to go! Malik and Doria . . . the container blew! We can't stay here, can't you feel the air leaving? There's a massive breach somewhere, and everyone still alive on this ship will be coming this way!"

Jantine turned to look at JonB, wondering how he could fail to comprehend the threat posed by Omegas willing to kill. The look of sheer terror in his eyes was sobering, and although everything he was saying was true, it paled in comparison to what might happen without a support Gamma to help the Omegas deal with the emotional ramifications of what they'd just done.

Jantine didn't say anything; she just tightened her grip on her rifle and started walking toward the shuttle. She saw Carlton heading up the ramp, and Crassus was already on station outside.

By the time Jantine, Artemus, and JonB reached the shuttle, a helmet-less Jarl was walking unsteadily down the cargo ramp. His hands were empty, and there were spots of blood on his pale face.

Jantine stopped and waved the others inside. From the base of the ramp, she could see the Omegas and Carlton excitedly shucking their packs and moving to examine the bulky piece of equipment she'd seen earlier. It looked like a sleeper unit, but it was three times the normal size.

Jarl's last step sent him crashing into one of the piston assemblies used to retract the ramp, and Jantine saw his eyes were wide and fixed. His encounter suit was covered in puckered scars, each one giving her another reason to get her team off the *Valiant* as soon as possible.

"Boss, shu . . . shuttle secured."

Jantine didn't know what to say. Jarl's normal rough whisper was full of something she'd never heard before. Pain, raw and unmasked. All she could do was take his report and try and live with the consequences of what she'd asked him to do.

Putting on her best command face, Jantine nodded up the ramp.

"Katra?"

"She'll live. I won't."

Jantine felt the darkness closing in again. This was Jarl, untouchable, indestructible Jarl. He'd done the impossible once again, but this time would be the last. Images of Malik, Doria, and Harren spun around Jarl's face, and the thought of another of her people—her friends, dying on this mission was almost too much to bear.

I can't do this. It's too big . . .

"Commander. Boss. You need to leave. Complete the mission."

Her mouth worked silently several times, almost apologizing, almost screaming her building rage. But Jarl's blue eyes were the cool center of a still pond, and if he could still stand after what had happened, so could she.

Jantine pulled a spare energizer and some grenades from her harness and handed them to Jarl. He waved off the energizer, instead pulling his hand pulser from its chest sheath and holding it out to her. She nodded, took the weapon, and tried to think of something, anything she could say to acknowledge his sacrifice. Before she could, Jarl took the grenades, straightened up as best he could and walked down the ramp.

"Jarl, wait." Jantine finally found her voice, even though it sounded strange in her ears. Removing her faceplate, she felt cold air moving past her cheeks.

Dammit JonB, why do you always have to be right?

The Gamma paused, and he stumbled slightly as he turned to face her. He smiled, then grunted in surprise when she pulled him into a tight embrace. She felt his hands come around her, then shift to tap her twice at the base of the neck and spine. When he whispered in her ear, it was the old Jarl speaking one last time.

"Rookie mistake, boss. Two touches, total paralysis. You'll have to do better."

Jantine buried her face in his neck, determined not to let her emotions overcome her. She needed Doria, needed Malik here to tell her what to do next. But Jarl had said it as well as anyone could, which made it that much harder to let go.

I have to do better.

Jantine closed her eyes and maintained the embrace for another three heartbeats. It was just long enough to start feeling uncomfortable, and she knew she was ready to go. Thinking her thanks to him, she turned without looking and walked up the ramp.

She was halfway up when she heard JonB complaining.

"How am I supposed to know what to do? Look at this place. Is there anything you didn't shoot at?"

Jantine looked around her new command. Close up, she saw that there was a small female form inside the sleeper unit. Carlton and the Omegas were fussing over a bank of monitors set unto the unit, but what drew Jantine's attention were the piled bodies of half a dozen enemy troopers.

As she walked up a twisting internal passage in search of JonB and the others, her feet brushed aside countless micro-slugs. The shuttle's interior was scored with thousands of shining scratches, but no craters like she'd seen on the bulkheads outside. At first there were occasional splashes of blood, but halfway up the ramp the walls were covered in dark red from floor to ceiling. Despite JonB's complaints, Jarl and Katra were too disciplined to fire at targets they couldn't hit, and at least one of them had scored a headshot.

How much of that blood is ours, and how much more will be spilled before we're through?

Following the Beta's voice, she came quickly to a control room. The rest of her team was crowded inside, and the Deltas were aiming every hand full of weapons at two enemies in restraints on the floor.

Katra looked even worse off than Jarl had. But despite the dried blood and cuts on her face she was still standing with her rifle clutched tightly in shaking hands, intent on two enemy troopers secured on the floor in front of her.

From the markings on their suits, Jantine recognized the captives from the brief vid image she'd seen earlier: the man who'd had guns pointed at him, and the woman who had been guarding his back.

JonB stopped talking as Jantine entered, and Crassus took the opportunity to rumble a report.

"They surrendered. The male's the one they're looking for. Says we need them to get off the ship."

Jantine examined the lined face of the man who'd gotten so many people killed. Captain Martin, if Crassus was correct, had a bruised face and wore a dark beard with many patches of white. He was definitely past his prime, but she recognized the haunted look in his eyes as one she imagined in her own.

Without taking her eyes from Martin, she called over her shoulder to JonB: "Prep the shuttle for launch. Artemus, go tell Carlton and the Omegas to dispose of the bodies and get secured."

"Okay, but these controls . . . it's going to be a bumpy ride, and even if I can get it flying I don't know for how long or how far."

"No excuses. Get it done."

JonB swallowed whatever he was going to say and got to work. His hands flew over the controls, searching for whatever switches were necessary to prep the ship for flight.

"Commander Jantine," said Crassus, "how long will Scout Jarl need to complete his sweep and get aboard."

Jantine let the question hang in the air, as she turned to regard the second prisoner. Whoever she was, the woman wasn't afraid, and Jantine had to give her credit for that.

"Jarl's not coming."

Katra's cry of rage was exactly the one Jantine wanted to voice, a raw knife-edged scream from the depths of her soul that made everyone in the compartment stop and stare. Before anyone could stop her, Katra stepped forward and drove the butt of her rifle into Martin's head. His neck snapped to the side, and he slumped in his restraints, but Jantine didn't think he was dead.

Yet.

Artemus pulled Katra away, using three hands to restrain the Gamma and the fourth to take her rifle away. Katra struggled against the Delta's strength, but the rage that drove her drained away as the enormity of what had happened settled in.

If the prisoner was bothered by the attack on her captain, she didn't let it show. The woman maintained eye contact with Jantine, narrowing her eyes slightly as if trying to divine some weakness in her captor. Jantine thought she was about to speak when JonB broke the silence.

"Commander, the shuttle's powered. The drive systems seem operational, but I can't initiate a launch sequence. There's just too much damage."

The prisoner smiled, and she spoke in a clear voice of authority.

"You'll need my command key for that. Or Captain Martin's, but I doubt he'll give it to you now."

I suppose it doesn't matter either way. We die here, or out in space, it's all the same. But I have to try, I owe them that.

"I am JTN-B34256-O. You are my prisoner, and any attempt to escape or harm one of my people will result in the deaths of you and your captain. Do you understand this?"

The prisoner laughed, seemingly unimpressed.

"We already tried to escape, and our own people started shooting at us. Considering how that turned out, I've got nothing to lose. Now, I'm assuming you're not going to untie me, so here's what you have to do."

Jantine studied the woman's face as she talked, searching for any signs of falsehood. But her face had none of the cues she normally looked for, and like the darker skinned young woman she'd examined earlier, it was just too alien for her to get an effective reading.

Doria, Malik, I need you now more than ever. How will I ever know who to trust, now that you're gone?

MIRA

MIRA WATCHED AS ONE OF THE GRAY-SKINNED monsters pulled her command key from the hard pouch on her left shoulder. She was still wondering how in the worlds the Colonials had found out about the Alpha, or even knew where to look for it. Martin had managed to keep the sleeping child's existence a secret from everyone aboard, apart from his immediate circle, yet these children showed up right on cue to reclaim it when everything seemed lost.

They're all so young. Even compared to all the middies aboard the Valiant, *their leader can't be any more than sixteen years old!*

The handsome, dark-haired boy they called Janbi accepted the key from the four-armed brute, then searched the board for where it was supposed to fit. Mira almost spoke up again, but the icy daggers stabbing her way from JTN-B34256-O's eyes kept her silent.

Those eyes were the worst part. The Colonial's face was impossibly beautiful—all of them were—but her blue eyes were like nothing Mira had ever seen before. They betrayed no emotion whatsoever, whether she was threatening Mira and the captain or discussing ammunition levels with one of the brutes.

I wonder what kind of gennie she is? She's clearly in command, but what does that mean? There's just so much we don't know about them.

Janbi gave a small shout of celebration and shoved the key home. Mira felt a familiar vibration through the floor: the cargo ramp closing and the outer doors sealing. She also saw flashes of light out the shuttle's forward windows and wondered how many more of her people were dying while she was relatively safe inside.

"Let's go, Janbi. We're wasting time. Is there anything else we need to know?"

"Is there a code for the bay doors?"

JTN-B34256-O inclined her head to Mira, who cleared her throat. So many bodies packed into the pilot's compartment was making the air a bit ripe.

"Input 'Harlan 4-9-3-8-Alpha-7-7' on the green buttons under the small monitor by your left hand. But first you'll want to . . ."

Janbi's hands moved faster than she thought possible, and the shuttle lurched to life before she could finish her thought. There was another flash of light outside, and JTN-B34256-O stepped over to a side window, looked outside, and tightened her jaw. Something that might have been an emotion flashed across her face, but she moved forward to sit in the copilot's chair without another word.

It was clear that Janbi had never flown a shuttle. Mira had been about to tell him that he needed to engage the force barrier before opening the launch bay doors, but he didn't give her the time and just released the doors without a second thought. Now everything not secured to the decking was being sucked outside, along with what was left of the *Valiant's* air.

Including us.

Mira felt waves of nausea as the shuttle's grav field dipped in and out of the flight deck's. Janbi had turned everything on at once, instead of waiting until the shuttle was clear of the bay doors.

As the shuttle raced towards the slowly widening doors, she felt a scream building in her throat, but none of the Colonials seemed concerned with the very real danger facing them. If anything, they seemed a bit bored, as if spaceflight were no more dangerous than sitting around talking in a well-lit room.

Who are you people? Do you have any idea of what can go wrong out here?

Just when she thought the shuttle was going to smash into the slowly opening doors, Janbi spun the ship on its side and they sailed through with centimeters to spare. But instead of making for open space, for some reason he swung around to follow the hull.

One of the equipment crates floating out in front of them got caught between the shuttle and *Valiant*. The shearing sound of metal against metal echoed throughout the cabin, and Mira wondered if it might not have been better to get shot in the head after all than to get killed by a joyriding gennie.

Even the tall gennie with the cuts on her face seemed unconcerned by the wild motions of the shuttle. Her blood-caked blonde hair gave her face a savage beauty, but she looked no more troubled than when she was blasting her way into the room while her partner took a full volley to the chest.

Mira turned and looked at the captain, whose unconscious face seemed younger than his normally stern expression. With the restraints effectively welding them to the bulkhead, the two SDF officers were probably safer than the gennies in the event of a collision. But at the speed Janbi was pushing the shuttle, she wondered if any of them would live long enough for it to matter.

Just my luck. First he flies a rock into my ship, now he's going to fly us into a rock. And for this, I escaped execution for treason?

If siding with Captain Martin over Captain Kołodziejski hadn't already sunk her career, collaborating with the Colonials certainly would. She took some small comfort in having made it this far in the first place, but it was only a matter of time before her luck ran out.

The gray monster standing closest to her seemed to stand a little taller, and Mira stared up into its broad face. It was smiling, and it seemed to be looking at something in the passage. From where she was secured Mira couldn't see what it was, until an even more horrifying creature crawled in on hands and knees to stare at her with four beady black eyes set into a round orange face.

Then the nose of the shuttle dipped, and Mira heard the blare of a collision warning. Then she was slammed back against the bulkhead as a herd of elephants landed on her chest. Even the orange monster grabbed at the bulkhead for support, and Mira saw its fingers dig furrows into an alloy that could survive a drop from orbit unscathed.

Impossibly, the creature pulled against the g-forces pressing Mira back, until its massive head loomed over her. Its tiny mouth opened, and a cloud of white mist came out of it and settled on her face. The whatever it was brought up its other hand until the fingers just brushed against her skin.

There was a fluttering sensation inside Mira's head, and then the pain in her chest went away. An unfamiliar woman's voice spoke to her from no direction in particular, and she felt a sensation of warmth wash over her.

≈*It is going to be alright. We are with you now. Do not worry.*≈

Mira screamed, and the world came crashing down around her. Thousands of images flooded her brain, and she could feel each one digging in and nestling alongside one of her memories. An image of a sunlit park came to mind. She and Debbi McAllister were walking home from school, whispering about the new boy in class and whether or not he was worth talking to. Then the scene twisted around to include the sight of a woman lying in a hospital bed, reaching out broken fingers to a little girl's face.

The universe exploded a second time, and another lifetime of memories came rushing into her. Over and over again she watched other people's lives in reverse, unsure of where Mira Harlan began or ended.

She saw herself meet the Builders for the first time, with Marta's memories fresh in her mind as she left the trauma center. The touch of their thoughts was like kissing a cloud, and she heard music in her soul that made her bones cry. She saw a smiling, dark-skinned boy, and kissed him on the cheek before turning away to hide her tears. Her heart broke, and she felt the pain and confusion in Harren's mind as the second impact tore him away from her and snapped his neck.

From somewhere far away, she smelled something sharp and acidic, and heard JTN-B34256-O shouting.

"What's wrong with her? What did you *do*?"

The deck pitched wildly, then all motion in the cabin stopped as the crushing thrust ended, and the lights dimmed to half-strength. The shuttle's grav shut down, but that was the least of Mira's problems.

Her body felt strange, as if it didn't belong to her anymore. Her skin itched all over, and the hurricane inside her head kept spinning. A dozen half-heard voices reminded her of how to make it slow down, if only for a little while. She could feel sweat beading on her forehead, with nowhere to go and no outside force to tell it what to do.

Artemus bent down, and two strong hands released the restraints holding her to the wall. Mira floated up from the floor, guided by the Delta's gentle touch. She felt the Builder's eyes still on her, and turned back to look at it. Its tiny mouth closed, and the memory of a smile appeared in her mind. Then its attention shifted, and a rainbow of warning sent her attention away from it and through Janbi's eyes to the tactical display.

Mira's head felt like someone was hitting it with a hammer, but somehow she could see through the boy's eyes as if they were her own. He was too busy working the controls to pay conscious attention, but the part of his mind that was always scanning and cataloging everything around him still worked just fine. The red danger of the debris field was well behind them, but five green triangles moved rapidly through it on an intercept course.

Outside the shuttle's forward window, a beautiful blue and white planet hung against a star-studded sky. Mira sensed the words forming in Janbi's mind right before he said them aloud, and felt elation from Katra, Jantine, Crassus and Artemus as they heard them.

"We made it everybody. Welcome to Earth."

JANTINE

YOU JERK. YOU STOLE MY LINE.

Jantine was staring at the Earther woman when the shuttle's wild flight came to a halt, but after JonB's announcement she turned and watched as the big blue planet swung into view. Despite everything that had happened, seeing it she finally had some hope that they'd live to see another day. A real sunrise, on a real planet. The planet—the only one that mattered.

Earth *was* humanity's home, and though they'd exiled the mods centuries ago, just to make it this far was still a dream come true.

Then a white hot knife of pain stabbed into her brain, and she couldn't get her helmet off fast enough. She pressed her hands tight against her ears, but nothing stopped the searing agony.

≈Oh shit!≈

The pain was momentary, and after blinking away tears Jantine recognized the voice in her head as that of the Earther.

But that's not possible . . .

"You idiot! Take evasive maneuvers! There's a Geyser spread closing in on us!"

Jantine turned her head to look at the shouting prisoner. She was floating free from her restraints and held in place by one of Artemus's hands. The Omega was still hovering in the corridor, and Jantine wished she had a support Gamma present so she could get an answer to her earlier question, or maybe tell her how the Earther was now able to talk inside her head.

The Omega. It did something to her, but what? And more importantly, why?

"Oh, those?" JonB hadn't seen the Omega's actions, and his smug tones were as annoying as ever. "Don't worry, I took care of them."

"What the hell are you talking about?" said the Earther. "You're just a kid, do you even have a clue about what's happening? We are all. Going. To die, if you don't get us away from here!"

The prisoner twisted around in Artemus's grasp, and the Delta dealt with the problem by simply letting go and stepping back. Free from the stabilizing influence of Artemus's personal gravity field, she spun around an internal axis for a moment until small jets fired from her hands and feet. She rocketed forward to the control console just ahead of the Delta's grasping hands and pulled a very surprised JonB out of his chair with one hand while grabbing the edge of the console with the other.

"Missiles. Missiles! If I don't get us out of . . ."

The woman's voice trailed off as she stared at something on the small holographic readout in front of her. She'd been about to press a button with her free hand when the look of panic on her face was replaced with one of astonishment.

Light flashed in the corner of Jantine's vision, but she didn't shift her focus from the woman, who made no move to resist as Artemus stepped forward and shoved her down into the pilot's chair. If she noticed Jantine, Katra, and Crassus pointing pulsers at her, she gave no sign.

JonB cleared his throat and took a tentative step forward.

"Like I was saying, I took care of them. We got some excellent scans of your missiles when you were firing them at the cargo slug. Malik's data feed recorded their maximum acceleration, targeting systems, and destructive capability."

Careful, JonB. Don't overplay your hand.

"Those, 'Geysers,' was it?" he said.

The woman in the pilot's seat nodded dumbly.

He continued: "The Geysers use a combination of mass detectors, microwave laser targeting, and ion sniffers, right? All I had to do was find a fragment in the debris field about the same size as us, dump some fuel, and lead them to it. This shuttle has fairly good sensor capabilities. It was easy."

JonB leaned forward until he was a few handspans away from the seated Earther.

"And I'm not a kid. I'm nearly fourteen."

Just then, the shuttle shifted again, and Jantine felt a deep vibration. The Earther's face went back to panic in a flash, and when it did the pain in Jantine's head was back. It was a gnawing, sinking feeling, and even though she knew the room wasn't spinning, she dropped her weapon and used both hands to grip the edges of her chair.

JonB's reaction was more evident; he grabbed his head with both hands and sank moaning to the floor. Katra was slapping the sides of her face, trailing lines of blood as her fingers moved back and forth. Even Artemus was affected, the normally stoic Delta's lips flattening into a tight grimace.

≈*nononono just a bunch of kids we're all going to die what the hell am I going to do have to get out get away get free let me go Let Me Go LET ME GO!*≈

Jantine shut her eyes tight and tried to force the words out of her head. She had enough anxiety of her own without an outside voice adding more troubles to her plate. She focused on her heartbeat, trying to reduce the universe to one sound she knew better than anything.

She heard a soft thump, and then the hiss of escaping air. Fearing the worst she opened her eyes and grabbed for the pulser floating in front of her. The pilot's chair was empty, and Jantine swung her arm to the left trying to cover the prisoner's escape path.

She'd almost forgotten about the Omega at entrance to the room, but it was as good as a wall in stopping the Earther's trajectory. Two big hands came up and caressed the sides of the woman's head, and as she stopped struggling Jantine felt the fear and doubt leave her mind as suddenly as they'd arrived.

Katra was already in motion, weaponless but no less deadly. Her hands were up and formed into claws, and the look on her face was pure rage. Artemus tried to intercept her, but he and Crassus both appeared to be having difficulty coordinating all six limbs. Jantine didn't know how to react to anything she was seeing but decided that firing her weapon was definitely the wrong call. She couldn't stop the Gamma's snarling attack, and, in any event, part of her wondered if it was even the right thing to do.

She can't be. It's just not possible . . .

Just as Katra was reaching to tear the unresisting Earther from the Omega's grasp, a massive orange hand let go of the woman's head and made a fist. Katra's breath left her in an explosive, bloody cough as the punch landed. She fell into a gasping heap, then toppled over onto the deck.

Jantine and JonB reached her at the same time, both desperate to help but not knowing what to do. Jarl said she'd survive her injuries, but that was before she'd suffered even more damage to an already compromised system. Jantine had felt the strength in that hand herself, had seen how terrible it could be when set to destruction. If the Omega had killed Katra, turned on one of its own in favor of the Earther, who would be next?

Katra let out an almost inaudible wheeze, and tiny bubbles of blood formed on her lips. JonB looked up from her at Jantine, and started shaking his head.

Jantine was on her feet and two steps toward the Omega before she realized what she was doing. But the big fist was gone, and the Omega was turning away from her to press its back against the bloody corridor wall. It still filled most of the available space, but there was enough room for Carlton to shove past shouting "Make room. Make room!"

Jantine felt him brush by her, still not believing her eyes. The Omega was staring at her as if nothing had happened, seemingly unconcerned with the Gamma dying on the deck.

"What do you want?" Jantine shouted. "Damn you, tell me what you want!"

"They're sorry. They didn't mean for any of this to happen. I'm sorry too, for what it's worth."

Jantine added hearing to the list of senses betraying her. The answer to her question was clear and calm, and coming from the mouth of the human woman.

"It's Carlton, right? Katra's left lung collapsed in the fighting, and her breastbone is cracked and pressing in on the other one. You need to re-inflate—"

"Shut up, Earther. I know what I have to do!"

The anger and pain in Carlton's voice combined with a wet tearing sound as he stripped away Katra's encounter suit. Jantine heard JonB gasp, and she used every bit of her will to keep her eyes on the Omega, instead of turning to watch.

This isn't happening. This isn't happening. This can't be happening. The humans on that ship were virus-free . . .

The human woman winced, shaking her head as if trying to dislodge something in her ear. She then raised a gauntleted hand and pointed at the Omega, who was slowly edging back down the corridor.

"I don't know how this is happening, but he—I guess it's he—wants you to know that none of this is your fault. The—look, is it okay if I just use my own words? She's smart, she'll understand. No, I don't think your way is better. What just happened was wrong, and you know it. Now let me do this, my way."

The impossibility of the situation was overwhelming, and Jantine sat down on the floor and took her head in her hands. Though she didn't want to, she could see the human woman's booted feet sink three centimeters to the floor and settle into place. There was a humming sound, and then the knees of the hardsuit bent until she was kneeling in front of her. The look of compassion on the woman's face was too much to take in, and Jantine closed her eyes and wished the world away.

It's not real. This is a dream. A horrible nightmare. Everyone is still alive, none of this is real. Wake up, wake up Wake up!

"I know you're afraid; I am too. This day just keeps getting crazier and crazier. An hour ago I was a junior officer wondering why in the worlds my captain was hiding out a few light minutes above the ecliptic. Then I was second in command of a dying starship, and then minutes later I was running for my life from my own crew to save the life of someone I've never even met."

She spoke loud enough for everyone to hear, but what Jantine objected to most was the warm feeling inside her head that accompanied them. She opened her eyes and saw the woman's strange face hovering in front of her.

Her expression was a mixture of concern and amusement, and there was something different about her eyes that Jantine couldn't quite place. They still had the same hardness about them Jantine had seen earlier, but they were a deeper brown somehow, and the corners were turned up in a way that made her think of home. Her cheeks were flushed, and sweat was beading up on her face.

It wasn't until she formed her lips into a lopsided smile that Jantine decided to punch her in the nose. There was a sharp crack, and when the first spots of blood began pooling under her gauntleted hand, Jantine stood and turned away.

"JonB."

At the sound of her voice the Beta looked up at her from the floor, where he was holding Katra's upper arms while Carlton inserted a small tube into the left side of her chest. There was blood everywhere, and Jantine saw at least a dozen ugly holes on her bare skin.

"You bith. You fuggin bith!"

The warm feeling in her mind was gone, replaced by a simmering anger Jantine knew all too well. If the Omegas wanted to play games with all of their lives, so be it. She still had a mission to complete.

Carlton bent forward and blew into the tube, and Jantine watched Katra's chest expand. The Gamma's eyes snapped open, and she gave a strangled cry while trying to sit up. Only JonB's genetically enhanced strength kept her from injuring herself further, and whatever Carlton injected her with next kept her from trying again.

"JonB, help me get her into one of the sleeping areas. There's a lot more I have to do if we're going to save her."

Jantine shook her head.

"Artemus can do that. I need JonB here."

JonB crawled away and let the Delta reach in to collect her in a gentle, cradling embrace. Jantine didn't turn to watch Carlton leave, keeping her attention instead on the blood-stained scientist. She assumed there would be some shuffling of positions behind her to allow the Delta access to the corridor, but she just didn't care how the other mods worked it out.

Jantine sat down in the second pilot's chair and examined the controls. "Which one of these can I use to find the sleepers' container?" she asked. "And why are we spinning?"

The last sliver of Earth's cool blue sphere slipped above the forward window as JonB reclaimed his seat and started studying the panel. He was silent for almost thirty seconds then pulled out his handheld from a thigh sheath. He frowned, and started tapping.

"Well?"

"I just need to . . . but that's not . . . Commander, it's gone!"

"Explain." The sinking feeling was back, but this time Jantine was fairly confident it wasn't forced on her by the Earther.

"That's just it. I can't. I mean, a fragment of the slug must have hit us when the decoy exploded, and that's what set us to spinning. But the container, it's just gone! We—I mean, the Omegas—tracked it clear of the debris field, and I should be able to pick up its trail from here. But there's nothing. No wreckage, no bodies, no trace whatsoever!"

"Scientist JonB, could the container have landed safely while we were escaping the Redstone dreadnaught?" Crassus's unexpected question focused Jantine's fear into something she could work with.

"No. If it was out here, the shuttle's sensors would pick it up. I'll need a few minutes to input Malik's pilot program into their core, but I don't have any idea of where it could have gone. I just don't know."

Jantine's patience ran out, and she got up out of the chair and walked over to JonB. He gave out a small cry when she spun the pilot's chair around until he was facing her, and she saw her own fear reflected in his eyes. But she didn't have time for fear anymore, or for any of his hypotheticals. She needed answers, and she knew of only one way to get them.

"Don't tell me what you don't know, JonB. Tell me where they are, and where we're supposed to be going. Crassus?"

"Commander."

The Delta was a solid presence at her side, and the pulser he had trained on the Earther captives gave her something solid to focus on.

"Have Artemus prepare a secure location for our prisoners. I don't care if the Omegas interfere, they can rot alongside them for all I care right now."

"But Commander Jantine, the Builders are—"

"I also don't want to hear any more about 'the Builders.' I am commanding this mission, and I will see us safely down to the surface without any more 'help' from them. Am I clear?"

Crassus was silent, and she could almost hear the thoughts forming in his head. When she started to feel a warmth building inside her mind, her hand pulser came out and was leveled at the female captive before she could even blink.

"None of that. Not now. If you have something to say, use your mouth!"

The woman nodded, and pulled her hand away from her bloody face. The Omega was still crouching in the entrance to the compartment, face impassive. She'd seen them angry before, and what passed for a smile. But whatever this expression was, she didn't trust their new "voice" enough to believe anything they had to tell her.

"We haff to leaf."

"What?" It took Jantine a moment to understand what the human woman was trying to say with her broken nose, but after a few words it was easy enough.

"We have to leave. Now. There's enemies out there trying to kill the Alpha. You have to—"

"Boss," JonB interrupted. "I found something, I think. There's a flight plan in the core for someplace called the Harrison Institute, in Central North America. Oh, and I can confirm the impact earlier. There's damage to our primary drive systems, but everything should hold together during reentry."

"Are you crazy? North America? You'll be shot down in seconds. Mars. Set course for Mars. . ."

The human's voice trailed off when Jantine waved the pulser in her face. But Jantine was still waiting for the rest of JonB's report, and when several more seconds passed without it, she prompted him.

"And the sleepers?"

The lights in the compartment came back up, and Jantine felt the ship's engines kick in. There was a momentary adjustment as the compartment's gravity returned, and Jantine wished JonB had a stronger sense of his environment as she wiped falling body fluids away from her face.

"Still no trace of them. But with more time, and better equipment . . ."

Jantine turned back to the front of the cabin and saw the stars swing by until the planet was back in sight. The second part of what the Earther had said finally fell into place, and with great effort, Jantine released the firing studs and lowered the pulser.

Alpha. She said enemies are trying to kill the Alpha.

"JonB, Get us down to the planet as fast as possible, but at least 100 kilometers away from any population center. I don't care how close it is to this Harrison Institute, just make sure that we aren't observed."

"You got it, boss. Plotting an insertion now."

Jantine turned and left the compartment, and she heard Crassus fall in behind her. She pointedly ignored the Omega's questioning stare, thankful that she was small enough to squeeze by without having to touch it. Crassus wedged himself through as best he could, but Jantine was too busy retracing her steps down the corridor to care.

By the time she reached the bottom, the shuttle was shaking as it reached the outer fringe of Earth's atmosphere. But even this momentous occasion was dwarfed by the sight of the second Omega sitting in the cargo area, staring with longing eyes at the small figure floating in a blue-green suspension matrix inside the sleeper unit.

From the reverence the Omega was showing, Jantine knew what the prisoner said had to be true. Jantine took a step closer, and then another. She couldn't quite bring herself to touch the gently humming sleeper unit, but seeing an Alpha in person for the first time, under these conditions, shook her worse than the violent motion of their descent.

What am I supposed to do now? Someone, please tell me what I'm supposed to do.

The acrid smell of burning plastic stung her nose, and JonB's excited shouting was barely audible over the much more immediate sound of Crassus's basso.

"Commander Jantine, I think something is wrong."

The shuttle lurched, and Jantine pitched forward into the sleeper unit. She hit her head on something, then fell to the deck as if pushed there. Then the shuttle stood on its nose, sending her sliding back up the blood-slick ramp.

Discarded micro-slugs scratched her face as the sounds of JonB's screaming came closer. Another change of direction slammed her into the wall, and then she was tumbling head over heels back down into the bay.

"COMMANDER!"

She tried to turn her head toward Crassus, but her neck was made of rubber. All she could manage was a pathetic gasp, and then the sound of tearing metal filled the room. Hot air washed over her, and Jantine felt herself sliding again until a big orange hand grabbed her arm and she jerked to a halt. Something popped in her shoulder, and Jantine flopped her head over enough to see the Omega holding on to the over-sized sleeper unit with its other hand, wincing as the crates of supplies it had carried the length of the *Valiant* broke loose and shattered against its broad back.

Shelters, ration packs and spare energizers rained down on them both, and Jantine tucked her chin into her chest to shield her eyes before something hard and heavy hit the back of her head.

Her last sight before everything went black was of a tiny, six-limbed figure sailing away from a ragged hole in the hull, waving its arms madly as it fell.

BOOK TWO

MIRA

Mira picked her way across a broad field of scorched grain. She'd heard this part of North America described as "rolling fields of gold," but she and the gennies had done more than enough rolling for the day.

We're alive. That's all that matters. I'm just hoping the miracles continue and we can find some sort of shelter before too much more time passes.

The column of smoke rising from the downed shuttle behind her was an apt summary to her day so far, and the craters their unplanned landing had left across the countryside would remind the Earth for years to come of the day the gennies came home.

Jantine was watching the sunset from one of the few untouched high spots on the horizon. Even dressed in shapeless brown coveralls, the gennie had an air of command Mira had tried to present for years. Out of her suit, out of her uniform, Lt. Commander Harlan was a rapidly fading memory, one being replaced by Mira the gennie-come-lately.

Mira reflexively squinted against the light of the setting sun, and she discovered another benefit of her changing biology. There was an extra layer of moisture sitting on her eyes that counteracted the harsh light, and though it was still a bit painful to stare at, she could now make out details on the surface that were hard to see even in space.

Despite the chaos of their crash, and the knowledge that she was fast becoming Fleet Enemy Number One, Mira found the open field around her very relaxing. For a change, the only thoughts buzzing around in her head right now were her own, instead of those the Omega had jammed into her brain. But like the column of smoke at her back, there were things about the current situation that needed to be addressed.

As she approached Jantine, she could "taste" the uncertainty lurking underneath the iron barrier of control the young leader maintained. She didn't know if it was a reaction to Mira's presence or that the girl never really relaxed. But three hours of downtime was all the group could afford; it was time for Jantine to make her decision.

One of Mira's new memories suggested that Jantine preferred that people just started talking instead of announcing themselves first. It was paired up with an image she'd always associated with authority: that of her father sitting behind his big desk with a stern look on his face.

"Janbi says it will fly. I have my doubts, but after his display in orbit I believe he means it."

A tiny smile played at the edges of Jantine's face, but her mind was full of pain and loss. Jantine's record of today's events was written in blood, and although she'd brought most of her people down alive, she was agonizing over those she'd failed to save.

Part of Mira wanted to smile at the gennie's discomfort— she was the enemy, after all. But the extra memories in her head were pushing her to project a feeling of well-being, even though Jantine had made it abundantly clear that she didn't welcome such efforts.

Not from me, anyway.

Jantine kept staring at the horizon. A layer of deep blue sat above a band of orange framing the distant tree line, and the clouds above were painted in purple. Evenings at flight school in Colorado had offered similar vistas, but Mira could now compare them to memories of a dozen different horizons on as many planets.

The original is definitely better. And she's seeing it for the first time. I just wish she could enjoy it.

"Katra?" Jantine's question was terse, but the sense of concern behind her words supplied the context Mira needed.

"Better. An hour in the shuttle's bio-bed dealt with most of her internal damage. We had to tweak it a bit to handle . . . her particular attributes, but the system worked just fine in the end."

Mira held back the words she wanted to say next, unsure of how Jantine would take them.

We Gammas heal fast, it seems.

Instead, she brushed her fingers across the smooth line of her now healed nose and waited for the proud girl to collect her thoughts.

Even while dealing with her pain, Jantine's mind was remarkable. The Gamma memories told her she shouldn't be able to sense whole images or thoughts, but Mira watched as Jantine replayed the frenzied action of the team's journey through the *Valiant* over and over again, searching for anything she might have overlooked, any opportunity she'd missed to save a life.

In Mira's opinion, there weren't any, but Jantine's unspoken pain was that her friends had died while she was paying attention to other things. Jantine was too new to command to understand that she couldn't fix everything, a lesson Midshipman Harlan had learned when Jantine was still in the crèche.

Doesn't mean you have to like it, though.

Mira wished she could speak openly with the girl. Tell her how it was okay to be afraid, or uncertain, as long as you understood what the right thing to do was and stayed the course. She'd had no mother or father to tell her these things, no older brothers to rub dirt in her hair or whale the tar out of some boy dumb enough to break her heart. Everything was new for Jantine, so everything hurt.

She decided to try a new tactic. If Jantine didn't want a shoulder to cry on, perhaps she could use a friend. Mira walked up the small rise and took a seat beside her. From

Jantine's mind came an intense image of spikes shooting out of the gennie's skin, and a cold mask fell across the girl's face as Jantine put a wall up around her thoughts.

I should probably stop using that term. Never liked it much anyway.

"I don't think we got off to a good start, Commander. My name is Mira, Mira Harlan. I was born about twelve hundred kilometers over yonder," Mira gestured off to the left in a generally southwestern direction, "and until a few hours ago I was a Lieutenant Commander in the System Defense Force. My life was primarily occupied with running training simulations for a crew just a little older than you are, and fixing whatever broke aboard the *Valiant*."

When Jantine didn't interrupt, she continued, intentionally trying to distance herself from the Colonial's guarded emotions.

"I'm not going to apologize for what happened to your people centuries ago. There really aren't any words. What we . . . what Earth has done is monstrous. But I can promise you that there are still good people here. I don't understand fully why you're here, or what's really going on with that little girl in the cargo hold, but we can't stay hidden out here forever."

A smile spread across Jantine's face. If anything, the setting sun made her even more beautiful, and Mira smiled herself at the thought of her brothers going ga-ga over the exotic off-worlder.

She'd probably kill Jim and Adam as examples to the others, but Sean might be able to keep up with her for a little while. Although come to think of it, Deb or Mar might be a better fit . . .

"You don't talk like a Gamma. Most of them would be afraid to sit this close to me, and they certainly would never speak their minds without permission."

As Jantine spoke, Mira's new memories confirmed them. The genetic caste system in the Colonies was ruthlessly insular, and all of the voices in her head were trying to get Mira to show proper respect to her "better."

From what Mira had learned in the Academy, Betas like Jantine were exceptionally rare. Mainly because of the low

Beta birthrates, but also due to the difficulties involved in taming new worlds. Only a handful of gennies made the cut—in general the Colonials were just a better variety of human being, one adapted carefully to their planet of birth on a world-by-world basis.

"Carlton said much the same thing. He's not sure I am a Gamma, not really. Thanks to my new best friends the Omegas, I'm transgenic like the rest of you, but for the most part I'm still a baseline human. I mean, I've got these crazy empathic skills, and about a dozen lifetimes of memories telling me how to do just about everything. It's like reading a book while someone else is speaking. I can't concentrate on any one voice well enough to understand it, but I still have a basic idea of what they're saying. I can almost hear your thoughts, but every time I try to project mine I get a massive headache and an even bigger scolding from a bunch of people who don't even exist.

"From what Carlton says, there's no real precedent for what's happened to me, and it's tearing him up inside that he can't nail down a proper classification. Besides, he's been pretty busy with Katra and the . . ."

This time, she couldn't shut out Jantine's spike of annoyance. It had flavors of anger, frustration, and fear, and for good reason.

As uncertain as Mira's position was in the Colonials' group dynamic, Jantine's was based entirely on the fact that she was the best genetic fit to lead her people to Earth. Her life so far had been spent training for a mission to reunite the human race, with the full knowledge that she wasn't expected to succeed.

In a way, Captain Martin's plan has destroyed her life just as thoroughly as it has mine.

A kilometer behind them, in the cargo area of a mostly dead shuttlecraft, was an Alpha. A little girl locked into a centuries-long, dreamless sleep who would become their undisputed leader the moment she woke up, invalidating everything Jantine's people had fought and died for.

If Captain Martin's intel was correct, it was entirely likely that that sleeping child had no leadership training whatsoever, but short of waking her up and asking questions Mira had no way to confirm that. Her surface mind, the only part Mira could reach, was a blank slate. The prolonged hibernation seemed to have caused no damage, and it was equally likely that when fully conscious she'd have just the intelligence and personality of a normal eight year-old girl.

But Jantine doesn't know one way or the other, and her life is one of absolutes.

While Mira was thinking about what to say, Jantine turned her attention to the ground in front of her. Mira could see that she'd been poking at the soil, but Mira didn't know why until Jantine's right hand darted out and came up with a tiny, wriggling figure cradled between her thumb and forefinger.

"What do you call this?"

Mira started to squint again, but her eyes knew how to adjust their focus on small things as well as distant shiny ones, even if her brain needed more time to adjust to her expanded visual range.

"It's an ant. There must be a colony nearby."

Jantine gently placed the insect back on the ground. It took a moment to orient itself, and then it raced away as fast as its six legs could carry it.

"This was supposed to be us. A colony. Hidden inside the Earth until we were strong enough to venture forth. But like the ant, we are subject to outside forces beyond our control."

Mira didn't need transgenic powers to know Jantine was building to something. She was far more intelligent than any Earth girl would be at her age—certainly smarter than Mira herself had been.

"Think about what stories it will carry back to its fellows. Of the great pink thing that held it in place. Of the rushing wind that carried it from one pebble to another. Will it even have a vocabulary for what happened?"

Mira saw where Jantine was heading, and decided to ease the Beta's mind.

"But ants work together. They're never really alone. Even if an individual worker has a problem, the colony survives. They also have a queen, who works to protect them."

Well, that's about as ham-fisted an analogy as I can come up with, isn't it?

"I don't know. We don't have these where I come from. About twelve hundred light years, yonder."

Mira laughed as Jantine waved her arm toward the darkening sky. But then the young woman's thoughts took on a decidedly different flavor, and Mira regretted her earlier word choice.

"But we do have queens. And their rule is absolute. It's what they're there for."

The pair sat in silence for almost a minute. For Mira, the wait to speak was an eternity, but Jantine had said her piece, and was waiting for whatever the universe brought next.

She may have said it, but what has she decided?

Mira let the silence continue, wishing she had enough real experience as whatever it was she'd become to help Jantine. Implanted memories were fine as a guideline of what she was supposed to do, but those same memories told her the knowledge she had right now would fade in time, sinking to the lowest depths of her mind until it was time to pass them on to someone else.

The extra lifetimes she'd received had only survived by associating themselves with her own life experiences, and were for the most part inaccessible until something triggered one. It was just her dumb luck that she was two decades older than most gammas were when a transfer was made, and had more memories to match them up to.

An empathic Gamma child was born with the ability to reach another's mind, and was trained for years by other Gammas in how to hone that ability. Mira had the lessons they received over a decade crammed into her skull all at once, and the Builders were as surprised as she was that the process had worked.

They just wanted someone to talk to. Lucky me. And if I can't get a soldier like Jantine to open up, I've got no hope of cracking open one of those big orange skulls without a hammer as big as a mountain.

"We should get back. Janbi and I were able to salvage part of the data core, but he figures we lost about half the information in the crash. And the Omegas are . . . impatient for your decision."

It was Jantine's turn to laugh. The Beta stood up, folding the wrapper of a ration bar into a pocket and then brushing dirt and crumbs off her coveralls with quick, efficient motions. Watching her, Mira was sure it would take an ultrascanner to find any particles she'd missed.

"Now I know you're not a Gamma. One of them would have started the report with the Omegas. But you're right, we do need to get back."

Jantine started back to the shuttle, and was a few meters away before Mira rolled to her feet and followed. As she drew even with her, Mira could feel the walls Jantine had erected coming down, and chanced sending her a wave of encouragement. She felt, rather than saw a smile widen in response.

"What do you want to be called?"

Unsure of how to answer Jantine's question, Mira searched the memories for some clue as to her meaning. Finding none, she quickened her steps to try and get a reading from the girl's face. Jantine's rare smiles had a mischievous quality, and for the first time she seemed truly happy.

"We choose our names in the Outer Colonies. The designations don't really matter unless you're ready for a pairing, and only traditionalists insist on them. But Lieutenant Commander Mira Harlan of the System Defense Force ship *Valiant* is going to break Artemus's mouth. And among friends, we speak as equals whenever possible."

The last rays of the sun had turned the shuttle into a beacon of reflected fire, though only a few wisps of smoke remained. Mira's enhanced eyesight could pick out Artemus and the Omegas and moving the bulky sleeper unit through a smoothed and widened hole in the vessel's side, with Carlton and a now upright Katra watching them.

"Mira. Mira will be fine."

Jantine stopped walking, and Mira was several steps past her before she realized what had happened. Turning back, she saw a hint of the uncertainty and fear Jantine had worked so hard to master in her eyes. Mira walked back to stand at her side and was surprised when Jantine took one of her hands in her own.

"Mira, I don't want to open that sleeper unit, not until we find out what happened to the others and are someplace safe. Can we trust the people of this Harrison Institute? Really trust them?"

Mira didn't need help from borrowed memories to answer this one.

"I have no idea. I can only tell you that the captain trusted them. The names of his network were in that data core, and who knows what we'll be able to salvage given time."

Jantine held Mira's hand for a few more seconds before continuing.

"Then what am I supposed to do?"

Now Jantine looked like a frightened teenager was supposed to, and the Gamma part of her was appalled at the lack of confidence the Beta was displaying. But Mirabelle Agnes Harlan from Roswell, New Mexico thought it was a good thing, and did what any big sister would do.

She lied.

"I can only tell you what the captain told me, when I came aboard the *Valiant* for the first time. The ship was so big, you see, and I'd never been part of a command team before.

"He took me aside, and said, 'Harlan, I'm about to give you the most important piece of advice I've ever received, but I'm only going to say this once. So listen carefully. You're going to screw up. You're going to make a lot of bad calls, and some may even get people killed. You'll stay up at night trying to figure out what you could have done better, but the answer is always going to be the same.'

"'Absolutely nothing. You're in command now. You're the one with the answers, even when they're wrong. Feel free to listen to other people's opinions, but your first instincts are going to be right pretty much every time. You're going to fight it, you're going to hate yourself, but the decision you know has to be made is always the right one.'"

Mira paused for effect, trying to summon up the twinkle in the Old Man's eye when he talked. She'd used her best approximation of his voice, but the smile was the real key.

It made the lies that much more believable.

"Now, personally, I thought he was full of crap. It was my job to keep people alive, no matter what the regs said. But you and I both know that's not always an option, and as officers the only thing we're ultimately responsible for is keeping ourselves alive as long as possible, so that the people who look to us for leadership know what they're supposed to do."

I fired the that first salvo of missiles at your vessel. It was the right thing to do, even though it ultimately killed your friends Malik and Doria and Harren. Jarl died rescuing me from my own people, and Crassus is dead because I put that Alpha on the shuttle. And I'd do it all again, because it was the right thing to do.

"I can't tell you what to do, Jantine. You're in charge. But I can tell you one thing that the rest of them won't." Mira gestured at the shuttle. The warm, caramel flavor of Carlton's thoughts spiked in her mind, as did the icy peppermint of Katra's disapproval.

"And what is that?"

"On Earth, we pick who to follow by their actions, not their looks. No matter what happens, you've earned their respect, and no one can take that away from you."

Jantine nodded, and Mira could feel the wall around her mind going back up again. Carlton and Katra were coming closer, and as she turned to look at them, Jantine's hand slipped out of her grasp as the last emotional bricks fell into place.

Do what you think is best, Jantine. But the real truth is that thing in there terrifies me, and I hope it never wakes up.

JANTINE

JANTINE LOOKED PAST MIRA TO THE CAPTURED Earther shuttle, and she didn't like what she saw. It wasn't the damage to their escape craft, or the concerned faces of Carlton and Katra as they walked to meet her. It wasn't even the Omegas standing next to that damned sleeper unit with Artemus watching over them.

It was the sinking feeling that someone was about to give her some more bad news, and there was nothing she could do about it.

Carlton spoke first. Now that they'd reached the surface, the Beta was much more himself than he had been aboard the *Valiant*. How much of that was having a puzzle to solve or patients to treat, she couldn't say. Mira said they'd been talking, so his mood must have softened some from their initial encounter.

A lot of things have changed in the last few hours, for all of us.

"Commander. There's something you should see."

"What is it?" Jantine was surprised to hear Mira ask the same question, but not as much as Carlton. The civvie's mouth pumped soundlessly for a few seconds as he processed both their faces, trying to decide if Mira actually outranked him.

Katra had no such qualms. She stared Mira straight in the eyes as she spoke, though the words were meant for Jantine.

"Transmitter in the unit. Started pinging when we moved it."

Jantine cocked her head toward Mira, noting that Carlton was now studying all three women's features for some clue as to who was in charge.

Or, he could just be staring at Mira.

The virus was still changing the Earther's face. The odd spots on her face were already gone, and her eyes were changing color. She would never look like a true child of the stars; she was too tall for one thing, with hard muscles formed and refined on the home planet. Plus, no amount of genetic restructuring would change the way she acted. Her culture promised her she could have anything she wanted, provided she had the will to take it.

And just what is it you want now, Mira?

At the moment, the Earther had her hands in the air, palms out, shaking her head in denial.

"Don't look at me," Mira said. "I saw that thing for the first time about four hours ago. But a hidden transmitter would definitely explain . . ."

Mira chewed her lower lip, seemingly unaware of the three mods waiting for her to finish her sentence. The unguarded expression was an odd thing to watch, especially in an otherwise disciplined person. Jantine wondered how many other foreign mannerisms she'd have to learn before she could fully understand her new team member.

That's definitely the direction we're heading in, at least if I still have any say in the matter.

"Mira, what is it?"

Jantine's prompt shook the Earther out of whatever reverie she'd slipped into. Jantine felt a touch of embarrassment brush her mind; despite her growing skill in empathic communication, Mira was having a hard time keeping her inner feelings a secret.

"Oh, sorry. I was thinking about whoever fired that last missile salvo. Until you crashed into us, the *Valiant* was for the most part completely undetectable. A transmitter on the sleeper unit would explain how they found us; Captain

Martin and I had just finished stowing it on the shuttle when Kołodziejski's capture order came through."

Mira's face took on a more serious expression, and her projected embarrassment shifted to urgent concern.

"Jantine, if it's active now, Janbi's trick to cover our tracks up there may not last much longer. Carlton, do you know where it is?"

Carlton raised his hands and gave a small shrug. He turned back to look at the sleeper unit before talking, and his voice had the same sort of distracted quality Jantine found so annoying in JonB.

"Probably, but the Omegas won't let me touch it. After we got it out of the bay, they pushed me aside and started . . . well, whatever it is they're doing now."

Jantine stepped out of the impromptu huddle the others had formed around her. The Omegas were sitting on the ground, backs to one another. One was facing the sleeper unit, and the other was looking in her general direction.

"Carlton, how did you detect the signal?"

"It was the Omegas, boss. That thing they do when they swing their heads, like on the ship. When they started again, I checked my handheld and found an RF signal just outside the range of the scattercomms. It's not one the Earthers normally use; I'm sure they can detect it, but I haven't seen anything like it before."

Carlton's explanation reminded Jantine of something, a half-remembered lesson from the crèche regarding the early days of the colonies. Of how ships sometimes would go missing on long voyages, only to be found waiting on the surface of an inhospitable planet years later by another expedition.

We didn't know the galaxy so well then, but we had no choice but to go on looking.

Jantine looked at the Omega facing her, trying to find some clue as to which one it might be. They were intentionally vague in that regard, letting the rest of society regard the Gammas as their "faces."

Well, you haven't got one now, have you? And I need answers.

"Mira. Will you help me speak to them?" Jantine wanted to make it an order, but still didn't know how to treat Mira.

"Of course. They've been pounding on the inside of my head since we started back. I can't promise I'll get it right, but it seemed to go well enough earlier when Janbi asked."

And what has my civvie scientist been up to that he needed the Omegas? Perhaps I was out in the field for too long.

But it was the other part of Mira's statement that troubled her.

"You have to tell us right away when they want something. They don't ask us for that many things, but when they do it's usually important."

"I'm sorry, I didn't know." Mira's face fell, and the embarrassment came back, underlaid with tastes of regret and fear. "I thought you were working something out on your own, and you didn't seem that interested in talking to me."

It was Jantine's turn to be embarrassed. She had treated the Earther poorly, resenting her new status and shifting some of the blame for what happened to her team onto Mira.

It's not like she's the one who killed them. And she's one of us now, sort of. We have to learn to work together.

Putting the matter aside, Jantine moved forward until she was close enough to get a good look at the Omega's face. Mira came up to stand behind her, and Jantine assumed the flicker of fear coming from the Earther meant Katra was nearby.

I'm going to have to deal with that, too.

Jantine readied herself. Her last two conversations with the Omegas had not gone well, but she thought she understood part of the reason why now.

Hopefully this one won't end in violence.

Burying her fear, she began.

"It's a distress beacon, isn't it?"

"Of course!" Before the Omegas, or rather, Mira could answer, Carlton's exclamation ruined the somber mood Jantine was trying to create. The Beta rushed toward the unit, but the Omega facing away from her raised an arm to block his path. Carlton stared at it with a shocked expression, and Artemus hurried over to pull him aside.

Then Mira started speaking, and the words had a distant quality to them Jantine recognized.

Here we go.

"Why have you not awakened the Adept? Wait, that can't be right. It's. . . the thought concept they're using doesn't make sense Jantine, I'm sorry."

The unfamiliar word didn't bother Jantine, she knew what they meant. And she felt a bit guilty, not because she'd delayed her decision, but because she took some pleasure that Mira wasn't quite as far advanced in her communications as she thought she was. Ignoring the Earther's commentary, Jantine continued with her questioning.

"It's not safe here. Whoever she is, we can't expose her to needless dangers. And our priority is the mission. We need to find the rest of the sleepers first."

"No."

No?

Jantine hadn't heard that word in some time, and having the Omegas finally voice their disobedience didn't make her like it any better.

"The distress call. What does it say?"

"S-A-198 must be awakened. You will instruct the others."

Jantine did her best to keep her temper under control. Nothing in her training had prepared her for this kind of insubordination, and the Omegas were the last members of her team she expected to give it.

"I give the orders on this mission. Tell me about the distress call."

When Mira did not answer right away Jantine turned and looked at the Earther. The older woman's face had a puzzled expression, and when she did speak, it was clear to Jantine that she was using her own words this time.

"I'm not sure they understand it either. But one of them is more agitated than the other. The memories . . . I've got nothing to work with for this situation."

"Just do your best, Mira. What do they want you to say?"

Mira's voice dropped to almost a whisper, and seemed even more distant than before.

"Cold. Cold star rising. Fire and death. S-A-198 must be awakened. It has been too long."

Jantine wanted to look Mira in the eyes, even if the other woman wasn't the one really speaking. Doria usually stood between the Omegas and whomever they were speaking to, but Mira had assumed a subordinate's position behind her. But Jantine's gaze was locked on the Omega's black eyes, and she felt if she looked away something bad was going to happen.

"And do you have any idea at all what that means?"

Mira's reply was a bit tentative, and as she spoke the differences between her and Doria became even more evident.

"Nope. They not using words per se to communicate; it's more like they're suggesting meanings and letting me know when I've got the right ones. But the images they're sharing with me don't many any sense at all. I'm seeing a sky full of stars, some mountains maybe. About all I can tell you for sure is that when you mentioned the sleepers, one of them was happy, and the other one was afraid."

Eyes still locked on the Omega's broad face, Jantine nodded. Delays in communication were common with Omegas, but Mira's different worldview was both helpful and a hindrance in this situation. When she thought of the right words to say, Jantine used her best command voice.

"I told you, it's not safe here. That distress signal will bring our enemies to us. We have to find a way to turn it off, and then we need to get to a place we can protect her."

"No danger. Safe here. S-A-198 must be awakened. They're . . . Jantine, he's lying!"

"What?"

"The one facing the unit, he believes you. But the other one. . . I think something is wrong with him. I think. . . he's scared."

Jantine's world was coming apart, one piece at a time. Not only was she on the verge of losing her command to an unknown, but now the Omegas were actively working against her. Lying to her. There were always things they did that didn't make sense, but this. . .

The Omega in question was on its feet before she could finish her thought. It was almost twice her height, and just one of its arms massed more than her entire body. In the dim light of the setting sun, shadows drew dark lines on its face, and Jantine felt Mira's fear pulling at her own.

She took a step back, chiding herself for the unconscious gesture. After seeing the Omegas in action aboard the *Valiant*, she knew there was nothing she could do to stop them if they really wanted to hurt her. Artemus couldn't possibly get to her in time, and even if he could get past the second Omega, it would only be to collect her corpse.

Then her fear was gone, replaced by a wave of support and confidence. Whatever it was seemed right, and as the feeling wrapped itself around the base of her mind, Jantine stood a little bit taller.

"I've made my decision. We must find a way to disable the transmitter, and once we are in a secure location, Carlton and JonB will—"

A hand touched her shoulder, and Mira's whispered words came from right behind her.

"Jantine, let me talk to him. I think I can get us out of this."

Angered by the interruption, Jantine shrugged the hand off.

"No. Don't do anything else. It won't hurt me. It can't."

"Are you sure about that? Because he's not."

Jantine didn't have any time to consider the implications of Mira's statement before a new voice added an unexpected complication to the situation.

"Commander, a word?"

The Omega spun its head to stare at JonB, who paled under its four-eyed scrutiny. The scientist was standing just inside the hole leading to the cargo area, holding himself steady on the sloping floor by gripping a protruding piece of conduit. He still had a few drops of Katra's blood on his face, but otherwise looked fine.

"What is it, JonB?" The words sounded a lot more confident than she felt, but Jantine refused to back down.

"Uh, not you, boss. Her." Without loosening his death grip on the conduit, JonB doubled up his right arm, pulling his wrist almost level with his shoulder and pointing at Mira.

"He's awake. Captain Martin, that is, and he wants to talk with you. If you can spare the time."

And now you're starting to do it. I'm still in charge here, JonB. Not the Omegas. And certainly not Mira Harlan!

"I think we're good, right? Everyone's said what they have to say?" Mira stepped in front of Jantine, staring down the Omega with steely eyes. Jantine felt a fresh wave of confidence as she passed by, one with familiar undertones.

But then she did something Doria would never have attempted; Mira reached up a hand and made a snapping noise with her fingers until the Omega turned away from JonB. Behind it, the second Omega rose to its feet, and Jantine thought she saw something like concern in its eyes.

The sound wasn't loud enough to be painful, and even with her muscular build Mira didn't appear to be a real threat to the Omega. But her intent to scold was apparent to everyone, and she didn't let it go with just the one gesture. She pointed a finger up at the Omega's face, and shook it several times for emphasis while she spoke.

"It's not nice to ignore someone when they're talking to you. Commander Jantine has very real concerns for your safety, for all of us. I know you're frustrated, but this is not the way." Lowering her finger, she nodded in JonB's direction.

"And you leave him alone; he's only trying to help. I'll be gone a few minutes, but we're not done talking about this."

Mira spun on her heel and walked over to the shuttle. The Omega followed Mira to the side of the ship and then gently boosted her up through the hole. Jantine heard the Earther say "thank you" before she leaned out over the edge of the hull and kissed the top of the Omega's orange head.

The Omega stood there with its hands spread out on the hull for almost a minute after JonB and Mira made their way further into the ship, just watching the space where she had been. When it turned around, its tiny mouth was pressed tight in something approximating a smile. It could have been the last sliver of sunlight painting everything with warm colors, but Jantine could have sworn its skin was a deeper shade, almost red in places.

Carlton started to say something, but Jantine waved her hand without looking at him, not wanting to spoil the moment.

Just then, work lights along the hull warmed to life, bathing the area in the broad-spectrum light of Colony A's secondary star. After so many hours basking in the warm yellow radiance of Sol, it was like gray paint had been splashed over everything.

By the time Jantine could distinguish colors again the Omega's face was back to normal. It walked over to the sleeper unit to rejoin its companion, but instead of turning to stare at Jantine, it raised its hand to the spot Mira had kissed. The second Omega did the same thing, and Jantine wondered how much of Mira's scolding had been delivered mentally so the Omegas could save some face in front of the other mods.

Whatever she's becoming, it's definitely not a Gamma. And the rest of us are going to have to change almost as much just to keep up with her. . .

MIRA

"IS SOMEONE GOING TO TELL ME WHAT ALL OF THAT WAS about? Or should I just stay terrified until my heart explodes?"

Janbi's question made Mira smile. He'd been busy since she last saw him, restoring grav in the corridors and completing an amazing clean-up job. The walls and floors no longer dripped with gore, and she wagered he'd done a better job than any middie work detail could have managed in the same amount of time.

Give this one another few hours, he'll probably come up with something to patch the hull as well.

In regards to his question, she could still feel the Builder's seething confusion behind her, a deep well of frustration that wouldn't be satisfied until the universe returned to the way it used to be. Mira's Gamma memories told her that most mods had difficulty distinguishing between one Omega and another, but she didn't need to see them to know who was who.

There was the one who'd changed her, and the one who thought doing so was a bad idea. The angry one, who still wanted to punch something with those big hands.

"I'm not exactly sure, Janbi. The Builders are . . . complex."

The boy's laugh was like a warm shower, setting her mind at ease. There was a small spike of annoyance when she'd spoken, but it faded quickly into the general aura of unshakable confidence he was projecting.

Oh, boyo. If you weren't half my age, Mama Harlan's little girl would be in trouble right now.

It wasn't just his looks that Mira found fascinating. Janbi's whole outlook was as different from the other mods as Artemus was physically from Carlton. He seemed out of place among the dour and brooding Colonials, though the longer she talked with Jantine the more she suspected the young leader was also a breed apart.

Maybe it's a Beta thing. Carlton seems fairly normal, but he can still get pretty intense at times.

"Well, if you figure it out, let me know. I never want to be on the wrong end of those two."

Mira thought about the perpetual dark mood the one she'd taken to calling "Grumpy" was in. The Omegas had experienced significant emotional trauma in the last few hours, but it had changed them in very different ways.

When "Happy" forced her body's transformation it was more of an accident than anything else. At first he'd just been curious about the different taste of her thoughts. But once he'd seen her up close, he acted on instinct, giving her both the Transgenic virus and the Gamma memories.

Including those of Doria. Wherever I go with these people, they're always going to be thinking of her. I don't even know what she looked like, and I feel like I'll never match up to their memories.

It seemed silly to be jealous of a fifteen-year-old girl she'd never met, but that's definitely how it felt. Having a selection of Doria's memories wasn't the same as talking with the Gamma or experiencing her thoughts, something every other personality fragment bouncing around in her head had done before passing on its knowledge to Doria.

Mira reached out to Janbi's shoulder, and a wave of raw desire rolled off him when they touched. Images that could make a courtesan blush flashed through his mind, and Mira couldn't help but be flattered.

Well that's good to know. They have normal human responses after all.

A memory fragment bubbled up—a private conversation between Doria and Malik—and Mira felt a touch of shame. It wasn't her fault the Gamma had assigned such an important meaning to the encounter. But it was something personal, something intense that was never meant to be shared with another. Mira was pretty sure the Builders didn't know about it either. Happy had just been carrying the memories; he didn't have the emotional vocabulary to understand them. But Mira did, and their meaning was clear to her. The Betas on this mission *were* different. Very different than those back "home."

"Janbi, tell me something. Why were you selected for this mission?"

Confusion warred with curiosity and passion in his mind, but the analytical ability that was his greatest strength trumped them all. Janbi considered her question carefully before answering.

"Actually, it's . . . never mind. I was chosen because I am the best."

"Best? Best at what?"

"Everything."

Janbi's confusion mixed with pride, and the combination twisted his face into something she wanted to stare at forever.

Oof, those eyes.

Pulling herself back to task, Mira pressed for more.

"Surely, there has to be more to it than that?"

Thinking about who in the Colonies would have made that decision, Mira was more afraid than ever of waking up S-A-198.

"My entire crèche was tested. I was selected, trained, and prepared to be a civilian adjunct to Jantine. Specifically Jantine, to answer your next question. One of the sleeper Betas is . . . was Malik's match."

Something in the way he said the word made her want to know more, but Janbi was already moving on to another topic.

"We should continue. Captain Martin—"

Mira pictured the captain as she'd last seen him, breathing uneasily in his cabin with Carlton removing a scanner from his head. She'd felt the pain he was in since re-entering the shuttle, but so far it was manageable.

"He's dying. I know, Janbi, and so does he. But this is important. I need to understand Jantine if I'm going to work with her. With all of you."

"My training tells me you are enemy combatants, but what I've seen—what I've learned in just a few hours with you—tells me a completely different story than the one our leaders have been feeding us. I have to know more."

The concern on Janbi's perfect features was real, and most of his salacious thoughts receded as he studied her face. Carlton had done something similar outside, and now that she'd experienced it again in his mind, she understood the feeling for what it was.

Pity. He knows I can never fully understand him, and that there's nothing he can do about it.

She could feel the captain down the corridor, managing his pain with thoughts of duty and how he could best make his death serve the human race. She might not agree with his decisions so far, but she could at least *understand* them, and that was a feeling she knew she'd have less and less during her time with the gennies.

"I'll help you if I can. But you're not one of us. Not yet. You're still an Earther at your core; you believe everything's going to work out for the best. It won't."

Janbi's stark acceptance of a futile universe seemed at odds with his deep curiosity about how it worked. She knew his mind was always seeking alternatives, and that he was capable of incredible intuitive leaps. But underneath it all was the cold certainty of his inevitable failure, and he was okay with that.

"But, we still have to try, Janbi. It's what makes us human."

"Are we, Commander? Are we really? What do you think those people on the ship thought when the Omegas tore them apart? I've lived my entire life with them, and I still can't believe what I saw. Think about when you first saw the Deltas. Did you think they were human, or monsters?"

Mira was about to say "human" but realized it would have been the Gamma memories talking. Janbi was right, they *were* monsters at first, and she'd recoiled from the Omega too until he shoved a dozen lifetimes of tolerance into her brain. Part of Mira wanted to believe she was a better person than that, but she'd been an officer long enough to know that people don't really change.

They just get better at fitting in.

Janbi took her silence as an invitation to continue.

"I don't think we are human, at least not what you mean by the term. We're something else. Something better. And until you accept that you're not one of them anymore, you'll never understand Jantine."

Mira detected nothing but honesty in Janbi's mind, wondered if she could do what he said. The longer she talked with any of the mods, the more her universe expanded. And locating her exact place in it was getting harder to do.

"We really shouldn't keep Captain Martin waiting." Janbi gestured down the corridor.

As much as Mira wanted to talk to the captain, there was still something she needed to ask Janbi. And given how much he'd altered her worldview already, she wasn't entirely sure she wanted to hear his answer.

"In a minute. This is important. When I asked you earlier why you were chosen for the mission, what I really meant was, why are you different from the others? None of them want to talk about this, or accept me without questions the way you do."

Janbi's mind went into overdrive, but Mira detected no particular emotion from him. It was a refreshing change, but she was a bit apprehensive about what kind of response required such intense contemplation.

"I don't think it was me in particular, although out of all my crèche I *was* the best suited for the mission. It was the combination of myself and Jantine that made me the only choice. We are compatible."

The nagging feeling was back. Janbi was saying more with the word "compatible" than she was hearing, and it was more than just a Beta vs human thing.

Or is it? Match. Compatible? It can't be. They're just kids!

"Janbi, are you married to her?"

Things that he'd said, that Jantine mentioned in passing, that Mira had seen but not understood in the Gamma memory dump started falling into place.

"I don't know what married means, but your context is correct. We are paired, or we will be if we can complete the mission and establish a colony. Our children, when it's safe to have them, will be of this world, and their children will be our ambassadors to humanity.

"Your other question is more interesting. I like you, Commander. I like you because you're *not* one of us. Not Beta, not Gamma. You're something different, something new, and I enjoy speaking with you. You almost make me believe I can change our fate, and that makes you a puzzle worth solving."

Mira knew he meant it, and as much as she hated herself for asking, she had to know for sure.

"Are you sure that's all of it? You have no other motives?"

Right on cue, all the boy's salacious thoughts resurfaced. And the knowledge that he knew she could sense their content was both embarrassing and very attractive. What's worse, she felt herself respond, if only as a courtesy to his wonderful smile.

Trou-ble.

"Oh, that. We will have sex, you and I. And our children will be even more impressive, I think, than those I will have with Jantine. But we don't have time for that right now. There are more important things to worry about than your pleasure."

Janbi took her hand from his shoulder, and raised it to his lips for a kiss. Mira felt her cheeks redden, embarrassed not only by the fact that she'd left it there throughout their conversation, but at the electric charge she felt when his breath touched her skin.

He was several meters down the corridor at an open door when the full impact of what he'd said hit her.

Wait, my pleasure? Why you little . . .

"Captain Martin, I've brought Commander Harlan as you requested. Do you need anything else?"

A wet, hacking cough preceded Martin's reply, and his pain banished all thoughts of Janbi from Mira's mind. She ran to the open cabin door, and saw the captain sitting up in bed and wiping blood away from his mouth.

"No, that's all right, son. Thank you. Just wait outsi—"

This close to the captain, his pain was almost overpowering. But Mira's mental companions knew a few tricks for dealing with it. She tugged on his memories until one from his childhood popped up, and she massaged it into a warm, soothing blanket to wrap around his mind.

ALOYSIUS

WELL, THAT'S NEW.

Martin's pain subsided, and the warm feeling that replaced it was more than a little nostalgic. He smelled something spicy that reminded him of cold winter afternoons spent watching the snow pile up outside while his great-grandfather explained how in his day, life was simpler, and "you boys best not forget where we came from!"

Opa. Haven't thought about him since…

Gerolt Maarten was one hundred and forty-seven years old when his great-grandson had entered the Academy, and almost lived long enough to attend his graduation. He did get to see Aloysius wear his uniform one time, on a visit home that also involved snowdrifts and hot cider.

Now, where did that come from, I wonder?

Martin opened his eyes, and saw Mira Harlan sitting beside him. For a moment, she was framed by a sky full of stars and an old oak tree, but then the familiar confines of his cabin surrounded them both. She was wearing a set of ship blues, but the last time he checked her name wasn't Marcus Callaway.

Apparently my pilot's clothes made it aboard, even if he didn't.

"You're out of uniform, Harlan."

Harlan's smile made him feel almost as good as whatever drugs the gennies were pumping into him. There was something about her face that seemed off, but his head was still fuzzy.

"Yes, sir. It was these or your formals, and I didn't think that appropriate at the time."

"Well, you'll get your command soon enough. Might as well get used to people calling you 'Captain.'"

Maybe it's her eyes. Were they always that color?

Admittedly, Martin hadn't spent a lot of time in Harlan's company, but there was something different about her. She was . . . softer somehow, as if some of her hard edges had been knocked off during their escape.

"I'm not so sure about that, sir. Since the last interaction I had with the fleet involved missiles and a bit of treason, I don't think either of us is in their good graces right now. Sir, Janbi said you wanted to talk to me?"

Martin grunted, then wished he hadn't. A fresh round of coughing brought up more blood, and Harlan had to ease him back into a sitting position. A fresh wave of warmth washed over him, and had the distinct impression it originated from her. He still didn't know what was bothering him about his second-in-command, but she was right. There were things to discuss.

"So that Carlton kid, he told you what's wrong with me?"

"Yes, sir. Vasogenic cerebral edema. Your brain's getting too big for your skull, thanks to all the hits to the head you took. I'd tell you that you should have kept your helmet on, but we were both pretty helpless by the time the mods captured the shuttle. But you also got shot a couple times and didn't tell anybody, and that's what's killing you."

Martin nodded, glad the pain in his head was finally gone.

"Wrong tense there, Harlan. I'm dead already. Only question is, what can I do to help you and those kids before I check out completely?"

Harlan squeezed his hand, and when she did, something like feathers tickled the back of his head. Her smile was infectious, and he was about to laugh when he remembered what happened the last time he tried it.

No sense making things worse. Didn't she used to have freckles? Maybe that was one of the others. It's hard to think straight right now.

"Sir, I need you to tell me about the Alpha. Specifically that sleeper unit. Where and when you found it, and what kind of shape it was in."

Martin chanced a look around his cabin. Most of his effects were back on the *Valiant*, but this shuttle had been his real home for a while now. Four months of detached duty with Horace Kołodziejski and his black hats while Bill Williams built him a crew he could trust, and then a month hiding out with the gennie on the other end of a hyper tunnel while things cooled off enough for him to return to the *Valiant*.

It seemed a reasonable enough place to die. His books were here, as well as his chess set. Gerolt claimed he'd carved it from a fallen tree after it had been split by lightning, but when one of the pawns was damaged a few years after the old man died, he'd found an identical replacement in an Amsterdam flea market.

"Sir?"

Harlan. Right. There was something I was going to tell her, something important.

"Sir? The Alpha?"

"I stole it. Off the *Tribune*. Horace was moving it around the system as an insurance policy in case our people found out about it. He was right, of course, but at the time he thought I was working for his side. When I saw my chance, I corralled a couple techs I could trust and we grabbed the thing and ran."

Harlan nodded, but her eyes were still fixed on his face. The feathers tickled him again, and her look of concentration intensified.

Is there something on my face?

"Anything else, sir? Did you detect any signals maybe when you moved it?"

Martin tried to remember what it was he needed to do. It was hard to think, when all he wanted to do was sleep.

"Did I ever tell you about my opa? He was full of crazy old sayings. My brother and I could predict which one was coming after a while, based on his mood. But his favorite of all was, '*de eersten zullen de laatsten zijn.*'"

Gerolt loved working with wood, but Martin never had the patience. The carved chess set was his favorite, and he always praised the boys for their skill at the game.

"Sir? Sir, I don't speak Dutch. You asked to see me, sir. Was there something you wanted to tell me? About the Alpha? The shuttle's computer core is damaged, and most of the proof you said was in there is corrupted."

Harlan? When did she get here? There was something I wanted to tell her, something important.

"Captain? I feel you slipping away, and I don't know how to help you. Is there something you want to tell me? Something important?"

Mira Harlan, that's her name. Top of her class. One of Maranova's "bright stars . . ."

Martin smiled. Harlan was a good kid. Bill Williams said she had potential, and he kept her on when he re-staffed the *Valiant.*

"We should probably bring her in, don't you think, Bill? She's got brains, and a good heart. She'll know what to do when the time comes."

Martin looked to his left, but Commander Williams was missing. He thought he heard someone talking, someone yelling, and then his world caught on fire. It was hard to breathe, and when the coughing started again something tore inside him. Strong hands held him up, and wiped something warm and wet from his face.

"Captain? Can you hear me?"

"Ha-Harlan, is that you?"

Martin blinked his eyes, but he couldn't make out where she was. Everything was white and gray clouds, and the pounding in his head wouldn't stop.

"It's me, sir. Don't try to talk. If you can, just think about what you want to say, and I'll try to translate it into terms I can understand."

"What's . . . what's happening to me?

"You've been injured, sir. You're dying. I can take away your pain, but when I do it clouds your mind. You called me in here to tell me something. Was it about the Alpha?"

Martin took in a breath to speak, but doing so sent pain throughout his chest. After another round of coughing he decided just to nod, and try doing what Harlan suggested.

Yes. The Alpha. You have to get it to safety.

Harlan's hand squeezed his, and the warmth in his mind went up a notch. Martin wasn't sure what exactly was happening, but at least the pain was getting easier to handle. Harlan's voice came from floating down from somewhere above the clouds.

"I know, sir, we're trying. There's a signal of some kind coming from the unit. I think it's what let Captain Kołodziejski locate the *Valiant*, but I don't know enough about what you were planning to turn it to our advantage. Can you tell me how to turn it off?"

Connect it to a power source. Damn. You have to get out of here. How long has it been transmitting?

Martin tried to get up, but his arms refused to do his bidding. Harlan squeezed his hand again, and then continued speaking in her far away voice.

"I'm going to go with too long. And things here are . . . complex. The Colonials are debating what to do about the Alpha, but your contacts are the most important thing right now. We found a course in the core for someplace called the Harrison Institute; near as I can tell it's about a thousand kilometers northeast from here.

"The shuttle will fly, but it's in no shape for a fight and these kids don't know the first thing about space warfare. They're smart, and lucky, but our people have been training for this a long time. They'll—we'll be picked off as soon as we break atmosphere."

A fresh round of coughing doubled Martin over and set his head spinning. He could feel Harlan's arms around him, but he couldn't summon the strength to do what had to be done. When he could breathe again, he put everything he had into three words.

"I'll . . . do . . . it."

"Sir, no. We can figure out a remote . . ."

"Only . . . play. Sacrifice . . . knight, save . . . queen."

Martin felt a small cold spot on the back of his neck, then another. Harlan started to speak several times but, for some reason, never finished. When he heard her voice again, it had undertones of sadness and resignation.

"What do you need me to do?"

JANTINE

JANTINE STARED AT THE SLEEPER UNIT AS CARLTON and an Omega fussed over its controls. Once JonB had righted the shuttle, it hadn't taken long to move the mods' remaining supplies outside— as well as the bulky sleeper unit back in.

A warm night breeze came in through the side of the shuttle and blew past her down the ramp. The image of Crassus sailing away into the open sky kept playing in her mind, and she was only half-listening to Mira speak.

". . . should keep him conscious long enough to get far away from here, but I can't say for sure. I've used a technique on him that will handle most of the pain, while keeping him lucid. He's still going to die, but he can at least provide a distraction and help us get away."

From what Jantine understood, Captain Martin's plan was a good one. And if Carlton said the captain was sound enough to pull it off, she believed him.

The bigger problem was what Carlton was doing right now. The choice to revive the Alpha was out of her hands entirely. Before discovering the distress signal, she could delay it indefinitely and maintain command of the mission. Now that there was no other option, she worried that the Omegas would be even harder to control.

The Omegas were getting easier to distinguish, just by the way they stood. One had its arms folded across its broad chest, glowering at the delay. The other was helping Carlton input the final wake-up commands, shoulders rounded and pointing at various readouts as they worked.

The team was back in their encounter suits, and Jantine had to admit she felt a bit more secure dressed for action. Artemus and Katra stood with weapons at the ready, watching the sky for attackers but still keeping an eye on the imperious Omega.

I'm not sure which bothers me more: a threat from above or the one standing in front of us.

Knowing she could do nothing about either, Jantine turned her attention to the newest member of her team. Even with her faceplate up, the sight of the woman wearing the white hard-suit reminded her of all the humans she'd had to kill to get to this moment.

And also of the one she hadn't killed quite yet, hopefully the last casualty of their arrival in the home system.

"Mira, can I talk to Captain Martin?"

The Earther nodded, and Jantine detected a hint of sadness in the gesture.

"I think he'd like that, actually. He has a lot of respect for you, for what you were able to do aboard the *Valiant*. As soon as Carlton and JonB are finished, I'll take you up. By the way, were you ever going to tell me I was saying it wrong?"

Jantine smiled at the light rebuke. Mira was beginning to understand mod humor, though it was doubtful she'd ever grasp the full reasons behind JonB's obstinance and the others' response to it.

"I was certain you'd figure it out, eventually. Which one talked?"

"Carlton. I asked him what S-A-198 meant, and then it all fell into place. Are you really going to marry him? You have to know you have a choice in the matter."

Jantine shook her head. While a distraction from the Alpha's imminent awakening was welcome, this particular topic was not among her favorites.

"Whether I do or not, that's a matter for another time. And you mistake my meaning. I don't want to see your captain, I want to *talk* to him."

Jantine raised her right hand, tapping the side of her helmet with a finger. Mira's eyes widened, and Jantine felt the Earther's soft touch in her mind.

"You're getting better at that."

"Thanks. It's not easy, believe me. There's nothing in the Gamma playbook that covers this, and I'm not sure I can do what you want. It . . . it doesn't work that way.

Jantine lowered her hand and turned away. Carlton pulled on a handle, gave it a half-turn, then pushed it back almost all the way. The Beta's expression was equal parts excitement and concern, and when he looked back at Jantine for approval, the other Omega stepped forward to block his view.

"On board your ship I discovered that our main communication methods are vulnerable to interference. If we can harness your abilities tactically, it would give us an unparalleled advantage. Empathic Gammas are not combat trained, and you are. And we're not going to have a better chance to practice than now."

Jantine took a step to the side and nodded at Carlton, who pushed the handle home. The sleeper unit started shaking, and after a few seconds she could feel the vibration in her bones.

"Mira? Anything?"

"I'm sorry, Jantine. The words are there, but I can't relay his thoughts."

"It's not a problem. We'll revisit this later. For now, we'll just use your radio, and I'll teach you how to use the scattercomms."

The bay became noticeably hotter, and despite herself Jantine couldn't take her attention away from the sleeper unit. What she was about to see was the most important event in the colonies, and she had only one chance to do this right.

A ring of lights strobed around the face of the unit, casting alternating shadows on the child within. Suspension fluid drained away from her face, and her pale skin almost glowed when the lights stopped moving. Then the dura-glass cover unlocked, sliding back with a series of warning chimes and another set of flashing lights.

A cloud of scented steam escaped the chamber, and Jantine's breath caught in her throat. She had to see, had to know, and when Mira turned on her radio Jantine nearly jumped out of her skin.

"Captain? Can you hear me? Commander Jantine wants to speak with you."

"I can hear you, Harlan. Is she listening now?"

"Yes, sir. Jantine?"

There was an odd buzzing sound accompanying each of Captain Martin's words, as if the tension she was feeling was interfering with the transmission. It felt wrong to be talking right now, but the feathery comfort of Mira's mind that accompanied her words set her at ease.

"Commander?"

"Yes, I can hear you. Both of you. Captain, I wanted to thank you for your sacrifice. You will be remembered well for this."

Carlton stepped up onto the sleeper unit, assisted by the less aggressive of the Omegas. Jantine moved forward herself, ducking under the orange arm that appeared in her way and very aware of the sound of five pulsers whining to life.

When she arrived at the base of the unit, "Carlton's" Omega offered her a broad hand while at the same time looking back over her shoulder.

Jantine floated off the floor up to Carlton's side. The Beta was removing sensor pads from the Alpha's skin and staring at her face. Up close, she looked even more delicate, not at all like the shadowy figures who'd dictated the course of her life over viewscreens since her earliest memories.

S-A-198's hairless head was oval in shape, and absolutely symmetrical. From her wide forehead to her tiny, pointed chin, she was a miniature vision of perfection. Even her almost translucent skin was flawless.

The sound of Captain Martin's voice over the radio made her scowl momentarily. How dare he distract her from so much beauty?

"Thank, you, Jantine, is it? But you have to know I'm not doing it for you. Despite what's happened, Harlan is one of my people, and she's the best chance we've got of getting your Alpha away from here and into the hands of those who can help."

Mira gasped: "Her mind, oh my God her mind!"

The Alpha's eyes snapped open, and her liquid brown eyes scanned both Jantine's face and Carlton's before fixating on the former.

Jantine was scared and alive and worried and delighted. Despite all her earlier concerns, she smiled, and her emotions doubled in intensity when the Alpha responded. The child's lips were plumping up, and her skin seemed to be thickening over her cheekbones.

The words were out of Jantine's mouth almost before she thought of what to say.

"I am JTN-B34256-O, commander of Expedition Force SS7. This is CRN-B34310-T. How do you want to be called, S-A-198?"

The sleeper unit gave one last chime, then fell silent. A broad pair of orange hands inserted themselves between Carlton and Jantine, who were still entranced by the Alpha's delicate face. The Omega gently pressed them aside, and S-A-198's tiny hands stretched feebly toward those of the hulking giant's. The Omega lifted her from the suspension chamber and then stepped back with the child gently cradled in its arms.

To her surprise, Jantine saw that it was the angry Omega who'd come forward to claim the child, rather than the one who had helped Jantine and Carlton climb up. The Alpha's head flopped toward Jantine, and her skin took on a more healthy color as blue-green suspension fluid poured from her mouth and nose. The Omega's chest compressed, and a white mist came out of its mouth and flowed over S-A-198's face.

For several terrible seconds, Jantine thought the child was going to die, until her chest started to rise and fall in a regular rhythm.

"Commander, it's so wonderful. Her mind is like sunlight, and she's, she's . . ."

Jantine heard the buzzing sound again, but before she could ask what Mira meant, one of the Alpha's arms came up and beckoned her forward. In her haste to comply, she almost stepped straight off the sleeper unit, but Carlton and the Omega were there to help her down. Jantine was dimly aware of Artemus, Katra and JonB staring at her, but she only had eyes for the Alpha.

She took a tentative step forward, then another, until she was standing just half a meter from the Omega. The mod crouched down until S-A-198 was at eye-level, and the child opened her mouth to speak. Her voice was barely above a whisper, but the sound of it sent a thrill throughout Jantine's body.

"Serene. I am called Serene. Where is J-A-197?"

Before Jantine could answer, the shuttle's engines powered up. Artemus and Katra were already halfway down the ramp, and Carlton and the Omega were hastily checking that the sleeper unit was fully secured. JonB was staring at the Alpha, but Jantine's swiveling head drew his attention away.

The face of the Omega holding Serene was also on a level with hers, and Jantine swore its small mouth twisted into a snarl. The orange giant spun around and pounded its way down the cargo ramp, and once she could no longer see Serene's eyes a deep sense of loss settled in her heart.

"Jantine!" Mira's shout brought her back to reality. "Captain Martin says we have hostiles inbound at three hundred kilometers Zulu and falling. It's now or never, Commander, let's go!"

Jantine looked down at the pulser in her hand, wondering when she'd drawn it. Looking up, she saw Mira using one hand to close her faceplate, and waving a weapon of her own in the other. A lifetime of training kicked in, and she gave the order to abandon ship.

"Move out, go, go, go!"

She was down the ramp in less than a second, pausing at the base while Carlton, the other Omega, and JonB exited. When the civvies were all on solid ground, she ran after them to the pile of supplies several hundred meters away.

The shuttle's maneuvering thrusters fired, and it rose unsteadily on columns of twisting air. Jantine could see internal lights shining through the hastily patched hole in its side, and when the cargo ramp closed the shuttle spun around and accelerated into the night sky.

Die well, Captain Martin.

Jantine followed the shuttle's course with her eyes. She'd spent some time outside the shuttle earlier memorizing and admiring the visible stars. As a new one rose to join them, she saw several other shining points of light race toward it.

"He knows, Commander. The last thing I got from his mind was that he wishes he'd had more time with you, and with her."

Mira's words were like a punch in the stomach, and Jantine took several long seconds to consider her options. Not wanting to see the end result of Martin's last act, she turned to follow the rest of the team.

Most of the other mods were racing away in pursuit of a tall, jumpsuited figure holding a tinier one. Only JonB and Mira were waiting for her, and the enormity of her loss was staggering.

"No, Mira. It's just Jantine now. I'm not the Commander anymore."

Jantine moved past JonB, and the Beta reached out a hand to her shoulder. She batted it away, and felt a tinge of regret at his hurt expression. He likely meant no offense, but she was in no mood to be comforted, especially by him.

But Mira Harlan was not so easily dismissed. The Earther's faceplate was open, and Jantine saw the same expression on her face that she'd used earlier to chastise the Omega.

"Like hell you're not." Mira was using almost the same tone with which she'd chastised the Omegas, and Jantine didn't like it one bit. Not just that the Earther was in a position to use it on her, but that like JonB, she was right. "Assuming the Omega puts her down sometime soon, that little girl may well be the most wonderful thing that will ever set foot on this planet. But there's no way she could ever do the things you've done today, and the others will see that soon enough. You're their leader, dammit. Act like it."

JonB was carefully avoiding Jantine's personal space as he moved into a position where he could see both hers and Mira's faces at the same time. Jantine wanted to tell him she was sorry, but she knew he'd never look for or expect an apology from her.

"You don't understand, Mira," he said. "You can't. It's like I told you earlier, this is who we are. Alphas direct, Betas serve. Gammas support, but I think the three of us can admit that's not who or what you're becoming. And that uncertainty is what will save us in the end."

Jantine was confused by JonB's words, but then she realized what the civvie was working up to. The cold brilliance of his plan was astounding, and once again she was impressed with his analysis of the situation.

Perhaps you and I really are compatible after all.

MIRA

"Wha . . . what?"

Mira wasn't sure what JonB was saying, but his thoughts had the same rock-solid certainty he'd had when announcing how he'd spoofed the missile strike, and then again with his certainty of their children together.

He really believes whatever he has in mind is going to work, and Jantine's on board without even hearing what it is.

"You're going to have to break it down for me. You two think a lot faster than I do, and I haven't got a clue as to what you're planning."

The three of them were alone now, and far enough away from the rest of the mods and their acute hearing for a bit of privacy.

"I told you before, Mira. You're not a Gamma, and you're certainly no Beta." Mira wanted to slap the smug smile off JonB's perfect face, but the certainty of his thoughts made her more curious than angry.

"But you are definitely a mod now, and completely new variety at that. From what we understand, spontaneous expressions of the T-virus among humans are exceedingly rare on your planet, and as a soldier—with your level of training—you are potentially more important than any Alpha. *Your* empathic abilities will revolutionize the order of battle, not to mention the advantages we'll have in dealing with outsiders. You, not S-A . . . I mean, Serene, need to be our leader."

Mira searched JonB's thoughts for any trace of humor, but found none. Both he and Jantine were convinced that his ridiculous plan had merit, even though Mira couldn't for the life of her figure out why, or even when they'd come up with it.

Looks like it's time to be the grown-up in this relationship.

"Let me get this straight. A little over five hours ago, Jantine had a gun trained on me. Three hours later, you, her thirteen year-old super-genius fiancé, blithely announced that not only were *we* going to have sex, but that our children would be the stuff of legend. And now both of you are telling me that—Oh, come on, really?"

In another universe, the expression on Jantine's face would be priceless comedy. Her nod, her smile, and the pleasantly surprised look in her eyes would leave a tri-vid audience in tears. But Mira could see past the mask the Beta wore and into her soul, and Jantine wasn't offended by the idea in the slightest.

In fact, she approved.

"Excellent thinking, JonB. We must lock in her variant as quickly as possible. You are fertile, correct? When did you last ovulate?"

"I am not having this conversation. Not now, not ever."

To punctuate her feelings on the matter, Mira sent a wave of disapproval into both the Beta's minds, wincing as it created an answering spike of pain in her own.

"Fascinating. How long has she been doing that?"

"Since before the crash. It's remarkable, isn't it?"

Mira couldn't believe either her ears or whatever sense carried their emotions into her brain. Not only was JonB revisiting some of his more exotic fantasies, but Jantine had her own imagination in overdrive on the same topic. And all the while, the Betas were calmly discussing both Mira's mental abilities and overthrowing the political structure of the Outer Colonies.

"What is wrong with you two? First, neither of you is my type, and I've a mind to give you both a psychic cold shower. Second, haven't each of you told me that crossing the Omegas was the last thing you wanted to do? They'll never agree to this, and once they discover your plan, what then? Kill them?"

The confidence JonB and Jantine had been projecting vanished in an instant. The Betas each took half a step back, as if even standing next to Mira would incur the Builders' eternal wrath.

"I'm sorry, I'm sorry. I didn't mean that. But you have to agree this is a ridiculous proposition."

"What do you mean, you didn't mean that? Why would you say such a thing?"

Jantine's voice was a quivering whisper. JonB moved to her side, and this time she didn't push him away. It took Mira almost a minute to figure out why they were so frightened, and that in itself was another condemnation of Colonial society. The two of them were shut down so completely that Mira couldn't get into either of their minds to put them at ease.

The Gamma memories gave her clear examples of what happened to mods that went rogue, especially those who threatened revolution. And while JonB wasn't advocating an overthrow per se, the distinction was fine enough that when she'd pressed the point what appeared to the Betas as a logical plan was completely undone by a simple exaggeration.

Can they really not know how to lie?

"It's just the way we talk here. No one wants to hurt the Builders, me especially. It's to prove a point, that's all. Everything's fine, really. I'm sorry. Please, I'm sorry. I just don't want you two to give up hope. Hope is all we have, in the end."

The platitudes seemed to be working, at least on Jantine. Her face regained its customary composure, but it was JonB who let his mental shields down first. Concern, uncertainty, and happiness were his immediate goals, and Mira was pleased to see that for once, his thoughts were directed outward.

"How will we do it?"

It was Mira's turn for shock. Whatever internal crisis it was that nearly shut her down, Jantine had made it through to the other side and was prepared to reclaim her position. Her words were spoken in a carefully neutral tone, and Jantine disengaged herself from her . . .

Just what am I supposed to call him now, intended? Betrothed? They seem to have made up their minds, at least about each other.

Whatever JonB was to Jantine, he was still the hyper-intelligent civilian scientist whose advice was meant to support her decisions.

Or does that change too, now that Serene is awake?

"As I see it, were Jantine or I to act directly, the others would have no choice but to lock us down. But you, Mira, have no official status in Colonial society. If you were to demonstrate sound leadership, and appeared to have support from the Betas, the others might well assume that Serene blesses your actions as well."

Mira studied JonB's face, wondering how smart the boy really was. His plan wouldn't stand up to any intense scrutiny, but from what she knew Gammas and Deltas cared more about carrying out orders than questioning them. Katra wasn't her biggest fan, but Artemus had "adopted" her almost as completely as had JonB.

Hopefully, not for the same reasons. If this works, we can keep things together long enough to locate the institute, and possibly get us some help.

"Mira?"

Her name hung in the night air. Jantine's voice wasn't yet back to its normal confident tone, but her mind was. With the question came a sense of urgency, and with a little concentration Mira could feel Katra's eyes scanning the plains for them.

"The plan has holes. Big ones. But so did Captain Martin's, and I signed on for that with even less information. We'll need to recruit Carlton for sure—I'll leave that to one of you. I like him and all, but he doesn't trust me. And Katra . . ." Mira looked in the direction where she'd detected Katra's thoughts. "If we're going to do this, we'll need to figure out if I—we—really can use my abilities as a secure communication network."

Despite the collected wisdom of the Gamma memories telling her it was impossible, Mira opened her mind to the two Betas, letting their emotions mingle with her own. Oddly enough, despite the time she'd been working with Jantine, it was JonB's thoughts that were easier to decipher.

≈*Oh, this feels wonderful! It's like holding hands, but without the hands. What happens if we . . .*≈

Mira regretted including him almost instantly, but Jantine gave JonB a mental punch in the arm that pushed most of his thoughts of "experimenting" aside.

It would be a lot easier, though, if I didn't get all *his thoughts at once. He really needs to . . . No. Not thinking about that. Definitely not . . .*

Mira waved the Betas forward, taking point on a leisurely walk into friendly territory. Katra was indeed looking for them, and the Gamma's rifle in her hands was a chilling reminder of what could go wrong if any of them slipped up. She put on her best smile and continued with their internal war council.

It was much harder for Mira to insert her thoughts into another mind than to decipher what they were thinking, and the pain it caused her was unlike anything she'd experienced before. To make it a bit easier, she imagined herself whispering the words directly into JonB and Jantine's ears.

≈*One thing at a time, young man. And never, understand me? Not. Ever. I need you focused on keeping us alive, not your sexual fantasies.*≈

≈*If it would help, JonB and I could copulate tonight. It is perhaps too early, but it would seem natural to the others.*≈

Mira wouldn't have believed Jantine was serious if she wasn't reading her mind. JonB was certainly interested in the plan, but before he could speak up Mira made another attempt to control the situation.

≈*I don't think that's necessary, but thank you. I think. We should spend tonight recruiting, not relaxing. Whatever you do, don't talk about your plan to make me your leader. Instead, talk about what good advice I've been giving you.*≈

≈*But that's not the plan . . .*≈

JonB's words carried a mixture of doubt and annoyance, but as far as Mira could tell he was willing to "listen."

≈*It is now. Hold up.*≈

"Jantine. Is anything wrong?"

Katra's question was half challenge, half concern, and Mira felt more than a little panic at how suddenly the Gamma had appeared in front of them.

Katra's eyes had a cold, calculating look that left Mira no doubt as to her feelings.

Betas may not be comfortable with telling lies, but Gammas are and do. This is going to be harder than I thought.

"No, Katra. Mira . . . was telling us about life on Earth."

Smooth. You're learning. And you hardly flinched at all when she didn't call you 'boss.'

"JonB, Carlton has found some machinery on the other side of the hill. I will take you there."

Mira's blood went cold at Katra's report. There were other reasons this part of North America was uninhabited, and although the chances of a Reclamation war machine being intact and operational in a Kansas wheat field was slim, it did exist. But before she could explain her fear, Jantine brought up another pressing matter.

"Good. The Omegas?"

Katra shrugged, indicating with her rifle their location. But Mira knew where they were already; in her mind she could feel the cool summer's day of Serene's thoughts thirty meters to her left, and close at hand the swirling pools of doubt and adoration that were the Omegas. With her eyes, she saw a soft glow behind some trees in the same general direction.

There was a shift in Jantine's mindset, which Mira read as a sense of determination before she shut her emotions down completely. It was a habit that, as an officer, she understood, but a dozen lifetimes of Gamma experiences found it rude and selfish. Examining those memories brought her a new realization about the Outer Colonies.

The Gamma empaths aren't there to help, not really. They're the thought police, and none of the other mods realize it.

"What kind of machines?"

JonB made no attempt to hide his pleasure. As instructed, he'd returned his fantasies to "storage," and applied himself to the more pressing business of survival. Like Jantine, he only wanted what was best for the group.

Katra gave another shrug. The starlight favored her long lines, and Mira's new eyes couldn't help but count the healed scars on the Gamma's encounter suit.

She's still hurting, but she won't let me see it. Can't, and still remain herself. Out of all of them, Katra will definitely be the hardest sell.

"He did not say. There are several buildings, and some odd containers in the area."

JonB made to move ahead before Jantine grabbed his arm. There was a brief flash of pleasure from him, then curiosity.

"Leave your pack, JonB. I need to do an inventory of our supplies. Whatever it is, Carlton's equipment will be enough."

Jantine turned her eyes to Mira and formed a question in her mind. Despite the pain, Mira opened her mind again.

≈*What is it, Commander?*≈

≈*Please relay to JonB. I don't think Mira's plan will work, but it has a better chance of success than yours. Start thinking of more alternatives. Do not attempt to initiate contact with me about any of this without approaching Mira first. Avoid scattercomms at all costs.*≈

Mira thought about the few items in her own bag, mainly rations drawn from the shuttle and a few of Captain Martin's personal effects. Everything else she "owned" was affixed to the outside of her hardsuit.

Jantine took JonB's pack from him, then snapped her head to the side. There was a brief flash of alarm from her, then appreciation. Katra's eyes flicked in the same direction, then returned to stare at Mira.

Mira felt Artemus approach long before hearing the Delta. The ease at which the big mod moved through the trees was impressive, and she was curious at what had tipped Jantine off.

Artemus slid out of the shadows and approached the impromptu conference. For a change, his lower hands held several dead birds instead of weapons.

"Scout Katra. Scientist JonB. Lieutenant Commander Harlan."

The Delta paused. It was slight, but the confusion in his mind told her more than any words could. A second later, he completed his deliberation and addressed Jantine.

"Governor Jantine. I have set up a two-kilometer perimeter line. Support Technician Carlton is very interested in his discovery, which he believes will allow us increased mobility."

Mira wasn't sure Jantine was comfortable with the new title, but sensed that she at least accepted it. Maybe it was because there wasn't really a colony for her to govern, but Artemus still wanted to follow her orders. And despite Serene's new status, Jantine was still the senior soldier present.

Well, that's somewhat debatable I guess, but I have even less interest in commanding these people than Katra does.

"What are those?"

Katra pointed her rifle at the dead birds.

"I believe these small animals may be edible. Lieutenant Commander Harlan, is this so?"

Mira remembered turkey hunts with her family as a child. Prairie chickens and pheasants weren't exactly the same, but she still knew how to clean and dress a bird. And since Artemus had apparently captured and killed them with his bare hands, when she was done there would be no annoying pellets to pick out of the final product.

"Yes, Guardian Artemus, thank you. I can show you how to prepare them if you wish."

Mira held out her hands for the birds, wondering if any of the mods had ever hunted before. Thankful he hadn't brought back a deer, she smiled and accepted them.

"I would appreciate that, but another time. There is still work to do to establish our camp."

"Artemus," said Jantine, "take JonB to Carlton. I will continue your patrol."

Artemus looked from Jantine to Katra, who gave him a small nod. Despite her efforts at control, Mira felt Jantine's annoyance spike. But it faded quickly, and the three Colonial soldiers split off in different directions, with JonB trailing after Artemus.

Mira called out to them while they were all still in hearing range: "JonB—all of you, really—please be careful with any machinery you find. Try to avoid activating anything without knowing what it does, and if you feel threatened, run. And if you can find a transport of some kind, remember that it has to be large enough to carry the Omegas."

"Of course," JonB said. "How long will it take to prepare the small animals? I wish to eat them as soon as possible."

"JonB, this is not our priority. There are enough ration packs for all of us."

One benefit to her new mental abilities was that Mira could "hear" the Betas bickering as they walked away, and she knew they were doing so more out of habit than annoyance. Something had happened between the two of them when they comforted one another, and despite the stress her earlier comments had caused she was happy they were getting along better. During their first encounter on the shuttle, Mira wasn't entirely sure Jantine wasn't going to shoot him.

She felt them move out of range, noting the distance. In time, she might be able to extend her abilities, but a two hundred meter radius seemed to be a hard limit.

"Do not get comfortable here, Earther," Katra said. "You are tolerated, nothing more. You are not one of us."

Katra's words matched her thoughts, both equally uncompromising. Mira had thought Jantine's mind inflexible at first, but Katra's was etched in stone. It wasn't hard to reconcile the sight of the warrior in front of her with the image of the Gamma fighting to breathe while she was bleeding out on the deck. Katra would never stop fighting until she was dead, and she would kill anyone who threatened her comrades.

A group that, as I am continually reminded, does not include me.

Mira shrugged, and held up the birds.

"Does this mean you don't want dinner? I think I saw some lemongrass earlier. Should be able to get something ready in about an hour."

Katra grunted, narrowing her eyes slightly. Though she didn't have Jantine's level of control, Katra's emotions were still difficult to isolate. Her anger was easy enough, but there was enough curiosity to give Mira some hope that the Gamma might eventually accept her.

That, or she's waiting until I finish cooking to kill me.

"It's fairly easy, once you know how. I remember my first time, though. Even though I wanted to be treated the same as my brothers, when Daddy handed me the bird I didn't understand what he wanted me to do with it. Once he showed me, I was sure I'd never be hungry again."

Mira filled the short distance to the mods' temporary camp describing her brothers' faces when she finally tried to clean the bird. As she talked, Katra's interest grew, and Mira was very pleased to feel the barrier between them coming down.

You're all so good at making hard choices, but not so much at making friends.

Her earlier assessment of the Omegas' positions was correct. "Happy" was sitting near the small pile of supplies that had survived the shuttle crash, while "Grumpy" was acting as a pillow for Serene. Mira felt the Alpha's attention on her as soon as she entered the small clearing, as well as flares of recognition from both the Omegas.

As before, Happy was relieved to be in her presence, and the mod's need for companionship was as powerful as ever. But Grumpy was a different matter entirely. Mira thought she could sense empathic activity in his mind, but he made no attempt to contact her.

Serene looked up into the Omega's face and smiled. Of all the mods Mira had seen so far, the child's face was the most alien. Shadows from a salvaged emergency light made her strange face seem even longer, and in the dim illumination her big brown eyes appeared nearly black. Grumpy certainly had no qualms about them, and from the way he was looking at Serene, Mira was certain she wasn't the only one in the clearing who could talk to the Omegas.

Oh, dear.

A snippet of Doria's conversation with Malik rose from her borrowed memories. She'd mentioned to him how few empaths there were in the outer colonies, mainly because only a handful were necessary depending on the size of a community. But Mira was starting to think there might be a different reason, and wasn't sure of the best way to ask Happy about the capabilities of a mature Alpha.

At her side, Mira felt Katra's defenses soften, and she detected love and devotion for the strange child. Mira felt a touch of embarrassment for the abrupt way in which she'd ended her story, but the Gamma didn't seem to care. This "softer side" of Katra seemed somehow appropriate, and Mira had to admit that it would be nice to love someone that much someday.

Just as long as it's not JonB. Trouble, trouble, trouble, that one.

Katra finally noticed the lull in conversation, and Mira sensed she was about to ask a question. One she'd been working on for a while now, from the feel of it.

"This family you speak of. Father. Brothers. Uncles. Where are they now? Were they aboard the ship, the *Valiant*?"

Mira wasn't sure which question Katra was more interested in, so she settled on the easy one.

"No. It's been a few years since I've seen them in person, but they are here, on Earth. There are Harlans spread out all over the place, actually, but most of our kin are still here in North America."

Mira thought she detected a bit of sadness behind Katra's eyes before she spoke.

"These words are old ones for us. Families. Kin. In the first days of a colony, they are necessary until the crèches are set up."

"And how does that make you feel, Katra?" Mira couldn't believe she'd used the clichéd words of a psychoanalyst, but they seemed appropriate to the moment.

Katra was silent for almost a minute, still looking at Serene lying back against Grumpy's legs. Happy repeated his request for communication, but Mira felt there was something here she should know, something important. She opened her mind to him, noting how much easier it was to do than sharing herself with the Betas.

≈*I need to speak with Katra now. Can you find me some water, and something to cook with? I promise, we'll talk soon.*≈

Mira did her best to imagine her mother's tall-sided stew pot, and also sent along the image of carrots and potatoes in the vain hope that there might be something similar in the pile of supplies. Happy sent a feeling of understanding, just as Katra's mind let go of the sadness she'd been holding back.

"Jarl is dead, Earther. There will be no family for me. And unless the Betas can find the sleepers, there are no more Gammas within a thousand light years."

The pain in Katra's voice was unbearable, and Mira wanted to pull her into a hug and never let her go. But two things stopped her: One, she was still wearing her strength enhancing hardsuit, and Katra might well interpret the gesture as an attack.

And secondly, Katra wasn't finished speaking, and her sadness had turned into cold anger.

"So to answer your question, I do not have time for feelings. I must protect those of us who still live. I do not think you are my enemy, but I do not wish to go to Harrison Institute. And if your presence here threatens Serene, I will kill you."

As the Gamma stalked away, Mira tried to remember waking up with only one person in her head. Of just being Lieutenant Harlan, who was a lot more like the woman walking away than either of them would ever admit.

She's right, I don't belong here. But I don't belong anywhere else either, and until we figure out who I really am, this will have to do.

Mira heard a crashing sound, and her gun was out before she had time to process the sight of Happy holding up a large metal container in one hand, and several brown things in the other. Her smile was something she didn't have to hold back, and she sent it to the Omega along with her thanks.

Wondering what she was going to use for firewood, Mira set the birds down and began taking off her hardsuit. If they were going to be here for a while, someone else could stand guard.

Besides, it's like Daddy said. "Grab hold, little girl. Bird's not going to skin itself."

JON-B34726-S

JON-B34726-S STUDIED THE GROUND IN FRONT OF him, memorizing the path ARS-D59007-C was taking. The Delta would have already selected a route free of obstacles, and it made sense for him to benefit from that experience.

JTN-B34256-O's last words to him were troubling, as they represented a definite change in their working relationship.

"Be careful."

Even in the middle of the battle aboard the Valiant, she had maintained a certain distance. But now that S-A-198—Serene—was awake, JTN-B34256-O's attitude toward him had definitely shifted, and he wasn't at all sure it was for the better.

Jantine. I must remember to call her Jantine. It's what she wants. What they all want.

"It is just ahead, Scientist JonB."

JON-B34726-S set his mouth in a tight smile. The other mods had been corrupting his name for nineteen days, two hours and five minutes now, and it still annoyed him. At least the Delta had the excuse that he was following orders, but the others were laughing at him every time they did it. Even Mira Harlan's mistaken pronunciation of "Janbi" was preferable, but since she'd shifted to the form the others were using, someone must have told her.

There are some things that should not change. We must be better than the humans, not the same. Isn't that the point of this mission?

"Are you experiencing discomfort, Scientist JonB?"

"No, it's all right, Artemus. I'm fine. What can you tell me about Carlton's discovery?"

Instead of answering, the Delta pointed through a gap in the trees with a lower hand. Just down a small hill was a landscape completely different from the grasslands. The ground itself was a different color: gray spotted with black instead of rich brown soil.

There were several buildings, one of which glowed from within. The area between was covered with long bars of metal, either laid down in lines on the ground or stacked in rusting piles. There were large, rectangular boxes made of metal as well, some lying flat on their sides and others with wheels attached to their bases and fitted onto the metal bars.

Even in its dilapidated state, this was the first sign of civilization he'd seen on Earth, and JON-B34726-S wondered how he'd missed it while they were descending from orbit.

I must have been distracted by all the screaming. But if this is an indication of their society, how did they ever launch a ship like the Valiant?

Mira Harlan said she was from this planet, and she seemed familiar with this continent in particular. She would know what this was, but Carlton had been here for some time already and would likely have a more scientific explanation for what he was seeing.

Increased mobility? From this collection of rusted garbage?

"I see," said JON-B34726-S. "Is it safe to go down there?"

"There is a substantial amount of hydrocarbon residue on the ground and most surfaces, but limited exposure will not be hazardous. I recommend you maintain suit integrity at all times."

"Understood, thank you."

A crumbling dirt path led down the hillside, one which JON-B34726-S suspected was not made by human feet. Artemus descended rapidly, kicking up dust and rocks as he went. The Delta then did a quick spin, checking for enemies at the base before lifting a top hand and motioning for JON-B34726-S to follow.

Let's see . . . it's about fifteen meters down, angle of almost fifty degrees. If I fall, I likely won't live long, but he would have carried me down if he thought I couldn't make it.

Trusting the Delta's earlier pledge of protection, he checked his helmet seals and placed a suited foot on the path. Easing himself onto the slope, JON-B34726-S saw several ledges along the path, and their irregular shapes suggested buried roots or rock outcroppings.

Well, if it will hold his weight . . .

JON-B34726-S took a moment to calculate the smallest number of jumps he could make to reach the bottom. Given his size and conditioning, he didn't trust himself to slide the entire length. But at the same time he was a Beta, and he took pride in his capabilities. Satisfied he'd chosen the optimum path, JON-B34726-S skipped down the hill in four uneven jumps, timing the last so that he landed right behind the Delta.

As soon as he reached the bottom, Artemus started moving toward the lit structure. JON-B34726-S followed, searching the area for possible signs of more advanced technology.

The metal bars he'd spotted from the top of the hill were of various compositions, and up close he could see that most of those on the ground were in better condition. There was a faint odor in the air he could not place—it reminded him of pre-exile artifacts he'd handled as a child.

Tires, if memory serves.

Looking around, he saw nothing like the textured black fragments he remembered from the Earth museum on Colony C, but he did notice more of the metal bars, including some arranged in a line leading into the illuminated building. JON-B34726-S kneeled down near the entrance, taking advantage of the extra light to conduct a closer examination.

The bars were spaced approximately 1.4 meters apart, and fastened to slabs of hard stone. JON-B34726-S ran his hand along both the metal and stone, and he found the latter to be a composite material of some kind.

I remember this from the museum as well. They made buildings out of something like this in the early years of Colony C. Crushed stone mixed with a binding agent. This site could be centuries old!

JON-B34726-S stood and looked back over the metal-filled plain. From ground level, he couldn't see the other end, but the line of bars and stones ran roughly a kilometer from where he stood, intersecting with multiple smaller angled sections of bars. When nothing else triggered a recollection, he turned and followed Artemus into the structure.

The interior was reminiscent of the launch bay of the *Valiant*, with dozens of scaffolds, machines, and work spaces. The tire smell was much stronger here, and several of the machines were surrounded by piles of black dust.

There was dust everywhere, in fact. Unlike the Earther vessel, most of these machines appeared abandoned and incomplete. Carlton had cleaned an area next to the largest of the machines.

The Beta was examining large wheels on the side of the machine when he noticed JON-B34726-S and Artemus enter. He had unpacked most of the collected Earther gear, including several of the power generators, and installed work lights on either side of the big machine.

"JonB, come look at this!"

Whatever the machine was, it was certainly impressive. It was tall, multicolored, and had handles and steps leading into an enclosed section at the far end.

JON-B34726-S walked the length of the building, marveling at both its new and old aspects. There were no comparable structures in the colonies; so much refined metal would have been re-purposed long before it could reach this state. Massive tools meant for human-sized workers were everywhere, and behind glass panels mounted on the wall he could see where Carlton had used his hands to reveal fading images. Not all the panels were intact, and like the large object many were coated with brightly colored pigments.

"What is it, Carlton?"

"It's an engine of some kind. They maintained it here, but look at this."

Carlton came forward and showed him a handheld. The image displayed was a scan of one of the glass panels, depicting a machine very like this one attached to a long line of containers, also on wheels.

"It's part of a transport system."

"Yes! And according to this," Carlton exchanged the image for another, displaying a series of lines drawn across the continent, "there's an interconnected network of these things all over this region. I think if we can get this one operational, perhaps some of the others as well, we can use them to get to Chicago and the institute."

JON-B34726-S nodded, appraising the condition of the machine. He walked around it, noting that though it was covered in dust, from the outside the engine appeared intact. He pulled himself up a ladder into the enclosed area and used a hand lamp to examine the control surfaces. After memorizing the positions of the machine's controls, JON-B34726-S joined Carlton in examining its underside. The engine's wheels each had a flange that rested snugly against the inner surface of the metal bars, with a large gear assembly joining each wheel to its duplicate on the other side.

Most of the bare surfaces on the machine were covered with an oily residue and exhibited none of the oxidation he'd seen on the metal outside. Reaching up and drawing a finger down a dust-caked panel, the resultant smear indicated the same coating had been applied to the entire machine, most likely as a preservative.

In fact, everything inside the structure appeared to be in very good shape, as opposed to the crumbling and rust-laden containers outside.

JON-B34726-S considered the implications of everything he'd seen so far, and thought the condition of the machine was encouraging. But Carlton was a support technician, and though his knowledge of contemporary equipment was extensive, he was no theorist.

"Carlton, what makes you so sure this machine can be restored? It may have been inactive for some time, perhaps centuries."

Carlton smiled and moved over to the pile of salvaged Earther equipment, then leaned down and picked something thick and rectangular up from the floor. "Is that . . . ?" JON-B34726-S couldn't complete the question. Such things hadn't existed in the colonies for centuries.

"Yes! It's a book! And it's not the only one I found."

Carlton nodded over his shoulder to a metal cabinet. His smile was bigger than ever, and JON-B34726-S couldn't help but share it. Carlton deposited the book on a workbench. Leaning in, JON-B34726-S saw an image of the same machine that rested behind them on the cover.

With the proper reverence due such an ancient treasure, JON-B34726-S opened the book. The pages were thin leaves of plastic bound together by heavy plastic rings, and the script was a bit hard to read at first. But after tracing the lines of text on a few pages with his finger, he came to a diagram showing the wheel and gear assembly he'd just been looking at.

The letters above the diagram were much larger, and as he scrutinized each one the meaning of the text below it became clear.

Ex 1450: Asynchronous traction motor and distributed power couplings.

Adjust the resting generator's main power output until all connected cars register a base charge of 1200v. Maintain output for a minimum of one hour to calibrate drive stems, then increase voltage until initial motion begins.

JON-B34726-S closed the book, resting his hand on the monochrome image of the machine on the cover. He looked at the open cabinet, noting crumpled sections of the door panels approximately the same size as a Delta's hands. He began tapping his fingers on the book, and looked over at the power generators they'd seized from the dead repair crews aboard the *Valiant*.

Yes, it should work. Assuming the bar path is still intact, of course, and we can find something big enough to hold us all.

"Scan it. Scan all of them, just in case. Make sure we've got a complete set of operation and maintenance instructions."

JON-B34726-S smiled. It wasn't ideal, but finding the engine was a promising development that gave the mods something they hadn't had before.

Hope. It looks like Mira Harlan may have had the right idea after all.

Thinking of the Earth woman made him remember his other objective for the evening. And a few long term personal goals, but as far as he knew Carlton couldn't help him with those.

"Carlton?"

"Yes, JonB?"

"Mira wants us to make sure and select containers in which the Omegas can rest comfortably. I'm not sure she knew something like this was here, but so far I have found her counsel to be remarkably insightful. Wouldn't you agree . . . ?"

MIRA

Mira hummed to herself, keeping the image of her mother wearing her favorite apron in the kitchen at the front of her mind. Whatever alien root vegetable Happy had given her was surprisingly fragrant, and as she peeled the last one she could almost hear her mother's pleasant drawl.

You have to be happy when you cook, Mirabelle. What you're doing keeps people alive, and people can't live on sadness. Put a little heart into everything you do, and there ain't nothing or no one can give you troubles unless you ask for it.

Annamarie Weston-Harlan was forty-three years old when she died, the mother of four sons and one precocious teenage daughter. The loss of her eldest son Brian put lines on her face that betrayed just how sick she was, but Mira remembered her mother best like this. Happy, alive, and full of down-home joy.

She worked the knife across the whatever it was by the light of a bed of coals, scraping off the skin with quick, sure motions. Seconds later it was cubed and into the pot, joining the others alongside some crushed lemongrass, salt, and a can of evaporated milk drawn from the shuttle's stores. The smell of the improvised sauce was heaven, and she turned her attention to the birds.

The Gamma memories were devoid of tasks like this, and she enjoyed the feeling of being her own woman again. To do something with her hands, with no other lives offering suggestions as to how to do it better, made her feel—for lack of a better word—human. Happy sat nearby, watching her cook in an eerie echo of Mira's own kitchen education. The Omega was basking in the happy glow she projected, drinking in the rich emotions that thoughts of her mother always summoned up. It was another area untouched by the Gamma memories, and Mira was determined to keep it that way.

Taking up one of the birds, Mira was keenly aware of Serene's attention, as well as Katra lurking in the trees. The Alpha child was sitting up on her own now, staring at her from across the clearing. She was wearing Marcus Callaway's uniform blouse as a belted dress, and in addition to foodstuffs, Mira was glad she'd had the foresight to take as many of the absent pilot's clothes as she could fit into a duty bag.

The sleeves were far too long for Serene's small arms, so Mira had done a quick bit of combat tailoring and cut them off at the elbow while Happy was collecting cooking supplies. Other than her first words to Jantine, Serene had yet to speak aloud, but Mira could feel her mind working behind those large, expressive eyes.

Mira had to admit to curiosity about what the Alpha was thinking, but the one time she'd attempted contact she slammed up against a mental barrier much stronger than the one Jantine maintained. The resulting headache was almost as bad as her first minutes as an empath, and Mira resolved to wait until Serene was ready to talk.

Plus, it's hard not to notice Grumpy crouching behind her, broadcasting a silent challenge to the universe: "Mine!"

Mira ignored the pair as best she could, focusing instead on the meal she was preparing. If Artemus had come back with turkeys, she'd have plucked and filleted the birds for grilling by now and called everyone for dinner. The process wasn't onerous, but even given how tired she was and the lack of both time and spices, she was thankful for the chance to improvise with these smaller birds.

Conscious of her audience, Mira stood up, positioned the first of the birds on the ground and got to work. With pheasants there was less usable meat, so there was no need to spend a lot of time worrying it off the carcass. She spread the wings and placed her feet on either side of the breast, grabbed the feet together, and gave an exploratory tug. She felt the wing under her left foot shift slightly, so she placed a little more weight on that side, bent her knees, and pulled.

The bird separated cleanly, with the backbone and entrails coming free with the half still in her hands. She set it aside, savoring the surprise in her spectators' minds at how fast it had transformed from a recognizable animal shape into a collection of parts. Katra's attention was completely focused on Mira's actions, and Happy was equally rapt as she cut away the wings to expose the bird's breast meat.

Thirty seconds later Mira had it washed and sliced into finger-sized pieces, and then she dropped them into the sauce. She repeated the cleaning process on the other two birds, this time setting the breasts aside for grilling. She almost asked Katra to come over and pull the last bird apart; her desire to do so was at the front of her mind and easy to read. Despite herself, the Gamma was impressed with Mira's skill, and Mira chalked the positive thoughts up as a point in her favor.

Looks like I can do something right after all.

The otherwise capable infiltrator was completely out of her element here in the most boring part of North America. Katra's hyper-vigilance was getting a hefty workout from crickets, night owls, and other small animals sharing the tree line with them, each encounter adding another sound or motion to her list of "things that won't kill us, yet."

It was odd to think of a trained assassin as a "city girl," but the label fit Katra better than anyone Mira had ever met. Jantine tried to hide it when she thought about the Gamma, but every time the two mods met, Jantine was thinking of ways to get Katra to both relax and think outside the box.

For her own part, Mira was glad Katra was the way she was. Like herself, Katra had been a training officer, and the secret to earning her respect was to demonstrate competence. Plus, despite her overt hostility Katra was always curious about the world around her, and that constant need for information gave Mira something to work with.

An owl took flight, and Mira sensed Katra's pleasure when she recognized and accepted the sound of its wings as a non-threat.

At least you didn't shoot at it this time. Before we leave here, the squirrel and field mouse populations will have even better stories to tell than Jantine's ant.

Happy noted it as well, but for the most part both Omegas ignored the sounds of the night. Mira knew their hearing range was far wider than even what her suit's pickups could detect; with four ears and a much larger brain, it pretty much had to be. But in general, the Omegas seemed immune to the trivia of normal existence, focusing instead on their projects and philosophies.

Builder is a good name for you two. Everything you do adds to the world, and you like making long-term plans.

As if sensing her interest, Happy's thoughts shifted into a pattern Mira recognized as "I want to talk to you." She placed the breasts onto a wire frame suspended over the coals by the gauntlets of her hardsuit. She wasn't sure what the frame's intended use was, but the Omega brought it to her with a sense of satisfaction as she was setting up her improvised kitchen, and Katra hadn't objected.

Sitting back on her heels, Mira opened her mind to the Omega while the food cooked. She let her mother's smile fade back into memory, and then she let the "others" rise to the surface. The hurricane inside her head was getting easier to tame, but Mira had doubts she'd ever come to accept the Gamma memories as her own.

≈*I am here with you. I am listening.*≈

Happy's thoughts were chaotic at first, until the Gamma memories took over and she was able to assign meaning to the concepts he was sharing. She felt ethereal fingers roaming around her thoughts, and an image of the Omega standing in a white room inside a glass case came to mind.

With the aid of those same memories, Mira partitioned herself, leaving enough awareness in her own body to keep an eye on the meal she was preparing. Across the camp, starlight and shadows framed Serene's odd face, who was still looking in her direction.

In the Omega's mind, his self-image was reduced in size until he was just over two meters tall. Mira found herself standing just on the other side of the glass, looking into his eyes. A wave of sadness poured into her, and she felt several other presences nearby.

Several meters away, Grumpy and Serene were sitting cross-legged on the floor. The other Omega was also reduced in size to a near-match for Serene's small form. Mira's mental eyes widened when the pair began playing patty-cake, and while neither spoke she recognized the memory as one of herself and Debbi McAllister playing in a sandbox.

With her own mind now supplying the scenery, the white room faded into green trees and a summer's day. Happy remained in the case, looking out at the other mods with his hands pressed up against the glass, still radiating sadness. Mira imagined the case expanding out to enclose her.

Inside, the sadness was much more intense, and she shared Happy's feeling of isolation.

≈*You're wrong, though. It doesn't have to be this way.*≈

Mira put her own hands on the glass, and a third child approached the pair as they played. At first it had Debbi's face, then the image shifted into a young Mira, and finally a small Happy. The combined child sat down and the sandbox melted away, replaced by a sidewalk covered in chalk drawings. When small Happy started bouncing a red rubber ball, Grumpy and Serene turned and smiled at him, the latter pulling a handful of jacks from a shirt pocket and scattering them on the ground.

≈*Go to them. I'm sure they won't mind the company.*≈

Happy shook his head, pressing even harder on the glass. Grumpy and Serene continued playing with the jacks, passing the ball between them and ignoring the other child. The young Happy stood up and started to blur around the edges. It faded from view, and then a group of adult Omegas walked into the scene.

The newcomers came up to the seated pair one by one, and Serene looked up into each of their faces and smiled. The Omegas started sitting down in circles around them, and no matter how many orange faces approached, Serene greeted each one with warmth and affection. All except for the last one, a stoop-shouldered, elderly version of Happy to whom Serene gave no greeting at all.

≈*Now that's not fair. Everything is new to her; you just have to give it time. Here, let me show you.*≈

Mira imagined a handle on the glass, and opened the case to lead Happy out and into the main hall of the Academy. Bright-faced cadets filed all around them, and Mira remembered and shared the pain and isolation she'd felt her first weeks there.

Dream Mira was thin and gangly and everything she'd tried so hard not to be over the last decade. The young girl raised her hand to wave before being carried away in the press of bodies, and Mira painted a few of the faces orange for effect before letting the scene focus on her father, standing proud and tall in his uniform as he waved goodbye to his only daughter.

Brian's death in a training accident had hurt him too, but instead of wasting away like Momma, he'd buried himself in duty until one day it was all he had. Four years later, his remaining children were grown and living their own lives, his wife was dead, and he took his own life. Mira and Happy stood by his casket as fighters thundered overhead, accepting a folded flag with numb fingers and saluting then-Captain Maranova with tears in their eyes.

≈*But it didn't have to be that way. He could have asked for help, told people how much he was hurting. I did, and so did the boys. We got through it together, and so will you.*≈

Mira's brothers raised their glasses and cheered as Happy went to fetch another round of drinks. When he came back, she pulled him into a hug, letting the joy she felt being part of a family soak into him and force out all the unhappy thoughts. Her brothers joined the embrace, which then turned into a laughing wrestling match that came to rest next to the campfire.

Mira turned the improvised basket over and gave the pot a quick stir. Katra had moved on, but she could feel Artemus and Jantine coming closer from opposite sides of the camp.

≈*You have a family too, a good one. I'm the one looking for a place at the table.*≈

The Omega sent her another image of the cemetery, but this time it was Mira handing the flag to Happy, as they stood next to five graves of assorted sizes.

Mira countered by envisioning a sunrise, distracting Happy until Carlton came to lead him away. She tugged on his memories of plans for the Earth colony, highlighting all the places where he and Grumpy had indicated other hands doing the work.

Mira realized she'd taken the analogy too far when Happy's memory of sealing the sleepers into their container came to the fore, and with it an even greater sense of loss. She was unceremoniously dumped out of his mind, and the sudden disconnect left her unprepared when Serene's consciousness brushed up against hers.

If joining with Happy was like navigating a choppy sea at night, Serene's mind was being caught in a hurricane on a small raft. Instead of a feathery touch, Mira felt sharp claws digging into her brain, searching for answers and casting aside anything that didn't relate to life in the Outer Colonies.

≈*Slow down—you're hurting me!*≈

If the Alpha heard her mental cry, she gave no sign of it. The onslaught continued, starting with Doria's memories of the mission briefings and then focusing on Colony B and the mods who lived there. Feeling herself slip away, Mira imagined a tall pillar of stone and chained a mental image of herself to its base. The pain lessened, but the rummaging continued unabated.

Though she was terrified, Mira sensed something familiar about the way her mind was being peeled back. It was almost the reverse of the process Happy had used to give her the Gamma memories, and true architect of her situation was revealed.

She's got help, and Grumpy likes me even less than Katra does.

Not knowing what else to do, Mira imagined an ear-split-ting emergency claxon, and sent out a mental mayday with all the strength she had left. She felt Jantine, Katra, and Artemus respond to her call for help, but it was Happy who got to her first.

Mira felt a broad hand slide under her shoulder blades, and the hurricane was gone. But Serene's mental talons were still ripping away the parts of her life attached to the Gamma memories, and Happy had even less of an idea of how to stop her than Mira did.

But there was one thing the Alpha couldn't get at, because she'd never had a mother of her own. The warm smell of the stewpot rose in her mind, and eight year old Mira climbed up on her stool and reached for the metal handle to raise the lid and check out what they'd made. Momma's warning came too late, and Mira jerked her hand away and fell backwards to the floor.

Howling at the pain of the burn, Mira opened her eyes to the night sky just as Jantine entered the clearing. The waffle pattern of the wire frame was seared into her palm, and the smell of her own flesh combined with the roasting pheasant filled the air. The meat was resting directly on the coals now, and blackening around the edges.

Happy was a warm presence at her back, and across the clearing Serene was sprawled unconscious against Grumpy in similar fashion. The Omega's cold hatred came off him in waves, but for the moment he was more concerned with Serene than any thoughts of revenge.

The pain of her burn was pure agony, but it was nothing compared to losing so many parts of herself at once. There were holes in her life now, empty spaces where her childhood used to be. Any memories not directly related to her family or the Academy were just gone, and the words were out of her mouth before she knew what she was saying.

"She took them. The Gamma memories. They went into my mind and just took them!"

Thanks to her new and improved biology, the burn on her hand was already healing, and a Mira felt a slight rush as her body flooded with endorphins. But while it helped to dull her physical pain, it only magnified the feeling of being in two places at once.

Part of me is over there now, locked up in that little girl's head. Is what's left enough to make a whole me?

Jantine's face had turned to stone, and the light of the coals made her expression even more dramatic. But it was nothing compared to the storm brewing in her mind, and Mira sent her what she thought was a wave of comfort and acceptance before the Beta acted on any of her murderous thoughts.

"It's all right, Jantine. It's all right. They weren't mine anyway. Don't do anything rash until I figure out how bad it is."

"This is not done. Ever. She must be held accountable."

The logical consequences of what she was thinking hit Jantine like a landslide, and the Beta shut herself down so completely that Happy's other hand had to reach out to catch her before she fell into the fire. The Omega drew both women into a tight embrace, but as he did one of Jantine's feet bumped the pot, knocking it over. A wave of scented liquid spilled onto the burning pheasant breasts and extinguished the coals.

Years of therapy after Brian's death had taught Mira a couple coping mechanisms for impossible situations. One was to shut down all emotion until she was in a safe environment, and another was to turn pain into laughter.

Mira started laughing, drawing a puzzled stare from Artemus as he crashed through the trees. The sight of the Delta's expression and a weapon in each of his four hands only made her laugh harder, and sensing Katra rushing toward the camp in a similar state of alarm only added to the sheer absurdity of the scene.

Dinner's served, everyone. Come and get it!

The laughter helped Mira push back feelings of outrage from the mods around her—an emotion she was ill-equipped to deal with without the Gamma memories. Only Happy knew the true extent of what Serene had done, and he did his best to shield her from their feelings.

Jantine recovered quickly, and pushed her way out of Happy's arms. That she was furious with Serene and Grumpy didn't make Mira feel any better. If anything, Mira could sense Jantine's emotions even stronger than before.

Despite Happy's help and her endorphin rush, Mira's head was pounding. She knew she had only one chance to stop Jantine from starting a fight she couldn't possibly win, even though the Alpha deserved everything Jantine was thinking about doing to her.

"Jantine, Stop. We can get through this. Just don't push her right now, Grumpy's right on the edge and I don't know what he'll do next."

"Grumpy? What is grumpy? Another Earther thing I am required to learn?"

Mira stood on shaky legs, grateful that Happy was there to keep her from falling. "It's what I've been calling the . . . Serene's Omega. Just to keep them straight in my head. Happy is this fella here."

Jantine stared at her, and Mira could feel a mental message forming in the Beta's mind. Unsure of what that might feel like, Mira waved her off.

"Just let me handle this. And keep the others back. It's . . . hard to be around you all right now."

Mira pushed gently on Happy's arm, then took a tentative step toward Serene. Jantine's anger was a bonfire behind her, one that kindled in Katra and Artemus as well as she explained what had happened. But Mira only had eyes for the strange alien child and her hulking guardian.

Out of habit, Mira reached for the Gamma memories for some clue as to how Grumpy would react to a confrontation. The cold emptiness in her mind was almost as frightening as the Omega scowling at her. She should be angry. Furious. But although she knew the words and understood the general concepts, her emotions were savaged as badly as her memories. All she had left was happiness, pain, disappointment, and fear—and a headache that would not go away.

After a few more steps, she stared into the eyes of the seated Omega, and spoke from her heart.

"That can never happen again. I would have given them to you gladly, if you'd asked. But you hurt me, very badly, and now I don't know how, or even if, I can help you."

Mira could feel Grumpy's anger, and tried to replicate it in herself. But it faded too fast, and she was about to continue her harangue when she realized why; Serene was awake, and every bit as upset as Mira. But the Alpha was more direct in her disapproval, and whatever she was doing to him went from subtle to sadistic in a flash. Even without a full connection, Mira could tell he was in agony, and she knew she had to do something to stop Serene from seriously damaging his mind.

"What are you doing? Stop that, it's not helping anyone! We have to learn to work together, or it's going to go very badly for us."

Grumpy's pain vanished, though he was visibly shaken. Mira's knowledge of the Omegas was spotty at best, but she could still remember all of her interactions with Happy, and Jantine's reaction to the mental assault gave her an idea of how serious the matter was for them.

Serene stood and looked up into Mira's face. Mira's first instinct was to kneel down and talk to her as she would a child, but was unwilling to cede any advantage to the Alpha she didn't have to.

"I am sorry. O-6913 told me no harm would come to you, and I believed him. You have been kind to me, and I see in your memories the kind of person you are. You should not have been made to suffer."

The thought of an alien child being able to remember things about her life she could not was agonizing, but Mira forced herself to remain calm.

Serene stepped forward and took one of Mira's hands in both of her own. The Alpha's skin was much warmer than Mira's, and in Serene's touch Mira felt an echo of the electric charge JonB's similar gesture had imparted.

Despite herself, Mira smiled. Serene did too, and Mira could sense genuine regret in her mind. Remembering how it had felt to have other people's lives forced upon her, Mira knew

Serene had to be more than a little out of sorts right now and hadn't meant to hurt Grumpy.

Then she felt it, and all Mira's sympathetic thoughts vanished in a heartbeat.

The Alpha's level of control was amazing, much more subtle than Mira's blundering efforts. But even though Serene was using the Gamma memories to guide her efforts, Mira's empathic ability was far stronger. Making note of her technique, Mira started building a wall to keep her out, while at the same time planning a verbal response. Putting aside any ethical concerns about what she'd done, Serene was still a child, and not quite in control of her actions.

Of course, now she's got a dozen lifetimes worth of memories in her head telling her what to do. Thirteen, counting mine. How much longer can she really be considered a child?

"It probably would have been fine, with a Gamma. Not right, not by a long shot. But I'm different, and what the two of you did is considered a serious crime on my planet."

Or it would be, if we had any telepaths of our own.

"As you say. I will think on how to make proper restitution. You and I are linked now, and harm done to you is harm to myself. As you say, we must do better in the future at expressing our desires."

These last words came with an empathic rebuke for Grumpy, and Mira couldn't let Serene have the final emotional word. She let go of Serene's hands, reaching out instead to the Omega's face.

Mira was impressed by how steady her fingers were. Grumpy's skin was much cooler than Serene's, and Mira focused as strong a burst of forgiveness as she could muster.

She was still upset, and she let him know it. But while they touched, Mira could sense all the confusion she'd suspected Grumpy was feeling regarding their very long, very stressful day. He honestly hadn't intended to hurt her, but at the same time he really didn't care that he had.

That, more than anything, made up Mira's mind to go forward with JonB's plan. She and the Betas would have to stay alert at all times to prevent any further mishaps, especially now that Serene had demonstrated an ability to enter their minds uninvited. The Alpha was too unpredictable to leave unsupervised, and Grumpy was far from an effective counselor.

Mira walked back to the extinguished cookfire, leaving Serene and Grumpy to work out their differences. Happy was sitting and staring at the remains of dinner with a sigh in his heart. Mira sent him a smile, and the memory of her mother's gumbo. She got one in return along with an image of herself, Carlton and Happy walking along a path eating ice cream.

It took her a moment to realize she was looking at one of her own memories, recovered and translated through the Omega's eyes. Skipping stones along the river with Debbi and Tommy Watson after a revival meeting, making plans for their future. Tommy didn't want Mira to go to the Academy, and that was the day Debbi realized he was never going to marry her, because he was in love with someone else.

Love. I can remember love!

The bittersweet memory of three friendships ending forever wasn't exactly appropriate to the situation, but Mira thought it was the most wonderful gift she'd ever received. She didn't trust her emotions, so she crushed herself to the Omega's chest for almost a minute, savoring that long-ago day when her world was simple and small.

Though it must have looked ridiculous to the other mods, she moved her hands up to his cheeks, then leaned in and kissed Happy on his lipless mouth. She sent him her thanks, along with an image of her mother's last family dinner, with him in the guest of honor's chair.

Stepping back, Mira thought about the scenes Happy had shared with her just before the attack. With only memories of her memories of what Colonial life was like, it was hard to be sure, but Mira had a strong sense that there was no real concept of privacy in their worlds. With Gammas and Alphas able to root out any secrets, it was no wonder that Jantine maintained such strong mental discipline. Even now, in conversation with Artemus and Katra, the Beta was pointedly avoiding looking in her direction, allowing her to deal with the Omegas in her own way.

A thought struck her, and she was about to share it with Happy when an image came into Artemus's mind. JonB and Carlton were in a building, working on a—

Oh, you clever, clever boys. That's perfect!

"Jantine?"

Jantine's conversation with Katra and Artemus died abruptly, and all three turned to look at Mira.

"You should ask Artemus what the other Betas are doing. I think you'll be pleasantly surprised."

A few seconds later a flash of annoyance mixed with laughter slipped past Jantine's shields. Apparently, Artemus hadn't yet told her what the boys were up to, and Jantine wasn't sure how to react to the news. But building a train solved a lot of their travel-related problems, and Mira was happy for any good news she could get.

We're all feeling our way blind today, and today just keeps getting longer.

Jantine and Artemus set off into the trees without Katra, with the former intent on seeing the engine for herself. Mira could tell Katra was upset that the meal she'd been preparing was ruined, and Mira resolved to cook her another one as soon as possible. Turning to the Omega, she smiled and opened her mind to him. Without Doria's direct experience as a guide, it was a little rough at first, but Happy supplied the missing mental steps for her. This time, instead of entering his mind, she held out her unburned hand, palm up.

"I'm Mira, Mira Harlan. What's your name?"

Happy simply stared back at her, mind in neutral. It wasn't until she repeated the words a second time that he understood what she was asking, and his reaction was not at all what she expected.

The Omega jumped to his feet, hands out and head shaking. Mira brushed aside his refusals, sending the concept of an introduction and a handshake again. Then she sat on the ground, and patted the space next to her.

"This is Kansas, my friend. You're not in the Colonies anymore. And among friends, we speak as equals. So what's your name, or do you want me to pick one for you?"

Happy didn't respond at first, but after a minute or so of silence he eased himself down next to her, and looked up at the sky. Mira followed his gaze, and started pointing at the stars.

"That one? It's called Vega. But if you look at the stars around it like so," Mira made a drawing motion with her finger, adding lines of light in her imagination, "you get the constellation Lyra. The ancients thought it looked like a lyre, a kind of harp the god Hermes gave to his brother Apollo."

Mira could tell that Katra was listening to her every word as well. Without openly acknowledging the Gamma's presence, Mira raised her voice so Katra could hear her better.

"And that one over there is Rukbat. It's the knee of Sagittarius. Most of what we can see of the constellation from here are actually clusters of more distant stars, but in the ancient world they had no way of knowing that. There are a lot of stories about how it was named, but my favorite involves . . ."

Happy did something to his eyes, and Mira's voice trailed off in wonder. She'd been happy just to look up at the stars and talk, seeing them now with her improved transgenic vision as if for the first time. But instead of the slightly better defined blobs she was enjoying moments before, through the Omega's eyes now saw Sagittarius A in all its multi-spectrum glory. The burning black hole at the center of the Milky Way galaxy was sending out radio waves across the millennia, to find two lost souls on an insignificant planet at the edge of everything.

Oh, wow.

It was several minutes before Happy returned the universe to an understandable state, during which Mira simply watched in silence. There were no words to describe what she'd seen, colors unknown to even the most sensitive instruments and rolling waves of energy dancing across the sky.

Happy sat beside her, truly content since the first time she'd tasted his thoughts. He saw the universe like this all the time, but only through her eyes was it magical.

There was something else new in his emotions. Curiosity. Not how she understood it, but something much deeper. He wanted to see everything through her eyes now, and experience the world he knew in a different way.

But more importantly, he wanted to hear the story she'd started. Mira leaned into his arm, closed her eyes, and remembered her father's voice.

"It was a long time ago, before humans sailed the stars or even understood what they were. In a land where gods walked the earth, a group of ordinary men set out on a quest aboard a ship called the Argo . . ."

JANTINE

"How much longer will the repairs to the tracks take this time, JonB?"

Jantine looked past the civvie towards the east, a seemingly unending expanse of green hills and blue sky. Sol was already high overhead when they arrived here, and it had moved several degrees while the train sat idle.

JonB's face was smudged with some black substance different from the dirt on his jumpsuit and forehead. He appeared not to notice, and Jantine had to admit she liked the way it looked.

"It depends on whether the tracks are intact under the soil. They should be: the foundation blocks are sunk deep into the ground. But we won't know for sure until we dig it out. Katra's forward survey found intact tracks coming out of the ground two kilometers ahead."

Katra had already relayed the results of her scouting mission to Jantine through the scattercomm, but the longer the team stayed in one place, the more exposed she felt. Not being in control was becoming the norm rather than the exception, and she didn't like it.

Working through the night, JonB, Carlton, and Mira had constructed a working transport, attached several empty containers to it, and got them moving towards Chicago. Mira had mentioned that she used to repair things aboard the *Valiant*, but when the three of them got to work, the woman's skill was truly impressive.

Another thing she's better at than the rest of us. Perhaps JonB's plan was not too far off the mark after all.

"Are we going to have to lay down new tracks again?"

Although the engine was running fine off the converted power cells, several kilometers from their starting point they'd had to stop when the rail line ran out of metal tracks, and again a few hours later when fallen trees blocked their path.

"Most likely not. But then again, we weren't expecting to do it the last time either. The system is in very good shape overall, but after four hundred years, I'm just happy we've made it this far."

It was a minor miracle, made possible only by the combined technical talents of JonB, Carlton, and Mira Harlan.

Although Mira had reached her own peace with Serene, what the Alpha had done, or allowed to happen, to the Earther still made Jantine uneasy. The woman seemed to be adapting well enough to yet another change in her status, and having a project to work on certainly helped.

In fact, Jantine had had to order her and the Betas to take a rest period before they started traveling, but after they'd slept a few hours, it had not taken much more work to make the engine fully operational. The adapted power cells required frequent recharging, but Sol had energy to spare.

"In answer to your first question, I think maybe two hours, if we, as Mira Harlan says, 'put our backs to it.' Possibly sooner, but I can't say for sure."

There was hesitation in JonB's voice, and Jantine could tell he wanted to ask her something else. Ever since Mira had joined their thoughts, she was more understanding of his peculiar mannerisms. At times, Jantine almost sensed what he was going to say on her own, but the rational part of her brain knew that couldn't be true.

We are what we are, nothing more. To expect more from life is to court disappointment and failure.

She let the silence linger, hoping he'd bring up his question without any prompting from her. His eyes focused on something over her shoulder, and she saw his jaw clench slightly as he made up his mind.

"Of course, this would go faster with an additional pair of hands. Jason and Artemus can only do so much."

Jason. One more change initiated by Mira Harlan's Earther ways.

Jantine wasn't really upset that the Omega had taken a name, or even that Mira had started telling her people stories of ancient Earth. She was as surprised as the rest of the team to hear the Omega announce his choice through Mira before they boarded the train, and after Jantine received a private explanation from the Earther it was at least understandable.

It did solve one of her problems with the Omegas: how to tell them apart. From where she stood, Jantine could see that Jason had painted a red stripe on his head and was playfully throwing dirt at Artemus as they worked to clear the tracks. Carlton was with them as well, smiling and laughing as he dodged head-sized clumps of packed soil. It was the happiest she'd seen the Beta since the death of his crèche-sib Harren, and if this was the ultimate result of Mira Harlan's meddling, it was a livable outcome.

Then again, the pendulum swings both ways.

Jantine turned and followed JonB's gaze to the other Omega, walking along the tracks at the rear of the train of transport vehicles with Serene. 0-6913 was leaning down to offer support to Serene, who was holding one of his fingers in her hand as she walked.

Serene was adapting well to Earth, gaining color and strength by the hour. She was still the most beautiful being Jantine had ever encountered, and her heart ached for harboring its thoughts of betrayal. But despite the additional lifetimes of experience she'd stolen from Mira, she was dangerously naïve, and not fit to lead their expedition.

As Jantine and JonB watched, Serene let go of 0-6913's hand and went tumbling down a low hill out of sight. She was alarmed at first, but then she heard the Alpha's sweet laughter, and saw her race back up the rise only to throw herself down it again. The Omega was too far away for Jantine to make out its expression, but she knew it had to be amazement.

"Will our children do that too?"

JonB's question was an interesting one. No matter how distasteful the thought of natural births was to both of them, until he could build gestation chambers and crèches, the colony's children would most likely run unfocused and wild just like Serene.

We'll have to find the sleepers first, and resolve our issues with the Earthers. But maybe . . .

Leaving the question unanswered, Jantine started walking toward the Alpha and her hulking escort. JonB did not follow her, for which she was thankful.

What I have to say is not for him to hear.

Serene repeated her tumbling fall one more time as Jantine approached, then she began examining something on the ground. Wondering if she'd found an ant, Jantine waited patiently to be acknowledged. 0-6913's glare wasn't the recognition she desired, and Serene would have to deal with her as senior military commander, if not as an equal.

"Jantine! Look what I found!"

Serene's smile was radiant, made more so by several spots of dirt on her face. Her borrowed clothing was similarly soiled, but as with JonB, on the whole Jantine found the imperfections pleasing.

What she wasn't expecting was for the child to run at her full speed, and wrap her arms around her waist in a tight embrace. 0-6913 started forward but then stopped as a glow of pure happiness enveloped all three mods.

Serene disengaged and held up a brightly colored plant for her inspection.

"Isn't it wonderful? It's called a *daisy*! Mira used to pull the petals off and sing a song about her friend Tommy. He loves me, he loves me not. He lo-oves me. Here, you can have this one, there are lots of them!"

Not knowing what else to do, Jantine took the plant from Serene and held it while the child began to twirl in place.

"I love it here. It's much better than the train car. How long can we stay?"

Jantine searched 0-6913's face for some clue as to how she should react. Serene's transformation was something she had no referent for, and her behavior was entirely at odds with the Alphas she'd interacted with during training. It was almost as if she'd suffered some sort of injury, and when the girl spiraled in for another hug, Jantine used her free hand to search Serene's head for a contusion. She could feel none on the surface, and the short stubble now forming on Serene's head scratched her fingers.

"JonB thinks it will be several hours. He would like to shorten that time if possible."

Jantine kept her eyes on 0-6913, willing him to follow her unspoken order. Serene's head moved under her hand, first to Jantine's face, then turning to look at the Omega. The emotions she was projecting changed subtly, and Jantine thought she detected a sense of urgency combined with determination.

The Omega's face seemed to tighten up, and it wasn't until Serene actually voiced whatever silent mental instructions she'd given the Omega aloud that Jantine understood.

Grumpy. Mira calls him Grumpy . . .

"Go. I will be safe with Jantine. She is my friend, too. The others need you more than I do."

From anger to frustration to cruelty, Jantine had seen a lot of expressions cross 0-6913's face in the last day. But she never expected to see total shock. Even when Doria was dying, the Omegas were stoic. It wasn't until they'd detected Serene's distress beacon that they started to change, and Jantine wondered yet again what might have happened if the mission had proceeded as planned.

Her next thought was both surprising and unexpected.

We would all of us have become ants. Smaller than we should be, and hidden from the world.

The Omega lowered his gaze and walked toward the other mods. Jantine followed him with her eyes and she saw JonB still standing where she'd left him. The Beta was gesturing to 0-6913 as he approached, but the Omega ignored him and plodded on to the front of the train.

"Will you walk with me, Jantine?" Serene's voice against her stomach was muffled, but Jantine could still hear her well enough. "We can pick more daisies, and talk."

Jantine looked down into the Alpha's big eyes, and she knew that despite her reservations she could deny the child nothing.

"Of course."

Serene gripped Jantine's left hand firmly and pulled the Beta after her as she started walking. Jantine kept her eyes moving, scanning the vegetation for the snakes Mira had warned about and wondering what she was supposed to do with the daisy in her hand.

"I am sorry, you know," Serene said.

The words took Jantine by surprise, mostly because the cloud of happiness that had surrounded Serene vanished abruptly as she spoke.

Keeping her face and thoughts neutral, Jantine erected her mental defenses. "About what?"

Since Malik's death, she'd come to miss his casual way of pulling the truth out of people. It was a skill she had trouble mastering, mainly because, unlike Malik, she trusted everyone to say what they meant the first time.

"About Mira. It was wrong, what happened. I wanted you to know that I understand that."

All Jantine could do was nod. This was certainly no child of the Colonies, and she had no protocols for speaking to an apologetic Alpha.

"But despite the pain it caused her, I'm not sad it happened. I understand so much more now, especially how hard this must be for you."

Serene let go of her hand and flopped down on her back in the tall grass. Jantine crouched beside her, still uncertain about what was going on.

"In what way?"

"There's so much I still don't know about the current Colonies, and my memories of life before I went to sleep are not all that clear. But the ones I have now are very complimentary of your abilities. O-6068 in particular has a great deal of trust in you."

"Jason. O-6068 is called Jason now."

When it hit her that she'd just reflexively and openly challenged an Alpha, Jantine felt dizzy. She sat down, fighting to keep control of her emotions and prepared for the worst. While none of the other mods could see them, Serene was well within her rights to discipline her.

"That's a nice name. Do you know what it means?"

Swallowing, Jantine forced herself to answer. Something was not right here, but the only way to determine what it was would be to continue this bizarre conversation.

"As I understand it, Jason was an explorer on ancient Earth. He led a team of warriors on a variety of missions, eventually returning home to seize control of a kingdom from his half-brother."

Serene nodded and closed her eyes.

"It means 'healer' in the language of that people," Serene said. "It's an old name, but the origin of yours is even older. It's from the same part of the world, but religious in nature. It means, 'God is gracious.'"

Where is this coming from? We do not teach these things in the crèche. . .

The answer came to Jantine in a rush, and she was glad she was sitting down when it did. Serene's eyes were open now, and she was looking at Jantine with an expression she'd come to know very well in the last day.

But Mira Harlan learned different things as a child than we did. And probably spent her time picking flowers and playing in sunlight.

"I see that you understand. I don't mean to pry, but I had to know. Yes, Mira's memories are very strong in me right now, and they tell me more than anything that I need your help. O-6913 keeps waiting for me to tell him what to do, and he is so convinced something bad will happen to me that he's pushing the rest of you away. Especially you, but we both know why."

Jantine nodded. There never was much hope that they could seize control of the group from Serene, but something in the way she was speaking made the Beta think that perhaps it wasn't necessary.

"I'm not upset, or mad, as Mira would say. Especially not after what I've done, however well-intentioned it was. But it's precisely that mistake that lets me understand why you were plotting against me."

"We didn't want . . . you shouldn't blame . . . it was for . . . for . . ."

Jantine couldn't make the words come out. She felt her control slipping, and years of conditioning told her what was going to happen next: Serene would kill her.

But Serene didn't, though how Jantine felt now, staying alive was worse. Instead, the Alpha crawled over and laid her head in Jantine's lap and started to cry.

Jantine put her hand on the Alpha's head again, fighting to keep her own emotions in check. Between her sobs, Serene was still speaking.

"I don't know what to do. All of them are in my head, telling me you need to be punished. But Mira's there too, and Doria, and they keep asking me why."

Jantine felt even worse.

"Why, Jantine. Why does it have to be this way?"

Jantine didn't know the answer, but she knew what Mira would do. She pulled Serene up from her lap into a hug, and kissed the crying child on the top of her head.

Serene hugged her back with surprising strength, and for a moment Jantine thought she'd decided to kill her after all. But she kept on crying instead, until her sobs were replaced by long, wet sniffles.

Jantine felt the urge to start rocking, and the motion made her feel better. Serene's happy aura returned, and Jantine could make out two words whispered into the folds of her jumpsuit.

"Thank you."

"It's all right. It's all right. If you have to do it, I understand."

Serene's head shifted under her cheek, and Jantine pulled her own head back to look into her eyes. The child's face was puffy and red, but Mira Harlan's smile was firmly in place on her tiny lips.

"Don't be silly. If I kill you, who's going to help me find the sleepers? Also, I think JonB would be sad if you died, and I'm done hurting people. It's not very nice, and I want to be a nice person from now on."

Jantine couldn't help smiling herself. But before she could thank the Alpha for her life, Serene wiggled her fingers against Jantine's side, causing her to give out a very un-leader-like shriek. She tried to roll away, but Serene's grip was secure, and her laughter was infectious.

Oh, child of Earth and sky. What have you done to me, and what strange creatures are we becoming . . .

MIRA

"MAY I SPEAK?"

Katra's voice was strained, as if the words pained her. Mira wasn't sure what she wanted, as the Gamma's arrival in the train's control cab was wholly unexpected.

After last night, Jantine's instructions were that all the mods should practice and maintain mental shields. Katra's military mind had taken to it much faster than the others. After only a brief demonstration of what Jantine wanted, Katra vanished completely from Mira's perception.

It had been fun to track her movement during the train's frequent stops by how frightened JonB and Carlton were by her frequent mock ambushes, but over time Mira had found it necessary to close off her perceptions and do her best to minimize her interactions with the others. Something was wrong, and without the Gamma memories to guide her, the pain in her head was getting worse as the day went on. Now Katra wanted to talk, and so far her conversations had been full of strong emotions.

But it's not like I can say no, is it? If she genuinely wants help with something, I have to at least listen. And until we get the tracks dug out, we're not going anywhere.

"Of course. Please, sit down."

The train's cab was easily twice the size of their escape shuttle's pilot deck, and it was set up more like living quarters than a working control center. Mira was sitting at a small table on the side of the room. She waved Katra into an identical one.

The Gamma wrinkled her nose as she sat, and Mira was reminded of how long she'd been hiding in here.

Katra looked around the otherwise shining compartment, searching for hidden enemies. Once her visual survey was complete, she focused her attention on the table itself, and Captain Martin's chessboard.

Mira had voiced reservations about taking the carved wooden set with her from the shuttle, but the captain had insisted that she have it. "You need something non-regulation about you, Harlan. It gives people a reason to stop and talk."

Looks like you're right again, sir.

Mira savored the memory of Aloysius Martin's voice in her head. It hurt to remember how he was at the end, half-blind and near death. But once Jason had helped her rewire his brain a bit, he was as alert as ever.

"You do not want me here. I will leave."

Katra stood up, but Mira sent her a mental apology and raised her hand. The effort sent fresh spikes of pain into her brain, and she closed her left eyelid tight against the flashing stars.

"No, it's all right. A painful memory, that's all. Please, stay. What can I help you with?"

Katra looked uncertain, but she took her chair anyway. She was still nervous about something, and Mira chanced another probe into her mind. The Gamma's shields were still in place, and the resulting pain in her own head let her know what a fantastic idea it was to stop trying for a while.

Now if I can just get the others to stop thinking so darned loud, that'll work out nicely.

"Do you play this game?"

It seemed an odd question to ask someone sitting in front of a chess set, but from her limited experience of the woman Mira knew Katra took nothing at face value.

"A little. This belonged to Captain Martin, he thought I should have it when he . . ."

Mira couldn't finish her sentence. She knew her commanding officer was dead, but all the training in the world couldn't make her like it.

"I am sorry to have killed him. Jantine says he was an honorable man."

Katra's words left her a different kind of speechless. Even though the mods' arrival in the solar system had killed dozens, if not hundreds of Mira's crewmates, it was an accidental encounter. And the Gamma had no way of knowing that Mira was directly responsible for the deaths of at least three of her friends, and bore a large share of the blame for the others.

And she's apologizing to me?

"Captain Martin used to say that apologizing was a sign of weakness. We used to say belowdecks that he was full of crap, but what I think he meant instead was 'if you didn't do anything wrong, don't worry about it.' Also full of crap, but it's a bit more honest."

Katra reached out her hand and collected two pawns from the board. One white, and one black.

Oh. Okay, here we go. She's found a way to kick my butt and leave no marks.

Katra closed her fists around the pieces and held them out for Mira to choose. The Gamma cocked her head as if listening to something, but Mira's brain already hurt too much to go looking around where she wasn't wanted. Tapping Katra's left hand with her finger revealed the white pawn, and the two women cleared the board and reset the pieces.

Mira didn't care too much about the outcome, so she selected a standard opening from memory and moved a pawn forward.

Katra did not hesitate in her response, and moved one of her own. She stared at the piece for a while after letting it go, but she gave no indication she was unhappy with the move.

No fear. Good. At least, I think it is.

"It is a warrior's game. We learn to play in the crèche, but we do not have boards of this type."

Mira advanced her queen's knight, and Katra moved her pawn a second time, giving the piece a longer look.

"It was a gift from his grandfather, I think. The captain didn't talk about family in the wardroom much, but I do know he was a very old man, with very strong views on honoring one's past."

Mira moved her knight further into the center of the board, and Katra advanced a second black pawn to meet it.

"Your commander was a very wise man. It is important to honor traditions."

Mira advanced a second pawn of her own, which was quickly captured by Katra's first.

Oops.

Katra was studying the board intently now, keeping the captured piece in her right hand instead of setting it down on the table.

"When he did mention him, it was fondly. Some of his last words were about his 'opa,' a favorite saying of some kind."

Mira's queen took the field, capturing the black pawn that had invaded her side of the board. Mira set it aside, and noticed Katra's eyes following the motion of her hand before returning to the game.

"Do you remember the words?"

It was Katra's turn to move a knight, and Mira deployed one of her bishops.

"I think so. It was in Dutch, an old Earth language the captain tried to get us all to learn. I don't know what it means, but it was something like '*dursten zuln de latsen jin.*'"

Katra smiled, and Mira had the distinct impression it was the expression a wolf used when cornering a rabbit.

Katra's bishop came out of nowhere, placing Mira in check.

"I think you mean '*de eersten zullen de laatsten zijn.*' It was a favorite saying of Hendrik Trajectinus, Count of Solms, Commander of the *Garde te Voet*. A general in your 17th century."

Mira stared at Katra, uncertain she'd heard the mod correctly. Her accent was flawless, a near copy of the captain's, but to her knowledge Katra had never been to Earth before, especially not to the European Reclamation. Her king was in jeopardy, and an alien warrior woman knew more about Earth's military history than she did after top marks at the Academy. But all Mira could think about was the feeling in Captain Martin's mind as he'd said the same words, knowing he was about to die and trying to share something important with her.

"What does it mean?"

"It is a religious proverb, but also a military one. 'The last will be first, and the first last.' It speaks of service to the greater good, and of pride."

Matthew, 20:16. The parable of the workers in the vineyard. But why would the Captain choose that as his last message, in a language he knew I didn't speak?

"It is your move, Lieutenant Commander."

Mira numbly slid her bishop up to protect her king. Katra pressed the attack, taking the piece offered and sacrificing her bishop to Mira's knight on the contested space. Katra followed the move by castling, and then in a completely unexpected gesture tipped her king on its side before standing up.

"You are weary, we will speak another time."

Mira was out of her chair as well, but was tired enough that she hadn't noticed her left leg had fallen asleep. She stumbled forward into Katra's arms, who took her weight easily and steadied her on her feet.

Instead of thanking the mod, Mira simply held on, wanting to know more about what had just happened, and why.

Katra eased Mira back into her chair, and sat down herself. Mira made a show of massaging her leg for a few seconds while she tried to get a read on what Katra was thinking. Her shields were firmly in place, but her body language indicated she was definitely uncomfortable.

"You . . . Katra, what did you want? When you came in here, you wanted to ask me something, didn't you?"

"Last night, I was wrong to threaten you. I found your transformation unsettling, and I did not know what the future would bring. After Jarl, and Crassus . . . Jantine, Artemus and I are the only soldiers left. They have accepted you as one of us, but I needed to know more.

"When you were . . . assaulted by the Omega, it was your right to claim both their lives. Jantine could never act against an Alpha; Betas are born to serve. When she told us what happened, I stood aside and ordered Artemus to take no action as well. We would have killed you afterward, of course. But it was your right to try."

"I . . . Katra, I never . . ."

"But then you did something we still do not understand. You repaid horror with kindness, something no warrior of the Colonies ever does. And in a moment when you had every right to be vengeful, you turned enemies into allies."

She doesn't know. Can't know, if I want them to see me as a whole person. But I have to try and explain . . .

"You have to understand, Katra. It's . . . it's not our way to seek vengeance. It's not *my* way. I have fought battles before, and I've taken lives. Some of the people I've killed were men and women I trained myself, who at the time believed *they* were the ones doing the right thing. I even took a few shots at you on the flight deck if I'm not mistaken.

"But that's war, not vengeance. I don't hate you for what happened on the *Valiant*, and I don't hate Serene or Grumpy for what they did. It was an accident, nothing more. That proverb, do you know what it really means? It says that it doesn't matter what happens to you in life, but how you respond to the challenges it gives you *does*. It's about fairness, and compassion—"

The Gamma was the one now who looked like the wolf was coming for her, and was halfway to the door in a heartbeat. Mira wondered what Colonial taboo she'd blundered into this time.

"No, Katra, don't go . . ."

Katra froze in place, then fell easily into a ready stance. It took Mira a few seconds to realize that, however indirectly, she'd given Katra an order, and the Gamma had followed it.

She addressed me by my rank earlier, not as "Earther . . ."

"Katra, I'm not sure what to do here. I don't remember what I'm supposed to say, not anymore. Tell me what you want, and I'll try to help you. But you have to talk to me, please."

The Gamma only smiled and moved to the ladder leading down the side of the train. But she paused before leaving, face as composed and flawless as ever.

"I came to tell you, Mira Harlan of Earth, that I acknowledge you and your accomplishments. I look forward to fighting at your side, as does Artemus. We are at your service, until the end."

Did that just happen? How the heck am I supposed to respond to that?

"The black pawn. It is six grams heavier than any other piece of the same size. If you are studying the chessboard for a message from your captain, you might want to start there."

Mira looked to the two black pieces on her side of the board and out of the corner of her eye saw Katra slide down the ladder. She was almost afraid to pick up the pawn she'd captured, slightly smaller than the bishop next to it. Part of her was in awe at how skillfully Katra had manipulated the board to put it there, and the rest of her wanted to know what might be hidden inside.

She reached out and took the piece in her hand. Her eyes widened as she confirmed Katra's statement. It was hard to see, but there was a seam inside the carved groove on the pawn's base. It resisted her attempts to twist it open, and neither did it budge when she pulled on it.

Well, I'll be. Aloysius Martin, you old fox.

Whatever the captain had hidden inside, it meant enough to him that he'd altered or replaced one of his "opa's" custom pieces to keep it safe. And Mira knew one secret in particular he was willing to die to keep . . .

JANTINE

"I STILL DON'T UNDERSTAND WHY WE CAN'T USE THE bridge." Carlton's question was a fair one. If JonB hadn't warned them about the potential structural instability of the bridge, they wouldn't have stopped the train and may have been in Chicago by now.

The bridge in question was a narrow span across a wide river, one which the maps and Mira Harlan named Mississippi. There were ruins on both sides of the bridge, but across the river the crumbling piles of stone and rusting metal were slightly taller. The setting sun looked much different here than it had on the grasslands, and the shadows formed as it peeked through the remains of the city were edged with fire.

Unlike other bridges they'd crossed during the long day's journey, it was barely wider than the train, with just enough clearance for the engine to pass without incident. There were small islands of some sort paralleling the bridge, but Jantine didn't understand their function.

JonB and Mira had performed a quick survey of the structure, and returned some unsettling news. Not only was it decrepit, but it had been mined. JonB's quick thinking had saved them all, again, and Katra's perimeter survey had uncovered another problem.

The track system split into two paths several dozen meters in front of the ancient bridge, with the second spur traveling into the ruined city. While scouting for another path across the river, Katra found deep scratches cut into the metal of the tracks, and more leading into an underground tunnel.

"Carlton," Mira said, "do you remember what I told you about the Reclamation zones?" Mira's casual tone reminded Jantine again of the easy way Malik had handled this aspect of the mission for her, but she suspected the explanation was more for the wide-eyed Serene.

"What is this Reclamation?" Serene had been sleeping when Mira gave her pre-dawn history lesson, and was understandably curious. Carlton blanched at the memory, and thinking about what might be down in the tunnel made Jantine's blood hot.

Mira turned and looked at the Alpha. For some reason, the Earther hadn't been broadcasting her emotions for many hours, so Jantine had only visual cues to go by in determining her mood. Mira's expression fell somewhere between sadness and embarrassment, but she seemed willing to tell the story a second time.

"It's a . . . dark period of our history. Earth history, about half a century before you went into suspended animation. So far, there's been enough track for us to avoid the cities, even if it meant going a good distance out of our way. Most of the smaller towns and communities between Old Kansas and here were already abandoned when the war started, but the cities . . . I don't want to be sitting here all night if I can help it."

"What kind of war?"

Jantine saw Katra and Mira set their jaws at Serene's question, and she imagined each was thinking the same thing she was.

There is only one kind of war. The weapons may change, but the results are always the same.

Mira crouched in front of Serene, face carefully neutral. Despite her statements of forgiveness, the Earther still had to feel some resentment over what was taken from her. But having heard this story herself, Jantine knew that Mira was trying to put the best possible spin on an even greater atrocity.

"A bad one. One that should never have happened, but in hindsight most scholars believe it was inevitable. Earth was a much different place, then. We'd used up many of our resources, and we were surviving by taking what we could from the rest of the system. Mars and Titan had only been settled for a hundred years, and we'd already cut off contact with the Outer Colonies."

Serene nodded. There was no need to rehash the Exile, she knew more about it than anyone else present.

"But here on Earth, there were problems too big to ignore. The World Congress had dissolved, and nation-states were arming themselves with whatever they could buy, invent, or steal. Those who already had access to space could take whatever they wanted, and only a few were willing to protect those who could not."

"So what happened?"

Mira smiled and lowered herself the rest of the way to the ground. Face half in shadow, she looked up at Jantine before continuing her explanation. Jantine thought a simple question at her.

≈*Who will you need to scout the tunnel?*≈

≈*Katra and Jason. Carlton too, if you can spare him. I need someone with no military training.*≈

≈*Not JonB?*≈

≈*No, he's more valuable up here with you. If something happens to us . . .*≈

≈*Understood.*≈

"You have to understand," Mira said, "everyone was so afraid. If you didn't have a weapon, you were an easy victim for those who did. And once you had one, before too long someone else would get a bigger one. But there wasn't just an arms race, there was a knowledge race as well.

"Corporations were nearly as powerful as governments, and they sold their inventions to whoever had the most money. Most often one another, but there were enough spies on all sides to render any advantages moot in short order."

"I still don't understand," Serene said. "Why? And what's wrong with the bridge?"

Mira's smile was a brittle thing that threatened to crumble if she pressed her lips any tighter together. Jantine looked up and caught Katra's eye: she tapped her left cheek with her forefinger. The Gamma acknowledged the signal for communication and moved back from the rest of the group.

Jantine placed a hand on Serene's back, and leaned down to kiss her on the forehead. The Alpha stared at her with a confused look, until Jantine gestured toward Mira by wagging the fingers of her left hand. Mira patted the ground next to her to complete the message, and Serene moved forward to sit next to the Earther.

Jantine stepped away from the assembled mods, and she frowned when JonB tried to come with her. He narrowed his eyes and cocked one eyebrow, but when she mouthed "later" at him, he resumed his position against the train and simply watched her walk away.

Trust me, JonB. You don't want to know about this just yet.

"The weapons kept getting more and more destructive. Air superiority was still a deciding factor, so the great powers for the most part ignored what was going on down here on the surface. If one of them took a side in a corporate conflict, there's no telling what might have happened. But they didn't stop building their own weapons, and in the end all it took was one mistake to set the world on fire."

Jantine walked around the back of the train to the other side. The three cars attached to the engine were tall enough to block her line of sight to the mods gathered around Mira, and after she descended a small hill toward the ruins, she could no longer make out the Earther's words. There was nothing she could do about the Omega's acute hearing, but she was satisfied there was enough distance between her and the others to use the scattercomm undetected.

She ran a finger down her jawline and heard two clicks in her ear.

"How big would you say it was?"

"Possibly as large as the train engine," Katra whispered, "but more likely half that size. The marks were fresh, not weathered.

No more than one day. If it's one of Mira's war machines, it's still active."

Jantine didn't have to ask if Katra was sure—she wouldn't have brought it up in her scouting report if the Gamma didn't consider it a threat.

"Mira will lead. Yourself, Carlton, and Jason. Priority is to secure a clear path under the river, but I want no casualties. Withdraw if you feel the situation warrants it. Use the Earther comms, they have longer range. Mira will advise."

"Understood. Commander?"

"Speak freely."

"Why do we risk the Omega in this fashion?"

A good question, with no good answer. But there was an easy one, and though she didn't like it, it was good enough.

"Mira thinks it best to use a combination of artificial and natural senses. If someone else is using this transport system, we need to know about it. And as Mira says, these machines are very dangerous. If there is a potential danger in this region, we must eliminate it as soon as possible."

"Understood. Perimeter sweep ready in fifteen."

One click sounded in her ear, and Jantine disabled the scattercomm.

Jantine was in no particular hurry to rejoin the others, so she drew her hand pulser and sat down to watch her second sunset on Planet Earth. Even filtered through ruined buildings, Sol was a marvelous sight, and it provided more than enough illumination to field strip her weapon.

She checked each piece for defects in the red-orange light, and snapped in a fresh energizer as she reassembled the pistol. There was more than enough charge remaining in the old one, but Mira's earlier warnings were still echoing in her head, and she saw no reason to face them at anything less than maximum combat readiness.

"Terrible weapons, capable of reprogramming themselves to overcome any threats. But in the end, there was no greater threat to the war machines than the people who'd invented them, especially those who'd expressed transgenic traits . . ."

MIRA

Something crunched under Mira's boot, and the sound echoed off the tunnel's walls. So far, neither her own enhanced vision, the visor's optics, nor borrowing some of Jason's senses had detected anything more than a wide tunnel with ancient, rusting machinery.

Whatever made the scratches Katra found, it's definitely down here somewhere.

The darkness was almost a living thing, a deep, chilling black that clung to every surface like tar. But they weren't using active sensors, which meant that despite his Beta reflexes, Carlton tripped over every raised object in his path.

Mira put out a hand to catch him, but whatever it was he'd kicked went skittering to the left and clanked off the side of the tunnel.

Mira froze at the sound, and she felt both Katra's and Jason's awareness spike. Seeing the tunnel though the Omega's eyes wasn't much different than the dim outlines drawn by her visor, but she at least had a more complete idea of where the major obstacles and walls were. Plus, since the Omega wasn't wearing a protective suit, she had access to his sense of smell. So far, he'd only registered dust, rust, and ancient hydrocarbons, but there was always a chance she might notice something Jason would otherwise ignore.

In contrast to the other mods' cool resolve, Carlton's emotions were like a hammer pounding inside of her head. Carlton knew only the basics of how to use his encounter suit and, as such, had only Mira's hand to tell him where he was. He was completely out of his element, but Mira needed someone without military training for this patrol, who would be afraid of everything they encountered. She was hoping the Beta's subconscious mind would give them some advance warning of an attack, and she hated herself because of it.

I'll get you back alive, Carlton. I promise. But I need you to be scared a little while longer, just in case.

Mira sent a thought to Katra, wincing at the pain that followed.

≈*Katra. We're going to wait here a minute until Carlton can proceed.*≈

≈*Understood. Fifty meters, then back.*≈

Once she lowered her defenses and allowed Mira in, the Gamma was surprisingly easy to talk to. Mira suspected that all Gammas had some kind of low-level psychic sensitivity, but given how little Mira know about them, there was no way to know for sure. Whatever it was made her a good soldier, and as with Carlton's inexperience, it was something Mira needed right now.

She slid her hand up from the Beta's chest to his shoulder and then pressed him down to the floor. He resisted at first, fear spiking so high that she gasped with the pain. But then he relaxed just enough so she could think on her own again, and he crouched down next to her in a tight ball of nerves.

Sensing her discomfort, Jason sent her another recovered image from her past. This time it was one of herself and Tommy climbing down into the caves, about a month before she left Roswell forever. It was another inappropriate memory, but Mira was thankful for it all the same. Each one he was able to isolate and return to her was a gift that restored a bit of her emotional spectrum. A moment like this was something wonderful, and she was happy to have it back.

On the tour they'd taken during the day, the colors of the cave had been fascinating. Greens and reds and oranges formed in a place where the sun never shone, and only when humans had come blundering in with electric lighting and cameras did simple sedimentary deposits transform into works of art. At night, Tommy's ebony skin had been part of the darkness, and the occasional flashes of his teeth and eyes in the chemsticks they carried had made what they were doing more exciting.

Mira and Tommy had hidden a blanket and a bottle of his father's whiskey in a secluded grotto during the day, and tonight was going to be "special." She knew what Tommy wanted, and she'd more or less made up her mind to give it to him just so he wouldn't follow her around forever with his sad eyes.

But when they startled the bats, all thoughts of youthful indiscretion flew out with them into the night. Mira held on to Tommy as tight as she could when the leathery wings snapped by her head, and afterward the two teenagers laughed until they cried. Then Tommy made his move, but when his lips brushed hers she pulled away. The moment was gone, and as far as she knew the bottle and blanket were still stashed there, waiting for her to change her mind.

Maybe if I had, it would have been easier later. Maybe he wouldn't have . . .

The sound of the bats echoed in her mind again, but instead of tiny claws scratching at her ears and the musty smell she thought would never wash out of her hair, it was accompanied by the cold hiss of escaping air that even a first year middie feared.

≈*Katra. Stop.*≈

Jason was warning her of something, but there wasn't enough information to pass along. Katra didn't respond with words, but Mira felt the Gamma's awareness expanding. She knew what might be down here just like Mira did, but Mira had seen one of the death machines before during her military education in Colorado, right on the edge of the Reclamation zone.

And that should make me even more frightened than Carlton. Chalk another advantage up for the Transgenic virus, I guess. That, and having my brains scooped out.

Most of Katra's training involved sneaking up to the enemy and eliminating it before it knew she was there. Sealed up in her black encounter suit, Katra was nearly invisible when she wanted to be, but they'd agreed ahead of time that the mod shouldn't use her active camouflage save in emergencies. A stray electron here or there might make the difference between life and death when facing an adaptive killing machine with advanced sensor capabilities.

Down here, in the blackest night imaginable, there was nothing for her to aim at. No enemy to evade or capture, and with the Mississippi River a hundred meters over their heads, blowing their unseen foes up wasn't really an option. But she was still in control of herself, and Mira borrowed as much of that feeling as she could.

Mira's own senses were stretched to the limit, but despite her plan Carlton's fear was making it hard to concentrate. Whatever made Jason think of the bats was also screaming a warning at Carlton's subconscious mind, and that more than anything made her want to abort the mission.

Come on, you metal freak. Show yourself.

Part of her wanted to be wrong. The consequences of being right were too horrific, especially on top of everything that had happened in the last two days. But all the signs were there, and if there was a pre-Reclamation killing machine in the tunnel ahead of them, Mira and Katra needed to buy JonB enough time to either defuse the charges on the bridge or find some way to succeed where she'd failed.

The whine of Katra's pulse rifle coming to life told her that the time of "if" was over.

"Now, Carlton. Do it!"

The Beta's fear was nearly overpowering him, but with Mira drawing it away he was able to hit the switch on the device he'd been cradling for half a kilometer and roll it into the middle of the tunnel.

In terms of illumination, an infra-red heater was about the least effective device one could use on a battlefield. But when deployed against a mechanical monster that hunted by body heat, it leveled the odds faster than high explosive rounds.

Speaking of which . . .

The bloom of heat scrambled her visor's sensors, but Jason could still see just fine. As fifteen meters of robotic death powered up and uncoiled from a hiding place on the tunnel's ceiling, Mira relayed its movements mentally to Katra while she got a better grip on Carlton's shoulder and pulled him back toward the entrance.

Katra's pulser was firing nonstop, and the invisible packets of phased energy were tearing away large chunks of exoskeleton. She'd already crippled one of its legs, but according to the power usage Jason could see it had at least five more.

Thankful again that both of them had missed shooting one another during the firefight on the *Valiant*, Mira dropped a second infrared heater and sent Carlton a strong desire to run to the surface. She felt his terror recede as he left, and turned her full attention to the monster twisting around as it attempted to destroy whatever was damaging it.

The robot's strategy was a sound one, given the technology it was programmed to fight. It was immune to most conventional weapons; Mira's slugthrower would be little more than an annoyance to the monster. But it wouldn't take long for its adaptive subroutines to come up with a defense against phased plasma pulses, and it was time for Mira to begin the next stage of the attack plan.

Now that Carlton was far enough away, Mira stretched out her mind and made a full connection with Katra and Jason. Their thoughts melded with her own, until they were essentially one person with three different bodies and a single goal.

As Katra fell back to the second beacon, Jason picked up one of the decaying machines littering the tunnel and launched it at the robot's head. Katra rolled behind a rusted lump of metal and sent a pair of pulses at the monster's rear legs. Mira was momentarily dazzled by the way the pulses sparked as they encountered small bits of matter in the air, but Jason accepted it as a normal phenomenon, much like the X-ray bursts from Sagittarius-A he'd shown her last night.

The robot had a target and a direction now, and it bounded forward quickly enough to make Mira's heart skip a beat.

Only the confidence she felt in Katra's mind gave her the will to stand her ground. The Gamma sent two more pulses into the robot's exposed inner workings. As they impacted with a shower of sparks, she relocated to a new firing position with a fluid grace that even Jason admired.

The Omega launched another improvised missile at the robot then sprinted to the side of the tunnel. His already low body heat was completely masked by the heaters, but even an Omega's thick skin had limits. A pair of cobalt lasers converged on the spot he'd just vacated, burning deep holes in the concrete and giving the creature a hot-spot to target.

But despite their impressive power, every cadet knew that the lasers weren't the real threat. The microwave emitter powering up in the robot's head was, and Mira charged toward the robot to spring the final part of their ambush.

Apart from a genetic super-assassin and a gentle tele-pathic architect who could see almost the entire EM spectrum, Mira had another weapon that hadn't existed during the Reclamation.

A fully charged hardsuit, capable of amplifying her strength by a factor of five.

Maneuvers like this were best performed in zero-g, but the SDF spared no expense in training their officers, and she'd learned her craft under the watchful eye of a grizzled and scarred sergeant. Most of the security forces assigned to the *Valiant* came to the ship fresh out of training, with a host of bad groundside habits and poor suit discipline. But those under Mira's command either learned to use their suits at their intended level of performance or found another posting in the fleet.

For the last five years, the *Valiant* had maintained the highest efficiency ratings of any ship in active service. Her damage control teams went through equipment almost as fast as they did recruits, but once Mira raised the Clarke Cup over her head for the first time, she knew she would never give it back.

And just because my ship is dead is no excuse to slack off now.

Mira's first stride was at normal power, but her second launched her three meters into the air and toward the tunnel's curved wall. When she hit, instead of surrendering to gravity's pull she bent her knees and flipped out over the still thrashing robot, firing all her attitude control jets and coming to rest on the ancient machine's back.

Its response was immediate, and predictable. It stopped thrashing its legs, tail, and manipulator arms in a futile attempt to find Katra's firing position, and it rotated every appendage into a configuration that would let it tear Mira apart. But Mira was already gone, having applied a thick paste of thermite gel to the back of the robot's head.

Rocketing backwards, Mira drew a borrowed pulser pistol and held the firing studs down, remembering to shut her eyes just in time. The plasma discharge ignited the gel in a white-hot explosion, burning completely through the robot's head in seconds.

The robot was by no means disabled, but its energy weapons were now useless, and a hefty portion of its adaptive software was now tasked with reconfiguring itself to meet the threat of an airborne opponent.

Which gave Katra all the time in the world to completely discharge a fresh energizer into its exposed interior.

The machine fizzled and died in a cloud of smoke and electrical discharges. Mira twisted in midair and landed in a perfect three-point stance between the infrared lamps. She gave herself an imaginary pat on the back—the three of them had just defeated one of the most advanced weapons ever invented in less than thirty seconds without casualties, and now they could forget all about the bridge and take their time guiding the train through the tunnel.

Not bad for an old lady. If you're watching, Captain, I did the side proud.

Mira dissolved the three-way link and staggered as the pain in her head tripled. She closed her eyes against it, activating her suit's emergency lights with practiced hands.

Katra's spike of alarm added exponentially to Mira's headache, and the sight of Jason turning and running full out for the tunnel entrance was like a punch in the gut. But the Gamma's flare of emotion was gone in an instant, replaced by the cool emptiness she'd maintained during the battle.

The Gamma rose up from behind her cover, inserted a fresh energizer, and started firing over Mira's shoulder. Her thoughts weren't hard to decipher as she did, and it was Mira's turn to be alarmed.

≈*I think we should be going now, Lieutenant Commander.*≈

Even though she had an idea of what was there, Mira had to see it for herself. A second later she wished she hadn't and was running fill tilt at Jason's retreating back, with Katra just a few meters behind.

Oh, shit.

JANTINE

JANTINE WAS STANDING OUTSIDE THE ENGINE WITH
Serene when the Earther comm unit sputtered to life. The
child was wearing another one of Mira's modified garments,
this time a heavy cloth jacket with the sleeves removed. It was
near enough to the coveralls the Mods used for the child to
look almost dressed, and the Earther had assured her that "M.
Callaway" would not want the clothing back.

For once, O-6913 was not with her. The Omega was twenty
meters away, staring down the tracks Mira and her team had
followed to the tunnel mouth as if willing them to appear. It
wasn't a defensible position, but having seen the Omega shrug
off multiple barrages of micro-slugs, she wasn't worried about
him. Besides, Artemus was standing at the edge of the bridge,
with one pair of weapons pointed across the river and another
in the direction the Omega was facing. If any threat came at
them from either set of tracks, the Delta would know about it.

JonB and Serene were Jantine's real priority, and as ruthless
as Mira's risk assessment had been, Jantine had to agree with
it. Even with all the losses they'd sustained so far, the mission
could still proceed if the Betas and the Alpha child made it to
a place of safety.

But even before she heard Mira's voice on the comm, Jantine
suspected that it was not going to be good news.

"JonB! Detach the trailing car and get the locomotive onto the bridge right now!"

"What was that?"

JonB stood in the door to the engine compartment, hand-held in one hand and one of Mira's chess-pieces in the other.

"Don't think," Jantine said. "Obey. I will move the train."

JonB slid down the ladder and ran toward the rear of the train, while Jantine picked Serene up with her free arm. She could have waited for O-6913 to finish his charge up the tracks and claim her, but she wanted to hold the girl, as if it might be her last chance to do so.

"Casualties?" Jantine handed Serene off as she spoke into the comm, then she vaulted into the engine's cab. Mira's response was close to panic, and the thought that Jantine had lost another friend distracted her from which of the controls she was supposed to activate to get the train rolling again.

"Not yet, but . . . dammit, Katra, keep up!"

Jantine wanted very badly to see what was happening, but the "backup plan," as Mira had explained it, was for her to get Serene across the bridge as fast as possible, and not look back.

Which control was it? Why can't I remember?

Jantine was afraid, and she didn't know why. It wasn't until she heard Carlton's voice yelling from outside the cab that she understood the feeling might not be her own.

"We have to go. We have to GO!"

"Jantine. Jantine! Is the train moving? We can't hold them back much longer."

Them?

Mira's voice over the comm was enough to at least get Jantine's mind working again. If she couldn't remember the control, Carlton or JonB would. Her first responsibility was to get Serene out of danger, and that she could do with just a word.

Jantine hurried back to the ladder and looked outside. O-6913 had Serene cradled to his chest, and she could see real fear in the child's wide eyes. She waved the comm unit at the bridge.

"Run."

The Omega was moving before she finished the word, and Carlton was not far behind him. There was enough starlight for them to make their way onto the bridge without difficulty, and as Jantine watched them pass Artemus and move onto the rusted metal structure she raised the comm to her mouth.

"It will be soon. Do you need support?"

Artemus started across the bridge, and by the way the Delta's heavy footsteps shook the tracks, Jantine revisited her doubts as to how successful JonB's efforts to disable the detonation charges had been.

As if on cue, she heard hissing air from the rear of the train, accompanied by a soft clanking sound.

"Mira. Do you need support?"

Jason appeared out of the night, waving his arms over his head. The Omega did not turn and follow the rest of the mods onto the bridge but instead moved to the rear of the engine and braced himself against it. There was a squealing sound as the train started moving forward, and Serene and her fear were far enough away now that Jantine realized he too was carrying out Mira's orders the only way he knew how.

Jantine thought she heard something from the rear of the train, but the sound did not repeat. She marveled at the sight of an Omega doing the work of a one-hundred ton machine before turning her attention back to the control panel to find JonB already standing there.

The civvie had somehow entered through the entrance on the other side of the engine without her noticing, another indicator of just how paralyzing Serene's uncontrolled and contagious fear had been. The Beta's right hand reached out and threw several switches, and as the electric motors hummed to life, she noticed his face was flushed, his left arm was cradled against his chest, and there was a trail of blood leading from the entrance to where he was standing at the control panel.

Although she easily adjusted to the motion of the train moving down the tracks, Jantine was nearly pitched out of the cab when the engine rocked violently to the left. She caught herself before she slid completely out of the open portal, but she lost her grip on the comm unit. It fell to the ground and bounced toward the tracks, and over the squeal of metal wheels on rails she heard a distinct crunching sound.

From her position on the floor, Jantine was facing the rear of the train and had an excellent view of not only Jason pulling himself up to the top of the engine but also of lines of purple light illuminating two human-sized figures in the distance.

Before she could stand again, the train's brakes engaged and Jantine nearly joined the comm unit under the engine's wheels. Mira's chess pieces bounced past her head, and Jantine wondered why JonB had been carrying one of them when he ran toward the back of the train.

No time for that now. We have to get moving.

Jantine rolled back onto her feet, grabbed one of the supply packs that had slid to the back of the cab, and threw it to JonB as he turned toward her. He looked like he was about to say something, but Jantine didn't wait to find out what it was. Instead, she shouldered several packs of her own and stepped off the engine and down onto the bridge.

There was another hissing sound, this time much closer. Jantine looked for the source, and saw Jason separating the remaining cars from the engine. Another pair of purple lights flashed in the distance, and out of the corner of her eye Jantine thought she saw one of the figures rise into the air on a small column of flame.

Then Jason grabbed the bottom of the car in front of him and lifted. The boxy container they'd been bouncing around in since dawn came up off the tracks, and veins stood out on his arms as he found a better grip on the heavy weight. Jason took two staggering steps forward and then tilted the car to the left until it fell on its side with a loud crash. The car behind it jerked forward and jumped off the tracks as well, and came to rest with its length half on, half off the tracks.

Not content with simply tipping the container over, Jason braced himself against the nearest wheel assembly and pushed. Sparks flew off the steel bars as the container rotated until it was nearly perpendicular to its previous orientation. The trailing car separated with a shrieking, tearing sound, and rolled down the small hill toward the ruined city.

Then the bridge shook again, as O-6913 thundered past to join Jason. The Omegas each took hold of a long metal bar on the underside of the container, and pulled the protesting container back until its bottom surface came up against the metal support beams of the bridge's superstructure. On its side, the container nearly blocked access to the bridge, leaving only two meters of space and a slight inclined gap between them.

JonB landed beside Jantine with a small cry of pain, and she turned to look at him with incredulous eyes. He was lying on his side, helmet off, and facing away from her. When he rolled over, his face was even paler than usual. But what drew Jantine's attention was the blood-covered pack he was clutching to his chest with his right arm.

Jantine dropped the two she was carrying and rushed to his side. She lifted the pack away, expecting to see a horrible wound on his chest. Instead she saw a drying smear on the outside of his encounter suit, but no sign that the smart fabric had sealed over a puncture.

"I'm okay. I can't feel it. We should . . . we should get moving."

Jantine put her left arm under JonB's shoulders and reached for his face with her right, turning it to the side and trying to spot any head wounds hidden in his dark hair. The starry sky gave off enough light for travel and most operations, but she couldn't tell if he was bleeding or not.

An explosion shook the bridge, and yellow white light poured over the overturned car and dispelled the shadows for just a moment. Jantine blinked twice, fixing JonB's image in her mind, though in that brief glance she saw no blood in his hair or on his neck. She was about to ask him what had happened when a broad orange hand scooped her up and carried her away.

"No, wait. Put me down!"

Whichever one of the Omegas had tucked her under his arm ignored her shouted commands, and Jantine had a bouncing view of the river through the bridge's supports as he ran. She heard JonB grunt behind her, and then saw Katra skip by holding several grenades. The Gamma didn't slow down as she ran up one of the bridge's angled support beams, and then the Omega was past her, each step shaking the bridge until Jantine thought it might collapse just from the vibrations.

There was a second explosion across the river as the Omega reached the other side, and Jantine was unceremoniously deposited next to the tracks facing away from the bridge. She spun around, drew her hand pulser, and tried to spot Katra or Mira coming across. Two columns of flame and smoke stretched up to the sky, but she couldn't see either woman.

Serene was crying just off to her left, but her fear seemed to be back under control for now. The Alpha was clinging to one of Artemus's legs, and as soon as she recognized Jantine she disengaged and threw her arms around the Beta's waist.

Jantine was moving back onto the tracks at the time, helmet off and trying to get a better view as to what was happening on the bridge. The unexpected impact was enough to unbalance her, and she sat down hard between the tracks with Serene still clinging to her midsection. The other Omega was charging hard, straight in her direction, and not knowing what else to do, Jantine curled up around Serene and closed her eyes.

When there was no bone crushing impact, Jantine raised her head and saw the back of JonB's encounter suit just centimeters away. Serene stopped crying long enough to ask a question.

"What happened to your hand?"

Jantine didn't understand the question. Both her hands were on Serene's back, the left pressed against the child's spine and the right holding her pulser. She raised both, twisting her wrists in the starlight and trying to find some defect in her encounter suit.

"I fell down under the train, and it started moving," JonB said. "It's okay, I can't feel it. These suits have pain blocking medications."

His voice was flat, and full of the same artificial calm that Doria's had had at the end. Jantine tried to sit up, but with Serene in her arms she didn't have enough leverage to do more than raise her back up slightly.

When Jon B twisted around to help her, the stump of his left arm hit her in the face, and he started screaming.

KATRA

≈*ARE THEY CLEAR?*≈

≈*Yes. JonB and Jantine are across now. She is fine, but he is . . .*≈

≈*Doesn't matter. Tell me when we're done.*≈

Katra nodded, not sure if the gesture would translate over the mental link with Mira. There was nothing either of them could do about the Beta's injury, and the machines now perched on top of the overturned container car would kill everyone if they were not stopped.

The pair of killer machines seemed impervious to the flames and smoke surrounding them. Whatever Mira had used to detonate the cars was still burning hot enough that Katra's visor optics couldn't make out many details. One thing she was certain of, though, was that the machines' heads were swiveling back and forth in an attempt to locate her, in motions eerily similar to those the Omegas had used aboard the *Valiant*. Beyond them, the remains of a third machine were indistinguishable from the wreckage of the first container.

The one that had our supplies.

Katra didn't think Mira made the wrong decision in destroying the container; it had bought enough time for the rest of the mods to cross the bridge and for herself to climb inside the engine compartment. And although it had only eliminated one of the machines, it was an effective enough demonstration to make the other two pause before continuing their assault.

From where Katra was lying on one of the bridge's middle support frame, she had a good view of the entire span, including the packs Jantine had discarded when tending to JonB. If they were the ones from the engine compartment, among other things they contained the only replacement energizers in a thousand light years.

Katra wasted only a moment formulating a retrieval plan; it was clear to her that any such attempt would betray Mira's position in the engine to the enemy. Her rifle was of no use without a charge, but she definitely wouldn't be firing it if Mira wasn't around to perform another of her miraculous reversals.

Katra was not a strategist; in a society that produced Betas to plan and execute battle plans, few Gammas were. But she recognized this failing in herself at an early age, and hoping to unlock the intricacies of war, she'd studied it obsessively for many years. Her knowledge of military tactics and history was extensive, but it wasn't until very recently that she'd had an opportunity to apply it practically.

Now she faced machines that did what she could not; adapt to changing situations and conquer. Moltke the Elder, a classic Earth strategist, maintained that no battle plan survived contact with the enemy. On the other side of the equation, the robots epitomized the "utmost use of force" Moltke's mentor Clausewitz warned against.

The humans invented them to kill us, but they only succeeded in killing themselves.

≈*Get ready to move. Sixty seconds.*≈

Katra tightened her grip on the incendiary grenades in her hand. She wished there was more she could do to help Mira than offer a distraction, but the Earther's bewildering plans had kept both of them alive so far, and there was no reason to question them now.

Without Mira's relentless optimism and the "fool's luck" common in so many of the military leaders of Earth's past, Katra would probably have been killed several times over by now. Her continued survival was proof enough that trusting Mira was the best strategy, and if there was a way to survive this latest encounter, Katra was sure the woman would find it.

One of the machines extended a metal leg to the edge of the support frame, and another into the gap leading down to the edge of the bridge. Unlike the solid ground the burning container sat on, the bridge's surface level was a rusting nightmare of empty spaces and good intentions.

Mira's latest theory was that the demolition charges built into the bridge and the tracks in front of it were meant to contain the machines, and the structure's current condition spoke to at least one previous attempt by the robots at a crossing. It would have been far easier to clear out any potential blockages in the tunnel than to disarm the charges, even assuming they'd found them all. JonB was supposed to have temporarily disabled the otherwise effective defense against them, at least over part of the span.

If the fifty meters separating the train engine from the robots was any indication, he must have been at least partially successful. But that distance was only a tenth of the bridge's total length, and the machines could run much faster than people. As the fires died down, the time was running out for whatever contingency plan Mira was enacting inside the engine.

≈*Almost done. Any change?*≈

≈*Fire's almost out. They're testing the bridge.*≈

≈*Good. That's what we want them to do.*≈

Katra trusted that Mira either knew what she was doing or was lying to keep her calm. It was a very different style of command than she was used to, and despite her impending violent death, Katra had to admit that she liked it.

≈*I'm clear. Do it.*≈

Katra armed the first grenade and let it drop to the bridge's surface. She set the second to detonate after a five-second delay and set it down on the support beam she was using as a perch. She took two skipping, antigravity hops away from the grenade, and set up to observe the results on the next section of superstructure.

She didn't have long to wait. With the flames nearly extinguished, one of the machines was wedging itself between the overturned train car and the bridge's rusted frame. Metal shrieked as it extended two pairs of legs on either side of its body, shoving the container far enough back for the second machine to step cautiously down onto the tracks.

The grenades detonated on schedule, and as Mira had planned the machines charged forward to attack the twin heat sources but found themselves blocked from advancing by the engine. Mira grabbed the packs and dove off the side of the bridge, body heat masked by both the fires and her hardsuit.

Not for long, though. The machines started pushing the engine forward but found it much harder to move than the overturned container. The engine's wheels screamed in protest, and sparks flew as metal ground against metal. Meter by meter, the three technological relics advanced across the bridge.

Even filtered through her helmet, the sound was painful, and Mira's voice in her head was a welcome distraction.

≈*Five seconds. See you on the other side.*≈

Katra turned her back on the machines and selected a route down the superstructure to where the other mods were gathering around JonB. Jantine was holding his back to her chest, rocking back and forth while Carlton knelt in front of them.

Seeing the three Betas together was a painful reminder of the closeness she would never have now that Jarl was dead, and Katra tried to imagine herself in Jantine's place. She lingered a heartbeat too long on the fantasy of raising children with a compatible mate, and was caught unprepared when the bridge exploded.

As she tumbled headlong towards surface of the rushing river, Katra had just enough time to wonder how the encounter suit's impact systems would handle a fall from such a great height, and whether or not she'd remain conscious as she died.

BOOK THREE

MORDECAI

MORDECAI HARRISON WOKE UP TO AN URGENT knocking at his bedroom door. He gave what he felt was the only proper response: burying his face in his pillow and pretending he didn't hear anything. When the knock repeated, even that pleasure was denied him.

"Doctor Harrison. Doctor Harrison. There's something you need to see. Doctor, are you in there?"

"G'way. M'sleeping. Leave an old man alone, why don't you?"

When a third round of knocking started, Mordecai gave serious consideration to hiding under his bed. Paul Czegeny was an able assistant, but as the husband of Mordecai's grand-niece he enjoyed a few privileges most students did not.

Like the key sequence to my private quarters. Go away, Paul. I'm tired. Damned if I know what Chrissia sees in you anyway.

Tired was perhaps too mild a term from how worn out he felt. Four straight days of hearings, posturing, and screaming fits by the senior captains of the fleet was enough to wear down a man half his age, and that was without the daily trips up the elevator to the habitats. Floating back down on what-ever shuttle was flying near Old Chicago was the best part of his day now, if you took out the increasingly rare hours when he could sleep in his own bed.

"Mordecai, are you going to get out of bed or not? You're not going to want to miss this."

Surrendering to the inevitable, Mordecai rolled over and opened his eyes. When he swung his real leg off the bed and reached for his prosthetic, the room sensed his motions and brought up the lights just enough to aid his search but not enough to dazzle his remaining eye.

I should just let them replace the rest of me next time. It's getting harder and harder to get though the day without squinting. I hear the new model eyes can read signs on the moon, if the comsats are in the right locations.

"Mordecai?"

"I'm awake, Paul. What time is it in your universe?"

The artificial leg warmed at his touch, a feature he'd come to appreciate over the last year. He fitted it in place and waited for the pseudo-nerves to reacquaint themselves with those in his stump.

The leg they'd fitted him with during his rehabilitation was a cold and lifeless half-measure, little more than a jointed crutch. Once he'd learned to walk again, a "real" prosthetic was manufactured and calibrated to his gait, and there were almost five minutes every day when he didn't hate everything about it.

Almost everything. At least it's warm.

"Enter."

The door slid back into the wall, and light from the other side framed Paul waiting with a data cube in his hand.

"That couldn't wait? I've got a full day ahead of me chairing oversight committees and babysitting idiots with guns."

Paul took a step back while Mordecai stood up and shrugged into an old sweater he picked up from his chair. It hung low enough to hide the top of his prosthetic, but more importantly, it had a packet of stims in one of the pockets. The older man popped one in his mouth and chewed it as he shuffled out of his sleep chamber. When he entered his main living area, the smart room obediently dimmed the lights and began disinfecting the bed.

Yawning, Mordecai looked at Paul's tired face. His assistant was usually impeccably dressed and composed—a virtual spokesmodel for the Reclamation government. But something in the man's blue eyes told him that this was definitely not a social call.

He looks serious, for once.

"Fine, fine. Queue it up while I get some coffee. They do have coffee in your universe, don't they?"

"You'll sit and watch this, then we'll grab something on the go. And you should think about pants today; makes you look more professorial."

A harrumphing grunt marked Mordecai's full emergence from sleep. Paul's jokes were never funny unless he was awake enough to dislike them.

Paul slotted the cube into Mordecai's desk terminal then entered the sleep chamber to find him some clothes. As the sigil of the Harrison Institute for Applied Sciences coalesced above the desk, Mordecai called over his shoulder:

"Don't mess around with my system. All the clothes are stored according to precise axioms, and a novice like you will just make a mess of things. Take whatever's on top and come tell me what I'm supposed to be looking at."

Mordecai reached a shaking and spotted hand out to the image. The sigil dissolved in a shower of particles, only to reform into an image taken from what looked like one of the topside securecams.

The angle looks right, but I don't recognize the ruins. Little wonder, I suppose, as I haven't been up there in years.

"Keep watching. And I know you own socks, so don't think you're getting away with wearing one of these outfits. You can't just wear robes all the time, even in your own universe."

Paul's use of a Russellism made him chuckle. Mordecai knew he wasn't a devotee, but Paul did try to "keep the old man happy" over and above what was required of his position. Unfortunately, Paul lived in the same universe as almost everyone else and was decades away from being able to embrace his own continuum.

Now then, what's all this fuss about an empty courtyard?

Mordecai kept watching, pointedly ignoring Paul's failed efforts to divine where the real clothes were kept. Sooner or later he would ask for help, and his universe would align with Mordecai's. But the holo existed in another continuum altogether, neither concealing nor revealing anything of interest.

Mordecai turned his hand over and pushed his palm into the image to collapse it. With only one eye, a holo never looked right, and he wanted to understand what was important enough that someone had convinced Paul to interrupt his sleep. Nothing seemed to be happening, so he expanded the image to make sure the timestamp was accurate.

He almost fell out of his chair when it shifted from showing him shadowed ruins of gray and green to a wide sheet of vivid orange.

"Three Passions, what is that!"

"Keep watching."

In all of his one-hundred and seven years, Mordecai Harrison had never wanted to do anything more. As he watched, the orange plain resolved into a pair of strange, close-set protuberances. He reduced the image, and noticed they were irregular, almost organic in nature.

Then the plain shifted, and two eyes blinked at the securcam, one above the other and in sequence. A broad red line started just above the eyes and moved up its huge forehead, and when it turned away Mordecai could see the stripe continued down the creature's back side.

He also noted the extra pair of both eyes and ears on the other side of the creature's face. His rational mind knew what he was looking at; if there were other creatures in the universe that looked like a Transgenic Type 30, the human race had yet to encounter them. But at the same time, Mordecai's universe located them in another part of the galaxy.

"But that's . . . They're . . ."

"Keep watching."

Paul's voice was right behind him now, and he tsked at Mordecai's choice of display modes. He set down a full—and depressingly respectable—set of clothing on the desk, then reached into the image to pull it image back out to its original dimensions.

"You have to let the neural recorders do their job, Mordecai, or they'll never be able to fit you with a proper eye replace- ment. Plus, you're going to miss the most important part."

Paul placed a second hand in the holo, rotating it until Mordecai saw a side view of the Type 30 as it moved out of frame, only to return moments later leading a decidedly female form wearing some kind of black bodysuit, being half carried by a taller figure wearing an SDF hardsuit covered almost completely in pouches.

Both figures had unfamiliar objects in their free hands, held in such a fashion as to scream "weapon." The hardsuited figure's helmet turned slowly to survey the ruined courtyard, aided by the Type 30's hand pointing out the precise location of the securcam.

Black Bodysuit Woman slipped off the hardsuit's shoulder and slithered to the ground rather than falling. She held her weapon in both hands now, pointing it in the opposite direction of the hardsuited figure's weapon. From this angle, Mordecai couldn't make out a rank insignia on the red blaze, but whoever it was inside seemed to know what they were doing.

"How long ago was this taken?"

"Twenty minutes. They're still up there, waiting."

"Waiting? Waiting for what? And why isn't there any sound?"

More figures came into the frame now, conducted into full view and posed by the Type 30 so that they were all "looking" at the cam. Three more bodysuits came first, two male, one female. The second female was standing slightly in front of one of the males, while the other one pulled out a flat object and began tapping on it.

Then came a sight that confirmed everything for Mordecai, one he'd been waiting for all his life. A sixth black bodysuit, standing not quite as tall as the Type 30 but with an additional pair of muscular arms. Each of the creature's four hands was holding a weapon, one of which was an SDF heavy slugthrower.

A Type 6. They're here, they're really here!

Last to join the group was another Type 30, this one without a red stripe on its head. Mordecai noted that both Type 30s were wearing gray-brown jumpsuits, each of which had dozens of small holes on the chests and legs. Instead of a weapon, the one in back was carrying a small child of indeterminate gender, wearing an SDF duty blouse with the sleeves cut off.

The hardsuited figure approached the tapping male and collected whatever it was he had in his hands. Mordecai stabbed a finger at the volume controls, then looked away from the holo to check if they were working. According to the desk unit, it was registering full sound playback, exactly as recorded. Paul waved his hand away and reduced the volume to half without saying a word, then pointed back at the holo.

The hardsuited figure was standing directly in front of the securcam now. It raised its gauntlets to the suit's neck seals and released them with a quick twist. Mordecai's eyes widened at the return of sound to his universe, the soft hiss of escaping air.

They did all that, without saying a word?

As soon as the thought resolved in his mind, he dismissed it. Of course the people in the image were communicating, he just didn't know how.

Probably some variation of comms that the sniffers can't track, that's all. Why, I'll bet the answer is as simple as . . .

The helmet came off, and Mordecai's worlds collided. Doctor Mordecai Harrison, head of the Harrison Institute and tired old man had no reason to know anything about the woman in the holo. But Councilor Harrison, of the North American Reclamation and Senior Arbitrator of the SDF Allocations and Oversight committee knew exactly who she was, even before she announced herself in a clear contralto.

"I am Lieutenant Commander Mira Harlan. Despite what you may have heard, I am a loyal officer of the System Defense Force, and I am escorting an embassy from the Outer Colonies seeking asylum in your institute."

The most wanted woman in the Home System, and she just walks up to my back door and says hello. She looks different from her pictures, but not that much.

"Who else has seen this?"

"No one but our people."

Our people. Like all things worth saying, the words had many meanings. Paul could have meant the Reclamation. He could have meant Institute staff. But the urgency in his voice when waking Mordecai, and his insistence that he view this holo as soon as possible, spoke to a third intersection of universes.

One that expanded even further as Mira Harlan reached into a pouch on her belt and pulled out a small object. She raised it up high enough so the cam could capture it without distortion.

"I also bear a message, from a mutual friend. *De eersten zullen, de laatsten zijn.*"

He'd been wanting to hear that message for many months.

Mordecai was out of his chair and halfway toward the door when Paul spoke up.

"Mordecai!"

"What? What, man? I have to go to them, you know that!"

Paul simply reached for the pile of clothes he'd placed on the table and selected a pair of pants.

"They'll wait. I have a squad ready, and from what you told me after the accident, you've been waiting for this all your life. Might as well make a good impression, yes?"

Mordecai looked down at his bare knees, one real, one not, and smiled. Then he looked back at Paul, his pants, and the holographic image of a black chess piece floating over his desk. He walked over and reached for his clothes, thinking about Aloysius Martin and the way they'd parted.

Allie, you must still be pretty angry with me, if this is who you chose as your messenger . . .

MIRA

≈*HOW MUCH LONGER MUST WE WAIT?*≈

Jantine's thoughts weren't impatient; Mira could tell that she was just formulating plans. Mira appreciated that, just as she did the space the Beta had given her over the last few hours. It hadn't been an easy night, even with the Omegas carrying the wounded. But now that the sun was rising on yet another insane day, it made sense to work up more contingency plans.

Mira had no ready answer, but she knew that as soon as she took off her helmet there would be no going back. At least one group of people on Earth knew she was helping the Colonials, and the Omegas were hard to explain away. Artemus could perhaps be a clever costume, and no one had seen his face or gray skin yet. But three-and-a-half meter, orange-skinned giants with tree trunks for arms were definitely going to attract attention.

What she did know was that their party was no longer alone, and she sent that information along through the link.

≈*There's a group waiting a few meters below us. There must be a tunnel complex.*≈

Group was an approximate term. But "four people with guns" would only alarm Jantine further, and so far Mira had detected no hostility from them. Just anticipation, something she and her friends had in abundance.

Friends. Is that what we are, or is it something more? I told Jantine that I had family spread out across North America, but other than the memory I shared with Jason, I haven't seen the boys in-person since I graduated. That night was our last together as a family, and after what happened to the Valiant, *they probably think I'm dead.*

Jantine helped JonB to the ground and moved closer to Mira. At first she thought the Beta was going to say something, but then Mira saw the sun burst into life on her visor.

≈*Is it always like this?*≈

≈*The sunrise? I think so. It wasn't for a long time, after the wars. There was just too much particulate in the air. But the Reclamation has done their best to clean the planet up, and I suppose for those who pay attention every day is different in some way.*≈

This morning was certainly different from their last. Mira and the mods had spent yesterday traveling by train, and although they'd made good use of the frequent stops to repair track sections, walking all night after destroying the hunter-killers left them tired in mind and body. Her new muscles were processing fatigue poisons with only a few minutes of rest per hour, but the ration bars in her kit weren't formulated for her new metabolism. Without high-nutrition food to replenish her body's energy supply, she wouldn't make it many more kilometers.

Besides, some of us got blown up last night. Makes the sunrise seem downright tame in comparison.

Katra's injuries were serious, as was JonB's amputation. The thought of that sweet boy trapped beneath the train and losing his hand was horrifying, but getting to his feet afterward and continuing his work was beyond belief.

Katra was right. Betas are just . . . different.

If she'd known the Gamma couldn't swim, Mira might have planned differently. Her encounter suit had kept her from drowning, but Katra had hit the river's surface at a speed that made it effectively as hard as concrete, and only the suit was keeping her alive right now.

Both injured mods were surviving on a diet of stims and painkillers—two more things the group was running out of faster than she'd like.

The emotions of the group were a mixed bag, and the pain in Mira's head was making it hard to think. Katra and JonB were reflective, with the former operating at a heightened state of alertness. Carlton was trying not to be excited about meeting humans who weren't trying to kill him. Mira had to admit that would be a pleasant change.

On the other hand, Artemus was a blank slate. The Delta had a weapon pointed in every direction, and Mira got the distinct impression that if he could operate one with his feet, he'd have asked for another.

Serene was, well, serene. During the attack of the hunter-killers, her fear was uncontrolled and infectious. Mira was glad she'd been far enough away to miss the worst of the effects, but according to Jantine, even O-6913 had been affected. Mira felt partly responsible for that fear; Serene's well-founded terror was based on her own childhood memories of pre-Reclamation war stories.

That reality had proven far worse was another matter altogether. But Serene hadn't seen the robots in action, and every time Mira closed her eyes, the image of three house-sized death machines coming at her down the length of the tunnel with lasers blazing was there to remind her why people just didn't visit North America if they could avoid it.

At least this side of the river is supposed to be safe. Mostly.

The only calm ones around her were the Omegas, but Jason's concern for her and O-6913's unshakabale devotion to Serene were intense in their own ways. It felt as if her head was being squeezed, and sooner or later what was left of her mind would be pushed out and replaced with the thoughts and emotions of everyone around her.

Her eyes had stopped twitching, and she could, for the most part, hear clearly now. But using her abilities nonstop was almost as draining as the ten-hour overnight march they'd made to get here.

But I can't let them know how close I am to passing out. They're depending on me to get them through this.

Jantine was lost in the sunrise, mind refreshingly blank. But standing this close to the Beta reminded Mira of how tightly wound the girl was, and almost losing two more of her friends had to be taking its toll on her emotions. Sooner or later she'd slip again, and all that pain would come crashing down on Mira.

The sun was several degrees higher when Jantine's thoughts resumed, a delay felt keenly by both the rest of the mods and the guards beneath their feet.

≈*What can we expect from these people?*≈

≈*Honestly, I have no idea. Everything the captain knew is locked up inside that chess piece, and JonB's in no shape to continue his analysis. The only thing I do know is that this is where he wanted to bring Serene, so that he—*≈

At the mention of JonB, Jantine lost control of herself for an instant. Everything Mira thought was going on in her head came rushing out, and it was just too much. Jantine's memory of JonB's scream was enough to send her to the ground with one of her own.

Alarm spiked in the mods, adding fresh lances of pain to her agony. Mira could feel all of them coming closer, and their well-intentioned concern was just too much to bear. She struggled up to a kneeling position, one gauntleted hand on her head and the other waving off Jantine's offer of help. When her left hand brushed casually against Jantine's body, JonB's memories came at her as well, and Mira pitched forward, unable to see or hear.

And still the thoughts came. Serene's fear was back, overflowing her formidable mental defenses and putting everyone on edge. Katra hit the water again and again, screaming her anger at Jarl's loss every time. Carlton's confusion as to what was going on with her was somehow worse than the others' unguarded thoughts, as it deepened Mira's own and robbed her of control.

The ground shook, bouncing Mira's head against the dirt. She almost welcomed the pain, as it was something of her own to focus on. Every bit of brain power she had left was occupied with maintaining her control, not wanting her agony to infect the others like Serene's fear.

Then the fear was gone, replaced by a feather light touch she recognized.

≈*Jason. Am I dying?*≈

The Omega sent her reassurance, and the emotional onslaught stopped. The pain was still there, though, and despite Jason's efforts she still worried for her sanity.

≈*How am I supposed to deal with this? The parts of myself I have left aren't enough to make a whole person, and the rest of you keep leaking in through all the holes!*≈

Jason drew her back to the white plain of thought, where he and O-6913 were standing with a wide-eyed Serene between them.

"I'm supposed to tell you they're sorry, and that they never meant for this to happen. You hid your difficulties from us, from me, and I understand why now. But the memories . . . I think I know how we can help."

Mira didn't know how to respond. Serene was talking about her memories, stolen from her along with those of the Gammas that had trained Doria. Serene probably knew more about Mira's life than she did herself right now, and having to be rescued by the Alpha child was the ultimate embarrassment. But all Mira could do was hold on to what was left of herself and whimper.

Jason came forward and held out one of his hands. Despite the pain, Mira formed a thought image of herself, reaching up from the ground for the help he offered. But instead of pulling her to her feet, he yanked back his hand so fast a misty outline of herself came with it. The pain in her head lessened, and her understanding of the Omega's capabilities grew.

Jason brought his other hand up, and started squeezing transparent Mira into a square shape. It solidified into a thick cube of stone, but Mira still recognized it as being a part of herself. Jason set the stone down, stood next to it, and held out his hand again.

Mira crawled forward and reached for the stone. It was smooth and cool to the touch, and just being near it made her feel stronger. She traced the edges with her fingers, breathing in the dusty smell of the playa that came into being around her. The desert sun beat down on her naked back, and she looked lazily into Tommy's eyes as he reached behind him for another beer. His toned body glistened with sweat from their exertions, and she took the bottle he offered gladly.

"They say this is who you are," he said. "You are strong, and independent, and no one can take that away from you. When the pain is too much, come back here to this place and set down another stone."

Mira wanted to change the past, to lie and tell Tommy that she loved him too. But she was due to ship out for the *Valiant* in a few hours and didn't want anything to spoil her last day on Earth. Instead she made the same mistake all over again and drew him to her for another kiss.

Mira felt Serene's embarrassment, Jason's interest and O-6913's growing confusion. She wrapped them and Tommy and the playa all up and pressed them together, making a second stone to place alongside the first. The pain in her head went down a notch, and she could speak again, at least inside her mind.

"Thank you. All of you. Can you tell the others I'm all right? I just need a moment to myself."

Dream Serene and the Omegas faded from view, leaving her alone inside herself for the first time in days. The playa stretched out in all directions under a perfect blue sky, the ground cracked and dry under her feet. Her uniform was perfect, right down to the shiny new rank insignia on her collar. Only one thing could have made the memory better, and Mira was glad to find it there waiting for her in the beer cooler.

She reached in and pulled out a deep, rolling thunderclap, smiling as the hot wind of its passing blew through her close-cropped hair. The sky purpled, and a flash of lighting split it in half. Mira danced and jumped and left her clothes behind with her worries as the rain started to fall, laughing as the storm's power soaked into her bones and healed her soul.

When she opened her eyes, Serene was snuggled up against her while the Omegas stood guard. It would have been a touching moment were Mira not wearing full body armor, but Serene's aura of happiness chased away the worst of the pain.

And I wonder how all this looked to our friend on the other end of that video feed?

Jantine's relief was easy to pick out from the conflicting emotions on the other side of the Omegas, and Mira had the distinct impression she was being shielded from the more powerful thoughts aimed in her direction.

She kissed the top of Serene's head and helped her to stand up, resolving again to get the girl some real clothes at the earliest possible opportunity. It wasn't so much that she looked bad wearing cut-down uniforms, but her grass-stained knees and bare feet made her look like almost feral, and whoever was coming to meet them from underground would likely wonder why she wasn't armed and armored like the rest of the mods.

Once Serene was standing on her own, Mira rolled to her feet and sent another thank you to the Omegas. Jason was as happy as ever to feel the touch of her thoughts, but O-6913 surprised her by offering his own satisfaction.

Why, you old softy.

Mira smiled and pushed her way through to the others with Serene clinging to one of her gauntleted hands. She sent a wordless acknowledgement to Jantine, who then returned her attention to JonB.

Mira was about to say something when she detected a shift in the almost-forgotten emotions of the guards in the tunnels below. It was as if they were paying more attention to something, and although their minds had the same oily feel as Captain Martin's, she got a strong sense of respect mixed with wary preparedness.

"Get ready, everyone. They're coming up."

Mira drew her slugthrower then realized she had no direction other than "down" to aim it at. As if sensing her need, Jason lent her his eyes, and a complex web of power lines drew itself across the ground. There was a glowing network of them forming around a section of faded tile work, and she relayed the location to Jantine, Katra and Artemus.

Then a new mind appeared on her mental landscape, one completely free of worry or distractions. It was the eye of the storm in the emotional hurricane surrounding her, and she felt vaguely guilty about the gun in her hand.

The tiles split into a dozen triangular sections, each of which drew back slightly and fell away into darkness. From the hole they revealed came the sound of a whirring motor, and Jason's eyes supplied a power usage curve Mira recognized as a telescoping engineering platform. The top of a bright red safety cage emerged from the hole, followed by a shock of white hair framing one of the most striking male faces Mira had ever seen.

A wave of alarm ran through all of the mods save Serene, whose only reaction was to hold on tighter to Mira's free hand. Mira took a step in front of the child, and the girl shifted her hands around to the back of Mira's armored left leg.

The man in front of her was the source of the calm thoughts, and Mira borrowed as much of Jason's vision as she could to study his face. As if he'd orchestrated it, the rising sun was eclipsed by his wild halo of hair, making it hard to see him clearly.

The cream-colored eyepatch was easy enough to make out, as was the wide smile that formed as he took in the assembled mods. His skin was a shade darker than Tommy's, but that didn't mean all that much in the Reclamation. What was most interesting about him was that Mira detected no apprehension whatsoever about the guns pointed in his direction, or even how many hands were holding them.

Instead, she felt waves of pure joy radiating from his perfect awareness of the scene, which brought to mind Serene's initial moments of consciousness after emerging from suspended animation.

"Marvelous. Simply marvelous. You have no idea how glad I am you've come into my life."

The man stepped off the platform, and Mira noticed he was using a cane. One of his legs was alive with energy, and she was impressed by the sophisticated prosthetic. The skin on his right hand was mottled, and though she recognized the signs of long-healed burns, the fingers were strong and healthy.

"Lieutenant Harlan, how is Aloysius? I was expecting a message from him a few days ago, and I am very surprised to find you on my doorstep in his stead."

'Lieutenant' . . . *He doesn't know! Why, I bet no one knows, and that's got to be good for us.*

"Captain Martin sends his regrets. He wanted to be here, believe me, and . . ."

The lie felt wrong on her tongue, but Mira didn't know what else to do. She recognized the half-cape and brown and gold vestments of a senior Reclamation councilor, but she'd been away from Earth aboard the *Valiant* for a few years and had no idea who the man was. The clothing had a complicated sensor web built into the rich fabric, and when Jason clued her into the transmission beaming its way into his ear Mira knew this was no one she could hope to deceive for long.

". . . some kind of phased plasma weapons, but Harlan and the big one also have slugthrowers. I really wish you'd let me send the team up the accessway; I don't care who you think sent her, that woman is bad news."

Whoever the man was on the other end of the transmission, he wasn't one of the guards below her. Their emotions were more or less constant—anticipation, boredom, and a dash of concern for the man at the top of the scaffolding. There was none of the focused attention evident in the unknown speaker's voice.

For his part, the old man just shook his head, waiting for her to continue. Then Jantine stepped forward, and Mira was surprised by the combined trepidation and . . . *loathing? Jantine, what's wrong?*

Mira realized she hadn't actually sent the question to her when the Beta began speaking. The Jantine she'd come to know in the last two days was gone, at least temporarily, replaced by the battle commander who had blasted her way out of one of the most advanced warships of the fleet as if it was just another day at the office.

"I am JTN-B34256-O, called Jantine. Who are you, and whom do you represent?"

This did get a reaction out of the old man, and not the one she was respecting. Instead of surprise, it was relief, and a deep sense of longing.

The voice on the other end of the transmission, though, was far from calm.

"Mordecai, did I hear that right? Get out of there, get out of there right now!"

Mira's hand tightened on her pistol, but neither Jantine nor the old man was alarmed. Much to the consternation of the younger man on the other side of the transmission, he reached up his right hand to his ear and disconnected his associate in mid-sentence.

"What are you doing? You can't just—"

The motion cemented for Mira what she'd suspected from the first moment she'd seen the man's face—he was someone who made his own rules, and answered to no one.

"I am Mordecai Harrison. Doctor Harrison, if it matters, but there are those who prefer to call me 'Mister,' 'Councilor,' or 'that crazy old fool' depending on who I've offended most of late. May I see your face, Jantine? I dislike anonymity, and given the company you keep I'm sure there's no need to hide, yes?"

Jantine turned her visored head to Mira, who nodded.

"It's all right. I think we can trust him."

Mira wasn't completely sure that was true, but since he was the only person she'd met in the last two days who didn't make her head hurt, she was willing to take the chance.

Jantine unsealed her helmet, exposing her flawless alien features to Harrison. Mira saw his eyes shift between Jantine and herself, and she sensed a hint of surprise in his thoughts that he squelched almost immediately.

It took Mira a moment to figure out what it was, then she remembered that her own face had undergone changes when the virus turned her world upside down. Gone were the freckles Tommy used to tease her about, and her eyes had a more almond shape to them than before.

And who am I now? What am I?

"Fascinating. All of you, such wonderful diversity. Welcome, welcome to our world. And who is this, peeking at me from behind her fingers?"

Harrison's voice rose sharply at the end of his question, in an annoying tone Mira had last heard from one of her grandfathers. His smile was about as fatuous, but Mordecai Harrison's thoughts contained none of the condescension Seamus Harlan had for his son's offspring.

Too bad Serene doesn't realize what he's doing, or she'd probably teach Mordecai a few new tricks . . .

Mira hastily buried her thoughts, lest the barely trained empath clinging to her leg detect them and do something everyone would regret. Instead of introducing the girl, she tried steering the conversation in a different direction altogether.

"Doctor Harrison, two of our party are in serious need of medical attention. Are you here to grant our request for asylum, or should we make other arrangements?"

Harrison sighed, the deep exhalation of a man who'd known real disappointment. But his smile was still in place, and when he spoke it was without premeditation.

"I'm afraid that's somewhat of a loaded term at the moment, Lieutenant. Jantine's broadcast upset quite a few powerful people, and my own status in the Reclamation government works against me in this instance. As Private Citizen Harrison I can offer you every resource at my disposal, and do so gladly.

"But Councilor Harrison cannot accept your request, especially not with so many guns pointed at him. Can we lower them for a while, or possibly put them away? I assure you, you have nothing to fear from an old man like me."

Mira sent a burst of confirmation to the mods, wincing slightly as her perceptions brushed against Katra's and Artemus's thoughts. The Delta had half his weapons aimed down into the hole, but Katra's pulser was pointed directly at the back of Harrison's head, and Mira knew she never missed.

"Is this really one of your leaders? How can you allow this to happen? Captain Martin was near the end of his usefulness, but at least he died a warrior. This. . . cripple. . . is there no one else we can talk to?"

It took a moment for Mira to understand what Jantine had said. The loathing she'd felt from the Beta was now flavored with a dash of contempt Mira remembered from their first encounter.

Mira was shocked by the intensity of Jantine's disgust. The open-minded, tolerant friend for whom she'd risked her life had an ugliness in her that, for the first time, made Mira think of her as truly alien.

Jason detected Mira's confusion, and without prompting sent her a series of images from his life in the colonies. Dozens, hundreds of smiling faces, going about their lives in well-ordered patterns and working toward the good of all. It seemed like a perfect society, and Mira wasn't sure she understood what the Omega was showing her.

Then Jason "introduced" her to another few hundred faces, who performed much the same tasks with similar smiles. Then there were hundreds more, and hundreds after that. As a pair of dim stars spun across a green sky, she had the impression that many years were passing. Decades, in fact, and all the while Jason worked building fantastic structures impossible to imagine in Earth's deep gravity well. The night sky's stars changed subtly, and Mira witnessed with him the birth of O-6913, and then many years later that of Jantine.

Dear Lord. Jason, are you telling me that. . .

The Omega sent her a confirmation tinged with regret, one O-6913 echoed. She'd felt more maturity from Jason than any of the other mods, but she had no idea how to react to the fact that he'd lived so long that almost everyone he'd ever known was dead.

And not one of mod faces he showed me was any older than my father's. . .

Mira swallowed the beginnings of something that might have been anger, were she still capable of that emotion. She'd just learned yet another damning truth about Colonial society, but this time it was something she could change. Choosing her words carefully, she tried to explain the truth of life on Earth to her friend.

"Jantine, it is very common for people to live well past a century on Earth. Captain Martin was nearly sixty, with many more years ahead of him in the fleet. The fact that I was even considered for a command at my age is very unusual."

Jantine's response was incredulous, and immediate. She moved forward and grabbed Mira's arm, leaning in close to her ear to whisper her next question. Serene shifted to the other side of Mira's body but still clung tight to her legs.

"But why is he so selfish? A Gamma should have scanned his knowledge into the crèche long ago, instead of letting him linger on in this state. How can the next generation improve upon his works if they cannot experience them first-hand?"

"We have no Gammas, Jantine. We have respect for our elders, and the will to overcome adversity."

≈But . . .≈

Mira shook her head and pulled away. What she had to say was for all the mods, and her head hurt far to much to even attempt linking them all in at once.

"No buts. Not anymore. How do you think we survived the hunter-killers? Luck? I learned to fight them from a man almost as old as this one, who's still alive and could probably teach Artemus a thing or two about strength. You're not in the colonies anymore, and if you can't control your prejudices, you should let me do the talking from now on."

Jantine's jaw closed with an audible snap, and Mira felt the Beta's mental defenses go up. But not before a burst of annoyance smashed through her own, one strong enough to steal Mira's sight for several seconds until Jason could pull it away and add another stone to her wall.

When she could see again, Mira turned to face the man whose next words would decide the course of her future.

"Doctor Harrison, thank you for understanding, and for your offer of assistance. I think we can definitely arrive at a mutually acceptable diplomatic fiction. But if possible, can we discuss it in your medical facilities?"

Harrison gave the entire group another look.

"Of course," he said, "of course. But I'm afraid that the lift can't accommodate everyone at once, and your Type 6 and Type 30s may well be too much for it to handle. But I'm willing to—"

Jantine's anger boiled over, and this time she didn't bother to hide it.

"No, Earther. We go together, or not at all."

"Jantine, what are you doing! We can trust him."

"I will not let JonB and Katra out of my sight. Too many have been lost, and he cannot speak for all who dwell below."

"Jantine, Katra is going to die soon. We both know it, and so does she. This is not a negotiating tactic, because there are no more options. She needs help, and he can give it to us."

"Not without an escort. You need to stay with the Omegas, and Serene is certainly not going anywhere without one of us. Do you propose to send Carlton in there? Alone? Even he cannot be spared."

Mira stared at Jantine, not bothering to hide her annoyance. The Beta was staring daggers at Harrison, whose face and mind were still blissfully calm. Serene sent a confused feeler in her direction, but Mira didn't want to involve the Alpha just yet. Besides, Jantine was not so hard-headed that she'd let Katra, or even JonB die. Sooner or later, she'd have to realize that...

Serene's next sending was not a request, and pushed through both the Omega's shields and her own meager defense with no difficulty. It wasn't a shout, but it chased the rest of Mira's thoughts away with a question she should have thought of herself.

≈*Mira, I don't understand. The machine he used to reach the surface is bigger than the hole, and he knows that. Where are the other entrances?*≈

A moment after the pain faded, Mira felt like kicking herself. Jantine hadn't let Harrison finish, and although Serene didn't understand everything that was happening, she was still at least as intelligent as the Betas, and she had a dozen lifetimes of insight to draw upon.

≈*Bless you, child, for keeping a straight head. You've given her a way out.*≈

"Doctor Harrison, I believe you were about to mention an alternative to the lift?"

Now Harrison smiled even wider, and there was definitely a grandfatherly twinkle in his eye.

"Yes, well, I meant to say that I was willing to offer myself as a guarantee of sorts, while my assistant arranges for a closed transport to ferry us all inside. I think we can come up with something fairly easily to fit Miss Jantine's needs."

Despite his pleasant tone, Harrison's words did nothing to settle Jantine's fears. If anything, they just made her angrier.

"*Commander* Jantine. And I accept your parole on one condition."

Harrison cocked an eyebrow, a gesture that might have completely disarmed his smile if it weren't for his eyepatch. But Jantine's emotions were near the boiling point, and Mira wasn't sure that the Beta would accept any further compromises.

"Yes, what is it then?"

Mira could feel satisfaction from both Jantine and Harrison, and she was relieved that he was willing to at least listen. His assistant, on the other hand, was shouting into the transmitter as if mere willpower could reactivate it.

"*Are you out of your mind? I'm sending up the team now! Hold on, Mordecai, I'm coming to get you!*"

Mira felt the guards below go from practiced disinterest to focused alert in a heartbeat. Still trying to defuse the situation, Mira shook herself loose from Serene and turned her face toward the securcam. She was about to tell Harrison's assistant to stand down when Jantine dropped the proverbial other shoe.

"That you offer your unconditional surrender to my force, and place yourself under the dominion of The Outer Colonies. You and your institute are now prisoners of war, Councilor Harrison, and as such are bound by the terms of the Interstellar Compact and the Magellan Accords."

JANTINE

"No," JonB said.

Jantine turned to look at him, furious at his interruption. Mordecai Harrison remained where he was, neither accepting nor refusing her terms. The old man smiled his too-old smile and put more weight on the rod in his right hand, which Jantine still suspected was a new kind of weapon.

≈*Mira, relay. JonB, this is not the time.*≈

Mira did not comply, at least not in a way Jantine could detect. But JonB struggled to his feet with Carlton's help. His face was even paler than it had been last night, when he was screaming in pain at the full realization of his injury.

"No, Jantine. No terms. Not now. We're beaten, can't you see that?"

JonB took a tentative step toward Katra, then another. Carlton left him standing on unsteady legs, then bent and scooped up the unresisting Gamma. Katra's head rolled against the left side of his head, and their faceplates met with a clink. JonB took a third step toward the old human.

"Mira!"

"Listen to him, Jantine." Mira's words had the same tone of resignation as JonB's. "This is not the way."

Jantine had neither words nor training to answer this betrayal. Of all people, JonB was supposed to support her decisions. Question them, yes, but open defiance was not in his character. It wasn't why he was here.

Once Carlton had Katra in his arms, JonB gestured toward the old man. Carlton adjusted her arm so that her weapon rested on her stomach, then moved toward the platform that presumably led down to the Harrison institute.

Jantine found her voice, but the words that came out of her mouth were little more than a tight whisper.

"I will break you for this, JON-B34726-S."

"Why? What possible purpose would it serve? And to whom would you report me? Serene?"

"What does that mean?"

The urge to answer Serene's question was almost overpowering, but Jantine kept her eyes on JonB.

Mira started whispering to the Alpha, but to a Beta's ears she might as well have been shouting in the nearly silent courtyard. "It's a rhetorical question. He's trying to make a point to her, one she doesn't want to hear."

"But why?"

Jantine took a step forward, hand tightening on the handle of her pulser. JonB just shook his head, and Jantine's anger finally boiled over. All her frustration at his constant questioning, his knowing smiles, and the basic unfairness of his survival when Malik was dead raised her arm for a blow. The pulser flashed in the sun as she swung, nearly reaching his head before his remaining hand caught her wrist.

"Go ahead. I can't stop you, not for long. Kill me if you want to, I'm half dead already. But Katra is dying faster then I am, and I won't let you kill her, too."

Jantine's eyes flared, and her face twisted into a snarl. She wrenched her wrist from JonB's grasp and smacked him across the face with the back of her hand. The civvie went down in a heap, fresh blood running down his face and onto his encounter suit.

Something broke in her hand when it impacted JonB's nose, but despite the pain Jantine kept a firm grip on her weapon and set her aim right between his eyes. Her finger touched the first firing stud, and her thumb brushed the edge of the second.

≈*Jantine, STOP!*≈

At Mira's mental command, Jantine's anger drained out of her in a rush, and her body went rigid. A warm cloud enveloped her senses, and everything around her seemed very far away. She could still see JonB on the ground in front of her— still saw the old Earther with his inscrutable face staring at her. But she couldn't move, and after a few seconds, she was thinking clearly again.

With clarity came shame.

JonB. What have I done?

Mira was at her side, gently pulling the pulser from her clenched fingers. JonB wisely moved out of the line of fire, and Artemus helped him to his feet with one pair of hands while reaching out the other to collect her weapon and place it into his pack. Jantine felt Mira's gauntleted hands grab her arms, and when the Earth woman spoke, her breath was mere centimeters from the back of Jantine's neck.

"Just . . . Just . . . Hell, I don't know anymore. Just don't."

JonB put his hand up to his face, and jerked. Jantine's senses and body came back under her control as his nose cracked audibly. JonB coughed, bowed his head for a moment, then turned his battered face back to Jantine.

"Son, let me look at that," Harrison said. "Broken noses can be tricky, believe me. And . . . oh, for the love of Reason—put those weapons down, you fools. Now!"

Four Earthers wearing hardsuits of armor like Mira's entered the clearing. Artemus raised all four of his weapons, aiming each one at a mirrored faceplate.

Mira's hands came away from Jantine's arms, and the Earther took an unsteady step around Jantine toward Artemus. It was a noble gesture, but all four of his arms were over Mira's head, and she did nothing to impede his line of fire. Whatever mental hold she had on Jantine disappeared though, and she was free to speak.

"JonB, I—"

"Don't say anything you don't mean, Jantine. Because you're right. In the Colonies I'd be stripped down and scanned for this, then conveniently shuffled away to run a mine somewhere."

"I'm . . ."

Jantine felt a wave of something warm and pleasant from Mira, but it cut off almost immediately as the Earther gave out a groaning sob, then fell limp. The unfamiliar words of an apology died on her lips as Serene charged past her just ahead of Jason's thundering footsteps.

"Mira? Mira? Please don't be dead." Serene's voice tugged at Jantine's heart as Jason took Mira in his arms.

Artemus's face plate rested in Jantine's direction for several long seconds before the Delta threw down his weapons and sat on a piece of collapsed wall.

Mordecai Harrison stepped up to Jason, and for a moment Jantine thought the Omega would stomp him into the ground for daring to touch the woman in his arms. But instead the Omega knelt down and laid Mira on the ground, and Harrison knelt beside her under the watchful eyes of his guards.

It took Jantine half a heartbeat to locate JonB again, and when she did she saw he'd almost reached the platform. Carlton was standing on it with his back against the orange-striped railing, supporting Katra. The Gamma's pulser was on the ground, and JonB stepped over it as if it wasn't even there. Once he was on the platform as well, he grabbed for one of the rails and sagged against it.

"We're not in the Colonies, Jantine," he said. "Not anymore. Our mission is a failure, and it's time to start thinking for ourselves for a change. Come find me, when you're ready to talk. I really wish you would. But I'm going down there, and I don't care what you think about that."

The Beta hadn't bothered to wipe away any of his blood after adjusting his nose, and his face was already bruising where she'd struck him. But his gaze was fixed on Jantine, boring straight through her encounter suit and into her soul.

"Are you all right, Janbi?" Mordecai Harrison was standing now, and his voice was much stronger than his small frame seemed capable of generating.

"No, Doctor Harrison. I'm far from all right. But in time, I think I will be. And it's . . ."

JonB's battered face fell into his puzzle-solving expression for a moment, and when his smile returned, the intensity of his gaze dimmed. He was still looking at Jantine, but he seemed different somehow. And instead of the imperious correction Jantine expected to hear in his words, his voice was soft and thoughtful, containing more genuine emotion than she'd ever heard him express out loud.

"Actually, I take it back. Yes, why not? I am called Janbi. My name is Janbi, Mordecai, and I surrender myself into your care."

Jantine had no idea what she was supposed to do next. As the platform moved downward and out of sight, her failure was complete. Her choices had split the team apart, she'd lost the respect of her closest friends, and the worst part of it all was that JonB was right.

Again.

All she could do was wait, and hope that things resolved in her favor. Taking a cue from Artemus, Jantine sat down and let the world move according to its own schedule. Only Mordecai Harrison was looking at her, and his previous expression of practiced neutrality was replaced with one of concern.

Jantine looked to the sky. The Home Star's yellow-white radiance painted everything around her with the colors of morning, but it did nothing to help the pain in her heart.

Don't look to me for answers, Earther. I'm not their leader anymore. Mira is, and she's welcome to them. Assuming, that is, that I haven't killed her, too.

JANBI

JANBI LOOKED UP FROM HIS BORROWED DESK WHEN
Jantine entered the room, but he almost didn't recognize her
without her encounter suit or coveralls. Dressed in soft white
garments bearing the logo of the Institute, she carried none of
her habitual swagger, nor the air of command he'd come to
associate with her every move.

The mod standing in front of him just looked tired, almost
as tired as he felt himself. He knew what he was feeling was
the combined after-effects of the stims and whatever Mordecai
had given him to sleep, a state the old doctor had predicted
would be "one monster of a hangover." But Jantine's face had
changed since he last saw her, and despite the pain in her eyes
Janbi had to admit he liked it.

*She's finally accepted it. We failed in our mission, and as such no
longer have purpose. And it terrifies her, almost as much as it does me.*

Janbi set his handheld aside and dimmed the panel, letting
the search routines he'd worked out do their job. He leaned
back in his chair and smiled, hoping his new face wasn't too
hideous to look at.

"JonB . . . Janbi, I'm sorry. I shouldn't have struck you. You
were right."

He hadn't expected a full apology, it would take the Beta
much more than a few hours to come to terms with the

mistakes she'd made. But although he expected her to have more to say than that, he decided not to punish her for being who and what she was.

It's not her fault they made us this way.

"Yes, I usually am," he said. "But I didn't ask you to come to me to make you feel bad. I just wanted to talk to you. Really talk, for once, without any expectations or demands on either of us. Do you think that's possible?"

Jantine was silent for fourteen and a half seconds then nodded. Janbi got up from the desk and moved over to a pair of overstuffed chairs, easing himself down into one as best he could with only one hand.

When Jantine realized what he was doing, she started to help him but then stopped when her eyes registered his bandage-wrapped stump. As if in sympathy, she raised her own injured hand to her chest and then quickly moved it behind her body as if the sight of it might offend him.

When she sat down in the chair opposite him, Janbi saw a hint of her former self. Jantine was careful not to touch the sides of the chair, and she selected the exact center of the cushion to perch on instead of sinking into its comfort as he'd done. Her left hand brushed away invisible specks of dirt, and she kept her back perfectly straight.

Janbi smiled again, a bit wider this time. It was enough to make his nose sting, but Mordecai assured him it would heal straight and he'd have no problems breathing. Janbi hadn't mentioned to him how little time the process would take, and he wondered how the human doctor was reacting to Katra's much faster recuperative properties.

Janbi and Jantine sat silently for a while, each content to watch the other for signs as to what to do. In the end, it was Jantine who spoke first.

"I don't know what I'm supposed to say," she said.

"You don't have to say anything, if you don't want to. There aren't any rules now, not for us."

"But I'm supposed to know. Or if I don't, you're supposed to help me find the answers. None of this was covered in our education!"

It seemed to Janbi that Jantine was about to lose control. Given that the last time she'd acted impulsively she'd broken both his nose and her hand, he decided that perhaps they still needed some rules after all.

"Jantine, you know as well as I do that our mission was expected to fail. Just making it down to the surface put us far ahead of the projections, despite what it cost us."

Jantine rolled her lips inward, her jaw was trembling, and her left hand had a white-knuckled grip on her knee.

"But that's the problem with the Colonies," he said. "The Alphas, the Builders, even the older Betas think too big. The details are left for us to work out, and if I've learned anything from our time on Earth it's that the little things add up over time."

Without thinking about it, Janbi was using his hands to emphasize his words. Or more accurately, one hand and one stump, and despite her best efforts Jantine couldn't stop looking at his left arm.

"This? This is exactly what I'm talking about. On Earth, they can make me a new one. I talked about it with Mordecai, and for something like a hand the calibration time is just over a month. But back home, they'd push me aside for the next in line. And given how poorly you and I got along when we first met, JRD-B34721-S probably wouldn't last very long either."

Jantine's voice was almost a whisper, and her face was pale and drawn.

"I would never . . . I never asked for this. Any of this. I never wanted you to be hurt, I just . . ."

Janbi leaned forward, moving his right arm in front of the stump.

"That's right. No one ever asked us. In fact, I'll bet that until we decanted Serene, you'd never even met an Alpha in the flesh. But I have. There were four assigned to watch my crèche. And despite my early reservations, I'd rather be with her than any of them.

"Do you know what it was like, Jantine? Do you have any idea how they trained us?"

Jantine shook her head.

"Your picture was the first thing I saw every day when we woke from the rest cycle. I heard your voice during every meal. I knew everything about you before we even met, and when they told me why I'd been born, I was so proud.

"What does that make me, Jantine? Who am I supposed to be? Our genomes are perfectly compatible, but as people we couldn't be more different. They picked everyone else for this mission based on their merits, but I was *designed* for it."

Jantine sank back in her chair, making no attempt to hide her tears. Janbi didn't want to hurt her like this, but she needed to hear his story. Needed to hear all of it, no matter what it meant for their future.

"When you took a test, our crèche had half a cycle to study the same topic and get a higher score. Anyone who didn't was taken away. Even when there were only a few of us left, we had to be smarter than any Beta who'd come before us.

"You all think I'm arrogant, but what choice did I have? My entire life only has meaning based on how useful I can be to you, on a mission the Alphas knew might well fail. And for it to succeed, I had to challenge you at every turn, knowing how it made you feel. What does that say about me, about us?"

Jantine's sobs were like blows to his chest, and Janbi couldn't stand another second of it. He rolled out of his chair and stood in front of her, holding out his right hand.

When she reached for it, all he could think of was how right it had felt when the two of them comforted one another that first night after landing. He leaned back, pulling gently until she rose to meet him. Jantine flowed into his arms, and he held her as tightly as he could with only one hand. But she had more than enough strength for both of them, and they stood like that until she stopped crying, and a good while longer.

"I'm not telling you this because I want to hurt you, Jantine. But I've had a lot of time to think over the last few days, and I've made my decision. I'm not taking any more orders, not from the Alphas. Whatever happens to me from now on, I'm the one responsible for my actions."

Jantine inhaled through her nose, a long, sniffling sound that preceded a small gasp as she opened her mouth to speak. Her voice was muffled against the fabric of his soft garment, but he knew the sound of her voice so well he could have made out the words from across the room.

"What are you saying? Why are you telling me these things?"

Janbi rested his forehead on her hair, careful not to jostle his nose any more than he had to. Her smell was his entire world, and part of him wondered why he'd ever considered Mira Harlan as an acceptable partner.

"Our old lives are over. We don't have to follow their rules any more. No more plans, no more compatibility matrix. I want a real life, a human life. I want to be old, and weak, and read books that have nothing to do with science, or logic, or societal planning."

Jantine stiffened in his arms, and she pushed away slightly. Janbi took a step back, but when he saw the pain on her face he almost rushed to hug her again.

"I don't understand. Janbi, I don't know what you're saying to me, or what I'm supposed to do. That's why I came here. I don't know anything anymore, but I didn't want you . . ."

Jantine's eyes brimmed with a fresh round of tears, and before Janbi knew what he was doing his left hand came up to wipe them away. But instead of recoiling from his stump, Jantine took his arm in her hand and pressed it against her face. She closed her eyes, and let out another shuddering breath.

"I didn't want you to hate me."

It was Janbi's turn to fumble for words, but instead of letting his mouth run free, he stayed silent. He knew it was the wrong thing to do, but he was as trapped by his programming as she was.

Perhaps that's why we're so drawn to Mira. She never hides her reactions, even when we don't like what she has to say.

"Jantine, I'm saying you don't owe me anything. You are free to choose whatever partner you want. I don't know what life will be like here on Earth, but I want to. I want to know all of it, and I hope someday, when you're ready, you will too."

Jantine opened her eyes, and Janbi took her smile to mean that she would at least consider what he'd said.

Janbi pulled away when his handheld chimed an alert, stumbling toward the desk with unexpectedly weak knees. Jantine opened her mouth at his abrupt dismissal, but the flashing panel was something he couldn't ignore.

When she did speak, it was with her old voice, and Janbi couldn't help but feel sorry for yet another missed opportunity.

"What is it?"

Janbi didn't answer at first, working his way around the desk until he could set the handheld down and tap out a few commands. Luckily, the desk's holo display responded to his gesturing stump, and equations formed in letters of light above its polished surface.

"I think I might have found them. The Sleepers."

"What?"

Jantine's face was just on the other side of the holo, and her hands must have strayed into the projection. The equations spread out around them, and Janbi had to crane his neck to find the ones he needed to verify.

When he did, he shook the handheld very delicately, not wanting to disturb the image any more than it already was.

"I've been running a decryption program on the Earther communications network. Doctor Harrison gave me his access codes for the institute's library, from which I was able to decipher his clearance codes for the Reclamation council."

Jantine nodded, and Janbi knew she was extrapolating from his words the kinds of networks they could now access. It seemed that she too needed a challenge to pit herself against, which wasn't all that surprising given how he'd developed the same personality trait.

"Ever since we exited the debris field I've been trying to figure out what happened to the other container. After the crash the shuttle's core was too compromised to run this kind of search, but the ones they have here are a lot more powerful and we have access to a very sophisticated microwave communications grid.

"This program," he said, indicating the equations with his stump, "has analyzed all encrypted transmissions moving through the network for the last seven hours. And I'm fairly sure I know where they are."

"JonB, are you telling me you know where the sleepers landed?"

Janbi didn't take offense when Jantine used the mocking designation, taking it for an excited utterance.

"No. As far as I can tell, they haven't landed at all. I think one of the ships that fired missiles at us recovered it, and has been trying to find a way inside ever since. There are multiple transmissions referencing 'modules,' and quite a few of them contain the word 'Chimera.' If we can find that ship, we can find our people. Jantine, we don't have to be alone!"

Janbi put the handheld down, raised his hand into the holo and made a fist. The holo obediently disappeared, giving him an unobstructed view of Jantine's face.

Her eyes were alive, and a tight smile teased the edges of her mouth. And the same eagerness she was feeling was alive in him as well. But he was completely unprepared when she leaned across the table, grabbed his head, and kissed him.

Janbi had to keep his hand on the desk to avoid falling, but he found it very pleasant to let Jantine maneuver herself around the side of the desk while maintaining contact with his mouth. Once they were next to one another, she drew him into an even tighter embrace than before, this time kissing him so forcefully that despite Mordecai Harrison's assurances, he couldn't breathe at all.

MIRA

"WELL, MY DEAR," MORDECAI HARRISON SAID, "YOU have some very interesting readings here. I'd like to talk to you about them, if you're feeling up to it."

Hearing Mordecai's Harrison's voice made Mira think of every time her grandfathers had come to visit. But unlike the Pappys Harlan, Mordecai wasn't here to hug her or slip her candy when her mother wasn't looking. He was a scientist, and if Captain Martin was correct, he was the foremost expert on the Transgenic virus in a thousand light years.

But from where she was lying on her bed, watching him absently tug on his wild white hair while his staff moved around the Institute's infirmary, he looked more like a character from a fairy tale than a preeminent scientist and statesman.

"I'm a lot better now that I've had some rest. My head's a bit fuzzy, but it doesn't feel like it's going to explode anymore. After the last few days, that's one heck of an improvement."

Mordecai's smile was as devastating as his voice, and Mira was having problems reconciling the avuncular professor with the High Councilor. She didn't remember his selection to the council, or even if she'd voted for him. But it was easy enough to see how he'd earned the total respect of all the Institute's staff.

I just wish the captain had told me more about you before everything got turned upside-down.

To be perfectly honest, Mira felt great. Part of it was being out of her hardsuit, but another factor was the incredibly soft and decidedly non-regulation hospital clothes she had on. They were some kind of cotton blend, with an almost invisible set of seams on each side so the attendants could "open her up" if necessary to attach more ice-cold probes. They'd removed most of those before she went to sleep, but Mira could still feel a couple of them in uncomfortable places on her chest and back.

"Well, that's the thing. You were dangerously dehydrated, and even though we pumped you full of fluids, you burned through every kind of sedative we tried to keep you asleep. So Paul had the bright idea to get you drunk instead. Apologies if you're not a bourbon fan, but since we had some on hand it easy to synthesize and introduce into your bloodstream."

"Umm, thanks?"

The last time she'd done any serious drinking was with Tommy, and she only remembered that because of the ribbing her fellow cadets gave her when she came back on duty with a very distinctive body odor. Mira offered up a silent prayer that she wouldn't have the same reaction this time.

"Paul's a fairly intuitive fellow. In another forty years or so, he might even be ready to take over this place from me. If I'm tired of it by then, that is."

A tall man snorted from several meters away, where he was examining a bank of monitors attached to Katra's biobed. The Gamma's injuries were far more extensive than anyone but Janbi and Carlton knew, but apparently she'd threatened them in some pretty inventive ways not to tell Jantine during their starlight run.

"He's just jealous because I'm so much better looking than he is. Hello, Lieutenant Harlan. I'm Paul Czegeny, but apparently you know that already."

Mira smiled. He was good-looking, if a bit skinny for her taste. But compared to the faces she'd been looking at for the last three days, he was a duck among swans.

"Not your last name, but I do recognize your voice. It's . . . complicated."

Paul shrugged in a very Harrison-like manner, and she wondered how long the two men had been working together. Mordecai held out a medicomp to Paul, leaning against her bed for support as he put his cane aside. The younger man swiveled his head between the monitors and the smaller device, then gave another shrug. His expression wasn't quite a frown, but it conveyed a similar message.

They don't know what to make of me. And as long as I'm sidelined by Paul's whiskey derivative, I can't use my abilities to figure out why. I can almost feel them, but after my emotional overload up on the surface, I'm okay with that for now.

Mira took a few seconds to consider this new development. It seemed foolish for her abilities to be counteracted by such a common substance, but she didn't have any referents for intoxicants in the Colonies. She'd have to ask Carlton the next time he stopped by to check on Katra. Bringing the matter up to Serene didn't seem right, especially if her current state gave her any advantages she didn't know about yet.

Paul stepped forward and took the medicomp from Mordecai, but he didn't seem pleased with what he saw.

"So as near as I can figure, Miss Harlan, you have two active strains of the T-Virus in your system. Neither matches the one your friend the Type 13 has, and—"

"Katra, Paul. And she's a Gamma, not a Type 13. Whatever information you have on the Colonials needs to be updated."

If Paul was chagrined by her words, he gave no sign of it. "Your friend Katra the Gamma, then. But you and she share some remarkable healing abilities that . . . that the young man who is so insistent on being called Janbi doesn't. Does she have . . ."

Paul waved the medicomp in a small circle near his head, and Mira smiled and shook her head.

"Okay, then. I can't explain either of you. But one of the active strains in your body matches the one in that little girl—Serene, is it? And unlike you, her readings are stable. Is she a Gamma too?

Interesting. Now I definitely need to talk to Carlton.

Mira wasn't sure whether or not to tell Paul the truth about Serene, but as she'd been prepared to hand the girl off to Mordecai sight unseen several days ago, she reasoned that there was nothing to be gained by silence.

"No. She's something else. An Alpha, but she does share my empathic abilities. More complicated stuff—I really don't understand it myself. Jantine, Janbi and Carlton are Betas; Artemus is a Delta. Jason and . . . well, the big fellas are Omegas, but don't expect a lot of conversation out of them. In fact, they're the reason I ended up like this, so if they ever decide to tell me why, I'll be sure to pass it along."

Paul nodded, entering data into the medicomp. She thought she detected a hint of curiosity from him, but it was nothing compared to the burst of curiosity she felt from Mordecai. It was strong enough to bring back a bit of her headache, but when she tried to "feel" more, nothing happened.

Good stuff, that bourbon.

"Are you sure about that, Mira?"

Huh?

"Sure about what?

"You said Serene was an Alpha. Is that true?"

Mira nodded. Jantine would be furious, but after what she pulled in the courtyard the Beta could lump it. Mira wasn't quite ready to forgive her yet, but if they couldn't trust Mordecai's people there wasn't really anything they could do about it.

"Yes, sir, I am. Captain Martin had more information, but he was sure this was the place to bring her. As for the virus, well he told me 'she wasn't done cooking.' Something about how she'd spent so long in suspended animation that the rest of the human race just moved on, and so did the virus. I'll admit, the distinction is a bit beyond me, but that's what he said. If we can get at the data he left for us, we'll know more."

"I've asked a friend to come to the institute to help with that," Mordecai said. "But I think I can explain what he meant, even if I can't explain how you ended up like this."

"I'm all ears, Mordecai. But my head's starting to hurt again, could I have some more of whatever it was you gave me? I don't recall dreaming about a glass and ice, so I'm assuming I didn't drink it."

Paul leaned forward and pushed a button on the side of her bed, and a few seconds later she was feeling no pain. It was just enough to knock the edges off the hurricane in her head, but not so much that she couldn't follow what Mordecai was saying.

"So it's like this. That girl, that marvelously strange girl, is from another world and another time. I can't say definitively where and when, but Paul, myself, and everyone here on Earth has a very stable strain of the T-virus. We see maybe a handful of minor expressions each year on Earth, and a few more in orbit. It's just enough to keep the grants coming in and rules in place about athletics and military service. I'm amazed that you have had such a complete transformation, but even more so that you've been infected twice."

"That's the part I don't understand, doctor. I'm not going to say that's impossible, since you're telling me it's true. But what they told us in school was that once you went active, you couldn't be infected again."

Mordecai's head was like a child's bobbing toy, and he started waving his hands around in the air as he spoke.

"I know! That's the best part. Serene's strain isn't causing your abilities, it's magnifying them. And none of the others are showing the same effects. You two are a couple of fascinating case studies, and I think we should keep you both under observation for a while just to make sure nothing happens to you."

Mira pushed herself up on the bed, feeling the sensors attached to her skin shifting. Then a spike of pain forced its way through the pleasant bourbon haze and past her strong desire not to be poked and prodded for the rest of her life. She closed her eyes and gasped, and she felt strong hands catch her before she could fall off the side of the bed.

≈Mira, what do you know about Chimera?≈

Mira was surprised by Janbi's sudden intrusion into her thoughts—and the very vivid mental image of his immediate surroundings that accompanied it. When she opened her eyes, Mordecai was shining some kind of small light on her face.

"Chimera? But that's a myth!" Her voice was much louder than she'd intended.

"Hmm? What's that, Mira?"

Harrison's upturned eyebrow was almost comical, but Mira was too confused by both Janbi's question and why he'd be asking it at this exact moment to answer him.

"Something above your paygrade, Mordecai," said a reedy voice from her Academy days. All activity in the room came to a halt. "And yours too, Harlan, but we'll get to that in a moment. Now, does one of you young people have an explanation as to why I had to come down the gravity well in the middle of the afternoon, instead of having a nice cup of tea in my wardroom?"

Mira was off the bed and standing at attention before she fully processed the appearance of Commodore Ykaterina Maranova in the room, resplendent in her dress blacks with the left half of her tunic almost completely covered in service ribbons.

In contrast, Mira's shapeless cotton outfit was woefully inadequate to receive a senior flag officer, but that didn't stop her from saluting. Or trying to, anyway. Between the fading pain of Janbi's unexpected message and the bourbon, she was having trouble standing up straight.

When Maranova stalked over and glared up at her, Mira felt just as awkward as she had on their first meeting, when, as a very junior midshipman, she arrived late and hung over for a fleet tactics symposium and had been called on to answer questions about the final days of the Tranquility uprising for the rest of a very long afternoon.

"What happened to your face, girl? It looks like someone took a brush and scoured off all your character."

Mira hadn't fully seen her own face for several days, save for chance glances at herself in the mods' faceplates. But she knew what the commodore meant.

"Well? How about it?"

"Ma'am, at 1245 ship time on July 17th, a then unidentified object made an unauthorized hyperspace emergence . . ."

YKATERINA

"HARLAN, I'VE LISTENED TO THIS STORY TWICE NOW, and it's still the biggest bunch of bullshit I've ever heard. Even the parts of it about me are bullshit, and damned if I don't believe every word."

Looking around the storage area at the variety of gennies present, Commodore Ykaterina Maranova felt every minute of her age.

Hell, all of the gennies added together might come close to my age, and that's a generous estimate.

They were something to see, she'd give them that. Tall ones with extra arms wearing slick black bodysuits, and even bigger ones in tattered coveralls with orange skin and decidedly inhuman faces, one of whom was serving as a living chair for a little girl with impossibly smooth skin and an oversized head.

The child, Serene, looked much different than she had the first time Maranova had seen her, floating in a sleeper unit aboard Aloysius Martin's shuttle a few weeks back. She was wearing a very baggy set of shapeless cotton scrubs like the ones Harlan and the more human-looking gennies had on.

That the Alpha child and Harlan were here and Aloysius wasn't stung a bit, but Martin was a career man, principled. That he'd gone out on his own terms said a lot about him, and those he trusted.

Here and now, Mira Harlan and the strange faces she'd surrounded herself with were watching her with a mixture of surprise and trepidation.

What the hell am I supposed to do with this lot? Harlan I have to arrest, I have to pretend Mordecai isn't committing treason against himself, and if I don't shoot the gennies for breaking the Exile I have to find someone to arrest me!

But far and away the worst part of watching beings from another star system interacting with humans was listening to one of her prize students speak on their behalf, and as one of them.

"Ma'am, I'm just as much a part of it as you are, and I don't understand it all either. But Captain Martin brought me into this, dropped your name, and sent me the long way round here to the Harrison Institute. I was in no way expecting you to walk in that door, but I'm glad you did."

Maranova snorted.

"That's all well and good, but it still doesn't explain why I'm here. Mordecai all but ordered me to come down and play a game of chess, and when I arrived what do I see but him giving care and comfort to not only one of my protégés but also the author of a transmission that has the fleet on high alert and me planted in orbit for the last three days trying to determine whether or not a state of war exists with the Outer Colonies.

"So here I am, waiting for an explanation no one seems to have. And let me tell you this for free, Mordecai, standing around while these children stare at me is definitely not my idea of a relaxing afternoon."

Maranova scanned the more normal faces among the gennies, in particular Jantine, or JTN-whatever the hell her number was. She'd cleaned up in a hurry, but there was no hiding her freshly fucked face, or the shit-eating grin on the one-handed boy standing next to her.

That girl would just as soon spit in my eye as shake my hand. There's some definite promise there.

"So what about it, Jantine? What's your play here?" Maranova watched Jantine cock her head, as if she was listening to something no one else could hear. If Harlan's story were true, the girl was probably asking Mira with her mind for clarification, and Maranova would be damned if she'd let a shavetail speak on her behalf.

"Don't ask Harlan, ask me. I'm the one you have to convince."

Jantine's look was pure ice, but she returned her focus to Maranova while contemplating her response. Maranova thought Harlan was going to pop a blood vessel trying not to explain it herself.

"I will have my people back, or die in the attempt. What this man, this Horass has done is unforgivable. He will die as well. After that it is up to you and your government."

Whore-Ass. Pretty much sums up that pissant Kołodziejski, and she's never even met him.

"That's a goal, not a plan. I need something to work with, if I'm going to help you."

"Ma'am, if I may?"

At least Harlan's voice hasn't changed. Still afraid of the sound of it, no matter how tall she stands.

"Lay it on me, Harlan. I've wasted enough time on this already, I might as well hear it all."

Mira Harlan wasn't a scared teenager anymore, nor was she a confident young woman reaching for the stars. Something had happened to her, recently by the feel of it, and Maranova didn't think it was just her transformation into a gennie.

You're half the woman you should be. You're definitely not the officer who's been trouncing my crew chiefs in fleet competency exercises over the last few years, so there must be something else about your transformation that you're not telling me.

Harlan's face had some eerie similarities to the little girl's, enough that Maranova almost believed the parts of her story she'd left out of the larger briefing. She hadn't believed Aloysius Martin at first either, until she'd seen the Alpha girl in suspended animation.

But hearing how Serene's face had been changing since emerging from the sleeper unit was almost as terrifying as the thought that the T-virus inside the child could transform Maranova into something else at any time.

"Ma'am, that's not the way they think. Jantine knows she has to get a ship, and some way to find Chimera. But she can't do either of those things right now, so she's not going to waste time making plans until she knows what resources she has to work with."

Maranova wasn't ready to let Harlan off the hook just yet. There was too much at stake just to give away all her cards, and it was clear she wasn't going to get any help from "Councilor" Harrison.

Mordecai was having too much fun a just being in the room with his thesis subjects, drinking in every minute and preparing his next paper for publication. But the thoughtful looks he was giving the little girl when he thought no one could see told Maranova that the doctor shared at least some of her fears, and probably had a few of his own.

"More bullshit, this time with a whiff of horse thrown in. You want a ship, girl, you ask for it. You want resources and information, you ask for them. That's how this works. Or have you forgotten who I am, and what my rank actually means?"

Maranova wasn't sure if she was talking to Harlan, Jantine, or Serene, but all three of them stiffened.

Serene's look of concentration reminded her so much of Cadet Harlan that, for a second, Maranova thought she was looking back through time. It was something she'd worked for years to train out of the girl before shipping her off to Aloysius Martin.

Then the Alpha's too-large eyes narrowed, and the orange giant she wasn't sitting on straightened up.

Jantine's nostrils flared, and it looked like she was about to say something Maranova probably wouldn't like until her boyfriend put his hand on her shoulder. She bit back whatever it was with an expression of distaste, and then let it go when the big orange one with the red-striped head lumbered over.

"No, Jason," Harlan said. "I don't think that's a good idea."

Maranova wasn't sure what was more unnerving. Harlan's half of the conversation, or the big gennie reaching out a hand toward her head. That the brute was more than two meters taller than she was the deciding factor, and she took a step back.

"Harlan, start talking before I have to shoot . . . hell, someone already tried that, didn't they?"

Close-up, Maranova saw that what she had taken for tears in his clothing were actually hundreds of microslug punctures, but the orange skin underneath was unmarked. Somehow, the thought of a telepathic, four-eyed space monster being immune to the only weapon she had didn't make her feel any better.

"It's . . . it's hard to explain, Ma'am."

"Simplify it. That's an order, Harlan."

Even though "Jason" had stopped advancing, Maranova took another step back. Not only did it put her out of his immediate reach, but now he wasn't blocking her view of the other gennies. The second Omega was standing up now, too, with Serene cradled in one of his huge arms like a toy. The girl still had one of Mira Harlan's expressions on her face, but Maranova no longer found it nostalgic or amusing.

"This isn't going to work, Serene. Think about what happened the last time you tried it. The commodore's a lot older than I am, and she doesn't have an active expression. This is a very, very bad idea."

"Harlan . . ."

Maranova drew the name out. She did not like the direction in which things were heading. Harlan was standing in front of her now, arms held up as if to fend off the advancing monsters. Then the sharp-featured gennie who'd been in the biobed earlier appeared beside her out of nowhere, with a long, jagged fragment of ceroplastic in her hand.

Katra, that's her name. She's a Gamma, one of their soldiers.

"Do not make me kill you, Jason. I will not let Mira be hurt again."

When the girl spoke, Maranova felt very old indeed. Although the gennie's voice was soft, when she spoke it was with the tones of a seasoned veteran.

The rest of the gennies weren't any more inclined to challenge her. Instead, they stood at the edges of a ragged circle and tried very hard not to look at the troopers pouring into the room with their weapons drawn.

Harlan spread her arms in an attempt to capture every eye in the room. Maranova felt sunshine on her face, and swore she could taste the most delicious chocolate cake in the universe.

What the fuck just happened?

Maranova wasn't alone in her surprise; half the troopers were lowering their weapons, while the others switched their aim to Harlan. Mira's next words were right out of the Aloysius Martin playbook, and Ykaterina couldn't help but smile.

"Now just hold on, everybody. Let's not do anything we're going to regret later."

MIRA

OH, GREAT. TWENTY MORE BRAINS TO DEAL WITH, AS IF my head didn't hurt enough already.

Mira wanted to grab her slugthrower off her chest, but the borrowed clothes she was wearing were remarkably short on weaponry. Things were going straight to hell, again, and this time she couldn't even shoot back.

Mira kept transmitting her happy memories, wincing at the pain of influencing so many people at once while at the same time forming it into thick blocks for her wall.

≈I could use a little help here, fellas.≈

She could tell Jason was willing, but he and O-6913 were both firmly in Serene's grasp and ready to go digging in Commodore Maranova's brain for the location of Chimera. Part of her wanted to let them try, just to see if the old lady could shrug off their attempts and give them a mental kick in the ass. But the memory of how helpless she'd been to resist Serene's assault, even with the Gamma memories to assist, told her otherwise. Her next words had to be the right ones, and there wasn't a lot of time to figure them out.

"Seriously, no one's going to do anything but Calm. The Heck. Down. This is just a misunderstanding, isn't it Serene?"

The Alpha's face was a stone mask, and the image of her standing on O-6913's open palm with one hand on his shoulder was one Mira would never forget. Especially when Serene decided to ratchet up the tension in the room another notch. If the child was concerned by the troopers with guns, she gave no outward sign of it.

"No, it's not. The humans have stolen from us, and as Jantine says we must have our people back. You may think you're still one of them, but you're not. Don't resist us, Mira. You won't like what happens."

Katra tightened her grip on her improvised weapon, and a few drops of blood seeped through her clenched fingers. Mira didn't think the splintered piece of Mordecai's cane would puncture Jason's chest, but there was no doubt in Katra's mind as to the outcome of the encounter.

She's already planning her second attack, and wondering if she can get to Serene in time before Jantine shoots her.

Mira hadn't seen the Beta draw her weapon, and she had even less idea where she'd been hiding it. The Institute clothing was pocketless, and even Janbi was surprised at the sudden appearance of a pulser in her hand.

≈*Serene, don't do this. Let me talk to them.*≈

≈*No. Better that we die here than do nothing while the sleepers suffer. She knows where they are, or at least how to find out.*≈

"I can't say I think much of your new friends, Harlan. Although your girl Katra is growing on me. What are you going to do missy? Stab him in the eye?"

Jason's face was neutral, but he felt genuine surprise at the thought that Katra might actually hurt him. The commodore's voice was equal parts laughter and approbation.

"No, too much bone behind an eye," Katra said. "One of the ears is better—easier path to the brainstem. Plus, he'll stay in place as a shield while I take your gun."

Jason's tiny mouth fell open in shocked realization of her true intentions. Mira's headache doubled in strength as the Omega stopped his efforts to screen her in favor of defending himself against the Gamma's imminent attack.

"Katra, you're not helping."

"She asked nicely. Just trying to be polite."

The thought of Katra developing a sense of humor was frightening, almost moreso than how efficiently she'd planned to murder Jason with a piece of Mordecai Harrison's cane. The doctor was sitting on a cylindrical container, staring at the rest of his cane on the floor and wondering when she'd broken it.

Mira needed to regain control of the situation, and fast. Unfortunately, her abilities were already pushed to the maximum; anything else she tried would mean even more pain, and the very real possibility that she might lose parts of herself forever.

"Please, everyone, stand down. We don't have time for these games. No one wants this to escalate, and there's still a way for us to work together."

She knew Artemus was moving by the way the troopers shifted their attentions. Despite his size, the Delta was very graceful, and he moved between Jason and O-6913 fast enough to catch even Jantine by surprise. At the end of his maneuver, the Beta's pulser was planted squarely in the Delta's back and all four of Artemus's hands were empty and held up in surrender. Jantine snarled at him, but it was Janbi who ended up being the voice of reason.

"You're all fools. Blind, stupid fools, for convincing yourselves that your small piece of the truth is the right choice for everyone. Doctor Harrison only has one eye, and he sees more than any of you. And I've had just about enough of this nonsense."

Mira's eyes darted around the room, trying to gauge people's reactions to his words. She couldn't help but remember how close Captain Martin had come to talking down the troopers in the launch bay, and how quickly it had all gone to pieces when that pair of doomed techs decided to be heroes.

Janbi was walking very slowly over to Commodore Maranova, with a pleasant expression on his face. Jantine was staring daggers at his back, and Mira wondered what this latest disagreement would do to their relationship.

Now that they're lovers in fact, she probably won't shoot him. Probably. But I've seen a face like the one she's wearing before, and I definitely don't want to be within a kilometer of those two when they have this out later.

Jantine lowered her pulser, crouching to place it at her feet. Even now, she was unwilling to let one of the advanced weapons out of her sight. Her emotions were locked behind her mental barriers, but she did smile as she stood back up. Artemus turned his head to look at her, stretching his lower left hand behind him to rest it on her shoulder. Jantine put her own left hand on top of it, and returned to watching Janbi walk.

"Hello, Ykaterina. I'm Janbi. I'm the smart one around here."

Maranova responded with a chortle.

"Well, you've got a pair of balls on you, don't you boy? Damned if you aren't the cutest thing I've ever seen. If you were about ten years older, I expect Harlan here would snap you right up."

Janbi's face became thoughtful, and Mira voiced yet another refusal.

"Please, ma'am, don't encourage him. He's bad enough as it is."

"Actually, Jantine said she liked . . ."

"JANBI!"

Despite the guns, the threats voiced by Katra and Serene, and the larger questions about their shared future yet to be addressed, the sight of Jantine blushing was something Mira could never have predicted. But the Beta was definitely embarrassed, a more genuine emotion than Mira thought she was capable of expressing at a time like this, especially considering what happened between the two of them up on the surface.

What is it about that boy that makes it so hard to stay mad at him?

Janbi just shrugged.

"The facts are plain enough," he said. "Captain Horace Kołodziejski has gained control of three hundred of our people and ordered them taken to someplace called Chimera. While we do not know exactly where this is, you might. Serene and the Omegas think we should scoop the information out of your brain, but given what happened the last time they tried something like this I don't have much confidence in their plan."

Mira felt Jason's deep shame, and a lesser version of the same sentiment from O-6913. Serene was as guilt-free as ever, but Janbi's reminder was enough to shake the Omegas free of her sway.

At least for now. How does he always know the right thing to say?

"I'm not sure I'm keeping up with what you're saying, boy, but you've all got a lot to answer for."

"Oh, yes, we certainly do. But Jantine is correct; if your officer harms even one of the sleepers, we will kill him. And if his support in your fleet goes beyond the ships I saw a few days ago, he will soon force a war with our Colonies and none of this will matter."

Janbi's message wasn't lost on Maranova, and the commodore set her mouth in a frown. For the thousandth time since he flew off to protect her, Mira wished Captain Martin was still here to advise her. But their shared mentor was, and if anyone could avoid a war, it was her.

"All right, then. Put your guns down, boys and girls. Janbi here's about to tell us what happens next."

Janbi either took Maranova's mockery in stride or missed it entirely. His brain was working faster than Mira could keep up with, and she only caught small glimpses of his thoughts.

They were enough.

"Yes, I am," he said. "Commodore Maranova, I would like to request the use of your personal shuttle, several suits of that powered armor Mira likes to wear, some of your slug weapons, and a uniform that would fit Carlton. Nothing too flashy, just something he can wear without saluting everybody he meets. I'm assuming you still salute in your fleet; I never see Mira do it, but she hasn't had many chances in the last few days."

"Me? Why do I need a uniform?"

Carlton's confusion was echoed on Jantine's and Katra's faces. Serene was . . . pouting? Her expression indicated childish pique, and Mira wondered how many times she'd used it herself.

"Because I can't go to the Moon," Janbi said. "Doctor Harrison says my stump won't heal properly in microgravity."

Mira was glad to see that both the troopers and Katra were lowering their weapons. The difference between them was that even without her encounter suit, Katra could still kill half a dozen of them before they realized she was upon them.

Even untrained, Commodore Maranova's mental barriers were on par with Mordecai Harrison's, possibly even with Jantine's. But she had much less control over her face than either of the others, and when Janbi mentioned the Moon Mira know Maranova was holding something back.

Jantine needed more though, and she stepped in front of Artemus to get a better look at Janbi when she spoke.

"I thought you couldn't pinpoint the source of the coded transmissions?"

"I can't. Not without a few more verified sources. But there are only a few locations from which Captain Martin could have flown his shuttle unaided, and his navigational data shows several journeys in near-Earth orbit. If it was a satellite facility, he wouldn't have needed as many supplies as he had on board, so Chimera has to be on the Moon. However, I still need the exact location, which Commodore Maranova can supply."

"Anyone ever tell you you're an annoying little prick when you're right?" Maranova's grumble wasn't meant to carry, but she didn't have much experience dealing with a Beta's enhanced senses.

"Not in so many words, but yes. All the time, actually. So, Commodore, what's *your* play? Will you help us, or does everybody die badly?"

The commodore turned to Mira, who didn't need empathic senses to understand she wanted to know if Janbi could be trusted. It was a question she'd been asking herself ever since she'd first met the mods, and probably would for some time to come.

Mira nodded, which was enough for the older officer. Maranova turned back to Janbi. The move spoke volumes about her political savvy, and Mira thought that with enough time someone like the commodore was the perfect person to teach Serene some much needed self-restraint.

Assuming any of us are alive after today.

"All right, boy, you win. If you have Aloysius Martin's files, you'll probably figure it out soon enough anyway. But you have to understand that I didn't know about your missing people until just now. I definitely would have tried to stop Horace if I had."

Janbi moved forward and took the cane fragment from Katra's hand, ignoring the blood on her palm. Mira couldn't see any cuts in her skin, so the Gamma's incredible recuperative powers must have returned to full strength.

Janbi extended the piece of cane to Maranova point first, but he didn't let go when she grabbed the other end.

"But you did know about L-A-197, didn't you? Where was your contrition when your people were experimenting on Serene's partner?"

Janbi squeezed the same splintered section that had cut Katra's palm, driving hard shards of ceroplastic into his skin. The pain was enough to overwhelm whatever medication he'd been taking, and Mira felt with him not just this new wound, but the constant ache of his stump. How he was able to keep it from showing on his face was a mystery, but Mira realized that he'd rather feel pain right now than act on his anger.

Then she felt her own rage return, along with another stolen memory. She was finally angry at Serene and O-6913, but also at Trooper Jensen and Kołodziejski and Aloysius Martin for entangling her in this mess. She was angry at her father for taking his own life and leaving her to take care of her brothers by herself.

But mostly, she was angry with Tommy for how he'd hurt her when they parted for the last time, and how he'd taken his rage out on Debbi when Mira wasn't around.

Maranova must have seen some of the struggle in Janbi's eyes, because she stepped forward until the point of the cane was pressed against her chest. "I swear to you, to all of you, that we had no idea what kinds of experiments Horace was doing. A little over five years ago, an expedition commanded by Vice-Admiral James Worthy touched down on a frozen world about 700 light years from here. He returned home with wreckage from a destroyed ship, including the two sleeper units we've been arguing about ever since. When Aloysius told me the other Alpha was dead, I wanted to kill Captain Kołodziejski, then myself for not stopping him."

Maranova looked directly at Serene, as if seeking the child's forgiveness for her subordinate's actions.

"Mordecai over there can tell you I've spent the last few days trying to keep the SDF from tearing itself apart over how to interpret Jantine's transmission. There is definitely a faction calling for total war against the Outer Colonies, and Kołodziejski is its leading advocate."

Now that she could distinguish the deep currents of rage swirling around in the Alpha's complex emotions, Mira knew the commodore would be waiting until long after the sun died before she'd get any absolution from Serene.

"But if this got out, if it gets *out* . . ." Maranova raised her voice, ensuring that the armored troopers could also hear her, "preventing that conflict might be impossible. Time and distance have been keeping you safe so far, but if Kołodziejski's scientists really have weaponized the T-virus, I want it destroyed as much as you do. Earth can't afford another Transgenic War. Not after how long it's taken to forgive ourselves for the last one."

The room fell uncomfortably silent, until Katra stepped up and took the cane fragment away. She twisted her hands, and the ceroplastic shattered into dozens of long splinters.

Mira regained enough composure to form the greater part of her rage into another row of stones for her wall, then buried the rest of it in her gut for later.

"Janbi, what's your plan? From what I remember of Captain Kołodziejski, he's not a very patient person."

"You've got that right, Harlan. So how about it, boy? What do you have in mind?"

Janbi took a moment and looked around the room. To Mira's surprise, all of the mods were waiting to hear what he had to say, and more.

≈*Are you sure about this, Serene? He's not that much older than you are.*≈

The Alpha's answering thought came with a wave of comfort, and a healthy dose of laughter.

≈*As you're so fond of telling us, we're on your planet now, Mira. We should pick our leaders the human way from now on. And despite his arrogance, he is the best.*≈

Janbi stood up a bit taller, and Mira smiled. Serene must have shared their conversation with him, because the devilish smile Mira had been trying to forget was back with a vengeance.

"So here's what we have to do . . ."

BOOK FOUR

MIRA

"COPY THAT, CONTROL. COMING AROUND TO VECTOR six-bravo, velocity ten meters per. Touchdown in three minutes, on your mark."

"Confirmed, Clarke Six. Black King sends his regards to the queen, and requests she join him at her convenience. Over."

Mira cut the circuit, trying not to let her annoyance show. The woman responsible for bringing the shuttle in had either defeated Janbi's scramble program, or some bright-eyed officer was following procedure for a change and looking out a window.

Either way, it meant trouble. Mira turned her head and shouted down the shuttle's main corridor to Jantine.

"Get everyone closed up, we're going to go with the gas."

Jantine responded mentally, and Mira winced. The Beta was completely enamored of using that form of communication, no matter what difficulties it caused anyone else.

≈Noted. I hope the filters on these suits are everything you say they are.≈

Mira sighed, added another stone to her wall, and sent a reply though the pain.

≈Just keep your eyes open and weapons loose. We'll be completely helpless until we're tractored all the way in, and they might already have eyes on us.≈

≈*Understood.*≈

The Lunar surface was speeding beneath the shuttle as Mira sent the disarm codes to the hidden missile platforms lining the approach to Chimera base. Both her instruments and eyes told her she was flying straight into a crater wall, but she was on the beam with no deviation. Since she hadn't been blown out of space yet, the codes were authentic, and there was still a chance that whoever it was on the other end of the comm wasn't mobilizing the entire base against her.

Lots of variables. Still so many things that can go wrong.

"Control, sorry for the confusion. This is Clarke Three, not Six. No flag this trip, just pawns dropping off the mail. But I will convey Black King's regards, over. One minute to surface, the ball is yours."

Mira activated the autopilot and gave a sigh of relief as Chimera's computers took over the approach. She imagined the maneuvering jets firing to slow the shuttle, but she didn't check the instruments to confirm. She was already out of her chair and floating aft to join Artemus on the cargo ramp, sealing her helmet as she went.

Commodore, I sure hope your intel is good on this one. Because we'll make one messy terrain feature if they decide to divert us now.

Mira passed Carlton and Serene standing in the door of a stateroom, breathers on and ready to go. She knew they couldn't see her face inside the helmet, but she smiled at them anyway, knowing that the Alpha would pick it up and relay the sentiment.

Serene was, for the most part, cocooned in a hazard bag, waiting for Carlton to seal her in and carry her down to the mobile containment unit in the cargo bay. It was sweet irony that she'd be the most protected member of their group inside the unit, but completely shut off from the rest of the team while there. Even with an inactive stasis field, something about the unit's construction completely blocked mental communications, something she'd need to remember if they ever had to pull this stunt again.

For now, Mira had to keep her focus on the next few minutes, and the numbers counting down on her helmet display.

≈*Mira, we just crashed into the Lunar surface. It's fairly dark where I am, but I feel quite alive.*≈

From her position on the hull, Katra had a much better chance of surviving the next few minutes than anyone else. Mira was depending on her eyes to tell her when it was safe to act, and part of her wanted to be out there with her. But no one else could fly the shuttle, and despite their combat training none of the mods could pass for a fleet officer over a comm.

"Touchdown, Clarke Three. We have you in the green. Initiating core shutdown. Be advised you'll be on your own for a few minutes—you caught us during shift change and we're still trying to find some loaders to help you."

"Roger that, Control. Tell those crane monkeys there's a little something extra in it for them if they can get me back in the sky in under an hour. I left something simmering back home, and I'd hate for him to get cold, if you know what I mean."

Mira wished her abilities worked over comm lines so she could tell whether the laughter on the other end was with her or at her. Careers were going to end because of this op, but Mira still wanted to keep the body count as low as possible.

"Understood, Clarke Three. Welcome to Echo Base. I'll try and get you back in your own bed as soon as possible. Control out."

Something grabbed the bottom of the shuttle, causing a vibration strong enough to register through both the deck and her boots. The lights went out in the cargo bay, and Mira switched over to her suit's internal sensors while at the same time borrowing the use of Jason's eyes for Carlton and Serene. Artemus was still in his encounter suit, and from her experience sharing Katra's perceptions in the tunnel, she knew the Delta's visor was even better suited than hers to lightless combat.

≈*We are moving through a tunnel now, zero tolerance. I repeat, zero tolerance.*≈

Katra's check-in increased the pain in her head. Mira tried to shove it away, but acting as a communications relay again was stretching herself too thin. Her skull felt like an eggshell, and even though they'd be leaving Artemus and the Omegas behind for a while, this mission was only just beginning.

What Katra was saying seemed right; it made sense that the hidden entrance to a hidden base was the same diameter as a flag shuttle, and not a meter wider.

Even though she worried about increasing the load on her poor brain, she chanced a message to Carlton.

≈*Are we ready?*≈

If there was even one sleeper hidden inside the base, Carlton was the only one of the team who could bring them out of suspended animation safely. And for Janbi's plan to work, he'd have to do it in record time.

≈*She's locked in. Mira, can you explain something for me?*≈

≈*Make it fast.*≈

≈*Serene kissed me on the cheek before I sealed the hazard bag. Is all this kissing going to become a thing?*≈

Mira smiled at the image he unconsciously transmitted with his question, then blinked her eyes when the Alpha's chaste kiss on the cheek was replaced with a very sensual scene of Carlton walking in on Jantine and Janbi while they were having sex.

She wished he hadn't seen that, or that they'd seen him before he backed out of the room. From what she understood about Betas, they'd likely have invited him to join their love-making, and it couldn't have been easy for the emotionally isolated Carlton.

If Mira hadn't known better, everything she almost remembered or had been told about the social structure of the Outer Colonies would identify Carlton as a perfect Gamma. But he was born into a Beta crèche and came from a genetic line of incredibly talented technical specialists. In many ways, he'd had even less choice about his future than Janbi. Even so, only his superior skill with machinery had kept him on the mission rolls once some of his crèche-siblings were selected.

That, and his expendability. One more thing for the two of us to be angry about.

Mira moved closer to Carlton, opened her visor, and put a hand on his shoulder. What she had to say was probably better relayed mentally, but her head was already pounding, and the Beta could probably use some physical comforting.

"It's called being human, Carlton. You'll get used to it, and with the right person it's a lot of fun. I wouldn't worry about Serene, though. She was just wishing you luck, and trying to tell you how much faith she has that you'll keep her safe. I'm going dark now, so tuck in and hold on to something until I give you the all clear."

Carlton sent her a wordless acknowledgment, and she dissolved the sensory link, and the edges of the whirlwind pulled back enough for her to add another stone to her mental wall. It was getting taller all the time, but she kept finding new ways to add fresh layers to the top.

For example, though she needed to keep her attention focused on the base of the cargo ramp, Mira couldn't help but think about Carlton's confused emotions. He said the Omegas had helped him deal with Harren's death, but when she asked Jason about it, the Omega told her that O-6913 had done what was necessary at the time. And since the other Omega wasn't very receptive to her mental communications, she'd let the matter drop.

I definitely need to get all of these kids hooked up with some of Harrison's psychoanalysts. They've got a lifetime of bad programming to unlearn if they're ever going to fit in on Earth.

Mira returned her thoughts to the vibrations under her feet. Whatever was going to happen, it was going to be soon.

≈*Mira. We are approaching a barrier of some kind, and have travelled approximately four hundred meters on a declining slope.*≈

Mira did a quick calculation on the distances Katra supplied and realized that she was missing some information. Despite the pain, she pulled Katra and Jantine into a single conversation, careful not to overwhelm the former lest she lose her grip on the shuttle's hull.

≈*Katra, Can you send me your last clear memory of the crater wall? I'm trying to figure how deep we are, and —*≈

Katra replied at once, not only with the memory she'd requested, but with a real time image of her suit visor display. It was Jantine who provided context, though, and Mira gave herself a mental kick in the backside for not thinking of it sooner.

≈*Seven hundred eighty meters. Janbi interfaced our handhelds with both the encounter suit grav systems and the sensor suites of this Earther armor. I didn't see any reason why we should be as clumsy as the humans, if it comes down to a running fight.*≈

Although she approved of Janbi's initiative, she didn't like that neither he nor Jantine had told her about it, or Jantine's continuing derision of humans as being, well, sub-human.

≈*We talked about this, remember? We're all human no matter what the T-virus has done to us. We have to keep that in mind, or we'll never make this work.*≈

≈*As you say. Perhaps if we survive this mission you can remind me again. Katra, can you see any enemies from your position?*≈

≈*Negative. The barrier has opened, and there is a lighted chamber beyond with a track on the floor and what look like blast doors on the other side. There are neither any visible weapons systems nor any unloading equipment.*≈

The rumbling under her feet stopped, and Katra's head moved enough for Mira to watch the bay doors grind shut after the shuttle was clear. Atmospheric sensors on her visor showed increased pressure in the chamber, and Katra triggered the gas canisters.

As power returned to the shuttle, and the lights came on in the cargo bay, Mira dissolved the three-way link and sent one last message to the group.

≈*Get ready everybody. It's time.*≈

Ignoring the pounding in her head, Mira resealed her helmet, stepped forward, and activated the ramp controls. Through her external pickups, she heard a hissing sound as the shuttle's atmosphere started mingling with the thinner air outside, and sent a silent prayer eighty thousand kilometers into space.

All right, Commodore Maranova. Keep your eyes peeled for our signal, because no matter how friendly we get, we're not going to fit three hundred more people on this boat for the return trip. . .

KATRA

KATRA DROPPED FROM HER POSITION UNDERNEATH the hull to the top of the cargo tender holding the shuttle fast, reinforcing Mira's suspicion that they would not be using it as an escape vessel.

Still on the lookout for enemies, she reclaimed her slugthrower rifle from where it was racked next to the gas canisters, and waited. Jantine would join her soon if the bay was clear, and if it was not then she would find an enemy and kill it.

Katra wished she'd had more time to train with the unfamiliar weapon, but she'd seen enough of them in action aboard the *Valiant* to know the basics. Once Mira showed her how to maintain the rifle, she was as ready as she'd get without several days of living with the weapon.

And if we're not successful in several hours, I won't need weapons or anything else anymore.

There was no need for speculation at this point, either they would be attacked soon, or they wouldn't. At least here they'd be able to see the enemy coming.

As the cargo ramp lowered, Jantine skipped down the ramp with a tight grip on her own borrowed weapon.

Jantine's boots attached to the tender, something Katra had forgotten to do. It was a minor lapse in discipline, but she still didn't trust the Earther suits.

Katra inclined her head to Jantine, who repeated the gesture until the two mods' faceplates touched.

"Anything?"

"No."

The suit pickups recorded the sound of Mira's footsteps on the ramp, and then Katra heard the Earther's voice in her head again.

≈Jason says the securcams are on, but there's no movement in the corridors toward us. And no one's talking to me on the comm channel. We've been made.≈

Katra and Jantine rolled out from under the shuttle and into firing positions, which they held only long enough to verify the landing chamber was empty.

The Earther was already racing for the blast doors, and she pulled a round object from one of the pouches on her hip. Aside from her handheld, Katra's pouches contained only additional ammunition and replacement rifle components, but whatever Mira was carrying opened the doors within seconds.

Katra sprinted for the door, mirrored by Jantine from the other side of the shuttle. But while Jantine continued out into the now-revealed corridor of carved regolith, Katra put her back to the manufactured wall of the room she was in and looked back at the shuttle.

Carlton came rocketing down the ramp at the controls of the mobile stasis unit. It responded to his deft touch like a personal transport, and Katra smiled at the thought of the dour Beta riding into battle atop an armored duo-cycle.

A schematic of the base's corridors appeared on her visor, just ahead of Mira's voice in her head.

≈Jason says he's redirected the securcam feeds and also sent a map to your handhelds. I don't want to know how he did it, just that it worked.≈

≈Confirmed. I see Jantine down the corridor.≈

Jantine sent her own response a second later.

≈Clear. Tell Carlton to come ahead. We have one hundred ten meters of passage secured.≈

Katra waved Carlton ahead. Mira had probably relayed Jantine's order to him as well, but as long as the Beta complied it didn't matter how he'd received the message.

Over his shoulder at the shuttle, she saw Artemus and O-6913 come down the ramp. The Delta took up a defensive position at ramp's base, while the Omega crouched under the shuttle and examined the clamp preventing their escape. It would be good to have more options, and the Omegas had already demonstrated their ability to deal with Earther technology. Once Carlton hummed by on the mobile unit, Katra looked to Mira. The Earther held up a hand with four fingers extended, and started folding them in toward her gauntleted palm. When she made a fist, Katra rolled forward into the corridor, noting that Mira had used her suit's maneuvering jets to clear the blast doors before they closed.

Once on the other side, Katra felt her perceptions expand to include Jantine's, and then she heard the Beta's words in her own voice.

≈*Katra. One hundred meters left.*≈

Katra skipped past Carlton as he glided up to Jantine's position, then she lengthened her strides. It only took a few jumps to reach the next junction, and she used the last one to push off the corridor's ceiling and then activated her boots. She touched down on one knee in a secure firing position, letting the encounter suit inside the powered armor take the brunt of the impact.

She looked down both sides of the corridor, comparing what she was seeing to the map projected on her visor. The right passageway ended in another set of doors fifteen meters away, while the left branch curved around a corner and out of sight twenty meters in the other direction.

≈*Clear. Map is accurate. Do you see the indicator?*≈

Jason had placed a green dot on the nearer set of doors, indicating it as the most likely route to the lab complex. The corridor was almost five meters wide, and much better maintained than the roughly excavated one she was crouching in.

≈*Yes. Mira, we have a path.*≈

≈*Copy that. Before he moved out of range, Jason said he'd try to give us door control, and enough advance warning as he could of troop movements. Ykaterina's estimates have two hundred troopers stationed here, plus an equal number of scientists and a small cadre of fleet officers.*≈

Katra noted that Mira had not said "non-c.
Unlike the *Valiant*, there would be no innocent casualties he.
Just unfortunate ones, and she'd deal with them as they came.
There was more than enough ammunition secured about her
person to handle that many enemies, but she still longed for
the pulsers and energizers they'd left with Artemus to maintain their disguises as troopers.

But we can't use them on this op anyway. Might as well wish for
Crassus, Jarl, and Malik to return to life.

Katra felt a vague sense of unease, and she wondered
if she'd transmitted that last thought inadvertently. But
neither Jantine nor Mira offered any comment, and she
dismissed the feeling as what Mira referred to as "the
jitters." She felt exposed like this, carrying around an extra
hundred kilos of gear and unable to use her active camouflage. But this was the mission, and she'd carry it out to the
best of her ability.

A red light flashed on her visor, and at first Katra was unsure
what Jason was trying to tell her. Words appeared, and the
jitters doubled:

INCOMING COMM TRANSMISSION.

She recognized the voice instantly, even though she'd only
heard it once before. And despite her earlier statements, Katra
felt very real hatred come through the link from Mira, a sentiment she had no problem sharing.

"Hello, Miss Harlan. I don't know what you and your gennie
friends did to our cams and internal sensors, but there are only
so many places you can hide before I'll find you and put an
end to this ill-advised mutiny of yours. Enjoy what life you
have left, and here's a little something to watch while you wait.
Be seeing you."

Though she had never seen Captain Horace Kołodziejski's
face, Katra imagined it was wearing a smug grin. A vid image
appeared on half her visor, and she imagined filling that face
with a few hundred micro-slugs.

A tall, dark-skinned human wearing a uniform like Carlton's
was leaning over a sleeping mod attached to a tangled web
of monitoring devices. He touched something to the mod's

skin, then backed away quickly. Katra saw the shimmer of a transparent shield on the human's face, but her attention was drawn immediately to the mod on the table when the sound of the devices changed from a sedate, rhythmic beeping to a screaming staccato.

Black veins rose under the mod's skin, and he sat up screaming. Katra gasped when his forehead split open, revealing half a dozen black and vaguely eyelike growths. Then his chest burst open, heart and lungs extending outward on a blackened arm of flesh.

Mercifully, the screaming stopped, and the mod slumped forward over his legs. The devices switched over to a continuous tone, but the horror had not yet ended. The body kept twitching for several more seconds, skin cracking open over the veins and oozing dark fluid.

"Two hundred and ninety-three more to go, Miss Harlan. See you soon."

Katra dropped her rifle and removed her helmet just in time to avoid filling it with vomit. Luna's lower gravity sent her vomit bouncing everywhere, but she didn't care. All that mattered to her now was surviving long enough to reach the human in the vid and kill him with his own poisons.

Katra spat the remnants of her last meal from her mouth and used alternating fingers to blow her nose. When she was done, she heard something moving behind her, and she grabbed her rifle as she spun around to face it. But she misjudged the distance and forgot that her boots were magnetically locked to the metal floor. The rifle went sliding forward on a tide of vomit, leaving her empty-handed and on her back, staring up into Carlton's shocked face.

≈*He doesn't know. Mira, don't share that transmission with Carlton! He can't know that his—*≈

The three-way link dissolved before Katra could finish her warning, but over the direct connection she had with Mira came a painful jumble of images and feelings. Arid landscapes, lightless caves, and the taste of something sweet and frozen spun around a male Earther face that she never could make out before it faded away into another memory.

A fresh wave of nausea punished her chest, and as she lay coughing, Carlton's eyes went wide behind the transparent lenses of his breather. The Beta had climbed down from the mobile unit and was kneeling beside her, turning her head to the side. Katra caught a glimpse of Jantine bounding up the corridor before a new series of images began whirling inside her head.

Loss and pain Katra could deal with, she'd known more than enough of both in her short life. But there was something deeper binding Mira and the Earther together, and every time she caught a glimpse of his face it got worse. Finally, Mira returned to the images of the mod's death, but instead of the body on the table, she was focused on the dark-skinned man.

Katra watched as a lifetime of faces stacked together: smiles and frowns and shouts and ecstatic utterances. She felt content and scared and resolved and unhappy, until the faces solidified into a cruel glare of hate hidden behind a shimmering mask.

Jarl died in her heart all over again, but this time it was much worse. It was as if Jarl was on the table, while Horace Kołodziejski's mocking voice rang in her ears.

Mira's emotions vanished from Katra's head, leaving behind the deepest disappointment she'd ever known. But what confused her wasn't the sentiment; it was Mira's mental lament.

≈*Oh, Tommy. How could you?*≈

SERENE

≈. . . DON'T CARE IF IT'S SAFE OR NOT, GET HER OUT *of there. . .*≈

Serene's eyes widened at the first thoughts she'd detected in many minutes, and at the thumping sound that came through the top of the mobile unit. It was peaceful inside the doubled obfuscation of biohazard bag and isolation chamber, and for the first time since she'd awakened from deep sleep, she was alone with her own thoughts.

Mostly alone. The memory shards in her head were urging her to practice mental defenses, but all Serene wanted to do was play. Little Mirabelle Harlan was her favorite shard, and the two girls had danced in virtual sunlight often since the mission started.

Serene felt bad about having stolen the Gamma memories from Mira, especially since the longer she had them, the more indistinguishable they became from her own. Jason and O-6913 didn't want to tell Mira the process was irreversible, since it shouldn't have been possible for the human to get them in the first place. But as the hours and days went on, Serene knew that to rid herself of them would likely kill her.

And I so very much want to live.

The murmuring almost-voices in her head went silent, waiting for more input to start formulating Serene's next actions. From what Serene could tell from Doria's memories, the shards hadn't been this insistent with her, but the Gamma had also had a first class crèche system on Colony D preparing her for her role as a facilitator.

That was supposed to be us. Our colony, mine and L-A-197's. The first one attempted after the Earthers exiled us.

According to Commodore Maranova and Captain Martin's files, L-A-197 had died a year ago, most likely somewhere here in Chimera base. With so many other people in her head, it was hard to remember his features, but that didn't make her miss him any less. All she could summon were vague impressions, which kept forming themselves into images of Mira's father.

≈*—st do it, Carlton. We can't get the unit through this room anyway . . .*≈

The thoughts had no real "voice" to them, but Serene thought they were Jantine's. They didn't have the guarded chill she was used to in the Beta's mind, but Katra was much more direct in her statements and rarely dwelled on her words before speaking.

And Mira shouts all the time. Still, I should thank her for being able to hear them at all. I won't thank her for the headaches, though. Those are no fun at all!

There was a hissing sound above her, and the pleasant darkness outside her bag became a murky gray. A mod-shaped shadow broke the homogeny, but from the nature of its thoughts she already knew it was Carlton.

A very, very nervous Carlton.

"What's wrong? What's happened?" Serene said.

Her voice was muffled by the emergency breather, but as Carton undid the seals on the hazard bag and lifted her out, the device fell away to the floor. Serene watched it drop lazily to the sterile metal panels, then bounce up nearly to his knees.

Wherever they were, it was cold and dark and a little bit scary. She clung tightly to Carlton until he set her down on the floor, and it took a few seconds to pick out Jantine, Katra, and Mira's thoughts from the humming machinery around them.

When Carlton didn't answer her, the Gamma memories decided he either hadn't understood or didn't want to tell her. One of the shards suggested disciplining him for his lack of obedience, but Doria's counseled patience.

"Carlton, what's going on? Where are we?" Serene asked.

Her voice was louder than she'd intended it to be, but she didn't detect anyone else present besides Mira and the mods. There was something else nearby, though, something almost as omnipresent as the humming.

"We've found the sleepers," Carlton whispered. "Most of them, anyway. Jason's trying to get an accurate count now, but he and Artemus are having a bit of difficulty with O-6913."

His words let her put meaning to the shapes surrounding them. The containers were far too small to be the sleeper units she was familiar with, but the deep, unformed dreams of those within resonated inside her. These were Carlton's people, and somewhere in the darkness were some of his crèche siblings.

Carlton's excitement was tempered by fear, but his thoughts were unreadable. Sometime in the last few hours, Mira must have helped him with his control. Doria approved, several of the shards tsked, and a few others let their appreciation of Carlton's fine jawline momentarily cloud their judgment.

Serene pushed away all the other voices in her head save for Mirabelle, who really never left. What she wanted to say was nothing any stern, half-remembered mentor could help her with, but having a friend "nearby" made her less afraid.

But still, I have to ask.

"Are any of them my people?"

Carlton's emotions shifted to a dull shame tinged with dread, and she knew his whispered answer before he gave it. Despite days of close contact, the Beta still wouldn't look her directly in the eyes. In fact, he was looking pointedly away from her face.

"I don't think so, Serene. From what I understand, the units are all the same."

It was a slim hope, if any. She knew that the humans had only found two viable suspension chambers in the wreck, but they did like to keep secrets. She nodded and held up her hand to Carlton.

The Beta stared at the floor, uncertain as to what he was supposed to do. She folded her fingers into her palm several times, and sent him an image of herself holding his hand while they walked. Carlton shrugged and took her hand, but was neither pleased nor displeased to have physical contact with an Alpha.

So very different, this century. So much to learn.

Carlton led her carefully through the maze of units, pausing briefly at each one to scan its ID code. As they walked, Serene felt Jantine and Katra's emotions getting stronger, but nothing from Mira.

This made her frown, and Carlton must have noticed. His fear increased slightly, adding her possible displeasure to his ever-growing list of worries.

"What's wrong, Serene?"

Serene had several answers at the ready, but the one she most wanted to give was one she was sure he wouldn't understand. She wanted to speak directly with Mira's mind and gain some mature context, but the woman had closed herself off completely.

Serene settled on her third most pressing problem.

"I still don't know what's going on. Why are we being so careful?"

Carlton knelt down beside her. At first she thought he was finally going to talk to her as an equal the way Mira and Jantine did, but instead he rubbed away a spot of grease from a metal plate to reveal a mod designation.

Serene wanted an answer to her question, and the longer she had to wait, the more the memory shards directed her actions. She sent a probe at the sleeper's mind, surprised at how easy it was to decipher his true identity. The plate gave her his designation, but with the shards' help, she learned his identity much faster than Carlton could access the colony manifest through his handheld.

"TRN-G272489-A prefers to be called Trahn. Agricultural workers should not be your concern right now. What are you not telling me, Carlton?"

Serene's voice rose as she spoke. Not quite to a normal conversational level, but enough to indicate she was serious. Carlton's fear jumped to the front of his mind, and she caught a glimmer of his thoughts as he hurried to answer her question.

≈—at am I supposed to do? Mira, can you hear me? Hello?≈

"The humans know we're here, but not exactly where. Jantine wants us to be as careful as possible until we can secure this area."

Serene gave Carlton a hard stare, fighting the urge to force him into a straight answer. In the end, she borrowed from both Doria's and Mirabelle's memories for the right response.

"Carlton, you're scaring me. Please tell me what it is that you are afraid of. It's all right, I won't be angry with you."

Before the Beta could answer, a sound from the darkness sent his fear to new heights. She caught a terrifying image of a giant machine crawling on the ceiling, and of herself running as fast as she could from whatever else was hiding beyond the next row of sleepers.

But that fear was tempered by the arrival of Katra, who held out her right hand to Serene without lowering the Earther weapon in her left. It bothered her a little that Carlton was almost as afraid of the Gamma as the killer machine in his memory, but then she realized it was the powered armor Katra had on over her encounter suit.

He thinks she's an Earther!

Then Katra's faceplate lit up from within, and Serene could see her smiling. All the voices in her head save for Doria and Mirabelle were on a high state of alert, and Katra's carefully modulated words did nothing to calm either them or Carlton.

"Come with me, Serene. Carlton, Jantine says this room is secure. Get started."

Doria's memories helpfully supplied that Gamma infiltrators spent more time in their encounter suits than any other mod, and even wearing an Earther hardsuit over it, Katra was probably capable of some amazing feats. Mirabelle just wanted to put one on herself.

Serene didn't want to leave, not until she had an answer from Carlton. Mirabelle supplied an image of planting her feet and refusing to move, but Katra's gentle tug got Serene's feet moving, and rather than be dragged along, Serene hurried to keep up.

≈*Katra, what is Carlton afraid to tell me?*≈

It was much easier to speak directly to Katra's mind than to use words. Mira, real Mira, had said it was because Katra had a "highly developed super-ego."

≈*He doesn't know for sure. We haven't told him what we saw, but purpose of this base is to experiment on mods, and that frightens him.*≈

Serene pondered this for a few seconds, with the Gammas screaming in her head for more.

≈*Show me.*≈

Katra obliged her instantly, supplying not only the horrifying image of the human injecting the mod but also the effect it had had on Mira.

Several things Carlton had said made more sense now, especially if his unconscious intuition was working toward the truth Katra had just revealed. If the three soldiers had been shutting him out, he was bound to know something was going on, and it was only a matter of time before he figured it out.

≈*He's almost there now. Was there something special about that mod? And have the Builders seen this?*≈

Katra and Serene emerged from between two sleeper units to see Jantine and Mira crouching on either side of a clear pressure door. In the room beyond, the human from Katra's memory was standing in front of a workstation and looking in the other direction. Serene felt nothing from him, but she had access to Mira's memories, and knew much more about him than sight alone could tell her.

Thomas Sullivan Watson. Mira's Tommy. And given what he did in the transmission Katra shared with me, I can understand part of why Mira is so upset right now.

Jantine and Mira crouched at the door, and Serene could tell from their thoughts that they were ready to rush in. Beside her, Katra crouched down to Serene's height, and looked at the Alpha for several seconds before her visor went dark. In those moments, Serene saw that the Gamma's smile had changed, and her thoughts now had a distant feel to them.

≈*Yes, and yes. We're about to deal with both, provided Carlton can get us a little bit of backup.*≈

Serene didn't understand what Katra was saying at first, but then she saw it. A stray image of the Gamma rolling into the room with her weapon firing—not to kill, but maim.

She means to punish him. Good. But if I've learned anything from Mira, it's that punishments must be tempered with mercy, and we'll need to keep him alive long enough to figure out everything he's done.

Besides. Mira always liked Tommy Watson. At least, I think she did.

A quartet of new minds came to life behind her. They were hard, and cold, and Carlton was more than a little afraid as he spoke the words she'd heard after emerging from deep sleep.

"MAR-G250698-I. YHS-G267980-I. HJR-G259612-I. KAR-G262234-I. I am CRN-B3410-T. What are you called?"

This more than anything made up her mind. Today, everyone would live. The newly awakened Gammas needed to see the best of humanity in action, and a revenge murder, however justified, did not exemplify the life in the Colonies she remembered.

Maybe the ones that exist today are different, but I think we lived better lives when I left Colony B. And Mira has certainly shown us how to make more of ourselves than our genetics.

Mira stood up and slapped a device with red and green lights to the side of the door, and an energy field Serene hadn't seen dissolved into a shower of golden particles as it opened. Serene picked that moment to run forward, just ahead of Katra's grasping hands. Jantine tried to stop her, but Serene dropped to the floor and slid feet first under her arms.

Once inside the room, Serene rolled up to her feet and ran at Tommy's legs. She felt, not saw, Mira standing in the portal's empty entrance, more from the flashes of anger given off by Jantine and Katra as they were forced to lower their weapons.

Tommy was half turned around when she hit him in the knees, and the expression on his face was more tired than anything she'd seen in Mira's mind. He was a decade removed from their walks along the river, and the lines around his mouth and eyes spoke to a life lived not in happiness, but despair.

Tommy went down in heap, interrupting whatever had been mumbling into his throat recorder. Even though he outmassed her considerably, the moon's gravity had clearly taken its toll on his muscles, and Mira's memories painted him as more wallflower than warrior. He bounced hard both against his workstation and the floor but remained conscious enough to gasp out two words:

"Help . . . me . . ."

The lights in the room started flashing, and an alarm sounded. But she was close enough now to do what she wanted, and aided by Mirabelle and Doria, she slid easily into his dazed mind and turned it off.

≈*Sleep.*≈

It took her only a few seconds to find what she needed from his brain, and another to figure out how to make his mouth work.

"Alarm off. Secure from containment. I slipped, nothing more. We have enough people here to handle things."

≈*What are you doing?*≈

Mira's thoughts were relieved, incredulous, and shocked. Serene turned toward the doorway and saw Jantine and Katra push Mira to the side. Jantine won the skipping footrace to Tommy, and she hauled him up by his uniform. She shoved him roughly into his console, but Serene's mental hold on him was absolute.

And although the Gamma shards as a whole were aghast at what she'd done, Serene caught the slightest glimmer of approval from several of them.

Looks like I can do something right on my own, at least for now.

Though Serene was expecting questions, she didn't expect Jantine to shout at her.

"What did you do? What were you thinking!"

Serene stood and took several steps away from Jantine, who was trying to shake Tommy awake. He was aware of what was happening to him, but unable to react in any way.

"Jantine, please stop. I'm sorry if I disobeyed, I just didn't want Katra to shoot him. Not in front of Mira."

Jantine's furious thoughts quickly returned to the cool, neutral state she worked so hard to maintain. But before the Beta could speak, Mira's voice reminded Serene there was still a lot about humans she didn't understand.

"Oh, honey," she said, "you have no idea what he's done. Not just to the mods, but to me personally, and to the people I love. Tommy is nothing to me but a handful of good memories and several I wish I could forget."

"But, the river. . ."

"Was a long, long time ago. And while you think you understand that memory, you're far too young to really know what . . . "

≈Katra, NO!≈

Mira's ability to control others was not as precise as Serene's, and Katra was fighting her every step of the way. She raised her rifle slowly, and Serene knew that even though it might destroy her, the Gamma was prepared to kill all of them for a clean shot at Tommy's unprotected head.

"He has . . . to pay . . ."

Everyone seemed to move in slow motion, and the lights dimmed a second time. There were no alarms this time, and Serene felt another four minds join those in the sleepers' chamber.

What have I done? And how can I stop it before it goes too far . . .

JANTINE

JANTINE STARED AT THE WHITE SUIT OF EARTHER
armor containing Katra, more specifically at the weapon in
her shaking hands. She'd never seen a Gamma this far out of
control, and if Jantine couldn't bring her back from the edge
it was unlikely either mod would live long enough to see
anything else.

*Is it too much to ask for just one thing on this mission to go
according to plan?*

"He has . . . to pay . . . for what he did."

Katra's voice over the suit's speakers was ragged, as if she
were fighting herself for each word. Given Mira's fixed stance,
outstretched hand, and abrupt mental silence, it was reasonable to assume Mira was somehow holding her in place.

"Katra—"

"No. Mira. No more forgiveness. He and his captain have
declared war on my entire people. He will kill all of us, and
that includes you. We have to stop him!"

Jantine saw herself and Mira mirrored in Katra's faceplate,
and she realized that Katra was staring down a reflected image
of herself in Jantine's. Whispering inside her helmet, Jantine
hoped things had settled down enough in the landing bay for
someone to come to her rescue.

"Jason, Artemus. I need you."

As soon as she spoke, she regretted not including O-6913, but it was hard to think of the Omega as an ally at the moment. That he cared for Serene was plain enough, but his loyalty to the rest of the mods was more than a little suspect. sJantine raised her hands to the suit's neck seals and released them. The inrush of cold air was just what she needed to help focus, and she turned back to face down her de facto second-in-command.

Mira and Katra hadn't moved, though the Gamma's rifle was still struggling upward. Before Jantine could move forward and disarm her, Serene padded forward in her ridiculous Earther shoes and pulled the muzzle of the slugthrower up until it was pointed at the center of her forehead.

It was exactly the distraction the newly awakened Gamma infiltrators needed to swarm Katra and immobilize her. Unlike Serene, they'd entered suspended animation fully mature and in peak physical condition, and the more modern sleeper units had been conditioning them for Earth's gravity for nearly a month. Even if she'd had complete control of her body, Katra was no match for eight other combat Gammas in their primes, especially when they picked her up and held her off the ground.

Mira slumped against a metal table that looked a lot like the one in Captain Kołodziejski's transmission. But Jantine had little time to wonder if it was the same surface, as Katra was now in full control of her mind once more.

"Release me at once! I am Senior Scout KTR-G245980-I. That human is a war criminal, and he must be executed immediately."

The Gammas holding Katra were a mix of genders and crèches, and though they were older by a few years, several reminded her strongly of Jarl. But while Jantine didn't know all of their faces as intimately as Malik would have, they certainly knew hers.

One of them worked the seals on Katra's helmet, revealing her wide eyes and snarling expression. The Gamma's hair was slick with sweat, and Jantine thought she detected a faint odor of bile.

The Gamma who'd removed Katra's helmet looked up from the disheveled mod in front of him, meeting Jantine's eyes from across the room. Ignoring Katra's curses and threats, he spoke in a strong, clear voice.

"Commander? I am MAR-G250698-I, called Marius. Carlton tells me that we are inside a hostile Lunar base. What are your orders?"

"Put her down. I have the prisoner under control. Serene, how long will he be like this?"

"He'll wake up whenever you want him to. Hello, Marius. Hello Yesha. Hello Hajira. Hello Karen. Hello—"

"You stupid girl, there's no time for this. He has to *die!*"

Katra surged forward, this time using her full, suit-assisted strength. But Jantine was prepared, and she met Katra's charge not with strength, but leverage. She grabbed a wrist in one hand and caught her under the shoulder with the other, using her own momentum to spin the Gamma into Mira's waiting arms. Mira reached down and touched a control on Katra's belt, and its gauntlets and joints locked into place.

Katra had knocked Serene to the floor as she passed, and it took all of Jantine's self-control not to backhand the Gamma. But the memory of Janbi's ruined face was enough of a reminder of how ragged her own emotions had been over the last few days.

Mira's voice sounded in Jantine's head, and for a second she shared in the entirely righteous rage that had consumed Katra. She felt her hand tightening on the Earther pistol in her hand and decided to return it to the holder on her chestplate.

≈*Katra. Katra. Listen to my thoughts. Let your anger go. This is not our way. I'm here with you. It's going to be all right.*≈

Jantine returned her attention to Marius and the awakened Gammas. One of the new arrivals was helping Serene up from the floor, and Jantine was about to thank him when she noticed his face wasn't quite right.

It was a mature face, not a fresh-faced mod just out of deep sleep. A human face, pressing a very human device against Serene's neck.

"You are a very bad man, and soon you will be dead."

Serene's words were calm and controlled, but Jantine could feel fear rolling off her in waves.

"How sweet. You gennies always say such nice things. I'll assume this is my missing test subject, and that's Harlan over there in the sealed suit, yes?

Horace Kołodziejski was as loathsome in person as Jantine had imagined. He was a thin, shifty-looking man, who'd somehow acquired a Colonial jumpsuit identical to the ones the Gammas were wearing. Given the transmission he'd sent out, it didn't take much imagination to figure out where it had come from, and as he pulled Serene close to his body Jantine saw a designation on his chest that made her blood run cold.

DRN-B34316. That would make the mod in the vid one of Carlton's sibs. . .

Jantine's jaw clenched, and she silently cursed herself for putting her weapon away. Marius turned at the sound of the human's voice, and Kołodziejski startled at the motion and backed himself into the wall. As quietly and with as little movement of her lips as she could, Jantine mouthed, "Not yet. Wait until she's free," and the Gammas took a step back.

Now that she could see Kołodziejski's face, she wondered what his plan really was. Despite his stolen garments, no one would ever mistake him for a mod. His face was too angular, his eyes too close together. In general, he gave off the impression of a skeleton trying to push its way out of an ill-fitting suit of skin.

Is he trying to escape? To free the other human? What's his play here?

Mira must have been thinking along similar lines.

"You won't get away with this, Captain," Mira said. "Commodore Maranova is—"

"A cloud of expanding atoms by now, I expect. When last I checked, she was flying blind straight into the teeth of my best two ships. And don't you lot get any ideas, you've seen my new T-virus in action, and I'm more than a little curious to see what it does to your little Alpha here."

Kołodziejski couldn't have frozen the mods in place more effectively if he'd used liquid nitrogen. Even Jantine was afraid to act, and she had no doubts whatsoever that the human would kill Serene anyway if he felt he had the upper hand.

But for now, she's alive. And he's not going anywhere.

The scenarios she could see resolving weren't at all to her liking, so Jantine decided to consult with her more level-headed advisors.

≈*Serene. Mira. Can you hear me?*≈

≈*Yes.*≈

Mira's thoughts were tinged with pain and fear, but Serene's were as cold as ice.

≈*Yes. Don't worry, Jantine. Help is on the way.*≈

≈*What?*≈

Before Serene could answer, Kołodziejski started sliding along the wall toward the portal to the sleeper chamber. To her dismay, the crowding Gammas parted and let him pass. Katra gave out a strangled moan, and Jantine's heart raced.

Then Jantine heard two clicks in her left ear, followed by Artemus's breathy rumble.

"Commander, I'm sorry. He got away from me and Jason. We're almost—"

The scattercom squealed in her ear as a competing frequency came into range. She spared a look around the room to see if anyone was using an Earther comm, and in the split second her eyes left the doorway, O-6913 appeared crouching on the other side.

The Omega's face was a mask of fury. Jantine's eyes widened, and she was opening her mouth to scream when she heard the hiss of the injector.

"I warned you gennie freaks, and now this is on y—"

Kołodziejski's head exploded in a spray of bone and blood as the Omega's hands came together. Serene slumped to the floor, and it was Katra who voiced the scream in Jantine's throat.

O-6913's mouth was open, and the interference in her ear climbed beyond her ability to register it as anything other than pain. Jantine felt her heart skip in her chest, and denied the double protection of SDF armor and Colonial encounter suit, her exposed face grew uncomfortably hot.

She dove behind the instrument console the dark skinned Earther had been working at, pulling his unresisting form after her. On the floor and out of the direct path of the Omega's ultrasonic scream, she felt its effects subside. It felt like a fire was burning inside her left ear, but her vision was unaffected and unblocked, giving her an ant's eye view of the very messy end of Captain Horace Kołodziejski.

Not satisfied with simply beheading the murderous human, O-6913 seized his corpse in his large orange hands and squeezed. Blood fountained from his neck and bounced off the ceiling, and when the Omega pulled his hands apart, what was left of Kołodziejski separated with them.

Katra's screams continued, and Jantine turned to look at the Gamma. Her face was red and flushed as well, but Jantine could do nothing to help her.

≈*StopstopstopstopStopSTOP!*≈

Whether Mira relayed her order, or the Omega heard it himself, O-6913 slumped to his side and closed his mouth. Katra's screams became sobs, and fell to her knees as Mira deactivated the suit restraints. Mira's own suit fell away from her as she raced to Serene's side, and Jantine recognized the emergency release system Mira had shown them during their suit training. Hard plates bounced off the floor as she took two short hops across the blood-drenched room.

Jantine returned her eyes to Serene's still form. The child was covered in human blood, her chest wasn't moving, and an angry red welt was spreading on her neck.

Jantine heard two voices rise above the growing confusion. The first was Mira's, calling for Carlton. But the second was a stranger's, and it took her a moment to realize it had come from behind her.

"What happened?"

A cold rage built behind Jantine's eyes, and she drew the pistol on her chest as she rolled over to face the scientist. He was still groggy from Serene's mental control, but he recognized the muzzle of a weapon pressed into the back of his neck well enough.

"Shut up, human. Or you're next."

MIRA

MIRA KNELT DOWN NEXT TO 0-6913, WATCHING Carlton work furiously to transfuse a barely conscious Serene with a device attached to his arm. That Serene wasn't dead already was a good sign, and the lack of black veins or exploding organs meant that either Kołodziejski was lying about what was in the injector, or that Tommy and his team of mad scientists had developed more than one T-Virus variant from the captured Alpha's blood.

Damn you, Tommy. Damn you for ever making me believe you cared about anything but yourself.

"Get back. All of you."

Artemus's basso rumble drew Mira's attention, and she saw him push through the group of Gammas crowding around Carlton while he worked. The Delta's voice was enough to deter most of them from interfering, but more than a few were offering to help, and the confusion over what had really happened was whipping them into a frenzy.

I can't do this. There's just too many of them.

"Mira . . ."

Serene's voice was barely a whisper, and from the scowl on Carlton's face, her brief return to consciousness wasn't what he'd hoped for. There was an SDF emergency kit open beside him, and the Beta was filling an injector with a green liquid of some kind. Mira had vague memories of an emergency medical seminar during which the instructor had warned about certain compounds that were only to be administered as a last resort.

The noise of the crowd intensified, as did their thoughts. Mira closed her eyes against the pain, but if dealing with a double handful of mods over the last few days had been stressful, several dozen was overwhelming.

"Mira . . . help. . . him . . . You need . . . to—"

Carlton pressed the injector to Serene's upper arm, and the child's fear spiked. Serene's eyes widened, and her unfocused panic was stronger than that of the crowd. Despite the pain, Mira reached out and brought both of them into a link. She regretted it instantly, but she borrowed some of Carlton's impossible calm to help her through the worst of it.

"Carlton. Wait. Let her finish . . ."

The Beta's eyes narrowed, but he paused.

"There is no wait, Mira. I'm going to lose her if I don't intubate. Plus, the longer she's awake, the worse her pain gets. It's already making the rest of them crazy, do you think we can deal with them if she dies?"

Mira's thoughts went immediately to Serene. She knew it was bad, but through Carlton's eyes, she saw just how close to death the child was. But Serene's fear of the injector was stronger even than her fear of death, and the Alpha bolstered Mira's efforts to remain calm. O-6913 seemed to relax a bit as well, but the Omega's shattered mind threatened to suck Mira in at any moment.

≈*Think about clouds, Mira. Big, white, fluffy clouds. That's all they need right now, something to distract them. But you have to help O-6913. It's all too much for him, what he did, what he wants to do. You have to—*≈

The injector hissed in Carlton's hands, and Mira felt the child's mind floating away.

"Dammit, Carlton! Not yet! Serene, I can't do this on my own. I don't know how—"

≈*Yes you do. You just don't . . . remember . . .*≈

Mira screamed as thoughts and images from over a dozen lifetimes exploded in her head.

Again. And this time, she had Serene's memories of the last few days as well. She was vaguely aware of Carlton yelling, but she couldn't make out the words over the rush of information trying to find a home in her already battered brain. It was worse this time, much worse, and even though all of her own memories were settling back into familiar places, they didn't quite fit the same way as they once had.

Mira collapsed onto O-6913's chest. That she no longer heard every stray thought in the room was a small comfort, but the continuing chaos in the Omega's mind was mounting a serious challenge on her renewed mental defenses.

So she thought about clouds instead. Billowing, fluffy clouds, dancing across the sky and sparkling in the sun. Above them was the deep blue of a Colorado sky over the mountains, and the feel of the wind in her hair as she sailed an ultralight over the plains helped smooth out the rough edges of two dozen very scared mods.

The storm in O-6913's head dissipated, as did the rumble of the crowd. Mira felt another mind nearby, and she opened her eyes to see Jason staring down at her, his right hand extended for support.

Mira smiled and sent him her thanks, taking another small pleasure in his realization that for the first time communicating directly with her mind didn't include pain. With the Omega's help, she sat up and took in the room.

Artemus had pushed the Gammas back, and on the other side of the crowd, Jantine had Tommy sprawled facedown on the floor with one slugthrower pressed into the middle of his spine and another against the back of his head.

A fresh wave of anger toward her former lover almost undid her newfound calm, but the Gamma memories were back and offering suggestions about how deal with her emotions. Mira found it amusing that almost all of them suggested using her rage to build a wall, and then went a step further by expanding her previous efforts to include a courtyard, a moat, and a grand dining hall.

If I'm going to save a princess, I might as well have a castle.

Carlton rolled Serene onto her stomach and began massaging her lower back. Despite O-6913's distress, and the very real possibility that Serene might die from whatever had been in the injector, it was Carlton and Katra who were Mira's immediate concerns.

The Beta was sweating profusely, and though his hands were fast and sure as he worked to keep the Alpha alive, his emotions were running wild. Mira recognized the symptoms; she'd experienced them herself when Jason activated her latent T-Virus. Whatever Serene had done to give her back her memories must have affected him as well, and there wasn't anything she could do to help him with the extra voices in his head other than to continue projecting an aura of calm she didn't share. His thoughts were more focused than ever, and the one that was foremost in his mind was also in Mira's.

She looks so small . . .

Katra was on the verge of fighting her way through her own people to kill Tommy, and although Mira mostly agreed with her, she owed it to Serene to find a peaceful solution.

"Katra," she said, "please come help Carlton. You can't do anything there."

The Gamma turned to her, incredulous, as if by even suggesting that she not carve her way through the press of bodies and wring Tommy's neck Mira was guilty by association. But after a moment, Katra's thoughts fell into a pattern that Mira had learned to associate with risk assessment.

"Trust me," Mira said, "he will face judgment for this. But if we kill him now, no one will ever know what he's done. I claim his life—for this, and other harms done to me."

Katra's eyes widened, and Mira wasn't sure if it was her use of "we" or "me" that most affected the Gamma. Whichever it was, Katra approved, and the visions in her head about what she wanted to do to Tommy were enough to add a drawbridge to her castle.

Mira drew back into herself, clinging desperately to Jason's towering sense of identity. Now that she was whole again, or at least mostly so, she could finally appreciate the incredible journey the Omega had taken in the last few days. From being the elder statesman of a doomed expedition, to a marginalized outsider, and back again to a trusted counselor, his transformation rivaled Janbi's in its completeness, and the Omega still didn't consider himself exceptional.

My friend, will you help me again? Our brother needs us.

In lieu of an answer, Mira found herself on a broad white plain, with her castle at her back and Jason by her side. The child version of O-6913 was several meters away, blurring in and out of sight. Mira reached one of her hands up to Jason, who shrank until one of his hands was barely larger than hers. Hand in hand, they walked forward and knelt beside O-6913's flickering form.

One of O-6913's arms was stretched out, and Mira opened herself to his perceptions. She was already accustomed to the confusion and pain in his mind, but she was not prepared for the thought-image he was trapped inside.

Kołodziejski was alive, and threatening Serene once more. But the Alpha's face kept shifting, becoming Crassus, then Jarl, then Doria.

"It's not his fault, you know," said an almost-familiar woman's voice from behind her. "He's so young, to have all this thrust upon him. His mind is shutting down, and you have to help him move on."

Mira expanded her perceptions until she could see the speaker without taking her eyes off of O-6913. To her surprise, it was a young girl with dark eyes and a wide smile whom she'd seen only in other people's minds.

"Doria?"

A slim boy about as tall as Jantine appeared next to Doria and spoke. "She worries a lot, doesn't she. It's a shame that she can't accept her strength."

"Hush, Malik. She's still alive, still finding her way. The clarity we have is denied her. For now."

Mira manifested another arm so she could take one of O-6913's hands in two of her own without letting go of Jason's. Drawing on the experience of the Gamma shards, she left the greater part of herself with the Omegas, and let her inner self rise up out of her body.

Mira turned, reveling in the freedom of an unencumbered mind. She could go anywhere, do anything, but she fought the urge to spread herself across the universe. Standing naked above the Omegas and herself, she was finally free to confront the one voice in her head that all of her friends wanted to hear.

"See," said Malik. "She understands now. Can we go?"

"No, Malik. We still have more to do, and in any event, I must stay behind."

"That hardly seems fair. Let the living sort out the living. Haven't we done enough?"

Mira smiled, taking in the truth of Malik's words. The image of Doria smiled in return, and the memory of the Beta dissipated, flowing back into her subconscious mind where it belonged.

"Hello, Mira. I'm Doria. I'm glad you're here to help my friends. None of this is your fault, but if I'd known of your existence, I'd have approved."

Doria floated over to Mira, impossibly beautiful and far more corporeal than a memory had any right to be. Mira felt awkward and ashamed and unworthy in comparison, until Doria touched her on the shoulder, and Mira realized that all her doubts were holding her back from a deeper understanding.

Doria flowed into her arms, kissing her neck and whispering into her ear.

"It's all right. I'm here with you. And we have work to do."

Mira had no idea how long they stayed like that. In the mindscape, it could have been a heartbeat or a lifetime. She had no memory of breaking their embrace, but her next thoughts were of O-6913, and how weak his thoughts were.

The Omega was still reaching out for Serene, Crassus, Jarl, and the rest, but he could no longer articulate his desires. Mira felt a sense of deep responsibility for those deaths, and when O-6913 recognized the tenor of her thoughts, she sensed his inescapable guilt.

"It's all right," said Mira. "Doria helped me, just as you did. We're all here with you now, and you don't have to face this alone."

Serene's three-day old sense of self separated from Mira, keeping one hand on her shoulder and reaching toward the Omega with the other.

"I'm going to be all right. He was a bad man, and if you hadn't done it, one of the rest of us would have. It's not your fault, and no matter what happens, we will be together always."

Mira wondered how much of Serene's words were her own, or carried over from the Alpha's inexpert attempt to heal her. Doria's image knelt beside Mira, and guided her hands to the Omega's face.

"Rest now, my friend. Let us carry your burden for a while, until it is time to pass it on."

Doria and Serene and Mira and a dozen other memory shards took form and placed their hands on the dying Omega, taking away his pain and confusion and sifting through all of his happiest memories. Mira saw her Doria-self as a child, reaching up with a shaking hand to greet him for the first time. Saw Jason pulling him from the floor of the crèche and enveloping him in a warm sense of belonging, explaining to him about Jantine and Janbi and Carlton and Katra and Artemus. As Mira watched O-6913 fade away, Doria hugged her, pulling all the parts of her mind back into one coherent whole named Mirabelle Agnes Harlan.

Kneeling alone in front of her castle, Mira spoke to no one in particular. "He should have had a name. Serene never needed one for him, and he didn't want the rest of us to know. But I refuse to remember him as Grumpy. He deserves better than that."

"Mira Darling, we all do."

The sound of her father's voice filled her mind, and despite the pain of her last memory of him, she looked up to see Captain Emmanuel Rogers Harlan in his dress blacks.

"There's my girl."

"Daddy, I—"

"It's all right, Mira Darling. I'm always here, just like Doria and all the rest. Ask us for help, and we'll give it."

Mira stood, now wearing a set of her own blacks. Mira thought she could see Captain Martin peeking around the corner of her castle, but she kept her attention on the man who was never there.

"Daddy, I'm not sure I can do this. I'm not a Gamma, not like she was. They need more than I can give them, and even though I have the memories, it's just too hard."

Emmanuel gave one of his infrequent smiles, and Mira saw more than a little of Brian in his face.

"I thought you understood, daughter-mine. Of course you're not a Gamma. That's not what they need. You're an Alpha. A new kind of Alpha, just like the rest of them. Jantine, Carlton, Katra, Janbi, they're so much more than their programming now, and it's all because of you. You've shown them another way to live, a way to choose their own futures.

"Jason will help you make them understand, as will Serene. But you have to go back now. She doesn't have much time left, and Carlton will need help understanding what's happening to him."

Mira knew he wasn't real. She knew her father was ten years dead, and that Doria and Aloysius Martin and Malik and all the others were just memories trying to help her get by. But the thought of letting her father fade away into white nothingness was too much to bear, and she crushed him to her with all her strength.

"I love you, Daddy. Please don't leave me alone again."

"You're not alone, Mira. I'm with you, now and forever. But you have to go now, before it's too late."

Emmanuel Harlan's embroidered chest melted away, shifting into a bloody and tattered coverall. Mira looked up into O-6913's face, and a despite the chaos around them, a sense of absolute peace spread through her.

"Goodbye, Brian. I forgive you."

The Omega's thin mouth closed in a smile, something his living flesh could never do. Then he was gone too, leaving her alone.

No. I'll never be alone again.

The real world snapped back into focus around her, but this time the chaos of the lab was well within her ability to cope. The hurricane in her head was gone, and everything was exactly as Mira had seen it last.

Damn.

"Carlton?"

≈Mira? I'm losing her. I can feel her slipping away. Doria says not to worry, and Harren is here and—≈

≈I know. It's going to be all right. I'm here with you. Here's what we have to do.≈

JANTINE

"MARIUS, KATRA, HELP US GET HER ON THE TABLE. WE don't have much time."

Mira's sudden order startled Jantine, and she nearly pulled the triggers on her weapons. It wasn't that she'd have minded killing the human, but Serene and Mira seemed to think he was worth keeping alive, and he was probably the only one left alive who knew what was in that vial.

From her vantage point, it was hard to see exactly what was going on, but then a crowd of legs parted and Serene rose up from the blood-soaked floor in Carlton's arms.

≈*Jantine, are you with me?*≈

≈*Yes, Mira.*≈

≈*Take a couple Gammas and secure Tommy in the next room. If the information Serene got from his mind is correct, there's maybe a dozen personnel left on base, and only a handful are troopers. The rest are either away in Tycho City, or launched with the* Indomitable *a few minutes ago.*≈

Jantine pulled one of the hand weapons away from the human's back and returned it to its place on her chestplate. Using her now-free hand, she grabbed the human's neck and pulled him from the floor. The room spun around her, and she altered her stance slightly to adjust for her damaged ear.

Still pressing the other weapon into his back, she leaned in and gave her best impression of Jarl's threatening whisper.

"One wrong move, and you're dead, human."

Whether out of fear or enlightened self-interest, the human complied, letting Jantine turn him away from the carnage and push him toward an exit on the far side of the laboratory.

Jantine gestured for two of the Gammas to follow, then shoved him a shuffling step forward. Even with the room spinning around her, Jantine was more graceful than Tommy, though being unable to hear out of her left ear would be a problem in a fight. She felt blood running down that side of her face, and wondered if Janbi's miracle doctor could build her a new ear.

"Open it. And no tricks, or you'll join your captain in whatever hell you two have made for yourselves."

The human raised a shaking hand to the door panel, but he paused before activating it.

"He wasn't my captain. He made us . . . this isn't what we set out to do. You have to believe me, I never meant to—"

Jantine smashed his face into the door and shoved the gun into his back so hard she worried that she might push it all the way through.

"Intentions mean nothing, human. I saw what you did. No one had a gun to your head, though if you'd prefer that I'll be happy to comply. Now open the door, or I'll pull this trigger and leave you to drown in your own blood. One more death isn't going to matter today."

The human's fingers fumbled blindly with the panel, opening it on his second try. The door opened, and he fell through into a sparsely furnished office. Keeping her weapon trained on him, Jantine waved one of the Gammas forward to cover the room's far exit. Jantine tipped her head toward the other mod, careful not to take her eyes off the blubbering human on the floor.

"What are you called?"

"Yesha, Commander. Are we going to execute this human?"

"No, please! It's not my fault!" Tommy whined. "They made me do it. I was trying to help you, honestly! Oh, God, please don't kill me pleasepleaseplease . . ."

"It's always excuses with you, isn't it Tommy?" Mira's voice from the doorway was flat and hard. "Never your fault. Well fuck you and your excuses. This time, you're the helpless victim, and it's us women who are in charge. Tell me where the antidote is, or I'll let Katra come in here and finish what she started."

"M-Mira?" The man—Tommy—sounded surprised to see her.

"Yes, that's right. M-Mira. Are you going to give me an answer, or do I have to go into your mind and rip it out?"

Jantine's eyes widened, and she turned away from the human to gauge Mira's intentions. The look of pure fury on her face was more pronounced than it had been at their first meeting, and even Jantine was surprised when she stepped forward and hauled Tommy to his feet.

"Well? Nothing to say? Oh, that's right, you don't speak Decent Human Being, do you? Only Chickenshit. Well maybe this will jog your memory."

Even without her suit, Mira was stronger than most humans, and her slap knocked his head back. Her next blow was a punch to his midsection, then her knee smashed into his groin. He dropped to the floor and curled up into a sobbing ball, but Mira wasn't done with him yet.

"Where is it? Where is the antidote! If that girl dies, they'll tear this system apart, and the universe will run red with blood. Tell me where it is!"

Mira punctuated each sentence with a kick, the last one coming dangerously close to the human's neck. He was barely able to speak, and what words he did get out weren't what she wanted to hear.

"I'm sorry . . . I'm sorry . . . I'm sorry . . ."

"Mira. Enough."

Mira spun around, rising half a meter from the floor. The look in her eyes was familiar, and when she spoke it struck Jantine that this is how she must have looked when she was beating on Janbi.

"It will never be enough, Jantine." Mira waved a hand at the man on the floor. "This. . . this thing doesn't deserve to walk around like a human being, not after what he did.

Serene's going to die if he doesn't help us, and I'm about out of options."

Jantine gave her weapon to Yesha, and then stepped forward to place a hand on Mira's shoulder.

"There has to be another way," she said. "You taught me that."

"No. Not with him. He deserves all this, and more."

"I don't underst—"

"Commander?" Yesha's voice drew Jantine's attention back to the man on the floor. "He's trying to say something."

"Only had ... one dose. Kołodziejski barged in, grabbed ... Couldn't stop him. Please, don't hurt me anymore. There isn't any more ... please ..."

Even with only one working ear, Jantine could make out what the human on the floor was saying, but Mira's perceptions went beyond the purely physical. From the look on her face, the human was telling the truth, but his words made no sense.

"Mira, what's he saying? I don't understand."

Mira shook off her hand and started back toward the other room. There was some sort of commotion behind her, and Jantine was tired of not knowing what was going on.

"Yesha, keep that safe for now," she said, gesturing to the human on the floor. "I'm sure we'll have more ... questions for him in a minute."

"Yes, Commander."

Jantine followed Mira, and part of her was pleased by the grim smile on the Gamma's face as she passed. Yesha had clearly enjoyed Mira's abuse of the human, and Jantine wondered if she'd have felt any different a few days earlier. She certainly hadn't cared when Katra struck Captain Martin, and this wasn't much different.

What was it Jarl had said at the end? I have to do better.

Mira was standing just inside the doorway, looking at something in the laboratory. Jantine slid around her, and saw Serene was sitting up on the table, arms around Carlton's shoulders and crying. Katra was crying too, something Jantine never imagined was possible.

"You bastards. You had no right." Mira's voice carried across the room, and Serene turned at the sound of it. Her eyes were red and puffy, and her skin several shades darker than it had been just minutes before. But what grabbed Jantine's attention were the child's eyes. Brilliant blue eyes, set in an otherwise unremarkable human face.

Understanding came in a flash, and Jantine was torn between weeping and returning to the office to finish kicking Tommy to death. But it was Mira who said the words aloud, and when she did everything changed.

"The injector. It wasn't the virus, it was the antidote. But the active strain in her blood . . . our blood . . . it didn't distinguish between the two."

Across the room, Carlton nodded, his own eyes brimming with unshed tears.

"Yes. Congratulations, everyone. The humans finally found a way to reverse the effects of the Transgenic virus."

MIRA

MIRA COULDN'T BELIEVE THEY'D ACTUALLY DONE IT. Captain Martin had hinted at the possibility of a vaccine, but not a cure.

They've created a more terrible weapon than the virus variant that that kills instantly, and they have no idea what a good job they've done. We have to shut this place down, and pray no other samples have made it off the base.

If she didn't have the memories of an unchanged, happy, and transgenic Serene in her head, Mira would never assume the little girl in front of her was ever anything more than human. Her head was rounder in shape, and her eyes near copies of Mira's own.

My old ones, anyway.

Mira was almost afraid to be near her, ashamed of her birth planet, of Tommy, and the uniform she once wore with pride. But Serene's need for companionship was apparent even without empathic abilities, and Carlton had no experience with human children.

At least, none of his own. Not sure how I feel about being on intimate terms with him as well, but we'll figure it out, in time.

Mira stepped forward, glad that she'd shed her armor earlier. The Gammas had removed the Omega's—Brian's—body, but Kołodziejski's blood still coated most of the exposed surfaces in the room, including Serene. When the little girl leapt awkwardly into Mira's arms, the impact was enough to force her back a step.

Mira just held her, letting Serene cry herself out against her neck. Nothing she could say would make up for what she'd lost, just as there was no real way for Serene or Brian to apologize for ripping apart Mira's mind.

If she hadn't given them all back, my memories would be lost now. But thanking her seems so petty, and no matter what, I still love her. How can I not? Like she said, I'm a part of her, and she of me.

"What do you want to do, Serene? How can I help you?"

≈*Can you still hear my thoughts?*≈

Serene gave no response to either query, and Mira did not press her for one. She could remember now being cold and scared and feeling like the world was ending, and although there was no going back for Serene, she was still part of a larger community that loved her.

Larger. Right.

"Carlton, I need you to take Serene for a while."

"Why?"

"Jantine, Katra, and I still have some work to do. Artemus and Jason can help you deal with her, and I'm sure some of the sleeper Gammas can as well."

Mira could tell from his reaction that Carlton hadn't thought of that possibility. She wanted to tell him it was going to be okay, but if experience told her anything, it was that there were a dozen other voices in his head giving him advice right now, including one that sounded a lot like her.

Mira shifted her right arm to support Serene's weight, and used her left hand to gently pry the girl's arms from around her neck. As she'd expected her to, Serene resisted, burying her face into Mira's shoulders.

"No, I want to stay with you."

Even her voice is different now. So young.

"I have to go, Serene. I still have work to do. But when this is over, I promise we'll spend time together, all right? Just you and me, for as long as you like."

Serene sniffed, and she pulled her head up to look at Mira's face. It could have been a trick of the light, but her hair looked a few shades darker than before, and Mira had an urge to ruffle her fingers through it.

"Can Jason come, too?"

Mira gave in to her impulse, adding a smile to the action.

"Of course he can. If he wants to. Jason's got a lot of work to do as well, helping Carlton with the sleepers, but I think he'd like that. Can you be strong for me until I get back?"

Serene sniffed again and nodded. Mira nodded back and offloaded her into Carlton's waiting arms. He laid her down on the biobed and gave her a mild sedative. Serene tucked her hands under her head, closed her eyes, and fell asleep.

Carlton looked up at Mira and smiled.

"I don't think I'll ever be able to do that as well as you."

"Well, I've never done it before just now, so I think you'll be okay. Whatever you do, don't let her out of your sight. There are still hostiles in the base, so don't use any tech you're not sure of. I might be out of mental communication range, so send a Gamma to ask for help if you have to."

"All right. Hurry back."

"I will."

Katra bristled at the side of the room, and her thoughts were easy to read. She wanted to kill something, or specifically, someone, for what was done to Serene. Kołodziejski was dead, so Tommy was the only target left for her anger.

And since I just kicked him half to death, it wouldn't take much to finish the job. We'll have to leave by the other door.

Mira collected the scattered pieces of her armor and began reassembling her hardsuit. The emergency shutdown she'd performed didn't seem to have damaged any of its components, and while she snapped the familiar white and red pieces into place, she watched Katra for any change in her demeanor while keeping a cadence in her head.

Right shin, left shin, front and back. SDF troopers got the knack.

Right thigh, left thigh, up the leg. SDF enemies gonna beg.

By the time she'd finished, Jantine had reclaimed both her helmet and Katra's, but the Gamma refused to take it from her. Instead, Katra withdrew the supple black hood of her encounter suit from a hard pouch and pulled it over her head. A second later her visor appeared from another pouch and snapped into place without ceremony.

Jantine simply shrugged and put on the glossy white helmet that matched her suit. When Mira pulled her induction pistol from her chest plate, both Jantine and Katra did as well, following suit when Mira checked the ammunition canister, triggered the acceleration module, and watched the indicator light cycle from amber to green.

Awarding each of them forty points for following proper weapon discipline, she nodded to her new strike team and prepared herself for action. They might not win the Clarke Cup, but Mira would take them at her back any day.

"All right, ladies, let's go."

Jantine fell in behind her, but Katra didn't budge. Mira was two steps from the portal leading to the sleepers' chamber when Katra voiced her objection.

"No. There are still threats here."

"And Artemus and eight other Gammas to deal with them," Jantine said, speaking up faster than Mira expected. The Beta was back in command mode, at least for a little while.

"I . . . we need you with us. And after the beating Mira just gave that one," she said, hooking a thumb over her shoulder, "he's not going anywhere for a while."

Katra scowled and remained where she was.

"There are still at least a dozen people in this facility," Mira said. "I don't know what side everybody's on yet, but I do know that they can't lie to me. And if I can save more lives today, I have to at least try. Serene sacrificed a lot to get us this intel. We need to put it to good use. I need you at my back to do this, can I count on you?"

Katra simply nodded. Her scowl did not diminish, but at least she started moving. Then, proving that she was always paying attention, Katra triggered a belt control and her hardsuit came apart as she took her first skipping step, and her second one carried her past Mira into the sleeper chamber.

There was a clattering sound as the induction pistol hit the floor, and Artemus tossed her both a pulse rifle and a Colonial hand weapon. The latter disappeared almost instantly, then a second later there was a shimmering effect as Katra passed one of the suspension units. A second after that, she melded into the darkness as if she'd never existed.

Mira formed a three-way link between herself, Jantine, and Katra. The other mods were calm and focused, and they sent her their readiness for orders. Mira was pleased that their emotions no longer threatened to crack her skull open, and she moved into the larger chamber with Jantine a step behind her.

≈*Jason's map indicated a control chamber one level up. Katra, do you think you can find it?*≈

A wordless affirmation was the Gamma's only reply, and quicker than Mira expected, she slipped out of her mental communications range. All Mira could do was follow, pausing at the corridor entrance and scanning the opposite direction for anything Katra might have ignored.

There was nothing there.

≈*Jantine. I hate to even ask it, but can Katra hold it together?*≈

≈*Of course. Katra's the best. It's why she's here. Jarl was better at takedowns, but no one matches her on patrol. Those mods back there are going to be the best trained infiltrators this side of the colonies.*≈

Jantine's response was tinged with amusement, and Mira was pleased again to note that it held none of the contempt it might have a few days earlier.

Is this my command, then? I still feel like an SDF officer, but other than Commodore Maranova, everyone from the fleet I've met since leaving the Valiant *has pulled a weapon on me. They've branded me a traitor, and if being a patriot means associating with trash like Kołodziejski and Tommy, I don't think I even care.*

The realization of her fall from grace stung, but Mira heard Emmanuel's chuckle in the back of her mind. If her mental father figure approved of her choices, then the rest of the fleet didn't matter.

As they approached an autolift, Jantine pulled up short, and through her eyes Mira saw a different view of an emergency panel Mira had seen earlier and dismissed. She'd entirely missed the pattern of scratches Jantine had seen from meters away, and Mira resolved to enroll herself in Katra's scout school when this was all over.

≈What does it mean? Does she want us to follow, or is it a warning? None of my mod memories are combat-related.≈

≈You're doing fine. We follow. This is one of Jarl's marks, actually. She really cared for him, and I guess this is her way of keeping him alive. I'll lead for now.≈

Mira still remembered the depth of Katra's pain from the few seconds she'd let it overwhelm her that first night, and the echoes of it when they'd spoken on the train. Mira had never met Jarl save in battle, and she still didn't know if any of the slugs that killed him had come from her guns.

If Jantine was still grieving for Jarl, or any of her dead, it didn't show. Her mind was focused on the task at hand and nothing else. The panel came off the wall easily, indicating Katra hadn't secured it from within. This part of the base wasn't on Jason's map, but Jantine skipped ahead into an accessway of pressure-sealed moon rock as if she'd been walking it for months.

Each new set of nearly invisible scratches she saw sent them moving in a different direction, until the map overlay appeared again in Mira's visor, just as Jantine finished climbing a slanted shaft to the next level. Katra's position was marked, just out of communications range.

≈Jantine, wait up.≈

The Beta paused at the top of the shaft for Mira to join her, then turned her head toward her. Mira leaned close and touched faceplates, only speaking after verifying all her comms were off.

"We've still got a long way to go, haven't we? To trusting one another, I mean. Until now, there's always been another goal, someplace we had to be and reasons why we couldn't talk about what's happened and heal."

"Mordecai Harrison said something to me before we left. I was angry at Janbi for staying behind, angry at you and Serene, and a bunch of other things that aren't important.

"Harrison told me that each of us makes our own universe and peoples it with our own fears. He said that the reason why

I was angry, why I'd lost control not once, but twice, is because I didn't believe in myself. Not my abilities, or training, but myself. And until I did, I'd never be the person I wanted to be."

It didn't happen often, but when Jantine spoke like this, Mira could see why the Colonial Alphas had shaped an entire generation of mods to follow her.

Jantine gestured at a section of wall with three small dots carved into it, each smaller than the other.

"This way, but quietly. Use your abilities."

Mira tried to keep her steps soft, wondering if her maneuvering jets would exceed the sound threshold Katra was trying to maintain. She thought about Harrison's once-removed advice, and then remembered another conversation she'd had with Jantine.

Or, more accurately, one she'd had with Doria.

≈*Do you remember what Doria told you, about what to do when things go wrong?*≈

An image of herself and Jantine sitting in folding chairs while the Omegas worked behind them formed in Mira's mind, and she shared it with Jantine. She felt Jantine's appreciation of her effort, tinged with a bit of sadness.

≈*Yes, and that's exactly what sprung into my mind when he said it. I was trying to be strong, but nothing was working right. I hated Janbi for how well he was adapting, and I loved him and feared him at the same time. But Serene was right: he's the best of us, and he was meant to be the person I turned to for help.*≈

Jantine crouched at a corner, her hand a few centimeters away from a curved, arrow-like symbol. Mira could feel Katra moving in and out of the edges of her perception, and sent her an acknowledgment. To her surprise, it wasn't the Gamma who answered, but Carlton.

≈*What is it? Are you back already?*≈

Mira's eyes widened, and she checked her location in the visor display. They'd traveled almost six hundred meters from the lab, well beyond her normal range.

≈*Carlton, how are you hearing me? Is Serene . . .*≈

Mira didn't even know how to ask the question, but Carlton supplied the answer she was looking for anyway.

≈No. She's completely virus-free, even the normal human variants are missing from her system. As for empathics, other than surface reads, I can't get anything from her. Harren says. . . Sorry, I'm not used to this.≈

≈Hold on for a second, will you? I'm with Jantine. Jantine, did you hear Carlton just now?≈

≈Carlton? Why would I . . . is he in the tunnels with us? Has something happened?≈

Mira tried to make sense of what was going on, but before she got anywhere with her thoughts, Katra came back into range and sent words and images into the shared link.

≈I have five hostiles in hardsuits guarding a collection of civvies and one female SDF officer. How soon can you tell me who to kill?≈

Mira sat down in the passage, trying to concentrate. She and Carlton shared more than an ability to communicate and read emotions. They shared the *same* ability, and more than a few of the same memories to boot.

And if I'm right, perhaps something else as well.

≈Carlton, I know the answer's probably yes, but do you still have Serene's scans from the Institute on your handheld?≈

≈Of course I do. Why?≈

≈Tommy's . . . that lab should have a genetic sequencer. You should run a scan of yourself and compare it to those readings. And mine, if you have them. Wait till I contact you to give me the results—I have an idea about what's going on.≈

Carlton sent her an acknowledgment, and then his thoughts disappeared as suddenly as they'd arrived. There'd be time enough to puzzle out why she was connected to the Beta like this later. Katra and Jantine needed her full attention right now.

≈Katra, what's your position?≈

≈One hundred ninety-five meters from you. That's your range, yes? The humans are thirty meters from here.≈

≈Copy that. Head back over there, we'll be up with you in a minute.≈

Jantine started to move down the passage, but Mira reached up and grabbed one of her arms. She held her still until Katra was back out of range. Jantine sent her caution and surprise, but she stopped anyway.

≈*They can wait a minute. What did you do? Did Mordecai say anything else?*≈

≈*I told him about Janbi. About who he was, both to me and the Colony. Can you see it in my mind? I don't want to get the words wrong.*≈

≈*I'll try. I've only ever done it with the Builders, so if it hurts you have to let me know.*≈

When Jantine signaled she was ready, Mira opened her mind, and pulled Jantine with her onto the white plain. They appeared standing at the edge of Mira's mind castle, bare feet resting on green grass. Mira was surprised to see a second towering structure nearby, and also when Jantine's hand reached out to touch her face.

There was a look of wonder on the Beta's face that never seemed to reach her real one. Her hand was cold, like glass, but it warmed instantly when it moved across her skin.

"I like your new face better. But this one is all right, I guess."

Mira smiled, and Jantine did the same. She looked younger in the dreamscape, as if the cares of the real world never touched her here. Unlike Mira's castle, Jantine's tower was built to keep things in, and there were no doors.

"Who you are here is who you are inside. It's the universe Mordecai was talking about, created by your thoughts and desires. Just think about him, and we should—"

An image of Mordecai Harrison appeared beside them, mouth open as if frozen mid-sentence. Jantine raised her hand to touch his face, and the old man's mouth pulled back into a smile.

"Good. It's not right to be alone. My wife and I were together for almost eighty years. In all that time, I never felt good enough for her, and when she died I was lost for a while."

Mordecai's voice was warm and soft, and it seemed to fill all the space around them. His right hand gestured to his eye patch, and then down to his leg. Jantine mirrored the gesture, and her lips were moving when he spoke again.

"We caught the men who killed her, who did this to me. They were separatists. Young fools who didn't want old men like me telling them what to do with their lives. They killed my wife and burned my body, and instead of doing the same to them we locked them away and put happy thoughts back into their heads.

"But no matter how long they live, no matter what kind of productive lives they might someday lead, Almira will still be dead, and I had to let her go before I ended up the same way.

"My universe is full of possibilities, and if you want to be more than whatever thoughts were stuffed in this fragile thing . . ." Both Mordecai and Jantine reached up and poked the other in the forehead, ". . . you have to forgive yourself for being alive. It's not your fault. You didn't choose to live, you just did. And if you're anything like your young man over there, your universe is going to be a very, very interesting place."

Mordecai smiled, and his face faded away into whiteness. Jantine rose off the ground, arms stretched wide, and she flew around Mira in ever tightening circles before touching down in front of her.

"I've always wanted to do that. Your hardsuits, they can fly, yes? Once you learn how, that is."

Mira laughed, remembering her very similar urge the first time she went out on the *Valiant*'s hull. She and her team were there to check on power conduits, but every one of her people was watching to see what she'd do. Instead of giving them a show, she'd given them orders, saving her zero-g acrobatics for the Fleet Games.

"Oh, yes. And so much more. So what are you going to do?"

"Janbi wants to live on Earth. He wants us to be old, and tell people what to do. But I want this, all of this . . ." Jantine gestured, and the mindscape became the blackness of space, with stars and galaxies blazing in all their glory.

"And Janbi. He was right about that, too, when he offered to let me go. But I want him, so I'll kill more people and fight as hard as I can until I can be with him again. I believe in me, in him, and us. And you as well, so you'd better be right about who we can trust."

Mira returned the mindscape to white, and then dissolved the link and returned them back to the Moon. According to her visor, only a few seconds had passed, which boded well for Katra's mood. Mira released Jantine's arm and carefully stood up.

≈*Well, let's go see about that.*≈

JANTINE

JANTINE SETTLED IN NEXT TO KATRA'S SLIM FORM, wishing she'd thought to shed her Earther armor as well. With full respect for Mira, it was awkward and bulky, though there were a few features she wished to try out someday. The maneuvering jets for one, but once interfaced with her handheld, its sensor suite was truly impressive.

As she shifted to get a better look at the rendered scene on Katra's handheld, a spike of pain from her ruined left ear made her wince, and an accompanying wave of vertigo caused her to lean into the Gamma. Luckily, the humans below them were too busy arguing with one another to hear the two mods tumble into the side of the passage, but it was definitely more noise than she'd intended to make while observing them.

≈*Jantine, are you all right?*≈

Through the three-way link, she saw Mira's view of the pressure door leading into the compartment, and could also feel Katra's concern and fierce devotion to her. The Gamma set her handheld down and helped return Jantine to a crouching position. After a moment, the dizziness and pain subsided, and she returned her attention to the surveillance.

≈*I'm fine. Another of them is gesturing at the door now, but the civvies are still in restraints. I don't think the female officer is with them, given her posture.*≈

In truth, it was hard to tell anything from an image rendered from ultrasonic sensor data, but Jantine had made do with less information in the past. The armored humans were definitely arguing, and the others were either tied to chairs or refusing to leave them.

≈*I'm definitely picking up mixed emotions, but it's hard to distinguish who's who from this side of the door. I'm going to have to get line of sight for an accurate read. Are you two ready?*≈

Katra nodded, powering down the handheld and stowing it in a thigh sheath. She checked her pulse rifle's charge one last time before turning on her active camouflage, and faded from sight.

True infiltrators like Katra didn't simply blend in, they *became* the space they inhabited. Jantine had never been this close to an active system before, at least not one she was aware of in advance. The urge to poke Katra to see if she was still real was strong, but their mission had to take precedence.

And since I'm the distraction of the hour, I need to focus on the fact that while there are only a couple of drawn weapons in there, all of the enemy are probably as heavily armed as I am.

The natural passage the two mods were in was separated from the mechanical crawlspace above the control room by one of the omnipresent magnetic grates the Earthers used to build this base instead of proper grav plating. It was easily removed, allowing Jantine to slip into the crawlspace and move forward to retrieve the sensor Katra had placed earlier.

It was impossible to tell exactly where Mira's thoughts were coming from, but the Earther's eyes told her she was about a meter away from the pressure door leading from the main corridor to the control room.

It was Mira's eyes she needed now, or more accurately, her experience.

≈*I'm in position.*≈

Jantine was lying prone next to a gently humming machine, and she imagined the air it was circulating running over the skin of her suit. While she had no direct information on where the people in the room were, all of them had to breathe something, and once she installed the gas canister, the humans in suits would either have to come up here through the maintenance hatch into Katra's line of fire, or open the hatch and step into Mira's.

≈*Okay. Jantine, press the red switch on top of the unit, and then pull the handle on the side toward you. The control center's systems are independent from the main base recyclers, and with that many people moving around down there, the CO2 alarms will go off almost immediately. They'll revive as soon as they're exposed to fresh air, so we'll have to move fast.*≈

≈*It's cycling now. And Mira?*≈

≈*Yes?*≈

≈*Thank you for letting me fly.*≈

Mira's answer was the memory of a smile. Jantine edged forward on her elbows until she was at the edge of the maintenance hatch, and then she drew her induction pistol from the chest plate before lying flat again.

≈*Something's definitely happening in there. Tempers are flaring, and . . . the hatch is opening! Get ready to go in.*≈

Katra appeared at the hatch with her rifle in one hand and the release handle in the other.

≈*Go, Go, Go!*≈

At Mira's signal, Katra twisted the handle and threw the hatch open, and Jantine slithered down into the room. One of the armored humans pointed a weapon straight at her but was shocked enough by her appearance that she was able to easily knock it out of his hands and force him to the floor.

The suited human at the door took a step forward then fell flat on the floor, and Jantine felt Mira's satisfaction through the link. Another was turning to see what happened when Mira's external speakers sent her voice booming into the room.

"This is Lieutenant Commander Mira Harlan, ordering you to stand down. I know some of you don't agree with Captain Kołodziejski's methods, and you probably already know that there is a fleet in orbit prepared to utterly destroy this base unless you comply. Put down your weapons and deactivate your hardsuits, and you will not be harmed."

≈*Mira, which ones can I shoot?*≈

≈*None of them, it seems. Jantine dealt with the leader, and the three still active don't want to be here any more than we do.*≈

Jantine smiled at Katra's flash of disappointment. The Gamma dropped to the floor, and a moment later the humans followed Mira's order. Jantine removed her helmet, relishing the feel of cold air on her face.

"Identify yourselves for the record."

The three standing troopers kept their attention on Mira as she came into the room, following her weapon with their eyes as she waved them toward the wall. Once they were up against it, she aimed the pistol at the chest of the man on the far left. He swallowed noisily before answering.

"Sergeant James Hardesty," he said.

The other two quickly followed suit.

"Corporal Nils Mikkelson."

"Corporal Janice Walters."

Katra moved to the black-clad human woman sitting at the control console and shoved her roughly to the floor. She came to rest awkwardly on pieces of the troopers' discarded armor, but she made no move to adjust to a more comfortable position. Jantine shot Katra a questioning glance.

"She was about to activate a control," Katra said. "Now she cannot."

Jantine shrugged, then collected weapons from the floor and tossed them out into the corridor. When she reached the other side of the room, she turned and looked at the humans who were still seated. As they'd suspected, all six were secured to their chairs with their hands behind them. Some sort of clear material held their mouths shut.

≈*Mira, what about these civvies?*≈

≈*Two of them are, or rather, were Kolodziejski's spies. The woman on the floor had a spike of fear when she heard my name, I think she's the control officer I was talking to before. She wants to tell me something, but she is terrified of Katra.*≈

While she couldn't sense Katra's underlying emotions like Mira did, the Gamma's response gave Jantine a fairly good idea of what she was feeling.

≈*Good. Shall I shoot the spies?*≈

Jantine was only mildly surprised by Katra's bloodlust, but it had been a trying day for everyone, and the Gamma's opportunities for physical release had been few.

≈Not just yet. We want them to confess first. Jantine, there's a belt control shaped like a . . . I forget sometimes. It looks like this.≈

Mira sent an image of a pair of slightly raised concentric circles, and of her hand turning it two rotations to the left. When Jantine turned the first of her downed opponents over to reach it, the man's face was slack and lifeless. Assuming he was somehow incapacitated by Mira's abilities, she activated the control as she'd been shown, and the man's suit went completely rigid. She picked him up and moved him away from the uniformed woman on the floor.

Once he was safely out of reach, she removed the helmet from the second, revealing a bald, dark-skinned woman. Jantine repeated the process, then stood where she could see both the corridor and the humans standing against the wall.

"So, who wants to tell me their story? My friends and I have come a long way to hear it, and we appreciate your cooperation.

≈Jantine, Carlton is sending Artemus and three Gammas to our position. He also wants to know how you're feeling.≈

≈I am fine. You will tell me about how you know this when we are finished, yes?≈

≈Of course. We're still trying to figure it out ourselves, but I don't think it's something you need to worry about. It may be . . . no, I don't want to speculate.≈

Jantine sent Mira her confidence and looked down the corridor for the other mods. But an unfamiliar voice behind her brought her attention back to the uniformed woman on the floor.

"Your fleet? It's gone. We recorded a massive explosion a few minutes ago, about the time we lost contact with the *Indomitable*. But we had nothing to do with that, I swear. And the whole time I was talking to you before, that pig Washburn"—the uniformed woman said, gesturing to the trooper Jantine had disabled—"had his pistol jammed into my ear. When I couldn't raise Captain Kołodziejski, he went crazy, and sealed us all in here."

Mira didn't directly acknowledge what the woman was saying, but Jantine had a sense of great sadness from her friend that could have meant several things. She hoped that whatever it was that was bothering Mira was something she'd share before too much time passed.

Katra moved forward and nudged the woman toward the other humans, and she crawled over without further complaint. As she moved, Jantine noted an angry bruise on the side of her face, far too developed to have been Katra's doing.

≈*Jantine, the Lieutenant on the left wants to say something. Take the tape off his mouth.*≈

Jantine stepped past Katra to the bound SDF officer and tore the transparent covering away.

"It's true, ma'am. When Captain Kołodziejski arrived a few days ago, he evacuated pretty much everyone to Tycho City. And when your voice came over the comm from the shuttle, he kind of lost it. This base has been staffed primarily with officers from *Indomitable* since we arrived, and they all cleared out when the ship lifted. We're alone down here, and it seems we're . . . what the hell is that!"

Artemus wedged himself through the portal, and once inside, he had to duck his head slightly to avoid scraping it on the ceiling. Mira slid to the side as he approached, and all three prisoners tried to press themselves into, and through, the wall. Jantine saw Marius and Yesha take up station outside.

"I am Defense Guardian Artemus, and you humans are now subject to the Interstellar Compact." When he spoke, he spread his arms wide, making sure the humans could see the weapons in all four hands.

"If you attempt to escape, you will be punished. If you attempt rebellion against my authority, you will be punished. If you take any action against my comrades in arms, you will be punished, and most likely killed. Do you understand these conditions of parole?"

The captured troopers nodded, but Jantine added her own warning to that of the Delta.

"He needs to hear you say it. Otherwise, you are still enemy combatants, and he's a very good shot."

Artemus turned his both his lower arms and one of the uppers until each of the weapons was pointed directly at a prisoner's head. All three were quick to respond with "yes" and "yes, sir", but Artemus wasn't done having fun just yet.

"I am Defense Guardian Artemus! There is no sir to yes at! Will you comply or not!"

"Yes, Defense Guardian Artemus!"

Artemus gave one of his rare smiles, showing his massive white teeth. "Good. Scout Marius, secure these prisoners, and those two on the floor as well. I will follow directly. Scout Yesha, up."

The slim female Gamma tossed one of the captured induction pistols up through the maintenance hatch, then followed it herself a moment later. Jantine heard her settle in next to the circulating machine, and several seconds later, she felt fresh air blowing on her face. Marius led the prisoners out into the hallway. *Why Artemus, you have a positive gift for command. We will need to work on this, but I see new opportunities ahead for you.*

"Commander. Lieutenant Commander. Will there be anything else?"

Jantine shook her head.

"You have performed admirably, Defense Guardian Artemus. Please see to our guests, and we'll talk soon."

The Delta nodded, and reversed his complicated entrance.

Mira waved Jantine to the command console and began activating controls. By the time Jantine sat, several holo displays were active, one of which showed the repeating signal they'd agreed upon with Commodore Maranova before launch.

Mira rested a gauntleted hand on Jantine's shoulder.

"If they're out there, any of them, this should do the trick. All we can do now is wait. Carlton says we'll need to get you down to Earth as soon as possible to deal with your ear, but he thinks the damage isn't irreversible."

Jantine thought about what Mira was saying, her eyes on the slowly bouncing signal announcing their presence to their allies. She didn't doubt that her friend was in contact with Carlton, but Mira hadn't indicated that the prisoner was lying earlier either. If Commodore Maranova's strike force really had been destroyed, the only vessel they had access to was the shuttle they came in on, and it was far too small to accommodate the sleepers.

The chair she was sitting in was much like the ones in the shuttle's control center, as was the console in front of her. She hadn't had time to familiarize herself with it completely, but if it was anything like the other ones she'd seen, there would be an internal transmitter.

Swiveling to face the uniformed woman on the floor. The woman shot her an angry look, but while Jantine was not quite as threatening as Artemus, she still liked to think she inspired respect.

"You, human. What is your name?"

"Lieutenant Lydia Daniels."

"How many humans can this base support?"

"I'm not sure I like the way you say humans."

Katra stepped forward, raising her rifle. Jantine stopped her with an upraised hand, which was enough to change the look in the human's eyes.

"Shall I call Artemus back in here to explain the rules again? Or can we discuss this like rational people?"

Before Daniels could answer, Mira removed the tape from another prisoner's mouth.

"Quit playing around, Lydia. These gennies mean business, and they probably saw that transmission the Captain made you send. Five hundred. It can support five hundred of us for almost a year, indefinitely if we can get enough oxygen out of the walls."

Yes, that will do nicely.

Mira continued releasing the humans, who were careful not to move too quickly around Katra. When Marius returned a few minutes later, he led away a still-fuming Lydia Daniels, four very cooperative and apologetic human scientists, and the two spies Mira had identified.

When all the humans were gone, Yesha came down out of the crawlspace, and with Mira's help, she sealed the hatch. Then Mira's face took on a strange look.

"Jantine, tell me what you're thinking."

Jantine was surprised.

"Don't you know?"

"It doesn't work like that. Not with you, anyway. Your mind is very well-ordered, and you don't let a lot rise to the surface."

"I'm thinking this is a good enough place as any for a colony. With the sleepers, we can hold it against any hostile force. There is food, air, and more than enough room for us to—I think you called it—'build some bridges' with the humans. "

"An excellent idea, Commander," Katra said. "But what about Janbi? Mordecai Harrison said he could not come to the Moon, possibly for many months."

Jantine pressed her lips together in a smile.

"Janbi will be our ambassador on Earth, as Mira will be to their military. And it will be good for the two of us to spend some time apart."

Mira nodded, and Jantine felt her trust and approval. Remaining on the moon might mean permanent hearing loss from her left side, but she was ready now to believe in herself, and be the person who made her own choices.

She was just about to tell Katra how much she appreciated her support when an unfamiliar female voice came from the command console.

"Aggie? Is that you?"

Mira's surprise was evident both on her face, and the amusement and recognition she shared through her link. Jantine wasn't positive, but her own recent experiences with desire hinted at a more personal relationship, one almost confirmed with the very different voice Mira used when answering the transmission.

"Mar? Where are you . . . are you on the *Clarke* now? When did you leave *City of Lights*?"

"There's a story there for later, but it's been a few days now. When you . . . When *Valiant* went dark, Captain Maddsen transferred about half his crew planetside. I was on the L6 station when Captain DeMarco and the Commodore arrived, and the captain seconded me to run his comms. I have her for you now, if you're ready."

"Give me a minute, Mar. I have something to do down here first."

"Copy that. Ping when you're ready. And Deb would want me to tell you that she never believed what they were saying. You should come visit her and the girls, when you get a chance."

"I will, Mar, thanks. See you soon."

Mira cut the circuit and leaned heavily against the console for several seconds. Jantine watched her face contort as her emotions leaked through her defenses. Sadness, regret, anger, and joy each had their turn, until she finally settled on hope.

She flashed Jantine a mischievous smile, and she chuckled before she spoke.

"Marya is . . . a friend. One of the first ones I made at the academy, and she married someone I care about a lot. Deb is . . . it's complicated. But you can trust her. She's almost family."

"You are our family, Mira," said Jantine. "If you love her, we will as well."

Jantine was surprised to see tears in Mira's eyes. But the Earther was still smiling, and after a moment she was ready to proceed.

"Are you sure about this, Jantine? It's not too late to change your mind."

"I am. This is why I'm here."

As she said the words, Jantine was finally convinced they were true. Instead of being a mantra handed down by the Alphas, it was now an empowering affirmation.

"Okay, here we go."

Mira reactivated the comm, but before she could say anything the shrill voice of Commodore Ykaterina Maranova filled the room.

"Harlan? Harlan, what's going on down there? What's the big idea about making us wait? Do you have any idea what's been going on up here?"

Jantine couldn't help but remember Janbi facing down the diminutive Earther with only one hand and a broken cane.

"I'm here, ma'am. We've been a bit busy as well. The base is under our control, and Captain Kołodziejski . . . is dead."

"Well good. And everyone else?"

"We are well, Commodore," Jantine said. "I wish to make a statement, not just to you but to your planet. Can you facilitate this?"

"Go ahead when you're ready, Jantine. We won the battle up here, so take as much time as you need. Marya here will make sure everyone with two ears and a heartbeat gets your message."

Jantine winced at the reminder of her injury, but Mira drew away her pain and placed a hand on her shoulder. Jantine covered it with one of her own, and prepared to deliver yet another worlds-changing proclamation.

"This is Governor Jantine. In accordance with Interstellar Compact and the Magellan Accords, I claim right of conquest over the section of Earth's moon known as Echo Base, in response to war crimes perpetrated against myself and my people by rogue officers of your military.

"In cooperation with the legitimate leadership of your System Defense Force, my forces have occupied this base, and hereby declare it to be an independent colony. Our ambassador is already in negotiations with the highest levels of your government, and we will not be displaced.

"Attempt no landings here without our permission. Do not seek to challenge our sovereignty. We have come to heal the rift caused between our two peoples by the misguided actions of our ancestors, but if necessary we will defend ourselves to the utmost of our abilities.

"You have been warned . . . ."

MORDECAI

MORDECAI STARED ACROSS THE BOARD AT JANBI, who was grinning wide enough to split his face in two. His nose was still a tad crooked, but something about it seemed to fit his face, giving it a comfortable imperfection that the rest of his people seemed to lack.

The Beta was waiting patiently for Mordecai's next move, with most of his white pieces arranged in front of him. On the board, only four of Mordecai's wooden army remained, surrounded by a besieging force of black pieces he'd barely managed to scratch.

It's not like I have much choice, now is it?

Mordecai moved his rook back to take the pawn threatening his king, unwilling to take direct action with that piece and blocked by his own knight from escaping.

Janbi quickly moved his bishop in for the kill, pulling the captured piece off the board and placing it into its correct position with the rest of the queen's retinue.

Neither player had spoken since hearing Jantine's announcement, though Janbi's smile spoke volumes as to his intentions.

Ambassador. Hah! Can't even tie his own shoes, and he's the second most important person on the planet. Who would have thought?

Mordecai felt a slight twinge of guilt for belittling Janbi's struggles on Earth, but it was hard to find anything not to like about the boy. In order to maintain the upper hand in their "negotiations," he had to at least think of him as an opponent, instead of someone he'd been waiting to meet all his life.

Besides, I'm not entirely sure he's not reading my mind. Did you hear that, Janbi? Smile if you're cheating . . .

Mordecai moved his knight to take the bishop, and Janbi's response was to move another pawn forward into the eighth rank. Mordecai scowled at the move he'd seen coming for at least fifteen minutes, and he waited for Janbi to ask for his queen back.

"How long have you known, Mordecai?"

"What? Are you reading my mind after all?"

Janbi shook his head.

"No, just your archives. And your personal journals, as well as those of your father. The analysis finished a few minutes ago, but we've been having so much fun I decided to wait to ask."

"Ask me what? Paul, did you have anything to do with this?"

Paul didn't shift from his position across the room, where he was waiting with a pair of dinner plates that by now must have been stone cold.

"Don't drag me into this, old man. I told you to take black."

That you did, my boy. That you did.

"The virus, Doctor. How long have you known where it came from?"

Mordecai's blood ran cold, and his heart leapt into his throat. Janbi had somehow uncovered his family's deepest secret, on his own, in only a couple of hours.

It took me sixty years, and I only confirmed the hypothesis this afternoon. Hell of Bad Reasoning, I haven't even written that down yet.

"Janbi, I'm not sure I like you anymore."

Mordecai's voice was calm, but it did nothing to disturb the Beta's smile.

"That's all right. You don't have to like me, just tell me the truth. How long have you known?"

Mordecai picked up the black queen and exchanged it for the intrepid pawn. Leaning back in his chair, he nodded at

Paul, and the younger man left the room quietly. A few seconds later, convinced that all electronic records of their conversation were now scrambled, Mordecai leaned forward and made his confession.

"To be honest, I don't know that I do. But I've suspected it for the last few years, and the samples I took of Serene's and Harlan's blood were the piece I was missing."

"So it is the ice world, then. Where they found Serene?"

"If not there, then wherever that colony ship stopped before it. We have no records of ever visiting it before, but Serene's virus was still active, in a way that we haven't seen since the very first expressions. It was changing her as we watched, adapting to whatever challenges she was facing. At first I thought it was because she was an Alpha, but Harlan was born right here on Earth and had the same strain of virus in her."

Janbi nodded.

"But even Harlan was an anomaly among anomalies. There had to be something else, some other factor that linked them together, and not the rest of you."

"It was the Omegas, wasn't it?"

Mordecai nodded.

"Even your Type 6s, the Deltas, they're still recognizably human. But the Omegas are so far removed from the base-line genome that they definitely qualify as an alien species, no matter what their origin. They were the first line to express on a planet other than Earth, and it would explain a lot if they had something to do with that ship crashing. Both Serene and Harlan were in near constant contact with one or the other of them since you kids landed, and despite the reverence your people have for them I think they know a lot more than they're telling you."

Janbi nodded and pushed himself away from the table with his good arm. Mordecai's eye went to the sensor coupling on his stump, wondering what it was that Janbi was going to do if the T-virus proved incompatible with a prosthetic nerve graft.

"That much is certain. I think Mira will be able to help us with that when she returns, but for now I think we should keep this between us. There may not be other Omegas among the sleepers, but if what you say is true it won't be long until some start developing here on Earth."

Mordecai hadn't considered that, and Janbi's matter-of-fact delivery made the idea all the more frightening.

"So what's your plan, son? How do you want to proceed?"

"Son. I like that. I never had a father, and you'll do well enough I guess."

This definitely affected Mordecai, who sat back in his chair and let out a long breath. He and Almira had never had children of their own, raising those of others when necessary and treating the whole planet as their family instead.

I think she'd have liked you, Janbi. I'm sure of it. But you frighten the hell out of me, and I'm sure you know that, too.

"But for now, I'm tired. I think I'll rest for a while."

Janbi stood and started to walk away from the table. Mordecai didn't know what to say to him, and as his universe changed at the will of another for the first time in years, he felt helpless to resist the Beta's pull.

"But, what about the game?"

Janbi turned back, and his crooked nose caught just the right amount of shadow to make his face seem much more mature. The Beta took two quick strides, then used his right hand to tip over first his king, then the queen he'd worked so skillfully to convert.

"I don't understand you, son. I really don't"

Janbi's boyish smile was as wide as ever, but when he spoke it was Mordecai who felt like a child.

"Good. That means we have something to work toward tomorrow. But as for the game, I already have a queen. I don't need another. I just needed to know how long you'd keep playing after you realized you couldn't win.

"Good night, Mordecai. We'll speak in the morning about damages due my people as a result of the Exile. I think I'd like to speak to the other Reclamation governors as well, can you arrange that?"

"Yes. Paul will set that up for us."

"Good then. And think about this for tomorrow, if you will: we sent out six other streamships, each with a team a lot like mine. Assuming they didn't also land in the middle of a civil war, that's twelve other Omegas out there somewhere who never met anyone like Mira Harlan, or learned what it means to be truly human. If all went according to plan, they're already dug in, and prepared to hide for a few hundred years and build up colonies with no outside influences whatsoever.

"What do you think they'll have in mind for the rest of us, when they finally do come out? I think we need to go to that ice planet as soon as possible, and find out what made that ship crash, and why. Because there's nothing I've ever heard of that can stop an Omega from getting what it wants, other than a kind word and an open heart."

Mordecai Harrison watched the young man who'd just destroyed his life's work walk out of his office. He felt old, and worn out, but for the first time in many months, he had something to look forward to with the dawn.

I only hope that you kids know what you're doing. Because if you can't help us fight whoever unleashed the virus on us centuries ago, the human race might be doomed after all . . .

ACKNOWLEDGMENTS

None of this would have been possible without Mark Teppo. He and I both have talked publicly about how I sold him this book, but it's hard to truly relate how much he inspired me to write the story in your hands today. Not only did he say no to two other pitches, but he drove me to understand what makes a truly great book, and why we should be publishing them. And while I'm not saying this book is perfect, it's certainly the best thing I've ever written or attempted.

Thanks also to my editors Fleetwood Robbins and Darin Bradley. While we didn't always see eye to eye, their ability to ask the right questions over and over until I understood them is why you have this book in your hands..

Homefront is a book about families, and I would be remiss if I didn't thank my own. So for the Magners, Fouseks, Pendletons, and Johnsons of the world, thank you so much for being there when I needed you. Living with a writer can be trying at times, I know. I can only hope that your patience is rewarded in my meager efforts.

And lastly, thank you, dear reader. No one gets to the acknowledgements page when reading a book without first finishing it, and certainly not without buying it. You fought along with me to the end, after taking a chance on an unknown author, a new fictional universe, and a rag-tag bunch of misfits doing the best they can to survive.

Let's do it again.

Scott James Magner has held down many jobs over the years, including circus promoter, warehouse manager, dog-sitter, professional role-playing gamer, and writer. He currently resides in Seattle with his partner of many years and several cats who don't understand why sitting down to write is not an invitation for lap-time.